Vagabonds

Josephine Cox

HEADLINE

First published in 1992
by Macdonald & Co (Publishers) Ltd

First published in paperback in 1992
by HEADLINE BOOK PUBLISHING

20 19 18 17 16 15 14

ISBN 0 7472 4062 0

Typeset by Keyboard Services, Luton

Printed and bound in Great Britain by
Cox & Wyman Ltd, Reading, Berkshire

HEADLINE BOOK PUBLISHING
A division of Hodder Headline PLC
338 Euston Road
London NW1 3BH

The story of Josephine Cox is as extraordinary as anything in her novels. Born in a cotton-mill house in Blackburn, Lancashire, she was one of ten children. Her parents, she says, brought out the worst in each other, and life was full of tragedy and hardship – but not without love and laughter. At the age of sixteen, Josephine met and married 'a caring and wonderful man' and had two sons. When the boys started school, she decided to go to college and eventually gained a place at Cambridge University, though was unable to take this up as it would have meant living away from home. However, she did go into teaching, while at the same time helping to renovate the derelict council house that was their home, coping with the problems caused by her mother's unhappy home life – and writing her first full-length novel. Not surprisingly, she then won the 'Superwoman of Great Britain' Award, for which her family had secretly entered her, and this coincided with the acceptance of her novel for publication.

Jo has given up teaching in order to write full time, and her seven previous novels have been immensely popular:

'Tension and drama . . . a book to read at one sitting!' *Prima*

'A classic is born' *Lancashire Evening Telegraph*

To three lovely women,
good friends whom I love very much:
Jane,
our delightful new daughter-in-law;
Madge,
a real trooper who is the salt of the earth;
Barbara Arnold,
who would happily scour the world for my books!
God bless them.

Part One

England 1885

Don't be afraid
When dark clouds gather.
Somewhere, the sunshine
Is breaking through.

J.C.

Chapter One

'Be off with you . . . we don't want no beggers at *this* door!' Cook's round, homely face was full of disgust as she glared at the young woman who was loitering on the outer step. 'Go on, I say . . . be off with you, afore I call the master. You'll show a clean pair of heels then, I'll be bound.' She had been up to her armpits in flour when the knock had come on the door. Now she began frantically wiping her chubby hands on her pinnie and flapping the corner of it towards the ragged, offending creature who seemed unwilling to make a move.

The young woman stood her ground and eyed the agitated cook with bold black eyes. 'I'm no "beggar"!' she retorted, drawing the tiny infant closer into her arms and reaching down to take the frail hand of the small child by her side. 'I don't want charity, missus. I'm willing to do good honest labour for a reasonable wage . . . and I'm a lot stronger than I look, so don't go thinking I'm afraid of hard, heavy work. I can do whatever's needed of me.' Molly was desperate, and it showed in her voice.

'Oh, it's work you're after, is it?' Cook's temper began to recede as she quietly regarded the young woman before her. 'These your two brats, are they?' She let her small, round eyes rove over the two children; the girl she ascertained to be somewhere in the region of three or

3

four years old, and the infant in arms probably not yet a year old. As for the young woman, she looked the most starved of all three. She was painfully thin, but had the kind of face that held a particular strength, with dark, striking eyes that somehow held a body mesmerized. Cook didn't hold with folks knocking on her kitchen door, especially when they might want something for nothing. 'Where's the father of these two?' she asked sharply.

'He's run off.'

'Run off . . . ? The devil he has.' Cook wasn't surprised. All men were the same in her eyes: either wasters or womanizers. The same thing applied whether they were beggars or kings. 'Well, I'm sorry, young lady . . . there's no place here for extra hands. Oh, we could do with somebody, I'm not denying that . . . but the master don't see it the same way as them that have to do the work.'

'Couldn't you at least *ask*?' Molly believed that beneath her sharp and unkind manner, the old lady might have a soft spot.

Cook shook her grey head. 'No. It wouldn't do no good.' Her small piggy eyes fell to the fair-haired child, who promptly smiled at her, melting her heart. 'Poor little tyke,' she said, thinking how all three made a sorry and pitiful sight. 'Look . . . wait here a minute,' she told the young woman. 'I know there's no work to be got, but there's a larder just bursting with certain goodies that would never be missed by them upstairs.' She jerked a podgy thumb heavenwards. 'I'll not be a minute,' she chuckled, tousling the child's unkempt curls before she turned to go quickly back into the kitchen.

As good as her word, the old dear returned within a

short time, bearing a strawberry basket tucked under her arm and filled with food from the larder: a crusty loaf, a tub of butter, two rosy apples, a chunk of pork pie and three slabs of her best cherry cake. 'Here, take this and make yourself scarce. If we're found out, there'll be *four* of us going down the road to beggary . . . you mark my words!' She thrust the basket over the young woman's outstretched arm and, without another word, stepped back into the relative safety of her own kitchen. 'Lord love and preserve us!' she was heard to mutter, before hastily making the sign of the cross on herself and shutting the door against the sight of that poor young woman with her two fatherless brats.

'Thanks very much, missus.' The young woman smiled and began walking away down the long narrow path that would lead her to the outer lane.

Satisfied that they were far enough away from the big house, she stopped and sat on the high bank beside the ditch. The children sat beside her, waiting for something to eat. Breaking two chunks of bread from the loaf, she gave a piece to each of the children. 'There you are, my beauties,' she said in a soft, loving voice. Then, at the sight of them both happily tucking in to the old cook's generous gift, she laughed aloud, throwing her arms round them and declaring with delight, 'Just follow your mammy's example . . . and you'll never go hungry. What . . . if that old woman had offered me a job in that big posh house, I'd have fainted on the very spot!' When the two children took pleasure in Molly's infectious laughter, she hugged them all the more tightly, her heart bursting with love and a prayer of thanks to the Lord that, somehow, he always managed to see them through the hard times.

From the window of the kitchen Cook had watched the pathetic ensemble as it went away down the path. 'There's always somebody worse off than yourself,' she murmured, feeling guilty that she had spoken so sharply to the young woman at first, because there was something about the creature that seemed to put her above the usual beggar or vagabond. She shook her head thoughtfully and turned her attention to the baking of the day's bread. But the image persisted awhile, until she deliberately pushed it from her mind. They'd be all right, she told herself, them sort had a way of surviving. She was astonished though, to think that a young woman of such attractive looks should be made to wander the streets like that. Oh, and what sort of a fellow would 'run off' and leave his woman and children to fend for themselves?

How much more astonished Cook would have been to learn that the 'vagabond' she had just dismissed from the house of Justice Caleb Crowther was no other than Molly . . . lost daughter of Emma Grady. Emma, the niece of Caleb Crowther, and now his bitter enemy.

'Oh, I say . . . such terrible tempers. And them being gentry and all.' The words were uttered in a soft and fearful whisper as, afraid yet strangely excited by the fearsome row that was raging inside Justice Crowther's study, the maid dithered by the door. A petite and plain woman with a thin, worn face and bright round eyes, she was burning with curiosity; yet she was also amazed by her own boldness in lingering here, her mind in turmoil and her ears singing in anticipation of the boxing they would get from Cook if she loitered in her duties.

Oh, but how dare she barge in on such a terrible

uproar with the master in as black a mood as ever she'd known, and the mistress giving him as good as she got? Why! The idea of disturbing them was *unthinkable*, and if a lowly scullery-maid such as she were suddenly to show her face with the intention of cleaning out the firegrate, like as not the two wolves at each other's throats on the other side of that door might just as easily turn on *her*! The thought was so real and terrifying that Amy clutched at her own throat and turned tail to scurry away. She would have liked to stay a while longer, but no matter; she had discovered enough.

As she went along the corridor and towards the stairs which led down to the kitchen, a wicked and devious smile came to her face. Even now, she could still hear the angry, raised voices behind her. The nearer she came to the narrow stairway, the faster went her thin little legs and the brighter shone her eyes. Oh, but she had such a tale to tell Cook! Such a juicy, satisfying tale!

'At last we know the worst. Emma Grady wants her pound of flesh right down to the blood and bones!' Caleb Crowther sank his ageing but still formidable figure into the leather-bound chair behind the desk, his piercing blue eyes marbled with fear as he glared at his wife's anxious face. 'Damn the woman!' he snarled, clenching his teeth and feverishly stroking his long thick fingers over the mass of iron-grey hair which covered the lower half of his ungainly features. 'When she was transported some twenty-two years ago to the other side of the world, I prayed we'd seen the last of her. But I was a fool. I should have known better. I should have made sure that she was *hanged*!' He fell forward on his desk, burying his balding head in the depths of his hands and making low, intermittent sounds that betrayed the hatred simmering inside him. Hatred, and something else . . . *fear*. The crippling fear that Emma Grady's return had wrought in him. 'Over three years since she set foot on these shores again. Uncertain years . . . littered with solicitors' correspondence and mounting fees to be paid at the end of it all.' He raised his head and began drumming his fingers impatiently on the desk-top. 'She has deliberately kept me guessing as to her real intentions . . . toyed with me . . . no doubt found it amusing to think of me squirming.' Suddenly he was sitting bolt upright in the chair, his narrowed eyes searching his wife's face as he judged her reaction to his next words. 'Now, she's moving in for the kill!' Snatching up the offending letter, he flung it across the desk. 'Read it, woman,' he snapped at his wife, 'this affects us all.'

'You seem very sure that she can hurt us . . . you surprise me. I thought you had prepared for every eventuality . . . including Emma Grady's possible return?' Agnes Crowther smiled knowingly, and with contempt.

It was a gesture that infuriated him. 'There'll be nothing for *any* of us to smile about if she succeeds in her little game,' he reminded her angrily, 'and make no mistake about it . . . she means to beggar us. We underestimated her once. We'd be downright idiots not to see her for the dangerous enemy she's become. Emma Grady went away a young, naïve creature who could be easily manipulated . . . she's returned an influential and powerful woman with a curiosity for certain answers and a thirst for revenge. Mark my words, she won't rest until she has us at her mercy!'

'Strange, don't you think . . . how the tables turn?'

There was cynicism in her voice, and a trace of fear. With calm deliberation, Agnes Crowther came forward from the casement window where she had been gazing across the beautifully tended lawns, quietly indulging in memories of long ago. Her troubled thoughts had carried her back some twenty-five years to when Emma Grady had played and walked on these same lawns; a young girl tormented by the fact that her beloved father, Thadius Grady, was wasting away. With his eventual passing, Emma's torment had not ceased. So many bad experiences had assailed her; so much tragedy and heartache that might have destroyed a lesser soul. 'What makes this letter frighten you so?' Agnes Crowther kept her unflinching gaze on his face. 'There have been others . . . and always you've satisfactorily dealt with them. Why should this one be any different?'

'Because it touches on deeper issues . . . deeds and titles regarding the mills that Thadius left to her. Up to now, her solicitor has been cleverly laying the groundwork . . . probing . . . making sure of his case regarding his client's claims. Now he's digging to the real issues, making demands . . . requesting certain documents. Uprooting things that go back too many years.'

'These . . . "documents" . . . surely you can supply them?' She let her gaze remain on his face a moment longer. Only now did she fear the worst. 'Or is there something there to incriminate you . . . to incriminate *all* of us?' She had always trusted his judgement in these matters; after all, he was a man of the law and well versed in such legalities. With a jolt, she was reminded of how he had cunningly secreted Emma's inheritance and almost lost it in the recession. It was true however that he had then salvaged enough to sell off the derelict

9

cotton mills and to buy a considerable share in the Lassater Shipping Line. If that enviable income were now denied them, it would be nothing short of disaster. Certainly, her husband's comparative pittance, as Justice of the Peace, would not sustain their pampered lifestyle. Suddenly incensed by the prospect of losing everything she valued, she rounded on him. 'This is *your* problem,' she told him in a cold voice. 'It was not me who chose to marry Emma off to an employee of my brother's, a man who was socially inferior to Emma Grady. Is it any wonder that it ended in tragedy? Though I must admit I never really believed that she had a hand in murdering the unfortunate fellow.' In her deepest heart, Agnes Crowther could never see her brother's daughter committing such a foul and cold-blooded crime; the girl was too loving, too warm and sensitive to ever deliberately hurt another soul. Yet it had been these very qualities which had alienated her from Emma. She had seen in her brother's child all of those admirable traits that were sadly lacking in her own daughter, Martha, who was almost the same age as Emma. She could not suppress her bitter resentment of the fact that while Emma was strong and forthright, Martha was weak and deceitful.

When Emma's mother had died in tragic circumstances, and later, when her father Thadius was gravely ill and brought Emma to live with him in this house, both Agnes and Martha had set about making Emma's life miserable.

After her brother's death, Agnes Crowther vented all her bitterness on Emma, not protesting at Martha's spiteful treatment of the girl, nor intervening when Emma was so unsuitably married off. All along, Agnes had suspected that her husband had deliberately planned to cheat Emma, yet she had not once argued on Emma's behalf. Not even when she realized that Caleb had played a hand in the verdict that demanded Emma's transportation as a convict.

For a long, uncomfortable moment it seemed as though Agnes Crowther might read the letter. But then she lifted her hand and joined it with the other at her breast, the fine bony fingers pointed upwards in that posture of prayer which had long been a familiar and peculiar trait of her unbending character. 'I will not demean myself by reading that mischievous letter, and thereby giving credence to Emma Grady's vindictive proposals.'

'You *will* read it!'

'I will not!'

'What are you saying, woman . . . that you refuse to support me in this bitter fight with Emma Grady? You seem to conveniently forget, my dear, that she is after all *your* kith and kin. And, more importantly, that the inheritance she now lays claim to should by rights have been left to *you* in the first place. Why your father struck you out of his will in favour of your younger brother, Thadius, is quite beyond me!'

'No doubt he had his reasons,' came the curt reply. She could have reminded him that the main reason she had been so cruelly disinherited was because she had stubbornly rebelled against her father's strong disapproval of Caleb Crowther. 'The man is little more than a fortune hunter,' he had warned his daughter, 'but mark my words . . . I will see to it that he never gets his hands on a penny of my money!' Agnes Crowther had loved her father. But, much to her later regret, she had loved Caleb more. She smiled now at the bitter irony of it all,

because even though Thadius had been the main bene-
ficiary in their father's will, he had foolishly appointed
Caleb as trustee and executor of his estate. As Caleb had
so often remarked in the months following Thadius's
passing, 'I could not have planned it better myself . . .
see how conveniently the inheritance has fallen into my
lap.' When the mills were later foreclosed by the banks
and the money almost gone, Caleb had felt no regrets for
Emma, who by now was 'safely' out of the way. His only
concerns were these: that he should salvage enough
money from the failing textile business to forge a new
company in his own name, which would serve to finally
sever the links between himself and Emma Grady, and
that he should cover all traces of his illegal acquisition of
Emma's fortune. He had believed himself to be cunning
and thorough. But now, with Emma returned, vengeful
and determined to expose his treachery, he had been
made wary and afraid. Yet he was equally determined
that she would not beggar him. He would see her ruined
first. *Or dead!* There was no remorse in Caleb Crowther's
heart for the callous way in which he had treated Emma
Grady. Only hatred, and now a deep haunting fear that
would not go away; he despised himself for harbouring
such fear. After all, she was only a woman, however rich
and influential she had become.

'So, you mean to defy me?'

'In this matter, I am afraid so.'

'Then you are a fool!' Infuriated, he got to his feet.
'Must I remind you that we're in this together. If I am to
be hounded by this upstart, I can assure you, my dear
. . . you will keep me company in the workhouse.'

'You think so?'

'I do indeed.'

12

With a wry little smile, Agnes Crowther turned away, her next words dripping softly in her wake as she moved gracefully across the room, a slim and regal figure in a bustled dress of dark blue silk. 'Oh, my dear . . . you know very well that the workhouse would not suit me. However, I must leave the matter of Emma Grady to you,' she told him icily. 'You know how hopeless I am at such things . . . and how I have no head for what is essentially "a man's business" . . . as you yourself have so painstakingly pointed out on the rare occasions when I have offered an opinion.'

'This is different,' he argued, with all the dignity he could muster in the face of her defiance. 'This concerns you as well as me.' He was puzzled by her bold attitude, but not altogether surprised. The further they had drifted apart over the years, the more independent and rebellious she had become. It was quite infuriating.

'And what would you have me do?' She turned at the door to sweep her cold, green gaze over his angry features. 'Should I go and see her? Put myself at her mercy and beg forgiveness for robbing her of her birthright, afterwards turning our backs on her when she was thrown into a prison cell, charged with murder? Do you think I should chastize her for seeking to hurt us? Or would you rather I tried to explain how sorry we are that we ignored her desperate pleas for help when she was labelled a criminal of the worst kind . . . faced with exile from the shores of her homeland when she was heavy with child . . . a child that was soon lost to her in unfortunate circumstances. And when she asks where her fortune has gone, what should I say? That it was squandered . . . but that enough was saved for investment in the Lassater Shipping Line . . . now a thriving and prosperous company, and one of Emma Grady's most bitter and dangerous rivals?' She smiled sweetly and quietly opened the door. 'Somehow I don't think I would be well received in my niece's house . . . do you, my dear?'

In a moment she was gone and the door was firmly closed behind her. Caleb Crowther went to the window, where he lit his pipe and furiously puffed on it. It seemed to him that, whilst his enemies began to close in on all sides, he stood alone, deserted and friendless. No matter, he thought defiantly, there were still those rats who had no choice but to stand by him . . . or go down with the sinking ship. He had not 'gone down' yet. Nor had he any intention of doing so. Certainly not because of Emma Grady! Or Emma Tanner as she was now called, since her marriage to that fellow Marlow.

In the privacy of the drawing-room, Agnes Crowther was also quietly meditating. Not too long ago it would have been unthinkable that she should defy her husband in such a way. But that was before she had discovered how deeply he had shamed her. She could not bring herself to forgive him for the way he had cheated on her, taking other women to his bed on those long journeys away as circuit judge and not even having the decency to deny it when she had confronted him. She could hear him now, lamely trying to justify his sordid affairs. 'You yourself are not altogether blameless, my dear,' he had told her. 'When a wife turns her husband away . . . fails to do her duty by him . . . then that same wife must not be surprised when he seeks his comfort elsewhere.' It was true that she did not enjoy his advances and his infidelity was only to be expected. But the idea that she should indulge in such undignified behaviour between the sheets was particularly obnoxious to her, considering that she was already in the autumn of her life. As for Caleb, he would never see sixty again and therefore should know better than to shamelessly cavort with members of the opposite sex. To make matters worse, it had come to her knowledge that he had even been seen in the company of street women. *Whores, no less.* She positively bristled at the thought, murmuring aloud, 'And you think I care what ruin Emma Grady brings down on you? You don't care what terrible shame you bring down on *me*, you old fornicator! And as for threatening me, let me tell you I will *not* be "keeping you company in the workhouse". These past years I have carefully put away a small nest-egg. You may rot in the workhouse, Justice Caleb Crowther . . . but I shall keep my dignity.' The thought pleased her and she chuckled deliciously.

It pleased her also to see her husband's astonishment at the manner in which she had stood up to him. At one time she would have been too afraid to be so bold, but, since Emma's return the tables had turned; however much he might deny it, Justice Crowther was quivering in his boots, and his wife, the long-suffering but equally devious creature, was emerging the stronger of the two.

'Why, you little fool . . . giggling and glorying in such a thing, when you should be trembling at what it could all mean!' Cook's reaction was not what the maid had expected, and she was completely taken aback when, after gleefully imparting the news of how she had heard the mistress saying that 'Caleb Crowther was a forni-cator and would rot in the workhouse without her, if Emma Grady was to ruin him', she had been angrily attacked by the normally amiable cook, whose chubby face had grown bright purple, the ladle in her fist sent whistling towards Amy's ear with intent to knock her sideways.

'*But it's true* . . . I swear it!' protested the astonished Amy. 'I ain't being fanciful . . . not this time. The mistress really *did* say all those things.' She kept her distance from Cook's anger, her bottom lip quivering and the curiosity gone from her eyes; in its place was the same expression Cook had seen on a big stray dog that she'd found sitting on the kitchen step some days ago. Lost it was, and starved of both food and affection. The constable had later returned it to its rightful owner, but Cook still recalled how it touched her old heart with its round, soulful eyes. 'Oh, you gormless thing,' she told the cowering maid, 'sit yourself down. I'll make us a brew of tea, and you can tell me what the mistress did say, word for word.' Amy waited until Cook had dropped the ladle on to the surface of the big pine table, then, quietly snivelling, she slid into one of the stand-chairs and pulled it up to the table. 'It were just as I told you,' she mumbled, carefully watching Cook's every move. She could do with a cup of tea now, she thought miserably, because the old bugger had frightened her so much that her mouth had gone all dry!

'You're a silly, innocent little fool,' Cook placed the tray on to the table and edged her ample frame into a chair set directly opposite the maid, 'but I shouldn't have jumped at you like that . . . and I'm sorry.' She cut a wedge of apple pie and scooped it on to a small china plate, which she then pushed in front of the little woman. 'Get that down you,' she ordered in a kindly voice, and, shaking her grey head, she added more severely, 'You'll never change, will you, eh? What were you when you first came to Breckleton House . . . fifteen . . . sixteen? That were over twenty years since, and you're still as daft as a brush!'

'I ain't daft.'

'Aye well . . . happen not "daft" . . . but you've still not learned the way of things.'

'What do you mean, Cook . . . the way of things?' Amy didn't feel quite so threatened now, so she took a hearty bite of the apple pie and leaned forward, the better to hear Cook's next words. For the life of her, she couldn't see what she'd done wrong.

'First of all . . . I don't doubt for a minute that the mistress said those things.' Cook smiled to reassure her. It was sad but true that Amy had never been what might be considered 'intelligent'. And the older she got, the less she seemed to stop and think things out. 'But there's some'at you need to realize, Amy, and it's this.' She chuckled good-humouredly when the maid began frantically nodding her head and urging Cook, between mouthfuls of pie, to 'go on . . . I'm listening.' Poor, misguided soul, thought Cook, as she went on in a discreet voice, 'What you heard upstairs . . . well, it could likely affect all our livelihoods, and that's a fact!'

''Ow d'yer mean?' The poor thing stopped chewing the pie. Somehow she wasn't enjoying it quite so much.

'Well, if you think about it . . . it's as plain as the nose on your face, Amy,' Cook said in slow, deliberate tones, the frown deepening in her forehead and causing Amy to grow anxious again. 'If Miss Emma does succeed in beggaring the master and he's left to live on what he gets from being a circuit judge, you and I both know it won't be enough for him to keep this big house . . . nor his servants.' She saw the light dawning in Amy's widened eyes, as she added cautiously, 'That means the house-keeper, the parlour maid . . . then me and you . . . we shall *all* of us end up in the workhouse together if the worst comes to the worst.'

'The *mistress* won't,' Amy thoughtfully corrected, ''cause I heard her say as how she had "a small nest-egg put away" . . . Oh, Cook! What shall we do? *I* ain't got no "nest-egg" put away, and I don't expect you have neither.'

For a short while there came no answer from Cook, who had lapsed into deep thought on the scullery maid's last words. Well, Amy was wrong, thought Cook, because a 'nest-egg' was just what she *had* got put away . . . safe and secure these many long years. But her 'nest-egg' wasn't bonds nor money, nor anything that might at first glance buy a roof over her head. Dear me, no! It was nothing more than a letter written to her by Mrs Manfred, the former housekeeper at Breckleton House. Poor Mrs Manfred who had been hanged over twenty years since for her part in the 'murder' of Miss Emma's husband, Gregory Denton. All the same, that letter was the roof over Cook's head in her old age, and the food in her belly, and a few guineas to make life comfortable too. It was a sad and sorry letter written by a gentle soul about to face the gallows and, as a body might want to do in such a terrible situation, Mrs Manfred had poured out all her innermost fears in that same letter. Not only her fears, but her dark suspicions regarding the master himself, whom she believed to know a great deal of the circumstances surrounding the death of *both* Miss Emma's parents. The letter indirectly accused Caleb Crowther of being a murderer, no less!

'I said . . . I don't expect *you've* got a nest-egg put by

any more than the rest of us . . . and as you told me yourself, you're well past sixty-five,' remarked Amy, who always regarded the elderly cook to be a fountain of all wisdom. 'So what will we do if the worst comes to the worst?' There were tears in her voice, and her eyes were suspiciously bright as they implored the round, aged face across the table. 'What shall we do, Cook? Where can we go?'

'Now don't you fret yourself,' warned Cook. 'The worst hasn't happened yet . . . and if it does, then we shall have to think again, won't we, eh?'

'Oh, Cook, d'you think Miss Emma really will take all the master's fortune away?'

'Well, if she does it'll be no more or less than he deserves. But you have to remember that Miss Emma's been back a while now, and she hasn't managed it yet.' She chuckled aloud and fell back in the chair, her great arms wrapped one around the other as she gleefully hugged herself. 'Oh, but hasn't it been a pretty thing to watch, eh . . . the master's face draining chalk-white every time one o' them letters from Miss Emma's solicitors comes a-tumbling through the door.' Her face was a study in delight as she revelled in Caleb Crowther's discomfort. 'But he's a crafty old fox . . . and he's had longer at the art of being devious than Miss Emma has. I'll wager the feud between 'em is coming to a head at long last.'

Suddenly, the elderly woman realized that it might be foolish to delay much longer in fetching out that particular nest-egg and collecting payment on it. But – just as it had done since Emma Grady's return – some deep instinct warned her to bide her time for as long as she could. The reasons were many. Firstly, the master was a dangerous man . . . a Justice . . . and if he were to learn of such a damning letter he might somehow steal it from her and see to it that she was locked away until she rotted; that was a fearsome prospect that gave her nightmares. It were a delicate situation, and one that she hadn't quite fathomed out. Of course, Emma herself might likely pay money to have the letter in her possession, but Cook had firmly resisted that particular course because it didn't seem right to ask *her* for money, besides which the letter referred to the suspicious deaths of both her parents and was bound to cause her a great deal of distress. Then there was the mistress, Agnes Crowther. Now, she would *certainly* be interested in the contents of that letter, but she was a stiff and easily shocked woman of rigid principles, and if she were to be asked for money against the letter, it might end up with its owner being flung in prison on a charge of blackmail.

No. The whole thing had to be done proper, decided Cook. For the minute, she had to watch how this wrangle was developing between Miss Emma and the master, and be sure to keep her distance from both of them. One thing was certain. She must be careful not to move in too quick, nor to leave it too late. It were a delicate thing indeed, that it was. Meanwhile, she was thoroughly enjoying the sight of the master squirming beneath the pressure of Miss Emma's boot.

Chapter Two

'D'you really mean to see him in the workhouse, Emma?' Nelly came into the garden where Emma was seated by the rose-arch, her quiet grey eyes gazing towards the distant green landscape and her thoughts reaching back over the years. There was sadness and regret in her downcast features. But when she saw the familiar and homely figure of Nelly, her face lit up in a lovely smile. 'I don't know, Nelly,' she replied, waiting for the other woman to be seated on the bench opposite. 'I do despise him for the things he's done . . . turning his back on me when I needed him most, betraying my father's trust in him, and using my inheritance as though it were his own. I can't forget these things and, God help me . . . I can't forgive him.'

'Oh, Emma gal, I do wish you would let the past go!' Nelly's brown eyes were beseeching, and Emma's heart was warmed by the sincere and loving soul that now implored her. 'Let it go, darling . . . before it becomes a blight on the happiness you've found with Marlow and the little lad.' Nelly blinked her eyes in the warm April sunshine as she prayed that, this time, Emma might be persuaded to leave her uncle, Caleb Crowther, to his own devices, and in time no doubt his wickedness would catch him up and be the end of him. To see the gentle Emma so bent on revenge was a terrible thing.

'It isn't so easy, Nelly,' murmured Emma. 'Oh, in time I might be able to forget . . . and perhaps even forgive all the things I've mentioned. But how can I forgive him for the worst thing of all?' Her voice fell to a whisper and the grey eyes softened with the threat of tears as she gazed longingly on the face of her beloved friend; a friend made in the fearful prison cell to which Caleb Crowther had committed Emma all those years before; a good and loyal friend who had helped her through her long, traumatic exile in Australia; a dear and cherished friend who, Emma hoped, would always be close by. In fact, Nelly was like the sister Emma had always longed for.

'Aw, Emma.' Nelly's gaze bathed Emma's troubled face. 'You're still brooding on that newborn girl-child, ain't you, eh?'

'I can't help it, Nelly. I try so hard to put it out of my mind, but it won't leave me. Not the sight and feel of that tiny, dark-haired bundle in my arms . . . nor the awful pain in my heart when the child was wrenched away and left in the gutter.' Emma's grey eyes shone like hardened steel and her voice stiffened with anger. '*He* did that, Nelly! . . . I begged him for help, but he left me in prison to rot. He could have arranged for me to at least have my baby in a safer place, where she might have had a chance to survive. Oh, Nelly, Nelly, how can I ever forgive him?' Now she could not hold back the tears that trickled down her face.

'All right, Emma, darling.' It hurt Nelly to see Emma's tears. 'Do what you must . . . but don't do anything you might live to regret, eh?'

Emma gave a small laugh as she wiped away the tears. 'Bless you, Nelly,' she said, 'you sound just like Marlow.

He thinks I'm only punishing myself by pursuing this business with Caleb Crowther.'

'Well! There you are then. And there ain't two people who love you more in all the world than me and your fella.' She shook her head and the wispy brown hair fluttered about her face. 'Tain't no good trying to reason with you though, is it . . . you're just as stubborn as you've allus been!' She chortled softly and the curve of her features was lost in a multitude of fine wrinkles. Nelly was not yet in her fortieth year, but the ravages of a hard life and earlier years of terrible neglect had written the passage of time cruelly on her. Even though she was considered shapeless and her face was more plain than pretty, there was something warm and delightful about her, a particular essence that endeared her to everyone she met. There was a world of joy and love in her merry brown eyes, and a childlike wisdom.

'I know that you and Marlow mean well and have only my interests at heart . . . but in this particular instance, I must follow my instincts. Caleb Crowther is a bad one, Nelly. It wouldn't seem right to let him go unpunished.' Emma rose to her feet. Slightly older than Nelly, she made a very pleasing figure, slight and softly curved in an expensive dress of blue taffeta with pretty white ruffles at the throat and cuffs. Her long chestnut-coloured hair was exquisitely coiled into the nape of her neck, where it was secured by two dainty mother-of-pearl combs. When she moved, it was with a natural grace and elegance. Now, as she began walking away, Nelly also got to her feet and quickly took up her place beside Emma.

Content and comfortable in each other's company, Emma and Nelly meandered through the garden, a lovely place of stately old trees and spreading shrubs already heavy with buds. At the farthest end, away from the house, there was a small orchard bursting with fruit trees of all descriptions. The entire garden was surrounded by a wall six feet high and supporting every kind of climbing flower imaginable: the beautiful cascading wisteria, the heavily scented jasmine, clematis, rambling roses and many more. One or two had already begun to open their buds in the April sunshine, but the whole magnificent panorama of colour and perfume would not be evident until mid-summer, when Emma would spend many contented hours in her favourite spot, the small paved area which was bound on three sides by tall, elegant spruce trees. In its middle was a small pond teeming with life, two fancy wrought-iron benches and a circular table. It was in this place that Nelly had found her just now.

From here, Emma could look across the garden and through the tall, wide gate with its open network of railings and scrolls. Beyond the gate was Corporation Park, an undulating expanse of green lawns and wide open spaces, the sight of which filled Emma's heart with nostalgia. It was here, in this lovely old house, that Emma had spent a good deal of her childhood with her beloved father, Thadius Grady. On returning to England, she had been delighted to see that the house on Park Street was up for sale. It seemed like the hand of Fate to her. She and Marlow had bought it, restored it to its former glory, and Emma spent many precious hours wandering from room to room and picturing herself as a child running free within its walls; a child without a mother, but cherished by the father who adored her, and cossetted by the unforgettable Mrs Manfred, who had come to be her nanny. It was in this house that Emma had known great happiness, then heartache when her father had told her of his plan to live at Breckleton House with the Crowther family.

Now, as Emma dwelt on these unpleasant memories, the pain was too much. Thank God for my own family, she thought, and for such a loyal friend as Nelly.

'I'm surprised Silas Trent don't take offence at the way you're badgering old Caleb Crowther,' remarked Nelly in her usual forthright manner. 'The old bugger is Silas's father-in-law after all.' Nelly intended to use every means at her disposal to dissuade Emma from feuding with her uncle because, although she herself loathed what that wicked man had done to Emma, Nelly could see nothing good coming of it all. She felt instinctively that it would be Emma herself who was likely to end up with a bloody nose, however much she was in the right.

Emma was not persuaded by Nelly's latest arguments regarding the man who was both a friend and business colleague and to whom she had recently sold the Australian-based trading company. 'Silas understands,' she replied, 'he knows it is something I have to do.'

Nelly shivered and made an unpleasant face. 'Y'know, Emma gal,' she said in a softer voice, 'I've allus regretted not having a father to talk to . . . somebody I could tek me troubles to when I were growing up . . . if y'know what I mean. But I'll tell you this, gal . . . I'd rather be orphaned and homeless than have a fella such as Caleb Crowther for me father!' Her mood was more indignant as she added, 'I might have understood Martha being swayed by her father's authority when she were younger . . . 'cause when all's said and done he's enough to frighten anybody. But it ain't as though she's still a snotty-nosed kid now, is it, eh? The woman's the wrong side o' forty, be buggered . . . and she still hangs on his every word!'

She hurried her pace to keep up with Emma, who had caught sight of her son's small dark head through the drawing-room window, where he was just about to be released from his afternoon's studies. Soon, he would be ready for full-time tutoring; thank goodness she and Marlow were in agreement that young Bill should not be forcibly sent away to boarding-school. 'When the time comes, we'll let the lad decide for himself,' Marlow had said, the 'time' being when Bill would be nine years old, Emma sighed. It did seem a long way off in the future, but she knew from experience how time had a nasty habit of running away all too quickly. Lately though, life had been good to her: she and Marlow were now man and wife, and they had a wonderful son in young Bill. Also, they were financially secure, what with the sale of her own business and the continuing success of Marlow's transporting concern along the Leeds and Liverpool Canal. In this last year alone he had increased his fleet of barges to twelve in all. Although Emma was always mindful of how fortunate she was, all the wealth and security in the world could never compensate for what she had lost.

Walking beside her, Nelly was aware of Emma's quiet thoughts; she heard the deep troubled sigh and knew at once that her dear friend was thinking of the newborn girl-child that was lost to her on a grim and terrible morning almost a lifetime ago. She knew also that Emma would always hold Caleb Crowther responsible, and rightly so. But, not for the first time, Nelly's

conscience troubled her, because all these years she had
allowed Emma to believe that her child was born dead,
when in fact she herself suspected that the little girl had
lived. The image rose in her mind now of how she had
embraced the unconscious Emma in the prison wagon
that sped them away after the birth, and of how, in the
vanishing distance, there had appeared an old woman
who had stooped to collect a bundle from the gutter, *a
bundle that cried out*. Nelly had never been certain, and
was loath to reveal her suspicions to Emma in case it
made her term of exile that much more unbearable.
Later, when Emma was a free woman, so many years
had passed it seemed futile to delve too deeply into what
was long gone and, to Nelly's mind, should be forgotten.

In a thoughtful attempt to dispel Emma's brooding
countenance, Nelly raised another issue that was close to
Emma's heart, that of a young woman, a thief they had
encountered at the Liverpool docks on their return to
England some three years ago. The unfortunate girl in
question had cunningly outwitted the police officer who
apprehended her then, much to Nelly and Emma's
relief, had made good her escape, giving Emma a cheeky
wink as she fled past them with a grubby child held fast
to her thin, ragged figure. Emma had since agonized
over the young woman's plight and when, a little over a
month ago, Nelly had caught sight of that pathetic soul
scouring the market-place here in Blackburn, Emma had
implored her to enquire after her, 'Nelly . . . we must find
her and make life more bearable for her and the child'.
She had not been surprised when Nelly pointed out, 'Oh,
but she has *two* nippers now . . . the first one big enough
to run as fast as ever her mammy can, and a little scrawny
thing clinging to her like a monkey.'

'What I *really* came to tell you' – Nelly's chirpy voice shattered Emma's painful thoughts – 'was that I didn't have no luck at all in finding that young woman. Nobody seems to know who she is . . . or, if they do, they're not about to tell no stranger.' She snorted with disgust. 'Hmh! . . . it ain't as though I look like a villain or a troublemaker, is it, eh . . . ? On top of which I even offered the buggers a handful of silver for any information regarding her whereabouts. Huh! . . . the way they stared at me anybody'd think I'd been sent by the law or some'at!' The idea was shocking to Nelly who, many years ago, had herself perfected the art of 'defying the law' at every opportunity.

'Did you find no one who might help?' asked Emma anxiously. 'Did you explain that you were on a kindly errand . . . that you meant her no harm?'

'Course I did . . . till I were blue in the face,' Nelly replied with an injured look, which soon gave way to a deep, thoughtful expression as she went on, 'Funny thing, though . . . how them bargees along the wharf clammed up the minute I described her, and I'll tell you what, Emma me old darling . . . I ain't finished with the buggers yet!'

'Oh, you *must* keep trying, Nelly . . . keep on trying till you find her,' urged Emma, her own troubles fading beneath the visions which now flitted through her mind: a young girl burdened with a child, both ragged and hungry-looking. It pained her to think that the poor unfortunate now had another mouth to feed and, according to Nelly, was 'every bit as thin and scruffy as the first time we saw her'. She recalled how the girl had winked at her even as she had led the police officer a merry dance. What a striking face she had, with those big black eyes and strong features. Something about her had touched Emma's heart. 'We mustn't give up,' she told Nelly now, 'I won't rest until we've found her.'

At that point, Emma's son came running from the house to greet her and she was saddened by the fact that she had not been blessed with more children. As she swept the laughing, sturdy little fellow into her arms, Emma felt a pang of guilt. He was so strong and healthy, so cherished and provided for. How very different must be the lives of those two children that Nelly had described. How hard must be the existence of a young mother who was made to steal in order to feed her babies. In her prayers, Emma never failed to give thanks to God for having made her life easier. Now she prayed he might help her to find this young woman so that life might also be made a little kinder for her.

Chapter Three

'Well, if it isn't Molly! A sight to brighten a fella's day. But I'm surprised you dare show your face in broad daylight, you tinker. What shameful antics have you been up to *now*, eh?' The friendly, taunting voice sailed along the wharf, causing the dark-haired young woman to stop and turn around. When her black, mischievous eyes alighted on the familiar brightly coloured barge moored nearby, she began sauntering towards it, her unhurried pace dictated by the tiny infant in her arms and her steps hindered by the slight, fair-haired girl trotting closely beside her. 'You're never meaning *me*, are you?' she laughed. 'Why! . . . I'm an angel if ever there was one.'

Straightening from his labours aboard the barge, the burly young man regarded her closely as she drew near. 'There were a fancy lady asking after you, Molly, my darling,' he said, with a lop-sided grin, 'done up like royalty she were . . . and real keen to make your acquaintance, I reckon.' Mick Darcy was mesmerized by Molly's dark beauty, and by that particular grace-ful way she had of moving. The nearer she came to him, the more his heart turned over. She may be painfully thin, he thought, and dressed in threadbare rags, but there was something magnificent about her; classy was how he would describe the lovely Molly.

Classy, and, as far as he was concerned, sadly un-
attainable.

Mick lost count of how many times that waster, Jack-
the-Lad, had run off and left her, only to return and put
his feet under Molly's table again. The truth was, she
loved the blighter. And love had a nasty way of blinding
a body until they saw only what they wanted to see. It
irked him though to see how Molly had been used by that
rascal time and again. By! If the fellow was here right
now, at this minute, likely as not he'd get the full weight
of a fist in his lying mouth! The bugger didn't deserve
such a loyal, bonny lass as Molly. Oh, if only she'd give
him the chance to look after her, he would make her
life that much more comfortable, treat her special, he
would. But her heart belonged to Jack-the-Lad, and
there seemed no way of winning it over. All the same, he
wouldn't give up. He wanted Molly, *loved* her. He had
patience enough to wait for the right moment in which to
make his move.

As she drew nearer, Molly could not help but be
impressed at the fine figure aboard the barge. Mick
Darcy was a tall, well-built man, and standing on the
deck at this moment, with the sunshine lightening his
earth-coloured curls and those long, strong legs wide
apart for balance against the rolling vessel, he made a
handsome sight.

With a wide, cheeky grin, Mick pushed the flat cap
back on his head and lowered his voice as she looked up
from the quayside. 'You little devil, Molly,' he laughed,
'what have you been up to, eh . . . that some fine lady
should be asking after you?'

'I ain 't been up to *nothing*,' she retorted good-
humouredly, hitching the dark-eyed child more securely

on to her bony hip and keeping a tight hold on the small girl by her side.

'Well, if you ain't been up to nothing . . . how come the gentry are stalking the market-place and offering good money to know your whereabouts, eh? You tell me *that*, sunshine . . . ! You must have been up to something.'

'*I tell you I ain't.*' She smiled and her dark beauty startled him. Then, laughing, she added, 'At least . . . no more than usual . . . a fat wallet or a fancy purse here and there, gently confiscated from them as can afford it. Only enough to keep body and soul together, mind.' Of a sudden, the small girl at her hand broke free. 'Now then, little Sal,' Molly warned in a sharp voice, 'don't you go wandering off . . . else like as not you'll end up in that there canal!' When the child broke into a run, Molly started after her. 'Stop her, Mick!' she yelled.

'Whoa, my little beauty!' Mick Darcy chuckled as he swept the frail, scruffy bundle into his arms and flung it high in the air. When it began laughing and squealing, he pressed it to the floor of his barge, playfully prodding its flat little belly until it curled in a heap and hid itself in a tight hug, at the same time letting out bursts of uncontrollable giggling. That is, until Mick came towards her, his fingers pointed from his forehead in the shape of two long horns and his voice wailing like that of a ghost. At that point, the twitching bundle clambered to its legs and ran screeching and laughing towards the galley hatch, where it disappeared into the quarters below.

'You terror, Mick Darcy,' chuckled Molly, who had delighted in the whole episode. 'The poor little thing'll have nightmares for weeks!' Taking care not to become entangled in the paraphernalia of ropes that cluttered the deck, she climbed aboard. 'Got the kettle on, have you?' she asked, going in the same direction as little Sal. 'My throat's parched.' She cast an accusing glance up to the blue, cloudless sky. 'There still ain't no sign of cooler weather,' she moaned. 'Have you ever known such a muggy, dry May in all your born days?'

'Can't say as I have . . . and I can't say as I haven't, Molly darling,' he replied, at the same time putting a strong lean hand on her shoulder and gently drawing her to a halt. 'There . . .' he stretched out his arms, 'give the babby to me. I don't want to see the pair of you tumbling headlong down that narrow flight of stairs.' His teeth showed white and straight against his tanned skin as he smiled down on her. 'Besides . . . knowing you, you'd like as not fall on my old mammy's best china, and she'd haunt me from the grave.'

'Huh! You ain't got no faith in me at all, have you, Mick Darcy?' She returned his smile and there was a wonderful warmth between them, which made Molly nervous and put her on her guard. She drew the child away. 'The little devil's wet her pants,' she warned, looking quickly aside when she saw the tenderness in those searching, amber eyes. 'Thanks all the same, Mick,' she said, starting her way towards the first step, 'but she's a bit touchy . . . teething she is . . . and she'll happen kick up a fuss.'

'Away with your excuses!' he told her, encouraged by the sight of the little one holding out her arms to him. 'Look there . . . the bairn's no fool, she knows she'll be safer with me,' he laughed. Whereupon Molly graciously handed the child over and they all descended to the lower cabin.

A few moments later, Molly was seated on the bench

by the table, with little Sal kneeling beside her. The smaller bairn was contentedly sleeping between two plump red cushions which Mick had carefully arranged in the narrow bunk that was just visible from the living quarters. Little Sal was growing excited by the increasing number of barges now navigating their way into the narrow waters fronting the many warehouses and cotton mills along Eanam Wharf; at the sight of each new arrival chugging in, little Sal would press her nose to the porthole and squeal with delight. From the galley, Mick could be heard whistling jauntily. Occasionally he would put his head round the wood panelling to reassure Molly and the girl. 'Won't be long now, my beauties . . . bacon and eggs, sunny side up.' The delicious aroma of sizzling bacon soon permeated every corner of the barge.

'You really don't have to feed us,' protested Molly, even though she hadn't eaten a proper meal in days and her stomach was rumbling with hunger.

'It's my pleasure,' he said, placing the hearty breakfast in front of her and little Sal, who suddenly lost all interest in the barges outside as she tucked into the meal with unashamed enthusiasm. 'If you'd only let me, Molly . . . I would take on the responsibility of you and the two bairns tomorrow.' His voice was quiet and serious as he studied her with imploring eyes.

'Well, we ain't your responsibility,' Molly was quick to remind him. 'We never could be . . . and you know it, Mick Darcy. These two little lasses and me . . . we belong to Jack.' She lowered her gaze and patted herself below the waist, 'Not forgetting the little one who's not yet shown its face.'

'*Oh, Molly!*' He put his breakfast plate on the table

and fell heavily on to the bench opposite. 'He's never left you with another?'

Molly nodded her head, and he could have sworn there was a merry twinkle in her black eyes. 'It happened when he found his way home just before Easter . . . "recovering from a run of bad fortune", he said . . . two weeks later he won a packet on the horses and went off to celebrate. I haven't seen him since.' She laughed out loud at the expression of horror on Mick's face. 'Oh, don't fret yourself,' she told him, beginning to enjoy her meal, 'if my calculations serve me right, the bairn should arrive some time round Christmas Eve . . . What d'you think to that, eh? It's not everybody as can look forward to such a special Christmas present, is it? Oh, and like as not, its daddy will have turned up long afore that.'

'The bugger deserves a thrashing!'

'Hey, watch your language afront of the little ones,' warned Molly with good humour. 'Come on, eat your breakfast and don't look so shocked . . . I'm not about to drop it here and now!' she laughingly reassured him.

'It wouldn't matter if you *did*, Molly darling . . . you know it would be made welcome.' There was a world of love in his voice.

'I know.' Long, slim fingers reached out to cover his hand in a warm gesture. 'You're a good friend to me and my bairns, Mick Darcy,' Molly murmured, 'and there's nobody else I'd ever share my troubles with. I can't deny what you say . . . Jack will never be any good . . . he'll always gamble his money away; he'll drift from place to place like the vagabond he is, and I know in my heart that there's no future for us together . . . he's not the kind to put down roots. But I love him. And I can't help the way I feel. Oh, it's not so bad . . . I can put up with his coming and going, and his gambling, because I know he'll aways come back, to hold me in his arms and tell me there's no other woman for him. It's only crumbs, I know . . . but it's all he can give, and it's enough. So long as he's faithful, and there's no other woman in his arms, I'll put up with all his failings.'

'And if there ever *was* another woman?' Mick had no reason to believe that Jack had deceived the trusting Molly, but the fellow was a worthless bounder who was capable of anything.

For a while, Molly remained silent, pushing the curled bacon round her plate with the prongs of the fork and deeply considering Mick's question. Of a sudden, she stabbed the fork into the bacon and raised her black, tempestuous eyes to his. 'I'd *kill* the pair of them,' she said with alarming calmness; after which she went on to finish her breakfast as though the subject had never arisen. All the same, her hands were trembling and her heart was beating furiously inside her at the thought of some other woman in her Jack's arms.

'I can't think how you ever got tangled up with the likes of him . . . you never have told me the full story.' Mick had seen the pain in Molly's eyes, and he called himself all kinds of a fool for having planted the seed of doubt in her mind with regard to her fellow. All the same though, he knew that Molly was no fool. The idea that Jack had ample opportunity to be unfaithful to her must have presented itself. 'You do realize that one of these days, Molly . . . he just may not come back?' Somewhere, in his deepest heart, he prayed for that day, but then he was filled with remorse, knowing how devastated Molly would be if ever Jack finally deserted her. He couldn't understand how she went on forgiving this man who used her badly at every turn. But then, love was a funny, unpredictable thing. Look at *him*, for example. Look how he adored Molly beyond all else, knowing that she would never look at any man other than Jack; Jack, who had lumbered her with three kids, and left her to fend for them as best she could, knowing full well that every time he went away there was always the danger that Molly and the young 'uns could be thrown on to the streets. However, if the truth were told, eviction might turn out to be the lesser of two evils, because that grim, God-forsaken place on Dock Street could never be called 'home'. If Molly were to lose that place she only had to ask and he would gladly take her in. But she *wouldn't* ask. He knew that, and it saddened him. Yet in spite of everything, he still loved and wanted her. So when it came right down to it, he did understand how one soul could adore another, even if it were a lost cause.

'You're wrong, Mick.' Molly's gaze was defiant, albeit a little desperate, he thought. 'Jack will *always* come back . . . he'd never leave us for good.' There came into her eyes a faraway look, and, as always, she was out of his reach. 'He loves us, you see.' Turning from Mick's earnest gaze, Molly looked out of the porthole, her dark eyes scanning the wharf as though searching for someone. When the infant stirred behind her, she quickly glanced round to assure herself that the child was safe enough. Then, facing Mick, she went on in a quiet voice, 'You don't have to tell me how worthless Jack is . . . I've known for a long time. You ask how I ever got "tangled up with the likes of him", and I can only tell you that he came to my help when I desperately needed someone. I were all alone in the world, Mick . . . very young and very frightened.' Here she paused. Images of an old woman came into her mind – a limping, bedraggled woman with thin, tousled hair and a kindly face that was ravaged by a rough life and a particular love for 'a drop o' the ol' stuff'. Old Sal Tanner had been Molly's anchor in life, her mammy, her friend, and the kindest, dearest, most cantankerous lady on God's earth. Leaning back in her seat, Molly fought down the tears. 'You know of old Sal Tanner . . . her as brought me up from a babe in arms?'

'I don't come from these parts but I know of old Sal right enough.' He smiled that broad smile which somehow disturbed Molly in spite of herself. 'Who *didn't* know of her? The old tramp's become a kind of legend in these 'ere parts. It's a strange story, Molly . . . how she always told that you belonged to the little people . . . how she found you in the gutter and all.' His voice grew more serious as he asked, 'Did she ever reveal your true parents?'

'She didn't know, bless her. She had strange ideas, did old Sal, but she was very special to me.' The memories came flooding back. 'There was this timepiece she used to keep hidden . . . a pretty, delicate little thing it were . . . with writing on the case. Old Sal would show it to me from time to time . . . almost afraid of it, she was . . . said it were right next to me when she found me in the gutter . . . "A sign from the little people", she claimed. At first, I believed everything she told me. But then, as I got older and realized that Sal's ideas were a bit stranger than other folks', I got to thinking about that there timepiece. I wondered about the writing on it, and promised myself that, one day, I'd learn to read. Then I might find out where I *really* came from, and where I belonged.'

'Where is it now . . . ? This timepiece? Will you show it to me?'

'It's gone . . . gone, long before Jack taught me to read.'

'Gone? You mean you sold it?'

Molly shook her head. 'No. I would never do that . . . not when old Sal made me promise never to part with it.'

'Then where is it?'

'Snatched from round my neck by Justice Crowther.'

'*Crowther!*' Mick recoiled in disgust. That was a name to foul anyone's lips. 'How in God's name did you tangle with *him*? Most folks know how to steer well clear of that particular devil.'

Molly told him everything: how, when she was very young, she'd found Justice Crowther's grandson dazed and wandering, and how he fell into the canal and would have drowned if she hadn't dived in and saved him. 'I didn't know who he were, till I took him to the cabin to recover . . . he didn't look like no gentry to me . . . dressed in filthy rags he were, and looking like the worst tramp.' Then she explained how it turned out that he'd been set upon by ruffians who had stripped him of his own posh clothes and swapped them for the rags he wore when she found him. 'Only a few days before, old Sal had left this wicked world and was lying in the mortuary . . . waiting for a pauper's grave unless I could come up with the money to bury her properly. Well, it were like Lady Luck smiled on me when she led that gentry lad to my door.' Molly told how she had contacted Justice Crowther's wife, and been reluctantly paid for the return of her grandson, Edward Trent – 'a really nice lad he was'. While Mick listened, enthralled and astonished, she went on to describe how Justice Crowther then blamed her for kidnapping his grandson, and hunted her down without mercy. 'It was the very night when he seized me and burned old Sal's cabin that he snatched the timepiece . . . when I was escaping from the prison-cart with Jack-the-Lad. He saved me, my Jack . . . kept me with him all the time we were on the run, even though I slowed him down and might have been the cause of both of us being captured and clapped in irons for the rest of our miserable lives.'

Mick shook his head. 'The story of how Justice Crowther's grandson was "brutally kidnapped" went far and wide . . . I remember something of it when I was working the Manchester waterways. But, my God, Molly . . . I didn't know . . . why haven't you ever told me all this before?'

'Because it's a dangerous thing to let loose. I've a feeling in my bones that if Justice Crowther were ever to find me . . . he'd *still* get pleasure from clapping me in irons. I only told you so you'd understand how much I owe Jack, and how he'll always come back.'

Mick nodded, though he was not convinced about Jack's loyalty. 'You say the timepiece was snatched from your neck, Molly?' When she nodded, he went on. 'Are you *sure* of that . . . ? I mean, could it not just have been accidentally broken in the struggle, and fallen to the ground?'

'No. Some time after, when we thought it might be safe, Jack and me went back and searched . . . Jack knew how much it meant to me. There was no sign of it. I'm convinced that Justice Crowther still has it . . . perhaps he thinks it might lead him to me in time.' She dipped her two fingers into the neck of her dress and drew out the black string that hung from her throat.

Knotted at the end of the loop was a tiny gold clasp in the shape of a petal cluster. 'When the chain was torn from my neck . . . this fastener got caught in my hair.'

'It's very little to go by, Molly.' Mick was surprised that she had not sold the pretty gold cluster. After all, it must be worth a guinea or so. Then he realised the depth of her love for old Sal Tanner, and the promise she had made the old woman. No, it was *not* surprising that Molly still cherished the tiny piece, for it obviously meant more than money to her. A sudden thought chilled him. 'Are you telling me that this fancy lady . . . the one who's been asking after you . . . is *sent by Justice Crowther* to root you out?'

Molly gave no answer for a moment, seemingly lost in deep, tormenting thoughts. She gently stroked the child's fair head and was suddenly fearful for the future. After a while, she looked up to meet Mick's anxious gaze with a rush of defiance. 'Who else could it be?' she asked. 'Of course she were sent by the Justice. But I tell you this, Mick Darcy . . . they can search high and low, but they'll not find me . . . I've learned when to keep my head down. And I've grown as crafty as a fox when it comes to dipping and diving.'

'You'd be safer moving away from these parts.' Mick was afraid for her. 'Come away with me, Molly . . . you and me . . . we could make a good life together.'

Molly got to her feet. 'You know my answer to that,' she said cuttingly, 'and if you want us to stay the good friends we are, don't ever ask me again.' She turned to draw the child into her arms. 'Come on, Sal my darling . . . it's high time we went.'

'Forget what I said, Molly . . . it's just that I'm afraid for you. You can understand that, can't you?'

Molly thought hard before answering. 'It's forgot then.' Her smile was warm, though not intimate. 'What I told you . . . about the Justice and all that . . . it won't go no further? There are times when a body can't tell friend from foe.'

'You can count on me.' He reached the infant before Molly did, and as he tenderly raised its sleeping form into his capable arms, his eyes were drawn to Molly, who was looking at him in a strangely unsettling way, her black eyes following his every move. When she realized that Mick had been made curious by her close observation of him, she was suddenly self-conscious and, irritated by the soft pink glow that suffused her neck and face, she quickly lowered her gaze to the floor.

Mick brought the child to her, yet made no attempt to give it into her arms. Instead, the two of them stood for a moment, he gazing down on her, and she with her eyes averted. When in a while she raised her eyes to his he was astonished to see them bright with tears. 'What is it, Molly, me darling?' he asked softly. 'Why were you watching me like that?'

Something in the tone of his voice cautioned her. She must never unwittingly give him hope. But, oh, what a grand, heartwarming sight he had made just now, when he had so lovingly raised her sleeping child into those strong arms; arms that were more used to raising the cripplingly heavy loads that lined the wharves. He was a good man, she thought. A better man than Jack could ever be, but she dared not tell him that, for fear he misunderstood. 'It's not important,' she said in a deliberately matter-of-fact voice. 'I were just thinking, that's all . . . just thinking.'

Before he could persist in his questions, Molly turned

away and climbed the steep, narrow steps that led up to the deck. Little Sal, full and comfortable from the hearty breakfast, trotted behind her mammy, and Mick brought up the rear, cradling the infant close to his chest. This was how it should be, he thought, me and Molly, with the bairns round us and Jack-the-Lad out of the picture altogether. Yet even while his fancies took hold of him, he knew that that was all they were. Fancies. All the same, it made him tremble to think how close he had come to frightening Molly away. He would watch his tongue in future. Somehow, he had to keep his emotions in check or he'd lose her friendship altogether. He couldn't bear the idea of not having her pay the occasional visit, when they could sit and share their troubles like two old friends. Such times were precious to him, and if he had to settle for that or nothing at all, then he would content himself with the strong friendship that existed between them.

As he watched Molly leaving the wharf, Mick's love for her was never stronger, a frustrating love, and one which he knew would continue to cause him pain. A spiral of anger rose in him, but it was tempered by a sneaking admiration. Molly was too independent by far! Too proud, and too bloody loyal to a man who wasn't worth salt. So what if Jack *had* saved Molly from the bobbies? Any man would have done the same, given the opportunity. God almighty . . . ! It didn't mean she had to devote her whole life to him because of it, and it didn't mean she had to close her eyes to his many failings.

At the corner of the warehouse, Molly glanced back. When she saw that Mick was still watching, she waved and smiled. Then she was gone. For a long, aching moment, Mick stared at the place where she had paused, before issuing a deep, weary sigh. 'Aw, Molly . . . my lovely Molly,' he murmured, but there was a smile in his voice, and in his heart a warm anticipation of their next meeting.

'Good morning . . . looks like we're in for another glorious day.' The fellow addressed Mick in a firm, friendly voice as he strode towards the front office of one of the bigger cotton mills.

'Top o' the morning to you, sir,' replied Mick, while observing how, even though the man was dressed in casual togs, they were not the togs of a labourer, but the easy attire of a gentry. This one was a puzzle, though, because he had a winning smile and a manner that was not hostile to the likes of himself. Growing curious, he clambered from the barge and sought out the advice of a bargee who was securing his vessel nearby. 'Who's that fellow?' he asked, adding with a chuckle, 'If he were fitted out in cords and rolled-up sleeves, I'd swear he was a bargee the same as you and me . . . there's something about his manner . . . and the cut of his swagger. Though I dare say he's never done a day's work in his life, eh?'

'Well now, that's where you'd be wrong, fella-me-lad!' The old sailor came forward to lean against the rail where he took off his cap, slung it over a nearby strut and leisurely proceeded to light up the tobacco in his pipe. Mick was amused to see how the old one was in no particular hurry to satisfy the curiosity of a stranger. In fact, he seemed to be positively relishing in withholding the information just that bit longer. When his pipe was lit and he himself engulfed in billowing grey smoke, he went on, 'That there fellow knows more about barges and working these waterways than you and me put together.' Here, he leaned over and pointed to the sign heading his barge. 'See that?'

'The sign, you mean?'

'Aye . . . see the name written there?'

Mick studied the sign, before reading it aloud – *'Tanner's Transporters'*. He glanced back to where he had seen the man disappear. 'You're never telling me that *he* owns this barge?'

'I am that. This barge . . . and nigh on a dozen more like it. And I'll tell you some'at else, matey, Marlow Tanner may not *look* as smooth and smarmy as the next gent . . . but he's a better gent than ever you're likely to find. A proper credit to the blokes who work for him. There ain't one of us who wouldn't stretch ourselves to the limit if he were to ask. Teks care of us he do . . . through thick and thin. You'll never find a better gaffer than Marlow Tanner.' He pursed his lips into a multitude of wrinkles and nodded his head as though agreeing with himself. 'And that's the very truth!' he concluded, making ready to resume his labours.

'A dozen such barges, you say?' Mick had been working this particular stretch of the Leeds and Liverpool Canal for almost a year now, and was curious to know how it was that he had not come across a 'Tanner Transporter' until today.

'Aye, that's right. Up until a year back, we were regular between here and the big docks . . . but the gaffer secured a juicy contract, which meant us coming up outta the Yorkshire side.' He chuckled, displaying a jagged row of tobacco-stained teeth, 'Earned us all a bob or two extra, that did.'

'I see.' That would explain why he hadn't shared a berth with one of these barges before. 'But didn't he lose the contract *this* side, if he shifted operations like that?'

'Naw . . . he's too bloody canny a businessman for that,' remonstrated the old one. Of a sudden, he was eyeing Mick's barge alongside. 'That yourn, is it?'

'It is.'

'And you've been working this particular stretch . . . ferrying cotton to the Liverpool Docks?'

'I have.'

The old one laughed out loud. 'Then *you've* been paid by Tanner . . . just like the rest of us . . . and all these single barge-owners hereabouts.'

Mick shook his head. 'No, old man. You've got it wrong . . . my pay packet comes from the owner of that there mill.' He pointed to the very building into which he had seen Marlow Tanner disappear. Suddenly, the light began to dawn. 'Well, I never . . . ! Are you saying *he* owns the mill?'

Thoroughly enjoying himself, the old fellow gleefully pointed out how Marlow Tanner not only secured every available barge-owner for the period of one year, but when the owner of the largest cotton mill loudly protested at what he claimed was a 'threat to free enterprise', he promptly bought the mill as well! 'Made the fellow an offer he'd a' been a fool to turn down.'

As Mick went thoughtfully back to his own barge, two things crossed his mind. One was paramount in his reckoning. If his own services had been secured for a year – which they had – and if the Tanner barges were now back in force – which they seemed to be – how long would it be before he was summoned to Marlow Tanner's office and told he was no longer needed? It was a daunting prospect, especially since the fellow was also busy buying up the mills that had hitherto supplied a living to the likes of himself.

Deeply concerned, Mick decided not to wait for Tanner to lay him off. He still had a living to make, and he wanted to make it *here* in these parts, where he could keep an eye on Molly. No, he couldn't afford to wait. The matter had to be settled. The sooner the better, to his mind. Straight away, Mick changed his direction and went hastily towards the mill office.

The other matter that had crossed his mind was the name *Tanner*. Surely it couldn't have a link to the old woman who had raised Molly from a child? No, he told himself. Old Sal Tanner was a drunk, a tramp who had no one but Molly . . . or so he had heard. He'd better watch his tongue, if he were to obtain more work from this fellow. Besides, Tanner was a common name hereabouts. He laughed softly to himself. The very idea that a mill owner, a wealthy fellow such as Marlow Tanner, was in any way connected with an old soak who imagined that 'the little people' had brought Molly to her, well, if he didn't want to be laughed at and run off the wharf, he'd best keep his foolish mouth shut!

Mick was still chuckling to himself as he entered the building. Some moments later, he was face to face with Marlow Tanner, a fine able-bodied fellow of some forty years and more, with sincere dark eyes and hair as black as coal. For a fleeting moment, Mick was put in mind of Molly's own similar dark features, and his heart ached a little.

'Sit down, Mr Darcy.' Marlow Tanner recalled greeting the young man earlier, and he had already guessed the nature of his urgent visit. 'No doubt you're wondering where you stand now that the year's secured work is almost finished?' When Mick answered that yes, this was so, Marlow Tanner immediately put him out of his misery by reassuring him, 'There'll always be work for them as wants it.'

As the discussion got underway, Mick's admiration and respect for this man was increased by the minute. He was pleasantly surprised at how quickly the older man put him at his ease. His surprise, however, would have turned to astonishment if he had known that Marlow Tanner was Molly's father.

There were things of the past that neither of them was aware of. Not Mick, nor Marlow. Nor certainly Molly, who had long given up the idea of ever finding her true parents.

Chapter Four

It was Christmas Eve. Blackburn Market had been a hive of activity all day long, but now the snow, which had been gently falling since late morning, was beginning to settle more thickly on the cobbles. Overhead the sky was grey with the promise of more severe weather.

As the snow grew thicker, the crowd of shoppers grew steadily thinner, with people cringing from the cold, scurrying away to the warmth of their own cheery firesides. Seeing their customers hastily depart, a number of stall-holders began to pack up their wares and load the waiting carts which would carry them home. The more seasoned and determined merchants, however, stood their ground, their lusty cries desperately tempting the remaining shoppers to 'Get yer hot chestnuts 'ere, missus' or 'rabbits for the Christmas pot . . . skinned and ready'. For those whose purses were fatter there was the offer of 'fresh, plump turkeys to grace any lady's table'.

At the sight of a well-heeled and expensively attired gentlewoman standing not six feet away, the man with the turkeys saw a likely customer and at once began besieging her with umpteen reasons as to why 'yer daren't go home without one, missus!' He was instantly struck dumb when back came a sharp retort in a broad Cockney voice, 'And I daren't bleedin' well go home *with* one, neither . . . else I'd be flung out the kitchen and no mistake!' Nelly might have gone on to explain that Emma would not thank her for interfering in what was Cook Parker's domain. But the outburst had provoked much laughter from the shoppers within hearing distance, so she merrily winked at the astonished stall-holder and wandered away to continue her browsing, finally coming to rest at the bric-à-brac stall where she purchased a small quantity of pretty coloured lace.

Not being naturally born to the genteel manners of a lady, Nelly loved to meander through the market, revelling in the shouts of the barrow-boys and other traders, and losing herself amongst the ordinary folk. She had another purpose also: to keep an eye out for the young woman who had crossed Emma's path and left such a deep, lasting impression on her; on Nelly too and that was a fact. Today, though, she had scoured the many faces which had thronged the market place, but none of them had matched the face of that young woman, with her strong, lean features and big black eyes that held a world of tragedy.

Over by the market clock stood the very person who was proving so elusive to Nelly: a poorly-dressed creature with a thin, anxious face and a belly swollen with new life. Beside her stood little Sal, a child of fair face and angelic blue eyes.

'There y'are, darling,' Molly told the child eagerly, 'the barrow-boy's making off soon . . . there'll be a few juicy titbits left lying on the ground when he's gone. You see if I'm not right.'

'Can we have a Christmas tree, Mammy?' Pinched by the cold, little Sal huddled into Molly's shawl.

'We'll see, sweetheart, but you're not to count on it,

mind.' Molly knew that even if they did 'find' a tree, it was more than she dared to drag it all the way back to Dock Street. Not with the birthing so close, and not with her feeling as weak as a kitten, the way she did. It was strange, she thought, how all the while she had been carrying little Sal and young Peggy, there hadn't been a day's discomfort. But *this* time it was different. Right from the start, she'd been violently ill of a morning, and the bairn seemed to lie so heavy inside her that it was like a dead weight pulling her down. There was something else too; a feeling that something wasn't quite right. She had scolded herself for even entertaining such depressing thoughts. 'The others were lasses . . . this little rascal must be a lad,' she had laughingly convinced herself. 'It's a known fact that fellas cause all the trouble in the world!'

'If we get a tree . . . I can put my rag dolly on it . . . then she can pretend to be a princess, like the ones we saw in the shop window.'

'Ssh, I've told you, we'll have to see.' Christmas was the worst time for Molly. It always hurt her when she couldn't provide the things that made a child's Christmas that much more special. But then, as far as she was concerned, Christmas was *not* special, it was no different from all the other days that ran into each other. Apart from the children's birthdays. She always made a little fuss then, because if anything at all was worthwhile in her life, it was her babies. Glancing down at the child, she softly called her name. 'Sal, you'd really love a proper tree, wouldn't you, darling?' When the fair, curly head nodded eagerly, Molly squeezed the tiny hand clutched in her own. 'Then your mammy will get you one, sweetheart,' she promised, thinking how it should be possible to pick up a few fallen branches and bundle them together to make a little tree.

Of a sudden Molly thought of Mick and was instantly beset by feelings of guilt. If she had taken up his kind invitation, their Christmas would have been that much brighter; there would have been proper food on the table, maybe even a fat, proud turkey. Little Sal would have had a tree. Molly quickly dismissed the pang of guilt. In her heart she believed that she had done right to turn down Mick's offer that she and the children spend Christmas aboard his barge; she had done right to tell him a lie, that Tilly Watson from next door had got there with an invitation before him, and that she had already accepted; so how could she be so ungrateful as to turn the woman down *now*, she had argued, after all the work she had put herself to? Like the gentleman he was, Mick had reluctantly agreed. 'I *did* do right!' Molly muttered under her breath. After all, what if she was enjoying a hearty Christmas in another fellow's home and Jack were to come back, only to find the house cold and empty. It wouldn't be right. Molly didn't fool herself that Jack was likely to come home laden with presents, but that didn't bother her none; Jack himself would be the best Christmas present, and the children would have their daddy for Christmas. Mick had been disappointed, but he'd get over it soon enough, she decided. Besides which, there were two other reasons why she could never have accepted. Firstly, the birthing was too near. Then there was this thing about Mick and her: him trying so desperately to hide his feelings for her when she only had to look in his eyes and his love was shining there like a beacon for all to see. It made her feel bad and un-comfortable. As though his pain was all her fault. Well, it wasn't, she told herself now, and much as she valued Mick's friendship, it might be better all round if she were to steer clear of him from now on.

A short time later, after filling their hessian bag with bruised but still edible titbits collected from the cobbles, Molly and little Sal were busy foraging for the longest branches from beneath the Christmas tree stall. Of a sudden, something happened to take Molly unawares and to put the fear of God in her. Something that triggered off a series of tragic events which no one, not even Molly, could have foreseen.

Having completed her small shopping expedition, Nelly was preparing to make her way home. The square was fast becoming deserted, and already the scavenging animals were slinking in to devour any juicy morsels that might be left lying beneath the food stalls. Feeling the effects of the cutting breeze that nipped at her face and froze her fingers, Nelly hurried towards the other side of the square, to where a line of horse-drawn carriages waited along Victoria Street for any would-be passengers. It was when Nelly stopped to glance about and make sure there were no traders' carts hurtling in her direction that she caught sight of the two bent figures busily collecting the strewn Christmas tree branches. 'It's her!' she muttered aloud. 'The *very* gal I've been searching for!' So excited was she that, in a moment, she might have called out. But caution and instinct warned her not to, for fear the young woman and her child were frightened off. Good Lord, Nelly told herself as she went on wary steps towards where Molly and little Sal were preparing to leave with their precious hoard, Emma would never forgive me if she knew I'd caught sight of the creature and then *lost* her.

It was little Sal who first saw the stealthily approaching
figure; Nelly's fox-fur neckpiece and fancy feathered hat
held her mesmerized. When Molly looked to see what
was so intriguing as to hold the child's attention in such a
way, her heart almost stopped beating at the sight of the
figure making its way towards her, and, to her mind,
looking devious into the bargain. 'Jesus, Mary and
Joseph . . . it's the gentry!' she cried, her black eyes
wide and fearful. 'Quick, Sal, *run*! Run as fast as your
legs'll take you!' Flinging the branches to the ground,
Molly grabbed the child's hand, chiding her when she
began crying for the precious Christmas tree which now
lay in ruins on the cobbles. '*Leave it!*' yelled Molly,
frantically tugging the sobbing girl away. 'The gentry's
after us . . . and if I'm caught it won't be a blessed *tree*
you'll be crying over . . . it'll be your poor mammy,
'cause they'll likely lock me up till I'm old and grey!'
There was real fear in Molly's heart as she took to her
heels, fear that lent wings to her feet as she and the
young one sped away over the cobbles with never a look
back.

'Stop! Stop!' Nelly took up pursuit, cursing at the long
heavy hem of her expensive dress and thinking how, if
she were twenty years younger and unencumbered by
the fancy attire of a 'gentlewoman', she would never
have been left so far behind.

Seeing that others, alerted by her cries, began to
follow the chase, she yelled for them to 'mind yer own
business . . . she *ain't no thief!* It's a private matter, so
bugger off!'

'Blow me down . . . she might look like a lady, but the
old trout sounds more like a sodding *fishwife*!' shouted
one, being frustrated at having the only excitement of

the day ended so abruptly. Just as quickly as they had joined in the fray and now looking somewhat affronted by the vehemence of Nelly's verbal attack, the pursuers loped off. All but a snotty-nosed lad who took great delight in pelting Nelly with anything he could lay his hands on – unfortunately for Nelly the articles included two split and not very fresh eggs which left their sticky mark all down the front of her skirt.

Nelly might have stopped to 'cuff your grubby ear'ole' but she still had sight of the two runaways and was bent on catching them if she could. In fact, if the truth were told, Nelly was thoroughly enjoying the entire episode. She couldn't remember when she'd felt so alive. Her mind rolled back to when she herself was no older than the unfortunate quarry she was now chasing and she couldn't help but chuckle at the memory of her own narrow escapes from the law and gentry alike. Oh, they were the days! Ducking and diving, grasping her opportunities as they came and never giving a tinker's cuss for the fact that she had neither home nor family. It was a hard life, but it had its moments, she recalled: the worst one being when the authorities clapped her in irons to be shipped off to Australia as a no-good vagrant and petty thief. The best moment was the fateful day when she met another poor soul who was branded with the same iron, but, unlike her, was as innocent as the day was long: Emma Grady. Her darling precious Emma, who had been her one and only family ever since.

'*Stop*, yer little fool!' she yelled now, her breath feeling cut off at its root and her steps already beginning to slow to a painful trot. 'It's a *lady* as wants ter talk ter you . . . Emma Grady as was, who's Emma Tanner now. She only wants to *help* you!' When she realized that the two ragamuffins were long gone, she repeated bad-temperedly, 'Wants to help you, she does . . . though Lord knows *why*. After the merry dance you've led me, you ungrateful urchin . . . I'd not cross the bloody road to help you, I wouldn't!' Yet she knew that her words were no more than hot air and frustration because now, after seeing how terrified the young woman was, and how she was foraging for the discarded bits of Christmas trees, and also that she was heavy with child, Nelly was as anxious as Emma to find her and do what she could to make her sorry lot that much easier. But she wouldn't find her again today. Not today. Maybe not ever again, now that the poor creature had the measure of her. She would be more on her guard than ever now, and that was a fact.

Despondent, Nelly gave up the chase and turned away, feeling both irritated and decidedly uncomfortable from the effects of her short burst at running. She promised herself that, now she was in her forties and a bit longer in the tooth than during her wilder days, chasing vagabonds would definitely *not* be one of her future activities. All the same, she would dearly have loved to talk with that young woman, if only to assure her that she had no reason to fear either herself or Emma, who, in Nelly's opinion, was one of God's chosen angels. 'Though she can be a real terror if she puts her mind to it,' she promptly reminded herself with a chuckle. 'And Lord only knows what she'll say when she sees me looking like something out of a shipwreck, with me hair bedraggled and me skirt stinking to high heaven of rotten eggs!' Anticipating a healthy exchange of words between herself and Emma, she promptly climbed into the nearest carriage and instructed the bemused driver, 'Park Street, my good fellow . . . and be quick about it!' When he appeared to hold his nose at the rich and unpleasant smell that wafted up his nostrils, she fell back into the seat, quietly chuckling. By God, when that young vagabond was finally brought to account for what happened today – and she *would*, of that Nelly was determined – she'd get the sharp end of Nelly's tongue and that was a fact! Still and all, even though Nelly had thoroughly enjoyed herself, there were serious issues here. She hoped the unfortunate young woman had not been too frightened by all the attention, nor pushed too far to her limit. After all, she had another little soul tripping along beside her, and the added burden of being heavy with child. On top of which, the pair of ragamuffins looked as starved as scarecrows, and couldn't have two penn'orth of strength between them. 'Ah, but they gave *you* a good run for your money, Nelly my gal, that they did,' she laughed, throwing a cutting look to the driver when he turned to regard this strange and smelly passenger. 'You look where you're bleeding well going!' she told him. 'Ain't you never seen a lady afore?'

'Quick, darling, run and fetch Tilly Watson . . . tell her to be as quick as ever she can!' Molly fought against the gripping pains that raged through her with a vengeance before spasmodically ebbing away, leaving her breathless and bathed in a film of sweat. The bairn was fighting to be born and there wasn't a moment to lose. It was the frantic chase through the market that had brought on the spasms, and at first Molly had hoped they might subside once she reached the relative safety of Dock Street, but, if anything, they had intensified. Molly's churning thoughts came to dwell on the woman who had chased her and Sal through the market. A gentry, but with a voice and manner that contradicted her fancy clothes. Molly recalled the words she had shouted after them, 'Stop, yer little fool . . . it's a *lady* as wants ter talk ter you. Emma Grady as was, who's Emma Tanner now!'

Molly knew she and little Sal had made a lucky escape, though she had wondered since whether the frantic run in her advanced condition had complicated matters for the poor mite inside her. Molly wasn't certain, because she had long felt that things were going wrong. All the same it was unfortunate, and whether the circumstances had brought her labour about that much more quickly, she really did not know. What she did know was that she and little Sal had done right to take to their heels. '*Emma Tanner*,' the woman had shouted, '*Emma Grady as was*.'

Molly's fears were threefold. Firstly, she knew the name Tanner well enough. Marlow Tanner was a big name hereabouts. She also knew that he was the brother of old Sal Tanner, whom Molly had adored, and who had suffered a great deal of heartache when her younger brother, Marlow, had 'gone orf to 'Merica ter seek 'is fortune'. Years she waited for him to return. Years of trouble and worry, when she never lost her faith in him. But when there came no word from him and she began to believe he had been 'snatched from the face of the earth', old Sal finally gave up hope of ever seeing him again. But she never blamed him, saying, 'My lad wouldn't desert me on purpose, Molly gal . . . if 'e ain't able ter come back an' see 'is old sister as fotched 'im up like both mam and dad to 'im, well . . . it's 'cause the poor bugger's lying dead on some foreign soil, or 'e's been swallered up by the ocean!'

Now though, Molly knew better. Marlow Tanner *had* deserted old Sal, because some time back he'd returned to his roots and built up a big fleet of trading barges along the Leeds and Liverpool Canal. Molly had seen him many a time, and many a time she had been tempted to accuse him on old Sal's behalf, and to tell him how his sister would have been buried in a pauper's grave, but for her. *She* had stood by old Sal, while *he* had deserted the darling woman. But Molly couldn't bring herself even to talk to him. She knew in her heart that old Sal would have forgiven him in a minute, but she never would! She loathed him; even the thought of conversing with him turned her stomach over.

Besides, in Molly's opinion, Marlow Tanner had made matters worse by marrying the one they called Emma Grady. In spite of the fact that the hated Justice Crowther had done nothing to stop her being transported as an accessory to murder, and there was now a feud said to be raging between them, Molly saw that particular woman as an enemy to be feared. After all, rumours ran rife and happen Emma and Caleb Crowther were not 'at each other's throats'. After all, he *was* her uncle when all was said and done, and there was no denying that Justice Caleb Crowther would like nothing better than to clap Molly in irons and leave her to rot. 'But oh, not if Molly keeps her wits about her!' Molly declared aloud now. 'They'll not catch me and mine while there's a breath in my body.'

Molly and the Justice had crossed paths on that particular night when he had snatched the precious timepiece from round her neck and burned old Sal's cabin to the ground. It was Molly's avowed intent that her enemies would never get the better of her, nor would the one who had joined them . . . old Sal's treacherous brother, Marlow.

Drenched in sweat and anxious for her baby, Molly waited for Tilly to come to her. The time for thinking was over. The child was on its way and there was much hard work ahead. If Tilly didn't hurry up, Molly knew she'd have to do it all on her own. There was no doubt that the birth was imminent. That in itself wasn't a bad thing, reasoned Molly, because this particular child had been the worst of all to bear. She would not be sorry to see it parted from her aching body and lying warm beside her. But it was hard! Dear God in heaven, it was hard to take such persistent and crippling pain; worst of all to make herself suppress the cries that might help to make the ordeal a little more bearable. But she must *not* cry out, not in front of little Sal, who would likely be horrified to hear her mammy in such pain.

As it was, the girl knew well enough that 'my babby' was on its way, for Molly had been careful to satisfy little Sal's curiosity regarding 'the bump' in her tummy; although she had kept her explanations short and simple, assuring the child that the babby she would insist was hers was a precious gift to her mammy and daddy from the Lord above and that the 'bump' was the cradle where the tiny being would stay warm and safe, until it was big and strong enough to come into the world and say hello. Little Sal was content with the explanation and never tired of hearing it. 'I hope she says hello to *me* first,' she had told Molly with an old-fashioned look in her soft blue eyes, ''cause I was here before Peggy, so my arms

62

arc bigger to hug the babby . . . and I won't let the babby fall, will I, Mammy?'

On Molly's frantic instruction, little Sal had raced out of the house to fetch Tilly Watson from next door. In a surprisingly short time she was back, with the small wiry figure in tow. 'Jesus, Mary and Joseph, Molly gal!' gasped Tilly, one look confirming her suspicions. 'You don't give a body much warning, do you, eh?' At once she ushered little Sal from the room, saying kindly, 'It's all right, sunshine . . . your mam'll be all right. Take yourself off to my place, child, and tell Joey to give you the eggs I've left on my plate. Seeing as you've dragged me away from 'em and they'll be cold and dried up when I get back.' Enthused by the prospect of an egg butty, little Sal promptly forgot about the 'babby' she had already claimed for her own, and went skipping out of the door, only to pop her head back round it a moment later to remind Tilly, 'You have to fetch me when the babby comes . . . you won't forget, will you?'

'*No, no, Sal!* Tilly won't forget.' Molly struggled on to the bed, gasping hard when the squeezing pain in her back became unbearable. 'Go on . . . go on, child!'

Sensing something beyond her understanding, and reassured by her mammy's promise – although puzzled why it should be given with such impatience – Sal quickly set off again. But not before she had discreetly glanced back at the sight of Tilly Watson's bedraggled brown head bent over the bed, and her thin bony hands busying themselves in helping Molly out of her garments. Sal didn't like that. Not at all, and, shutting out the image of her mammy's face all twisted and uncomfortable, she went on her way, her blue eyes thoughtful and a look of concern on her small, heartshaped face. She would have a word or two to tell that naughty babby when it came, hurting her mammy like that!

At the open door of Tilly Watson's house Sal paused, listening to the crescendo of noise emanating from inside, where the three younger Watson brood were indulging in a free-for-all, or, as Tilly called it when the three of them began wrestling in earnest, 'having a bloody bundle!' For a moment Sal was tempted to leave. However the thought of that fried egg just sitting on Tilly's plate and waiting for her was too much. Anyway, above the squeals and shouts could be heard the excited cries of little Peggy and the firm voice of Joey Watson, who had taken over the role of father since the demise of Tilly's husband. So, knowing that Joey would soon have things under control, little Sal entered the house, praying that none of the other children had pinched Tilly's precious egg, because if they *had*, she might just be ready to punch somebody on the nose and start them fighting all over again!

From across the road, and being careful to stay well out of sight, Jack-the-Lad watched the frail-looking girl go into Tilly Watson's house and close the door behind her. Chuckling softly, he circled the woman's waist with his arm and pulling her into him, he said quietly but with some amusement, 'That little lady ain't half as delicate as yer might think . . . and when it comes to her mam and young Peggy, just let anybody try and hurt 'em. *Then* you'd see what a little tiger that Sal can be.'

'Sal? . . . That your kid, is it?' The woman was past her prime, thickening in figure and brassy in countenance. She snuggled into his embrace.

'That's right, darling,' he confirmed, with an intimate

chuckle. 'Sal's the eldest, then there's Peggy. *Sodding gals!* Still . . . there's another on the way, so happen *that* one'll be a lad, eh?' He nuzzled her ear, and began pushing himself against her in a gently suggestive, rhythmic movement. 'Don't care much for gals,' he murmured. 'Well . . . not until they start bursting out in all the right places,' he laughed. 'Naw! Kids is a bloody nuisance . . . too much like responsibility, I say.' There he chuckled again and his voice fell to a sensuous whisper. 'I don't care much for 'em once the little buggers is here, but I can't deny I enjoy *making* 'em.'

'You randy bugger, Jack!' laughed the woman, playfully shaking him off. 'But I'm not complaining.'

'I should think not, sweetheart. Not after I've shown you a good time, eh?' He dug his hand into his trouser pocket and drew out a silver coin which he gave into her out-stretched hand. 'Get off down the boozer, gal,' he told her, gesturing towards the end of the street. 'Turn left at the bottom of Dock Street and you'll see the boozer on the corner . . . you can't miss it. Wait there till I fetch yer. Think on – you stay there till I fetch yer. Have yer got that?'

She nodded, but asked, 'How long d'you think you'll be?'

'No longer than necessary. It's Christmas, ain't it? I have to show me face . . . leave her a few bob . . . let the poor sod know I ain't dead or nothing.' He kissed her hard before thrusting her from him. 'Don't you fret, darling. I'll be down the boozer to fetch yer afore yer can say Jack Robinson. Then we'll find us a quiet dark place where we can have a bit o' rough and tumble, eh?'

Feigning embarrassment, she thumped him on the shoulder. 'Go on with you, Jack Tatt,' she said, 'no wonder they call you Jack-the-Lad!' She pushed the silver coin into her purse, then, without a backward glance, she bounced away to waddle at a furious pace down Dock Street, leaving her charming but devious colleague to saunter across the cobbles towards the house. Inside, in her terrible labour, Molly had cried out his name several times, only to be told by Tilly Watson, '*He* ain't coming to help you, my gal. The likes of that one don't even deserve thinking about!' Being a practical woman who could never understand what Molly saw in that useless man of hers, Tilly was loath to admit that, on this particular occasion, the good Molly might benefit from the sight of Jack's no-good face. Because on this particular occasion Molly needed her mind taken off the awful pain she was suffering and the unnaturally long time it was taking for the young 'un to show its face. She'd birthed many a newborn in her day, had Tilly Watson, and she had come across all kinds of complications. But none like this. There was something badly wrong here. Badly wrong, and very frightening. If the bairn didn't soon make an appearance, she might have to leave Molly and get help, but the thought of leaving Molly for even a moment was very frightening, because those few precious moments could mean the difference between life and death. For Molly, or the child. Or both.

Outside, Jack leaned against the wall and wondered what his reception might be. After all, he'd been gone a long time on his latest spree, and for all Molly knew he might be dead and buried. Of a sudden he was pierced by a stab of conscience, but like always, it was only momentary. 'Molly knew what she were tekking on . . . I never lied to her about the gypsy in me, never once,' he murmured to himself. Ah, but he *had* lied about other things, he reminded himself. Things that were just as precious to him as having his freedom when the wild blue yonder called; things like his insatiable appetite for a bawdy woman, and the need of a man to sow his wild oats before Old Father Time caught up with him. There was something else too, which he had never told Molly. One of the rare things in life that he was ashamed of. He hadn't the courage to tell her. Not yet anyway. All these things he had deliberately kept from Molly, because, trusting, genuine article that she was, Molly would neither understand nor forgive him. By! He trembled in his boots at the thought of her ever finding out how he had bedded one floozy after another; sometimes *two* at a time when he'd been too drunk to know any different. What! Molly might be an adoring and gentle soul, but she had one hell of a temper and would rip his eyes out if she knew how he was doing her down behind her back. He had only ever seen Molly's temper once, and that was enough. He remembered the occasion well and the remembering sent shivers down his spine. It was in that very boozer where he'd just sent the floozy. Him and Molly were not long wed, and he'd taken her into the bar to show her off to his drinking cronies, when in came a brazen hussy he'd been foolish enough to have a bit of a fling with, not two weeks before. The silly cow made a beeline for him. Thank Gawd for the fact that the floozy was legless drunk and couldn't remember his name, or the fur would really have flown, and no mistake! As it was, he managed to convince Molly that he was innocent as the day were long, and he had 'never clapped eyes on the silly bitch afore'.

Molly had never since broached the subject and he often wondered whether she believed his story, or whether she might just harbour a deal of suspicion towards him. However, she never showed it, and he made it his business to reassure her constantly of his undying love for her. Funny thing was, he *did* love Molly. He loved and respected her a great deal. She was a good woman, a good mother, and had always been exceptionally loyal to him. If the truth be told, Molly was the most beautiful creature he'd ever come across. If she had any faults at all, they were the strength of her love for him, and the way she trusted his word. Yes, Molly was good, while he was a waster, a womanizer, and too much of a bloody coward to face a man's responsibility towards his family. He was a useless wretch, no good at all, a Jack-the-Lad if ever there was one.

Jack's rugged, handsome face broke into a self-satisfied smile and suddenly all trace of self-recrimination was swamped by the good feeling that washed through him. It were no use fighting it. A Jack-the-Lad was what he was born to be, and a Jack-the-Lad was what he'd be till his dying day. He straightened up, spat into the palm of his hand and smoothed it over his unruly fair hair. Then, with a merry tune on his lips and a bright twinkle in his warm brown eyes, he went jauntily into the house.

Inside the bedroom, the scene that greeted Jack was a grim and serious one. Even before his shocked eyes had taken in what lay before him, he was made fearful by the atmosphere in the room. Slowly and silently he came forward, the merry tune stilled on his lips and a look of puzzled astonishment in his brown eyes.

The room, like the rest of the house, was sparsely furnished. There was a big old dresser and a broad, sturdy brown wardrobe; over by the window stood a marble wash-stand containing a bowl, a matching jug, and other bric-à-brac. At the far end of the room was a huge, high bed with four iron posts topped by spherical shiny brass knobs. Over the bed was a small, dark crucifix that Molly had found on the tip and which she would not let him throw away, and placed next to the bedhead was a little wooden cupboard with an unlit candle on top.

Jack's eyes were drawn first to Molly, who lay so still in the bed it frightened him, and whose dark, tousled head was turned sideways from him. At the foot of the bed lay a tiny bundle, tightly wrapped from head to toe, and horribly still also. Seated on the bed, her head bent to her hands and emitting a soft, crying sound was the woman he knew as Tilly Watson. It was she who looked up and saw him first. '*You!*' The word was a mere whisper, but it might have been a shouted accusation for the awful guilt it wrought in him. 'You're too late,' she said, 'always too late!' When she got to her feet and looked deep into his shocked eyes, it was with unconcealed malice. Without speaking another word, she collected the small, still bundle from the bed and, coming to where he had stopped in horror, she gently placed it into his arms. 'This is your son,' she told him in hostile voice, 'cursed he is . . . and barely breathing. The poor little soul nearly took his mam with him and all.' The next words were spat out in disgust. '*She needed you* . . . called out time and time again. I told her . . . you ain't worth the ground you walk on.'

When the door banged shut behind the furious woman, Jack made no move. In his arms he could feel the feather-light weight of the child and a faint warmth exuding through the shawl. Afraid and hesitant, he lowered his gaze to the tiny being now writhing in his arms. Instinctively, he drew back the shawl to reveal its tiny limbs. What he saw there shocked him to the core. The nausea had started like a clenched fist in the pit of his stomach. Now it spiralled up through him, touching every part of his being. The infant's legs were grotesquely odd, one shorter than the other, with a twisted foot, the sight of which was deeply repugnant to the man's senses.

Suddenly aware of the painful sobbing that filled the room and touched his sorry heart, Jack lifted his gaze towards the bed. Molly was looking at him: her big, black eyes were the most tragic he had ever seen and her tears were like purgatory to him. When she began to speak, he ventured forward. 'Look at him, Jack,' she pleaded brokenly, 'look at your son . . . *our* son.' The sorrow in her voice hung in the air like an enveloping vapour. 'Don't be afraid, Jack. Don't turn away from him . . . *please don't turn from him*.' For an endless moment she was silent, then in a painful whisper she told him, 'I needed you . . . *why* weren't you here?'

'Oh, Molly, can you ever forgive me?' He sat beside her, holding their son between them and reaching out a comforting hand. 'I'm no good for you, Molly . . . but I do love you. You *know* that, don't you?' Molly knew. He was here and that was enough. For now. Together they held the innocent babe. Together they cried. Together they took comfort from each other; but not even her beloved Jack's presence could dull the awful bitterness in Molly's heart when she had seen how dreadfully crippled their son was. It was too savage, too unfair. Yet hadn't she known all along that something was wrong? Known it, and been afraid. She told Jack as much now. '*Why* weren't you with me?' she murmured again, but deep in her heart she knew it would have made no difference to the outcome.

'There are two kinds of men in this world, Molly my love,' Jack said. 'There's the kind a woman can rely on to watch out for her and his kids . . . he'll provide for them and see them through the bad times. Then there's the likes of me.' He sighed and drew her closer. 'Like I said, Molly, I'm no good and I never will be. Oh, I love you and the kids right enough . . . but I'm too much of a coward to face up to my responsibilities. If I was anything of a man, I'd leave this house and never show my face again. Because if I was to stay and try as hard as ever I could, to be the man you deserve, I know it wouldn't work, Molly. I'd only end up making your life that much more miserable.' When she made no reply, he buried his head in her shoulder and for a while they remained silent, each lost in their own particular thoughts; she with her face pressed close to that of her child, and he with his arm embracing the two of them.

Molly offered the child her breast milk, but it had small appetite and soon, exhausted and emotionally spent, she drifted into a fretful sleep. For a while, Jack watched her and the infant. But he could not bring himself to touch it again. When it began softly whimpering, he fetched Tilly Watson. 'Don't wake Molly,' he told her, 'let the lass sleep.' After that, he went to the boozer on the corner. The tall, boldly-painted floozy had gone, so he emptied every coin from his pocket on to the counter. 'Let the booze run till the money's all gone,' he instructed the barman. Word had spread fast about Molly's crippled bairn, and the landlord understood Jack's forlorn mood.

At five minutes before midnight, they brought Jack

home and, with Tilly Watson's reluctant help, made him comfortable on the parlour couch. Soon after, Tilly returned to her own brood, who were temporarily subdued by the arrival of Peggy and little Sal.

In the dark early hours, Molly attended to her son. Then, carrying the lit candle, she went carefully down the stairs to the parlour. For a long, unhappy moment she stayed by the door, gazing down at the unconscious, spreadeagled form of her wretched husband. As she continued to gaze on his handsome face, he moaned and wrapped his arm over his shoulders like a child might do. A well of love bubbled up in Molly's tired heart. 'Oh, Jack! . . . Jack!' she chided softly. Molly suspected his pain was every bit as great as hers. But not his loneliness, she thought with a stab of bitterness, never his loneliness.

After a while, she turned away, her sorry heart that much heavier. There were so many things she had wanted to talk over with him. So much that was still unsaid. Dear God, didn't Jack know how much she needed him? Or that they could have helped each other so very much?

Lying in the dark, desperately tired yet too disturbed to sleep, Molly thought long on her son. She thought on the heartfelt words that Jack had spoken to her earlier. She recalled all manner of things from that fateful day, and, remembering with a small shock that it was Christmas, she cried for little Sal who would not have her tree after all.

Molly had known a good teacher in old Sal. 'Never let the buggers get yer down, Molly, gal', was her favourite instruction. 'Don't shed tears fer them as ain't worth it!' Molly smiled at the memory of that eccentric and cantankerous old darling. Her smile became a chuckle, but it wasn't long before the sound of Molly's soft laughter melted into sobs. Life was a trial. Her young bones ached like they were ninety years old and her heart felt like a lead weight inside her.

Suddenly, Molly had the strongest yearning to hold her newborn close to her heart. When he was tucked up in the bed beside her, she told him, 'Don't you worry, little fella . . . there's nothing for you to worry about. Not while you've got your mammy who loves you.' For the first time in as long as she could remember, Molly cried herself to sleep. Strangely for the first time also, she shed heartfelt tears for the parents she had never known.

It was Christmas. After a long, unsettled night of discomfort, Molly woke to a strange silence in the house. For a moment she was confused, but then she remembered that the girls were next door with Tilly Watson. One glance at the infant assured her that he was contentedly sleeping.

'Mammy . . . Mammy!' The sound of little Sal's voice gladdened Molly's heart. Suddenly the girls burst into the room and were running towards her; little Sal quickly hurling herself on to the bed, and Peggy, struggling to clamber up, only to have her chubby legs left dangling in mid-air as she clung tenaciously to the eiderdown, before slithering to the floorboards again. She was a sturdy child, more solid than little Sal, and having a bold, round face with large oval eyes, the same mud-brown colour as her thick, straight hair. She squealed with delight when Molly grabbed her two stocky arms and hoisted her on to the bed.

'Couldn't keep them away, Molly.' Tilly Watson stood at the foot of the bed, her thin, bony arms folded across her pinnie, and a smile on her mouth which Molly thought did not light up her eyes. 'By! You look better for a night's sleep, and that's a fact,' she told Molly. But there was something she was not telling, and Molly sensed it. 'I'll bet yer starving, aren't you eh . . . ? I'll tell you what, there's a bit of smoked bacon left in the larder. I'll fry it up with a piece of bread, and we'll top it off with a brew o' tea. Oh, I know it's not much, Molly . . . but it's the best we can do for now, eh?' She turned to leave.

'Wait a minute, Tilly.' Molly was afraid, but she had to ask. 'Something's worrying you . . . is it Jack?' It was there again. That feeling of nervousness and insecurity whenever Jack made his way home. Almost as though the happiness he brought was too good to last.

For a moment, Tilly Watson stood still, nervously twirling a knot of her skirt through her fingers. She brought her gaze to bear on the children, who were laughingly tumbling against each other and seemingly unaware of the tense atmosphere. Suddenly, the new-born was awake and thrashing his tiny arms in the air. Tilly swallowed hard and looked at Molly again; at the pitiful sight she made, with her reed-thin figure dressed in an old nightgown of Tilly's, and her surprisingly rich, black hair tousled about her ears. In her dark eyes there was more living than a woman twice her age should experience. Poor little bugger, thought Tilly, and how she wished it wasn't her who had to impart the sorry news. It *was* left to her, and there was only one way to tell it, and that was straight out. 'He's gone,' she said quietly, flinching inside when she saw the surprise, then sad resignation wash over Molly's face. 'I'm sorry, dearie, but the bugger's done a bunk. I can't say I didn't see it coming, and I dare say it'll be a long time, if ever, before he shows his cowardly face round these parts again.'

'Thank you, Tilly.' Molly glanced at the girls, her voice betraying nothing of her shocked thoughts. Thank goodness the children seemed not to have heard. 'I really am hungry . . . a bacon butty and a pot of tea will be fine.' Enough had been said in front of the children, and she didn't want Tilly to see just how hard the news of Jack's going had hit her. She had intended making the effort to get out of bed, but now the spirit had left her.

'Right then.' Tilly knew when she had been dismissed. She didn't mind, not in the circumstances. 'Poor little sod,' she murmured, closing the door behind her. 'What a bastard that man of hers is . . . to run off and leave 'em again, and after what she's been through . . . *Men!* I'd spit on 'em soon as look at 'em, and that's a bloody fact!'

At midday, Molly got up from her bed and checked that the newborn baby was sleeping soundly in his cot. After which, she put on the blue serge dress that had already seen her through four winters, and made her way downstairs.

'Now that's very foolish, Molly lass, if you don't mind my saying so,' Tilly Watson remarked with a wag of her finger. 'It'll serve you right if you start bleeding . . . and there's every danger of it, you mark my words. I do know what I'm talking about . . . I've seen more bairns born into this world than I can count. Most of the little blighters come easy, but . . .' she hesitated, afraid to harp on the awful circumstances of Molly's birthing,

'. . . well, you *have* been through a bad time, Molly, and Lord knows there ain't two-penn'orth of you.' Coming to where Molly had eased herself into the upright horse-hair armchair, she threw her hands up in despair, saying, 'You listen to what Tilly's saying, there's a good girl. Don't worry about the two lasses, because they'll be all right lost amongst my brood.' When she realized that Molly had no intention of going back up the stairs for a while, she shook her head and went to the door. Here she reached up to the nail where Molly's shawl hung, and taking it down she hurried across the room to fling it round Molly's small shoulders, saying with a degree of irritation, 'Very well, you must do as you think fit. Don't take no notice of me!' Her tone was unusually sarcastic.

'Aw, Tilly, don't take offence,' Molly pleaded, reaching out her hand and clutching the older woman's thin, muscular arm. 'I know you mean well, but I really am feeling stronger.'

'Huh! Stuff and nonsense!' Tilly snorted, taking Molly's frail-looking hand and putting it firmly back in her lap. 'Just *look* at yourself! What! I've seen *corpses* with more flesh on their bones and colour in their faces . . . you can't deny it. Not when you're sitting there, looking at me with them big black eyes that have lost the light God gave 'em. If you will insist on staying down here, my girl . . . then you must abide by two conditions.'

'Anything you say, Tilly.' Molly knew that if Tilly were to take her by the arm and escort her back upstairs, she would never find the strength to resist. Besides which, she was right to be concerned, because the mere effort of getting dressed and finding her way down to the parlour had all but drained Molly of her strength.

'First of all, you're not to move one step away from

this 'ere fireside.' She indicated to where her newly laid fire was already emitting a cheery glow. 'It'll warm your poor bones once it gets a proper hold,' she promised.

'You have my word, Tilly . . . I won't budge from this chair.' Molly couldn't, even if she wanted to, because she realized now that Tilly was right. She *had* got up from her bed too early.

'Right then. And think on, when I fetch you a bite to eat . . . happen a bowl of hot, nourishing soup . . . I want no argument about that neither. You'll eat every last morsel?' When Molly nodded, she appeared satisfied. 'Want to see the lasses too, I expect?' Without waiting for a reply, Tilly went to the fireplace where she took up the poker and began agitating the coals in the grate. When she swung round again, it was to see Molly staring up at the mantelpiece where, propped up against the brass candlestick-holder was a folded piece of paper, upon which was written the word MOLLY in big, black letters.

Molly's heart had turned somersaults when she saw her name glaring back at her. The name, *Molly*, had been the very first word that Jack had taught her to read. After that, she learned his name, and then the letters of the alphabet. Although it was a trying and laborious process, Jack had taught Molly the rudiments of reading and writing. She had loved him all the more for it.

'I forgot that were there,' Tilly said in a sullen manner. '*He* left it, afore he ran off!'

'You should have told me, Tilly. You should have told me straightaway.'

'Happen,' Tilly grudgingly conceded, 'but if I was to tell the truth and shame the devil . . . I hadn't made up my mind whether or not to burn the blessed thing!'

'Then shame on *you*,' Molly chided, but it was a gentle and kindly reprimand. 'Will you pass it to me now . . . or must I get it myself?'

'You stay where you are!' warned Tilly, reluctantly fetching the letter and giving it into Molly's outstretched hand. 'I'll leave you to read it then. But only ten minutes or so . . . then I'll be back with a bite to eat for you.' At the door she chuckled. 'And no doubt with the children in tow.' With a flourish of her skirt and a lingering look of disgust, she was gone.

Molly raised her quiet eyes from the closed note clutched in her hand. She wanted to open it and yet she was sorely tempted to fling it into the flames, where it would be quickly devoured. Instead she sat very still, gazing into the fire's glow and wondering how Jack might justify his leaving them all yet again, and at a time when they badly needed him. 'Oh, Jack . . . when will we ever be a proper family,' she murmured, now unable to stem the tears that rolled down her face. After a few moments she steeled herself to open the letter, and read:

Can't face you, Molly. Last night, I tried to drown it all in booze, but it was no good. *I'm* no good, as I've tried to tell you many times. I'm a waster, and like they say, I'm a Jack-the-Lad who'll never settle down.

It's not that I don't love you, Molly darling, because God knows *I do*. And that's the trouble, you see. *That's* what keeps fetching me back to hurt you and turn your poor world upside down. You know yourself, you'd be better off without a bastard like me.

If it were in my power, I'd have you done up

like the lady you are . . . with dandy clothes and a
fine house, with no worries to mar them lovely
black eyes. But it ain't in my power, and it never
will be. All I can bring you is trouble and
heartache. But because you've shown me how
things can be if only I might change me ways, and
because I love you more than I could ever love
any other woman, I'm asking you to be patient
with me, darling. Don't give up on me altogether.
But, if you find yourself a decent bloke while I'm
gone, then it'll be my loss. Don't miss out on any
chances because of me.

If I get lucky, I'll send some money, I promise.
Till then, God bless, and look after yourself.

Jack

You know, I always wanted a son to be proud of.
Life's a bastard, ain't it, Molly darling.

'Oh, and so are you, Jack. SO ARE YOU!' Molly
sobbed. There had risen in her a terrible rage as she read
the letter. Now the rage became a cold, hostile sensation, and pulling herself up by the arms of the chair,
she went on slow, painful steps to the fireplace. There
she screwed the letter into a hard, round ball and threw it
into the flames. 'You're so right,' she said in a contemp-
tuous whisper, and with bitterness in her heart such as
she had never known before. 'You *are* a bastard, Jack
. . . and a coward! And I don't care if I never see you
again!' She watched the letter blacken and curl. 'I hate
you. Don't come back. Don't *ever* come back!' She
thought of the good times they had known in the early

days, and that special way he had of making her laugh. In her mind she pictured his wayward fair hair and those dark brown eyes that twinkled. She recalled how passionate he was in lovemaking, yet so tender and thoughtful. He loved her. Molly knew that without any doubt, because it was not something that could be faked or hidden. And, God help her, she loved him. Enough to wait? She wondered. Enough to give him the one last chance he was asking? She tried to imagine what it would be like if she were never to see him again. Never to look into those laughing brown eyes, and never to have his arms embrace her. She weighed that pain against the pain he had caused her today, and which he caused her every time he left them. There was a greater pain now, because of their son, because of the children who might have had a proper Christmas, because he was too much of a coward to face life head on. Oh yes, there was pain and heartache, and bitterness. Yet beneath it all remained Molly's steadfast loyalty and love for Jack. Steadfast and deep-rooted. She couldn't deny it. Not yet. Maybe not ever.

Of a sudden, there was so much noise and confusion outside the room that Molly's turbulent thoughts were shattered. Above the din sailed little Sal's excited voice. '*Mammy . . . ! Mammy . . . !* See what we've got!'

Molly turned her head as the child ran into the parlour, and following behind was Tilly Watson with Peggy in her arms. '*Here's* something to buck you up,' she laughed, putting the child to the floor and pulling her to one side as all eyes turned on the door.

Molly was astonished when the figure of a man began pushing its way in. For a moment she couldn't see his face, because he was weighed down with a Christmas tree in one arm and a plump hen in the other. Her first thought was that *Jack* had come back to mend his ways and her heart warmed with gladness. She laughed out loud, the tumult at the door turning into a blur through her tears of joy.

'Happy Christmas!' he shouted, coming forward to the table where he laughingly off-loaded his wares, before swinging Molly into his arms. Her heart sank. It wasn't Jack. It was the bargee, Mick. Mick, with a broad smile on his handsome face, and two very excited children clinging to his trousers. *Mick, not Jack*. The realization cut through her like a knife.

'Come on, Molly sweetheart . . . let's have you resting!' he told Molly while leading her gently back to the chair. There was a special tenderness in his voice and a knowing look in his amber eyes, which told Molly that he knew what had happened: the night's trauma, the boy-child, even that her husband had deserted them. No doubt Tilly had sent her son, Joey, to let Mick know what had taken place here. Though Molly would be eternally grateful that the children would have a proper Christmas after all, she wished that it could have been Jack who had provided it. As it wasn't, she wondered how she could ever forgive him.

Chapter Five

'You pay me to advise you, Mr Crowther, and I am advising you now . . . stay as far away from Emma Tanner as you possibly can. Now that the date for the court hearing is set, you can only make matters worse should you even consider approaching her.' Mr Dunworthy leaned forward across his vast desk-top and, peering intently through his tiny spectacles at the grim-faced man before him, he repeated in a softer yet more penetrating voice, 'Stay away from Mrs Tanner, or be prepared to face the consequences.' His voice was authoritative and free of emotion, but in the privacy of his own thoughts, the man was only just beginning to realize how very much he disliked Caleb Crowther: once a justice who was feared and hated by all who were brought before him, but now retired and soon to be at the wrong end of a courtroom himself.

'To hell with it, man!' Springing from his chair with such anger that it was sent spinning on its axis, Caleb Crowther stormed back and forth across the office, his fists clenched tight behind his back and his head bowed to his chin. In spite of his fierce response to Mr Dunworthy's instruction to 'stay away from Mrs Tanner', there was an air of despondency about his bent countenance, and more than a suggestion of fear. Suddenly he swung round to face the small, fish-like face behind the desk. 'I *should* go and see the bitch . . . confront her and warn her off for her own good. This business is all wrong and you know it. The damned woman's vindictive . . . got her facts all wrong. If you ask me, her brains have been addled by the Australian sun. She spent too many years amongst the convicts . . . there's not a manjack who was ever transported that did not claim they were innocent. Emma Grady was no different!'

'So you're still convinced she had a hand in the murder of her husband?' Mr Dunworthy was not of the same mind. He never had been.

'*Of course* I'm convinced!' Caleb Crowther knew that Emma was not capable of such a heinous deed, but it had served him well to uphold her guilt. It served him well now. 'There is not the slightest doubt in my mind that she killed the unfortunate fellow . . . a most upright and respected citizen if ever there was one. Damn it, man, that was why I gave no objection when he approached me for Emma's hand in marriage.' He was very careful not to disclose that it was he himself who had put forward the proposal. His reasons had been twofold – firstly, he wanted Emma off his back because she was a thorn in his side, and secondly, she had been a constant painful reminder to him of her mother, Mary. God, how he had loved that woman, exquisite and desirable as she was. Also a temptress who drove him crazy with her insatiable appetite for other men. Not satisfied with her devoted husband, Thadius, Mary Grady had bewitched the young, virile Caleb Crowther, a man on his way up in the world. A man who, at the time, was able to lay the world at her feet. But he was married, and afraid to risk a scandal which would most certainly have wrecked his judicial career. When he refused to leave his wife, Agnes, it was then that Mary deliberately drove him to distraction by taking a lover: a bargee by the name of Bill Royston. Caleb Crowther visibly trembled as he remembered the terror and awful carnage that resulted.

'Sit down, Mr Crowther.' Mr Dunworthy was astonished to see the beads of perspiration break out on the other man's face. 'I'm afraid you're working yourself into a shocking state. Look . . . you must leave this matter with me. There is very little that you can do. Please rest assured . . . I will do all I can to safeguard your interests, Mr Crowther.'

'Yes, yes!' Caleb Crowther was appalled at having let his guard down in front of this eagle-eyed fellow. From now on, he would have to be very, very careful. For, if the terrible truth were ever to come out, of what happened all those years ago, well . . . it just did not bear thinking about. 'But believe me when I say there's an evil and vicious streak in Emma Grady . . . Emma Tanner now, since her marriage . . . a particularly nasty streak that stems from . . . from . . .' He could not bring himself to finish the sentence, or he would have said 'from her mother, Mary'.

He could not say it, because his deep, all-consuming passion for Emma's mother was still too alive in him. To betray her memory now would be tantamount to betraying himself. His courage was too small, his mind too filled with her image. What would she have said, he wondered now, if she knew how he had used her innocent daughter, Emma, for his own greedy, despicable ends? Married her off to an insignificant clerk so that he could be rid of her, and, if that wasn't punishment enough for the young, helpless girl, he had given over only a small part of her dowry, by duping the pitifully gullible young man who was to be her husband.

After the marriage Caleb Crowther had plundered Emma's entire inheritance. Then, when Emma's husband had met his untimely end and the law was baying for blood, he had made it his business to point the strongest accusing finger at Emma. Terrible things he had done against her. None of which he regretted. Only the thought of Mary had made him quake to his stomach, only the idea she might be watching from her grave; only the memory of what had taken place on a particular night some forty years and more before. Even now, the awful knowledge of it, and the part he himself had played, still brought nightmares. He felt the horror of it now. In a swift and trembling movement, he grabbed his hat from the desk and rammed it on his head. 'I must be away,' he told the surprised Dunworthy. 'Good day to you.'

As he strode from the room, leaving the door wide open behind him, Caleb Crowther could hear Mr Dunworthy's voice anxiously entreating him, 'Heed what I say, sir . . . make no attempts to approach your niece, or I might be obliged to wash my hands of this case altogether.'

The departing man made no outward response, other than to mutter angrily beneath his voice, 'The devil take you both, you pitiful fool . . . you and the bitch who would sink me to her level!' Once out on the street, he took a moment to quieten himself. He felt greatly agitated and spoiling for a fight. 'Stay *away* from her?' he sneered in a twisted smile. 'Not *me*, sir . . . ! Not the Justice Crowther!' Stepping out to the kerb he hailed a hire carriage, and, to the approaching driver who urged his ensemble towards what might be the likeliest fare of the day, Caleb Crowther made a formidable sight with his tall, bulky figure and large-boned face. This was made all the more awesome by the prolific and bushy growth of iron-grey hair that spread across his unpleasant features like a creeping mantle.

As the carriage clattered over the cobbles towards him, Caleb Crowther raised his arm across his forehead to shield his eyes from the late afternoon sun. He hated the summer and the tiresome August heat. It sought to rob a man of his dignity. On top of which, he was still smarting from Mr Dunworthy's instructions. So, when a small lad came careering into his path and foolishly rolled his wooden hoop into the gentleman's leg, the next thing he knew was the gentleman had whipped him sharply across the shoulders with his cane. There then followed a terrible uproar when the fearful lad began screaming for his father, who was some way behind. Seeing his son unjustly attacked, the incensed fellow launched himself at Caleb Crowther with vicious intent. The upshot was that he also got a cane sliced across his head, and was promptly taken into custody by a passing officer of the law, who had recognized the Justice Crowther. Therefore he lost no time in collaring the 'offender' who had dared set himself on such a solid and respected upholder of the law. By which time Caleb Crowther had climbed into the carriage and, with much irritation at having been so affronted, gave the astonished driver a curt instruction to 'make haste to Park Street – the Tanner residence'.

The Justice was so agitated that even when the horse and carriage went forward he could not relax, clinging as he did to the very edge of the seat and straining his narrowed eyes to the road ahead, as though he might will it to shrink so that in only a minute he could step down to the path that would lead him to Emma Tanner's front door. Yet he knew well enough that the journey through the busy centre of Blackburn and out on to the Preston New Road which would carry him to Corporation Park and the street beside it was all of three miles, with a deal of narrow roads and congested alleys to slow him down even before the carriage left the heart of Blackburn itself. He knew that. Yet still he could not settle.

It was when the carriage was making its way up Town Hall Street and on to King William Street that Caleb Crowther's searching eyes were drawn to the kerbside. There was something disturbingly familiar about the thin, dark-haired ragamuffin who was absorbed in arranging the colourful blooms which, now and then, she offered to strolling passers-by. 'Only a shilling . . . fresh as the morning,' she called out, and the two children happily playing beside her added their chirpy persuasion, 'Only a shilling . . . only a shilling,' whilst giggling uncontrollably in between. Molly smiled patiently at their antics.

Hearing the approach of a carriage, Molly hurriedly got to her feet and propelled the two small girls to a safer distance from the road, instructing them to 'stay there'. Then snatching up a particularly large bunch of flowers from the bucket, she approached the carriage, which had been forced to a slower pace by the many traders' barrows that lined the narrow, cobbled street. 'Fresh blooms, sir,' she called out, running alongside the carriage and holding up the flowers to the gent inside. 'Fresh blooms for the little lady,' she coaxed, peering inside to where Caleb Crowther was eyeing her intently, and desperately trying to recollect where he had seen the ragged creature before; he *had* seen her before, he was sure of it.

Deeply curious and strangely disturbed, Caleb Crowther leaned his ungainly form nearer to the open carriage doorway. Already there had been stirred in him a host of unsettling memories: of a dark and deadly night when he and his officers had scoured the canal banks for the criminal who had snatched his own grandson for a ransom. That same night he had found the culprit: a young street-urchin with big bold eyes as black as coal, and known to have been brought up by another no-good creature, who went by the name of Sal Tanner. Oh, but he had enjoyed snatching the young wretch from the makeshift home, which was a derelict workman's cabin on the canal banks. What a sight it made as it burned to the ground! However, his joy had been short-lived, for the urchin made good her getaway even before the prison cart had delivered her to the jail. He had never forgotten. *Never forgiven*, and he was not a man to leave old scores unsettled.

Instinctively, Caleb Crowther's hand went to his breast, his trembling fingers searching out the tiny and delicate timepiece that had once belonged to Mary Grady, the dead woman whom he was bound to love until the end of his days. All these years since the night he had torn it from the grubby neck of that street-urchin, he had agonized over how she had come by the timepiece, when he himself had seen Thadius Grady give it to his daughter Emma on his deathbed.

Caleb Crowther had argued with himself that the urchin could have stolen it, like the thief she surely was. But then, he reminded himself, how could she have stolen it when Emma Grady had been transported from

Her Majesty's prison to the other side of the world, some years before: at least as long ago as the urchin was aged in years.

Likely as not the old tramp, Sal Tanner, had stolen it. But no, he had decided against that theory, because all the time Emma Grady was incarcerated in jail in England, she had the timepiece with her. His discreet inquiries revealed the truth of that. *What then?* He had asked himself time and time again: how did Mary Grady's timepiece get from her daughter, Emma, into the hands of a street-urchin? For Caleb Crowther, only two real possibilities remained: one, Emma had either given it to someone inside the prison or it had been stolen there, when it afterwards changed hands again, and finally fell to Sal Tanner's thieving paws; or – and for Caleb Crowther this was the explanation that he had come to believe – the street-urchin was Emma Grady's *own daughter*!

Caleb Crowther had privileged information regarding Emma Grady's last moments before she was bundled into the prison wagon, and afterwards on to the convict ship in Liverpool Docks. It was discreetly reported to him that Emma had been delivered of a girl-child, on the cobbles, right outside the prison gates. The officer in charge, believing the child to be stillborn, had ordered Emma into the waggon, leaving the child behind at the mercy of scavenging dogs. It then happened – or so the officer thought (only *thought*) – that as the wagon sped him and his charges away, he might have heard the thin, painful wail of a newborn. However, he could not be sure, he said. As the years grew longer, his memory had become dimmer, until now he put it all down to a feeling of guilt and an over-active imagination.

Caleb Crowther, on the other hand, had been plagued by the whole episode ever since. After all, in the years when Emma Grady was safely out of the way, and he lived a high, handsome lifestyle at her expense, it disturbed him to think that there was at large a grubby alley urchin who was the legal heiress to everything he had robbed from Emma.

There was something else that crossed Caleb Crowther's deep and conniving mind, as he struggled to get a good look at the dark-haired girl who was now cajoling him to 'buy the pretty flowers'. The urchin who had long been a thorn in his side had encountered him on one other occasion, *previous* to his snatching her on that dark, unfortunate night when he had so foolishly lost her again.

The occasion in question was when he had believed himself to be securely hidden in a carriage which was discreetly stationed beside a certain public house called the Navigation. On that night he had with him a dubious and murderous villain who was on a particular errand for him: he was to commit one Gabe Drury to the murky depths of the canal, where his silence would be assured. Gabe had been unfortunate enough to see many years ago a particular 'gentry' leaving the site where heinous murders had been committed. Murders involving Mary Grady and her illicit lover, the bargee. Murders involving others, who as yet were undetected. It was Caleb Crowther's intention that they would remain so.

It had been imperative to Caleb Crowther that he silence the old drunk, Gabe Drury, once and for all. The deed was suitably executed. But on the night of its doing, *that same street urchin* had peeped inside his carriage. From that day to this, Caleb Crowther could never be sure whether he had been recognized. To his thinking, the surest way of safeguarding himself would have been to eliminate the luckless urchin; to dispatch her to the deep along with the luckless Gabe. But up until now, he had never again set eyes on her whom he suspected was Emma Grady's lost daughter. The irony of it all gave him a deal of satisfaction because he had been told by his own wife how desperate Emma had been to have another child. Now it was too late. For that very reason, he had not revealed his suspicions regarding the street urchin. The pleasure he got from thinking how a daughter of Emma Grady's was sleeping rough and scraping a living alongside thieves and vagabonds was too enjoyable. Besides, if he had his way, that particular urchin would never live to be old bones!

'Come on, sir . . . you'll not find fresher blooms in the whole of Blackburn. A shilling . . . only a shilling!' Molly took a breath as the carriage slowed to a creeping pace. The smile on her face was dazzling as she raised it to bestow on the gentry. A stab of astonishment made her gasp as she saw how intensely he was staring at her. For an awful second, their eyes met; his tiny eyes slitted to study her all the more closely, and her black eyes stretched wide with curiosity. The cry sprang to Molly's lips almost without her realizing. '*God Almighty . . . ! It's the Justice!*' For a second she was riveted with fear. Then all hell seemed let loose, as Caleb Crowther realized that here was the very urchin he had sought after all these years. '*Stop, thief!*' he yelled, in an effort to recruit the help of passers-by. But Molly was never an easy quarry and there was no one willing to take up the hunt. Not on such a hot and sultry day, when they had better things to do than wear themselves out helping a fancy gent in a carriage.

Before she took to her heels Molly flung the bunch of flowers in Caleb Crowther's face, causing him to stagger backwards on to the seat with a great thump that rocked the carriage violently. This in turn startled the horses, which reared into the harness, whinnying and thrashing. They started forward at breakneck speed as terrified screams rent the air and fleeing bodies scattered in all directions.

When at last the unhappy ensemble came to rest some considerable distance on, Caleb Crowther struggled to the doorway where he peered up and down the street, cursing all the while and lashing out with his cane at anyone who ventured a helping hand. All he craved was to have the black-eyed vagabond in his grasp. But it was not to be on this occasion: Molly and her young ones were long gone. And safe. For the moment.

Heaping hell and damnation down on everybody's heads, the trembling and furious Caleb Crowther fell back on to the carriage seat, threatening the hapless driver with all manner of charges should he be reckless enough to persist in demanding a fare. 'Get me to Breckleton House, you fool!' he ordered churlishly. 'At a steady trot, or you'll face the consequences!'

As they went sedately along, Caleb Crowther's temper was not improved. He would not give Emma Tanner the satisfaction of seeing him so shaken, he mused. But she would keep. Until he could confront her with a cool and level head.

The court hearing had been set for early in January 1887, so for the remainder of this year he must carefully examine all the possibilities which would enable him to bring that particular vixen to heel. There was time enough. Besides, if he had learned anything at all during his dealings with the 'lower' orders, he had learned one thing above all else, and it was this: *there were more ways than one to skin a cat!*

Meanwhile, whatever Emma Tanner was up to at this moment, he hoped against hope that life would treat her badly and hound her with all manner of misfortune.

Molly was shocked. The news was awful and, even though she considered Emma Tanner to be her sworn enemy, Molly's heart went out to her as Tilly Watson's tale unfurled.

'So there you are, Molly,' concluded Tilly with a grave shake of her head, 'it doesn't matter whether you're a lady or a washerwoman, rich or poor . . . when your child's taken from you in such tragic circumstances, the pain is just the same for one as it is for the other.' She leaned back in the horse-hair armchair and stared at Molly seated opposite, whose dark eyes were moist with tears. 'You know, Molly . . . it's a strange thing how life has a way of turning full circle.'

'What do you mean?' asked Molly quietly, afterwards glancing at the door to make certain the children had not crept down from their bedroom. When Tilly had come in from next door to relate how Emma's son had been killed in a shocking accident, Molly had quickly taken the girls away to their beds. There was enough heartache in their little world without them listening to others' tragedies.

'What I mean is this . . . there's an old saying which warns, "Be sure, your sins will find you out". There's another . . . "Vengeance is mine, saith the Lord".'

'You're talking in riddles, Tilly,' chided Molly, 'what are you getting at?'

'Well, I'll tell you. I'll tell you something now that I've never told anybody . . . not for a long time anyway.' She had lowered her voice to a whisper, glancing behind her towards the door, as though fearful of being overheard.

'Go on.' Molly was intrigued. She knew that Tilly Watson liked a 'drop of the old gin'. She knew that Ada Loughton had been the one to come round to Tilly's house with the dreadful news concerning Emma Tanner's son. She also knew that whenever Ada Loughton paid a visit to her old friend, like as not there was a bottle of gin tucked discreetly under her shawl. The result being that, some hours later, Ada Loughton would waddle away down Dock Street, swaying from side to side and singing out like an old sailor. As for Tilly, the gin always loosened her tongue, like it had now.

'What's on your mind?' insisted Molly.

'You promise it won't go no further, if I tell you?' demanded Tilly, casting an anxious look about.

'Promise,' Molly reassured her, 'and who would I tell anyway, Tilly?'

'You might tell the bargee, Mick. After all, he has been calling on you a lot of late . . . and the two of you seem to be getting real chummy-like.' She fell forward, throwing her arms about and loudly cackling. When Molly glanced towards the door, Tilly noticed. At once, she fell silent, pressing a bony finger to her lips and afterwards whispering, 'Sorry, young 'un . . . I forgot the lasses were asleep.' When Molly nodded her head and said nothing, she went on in hushed and secretive tones, 'You know how Emma Tanner . . . Emma Grady as she was then . . . was convicted of having a hand in her husband's murder?'

'Yes. I've heard it said,' agreed Molly. It only confirmed what she already believed – that Emma Tanner

95

had the bad blood of Justice Crowther running through her veins.

'You know *that* much, Molly girl,' chuckled Tilly softly, 'but there's something you don't know. *I was there . . . I SAW IT ALL!*' She revelled in the way Molly's big eyes opened wide with astonishment. 'And my old man with me . . . Lord rest his soul!' She quickly made the sign of the cross on herself. 'We saw the buggers struggling atop the stairs . . . Emma, her husband, Gregory Denton . . . and that old nanny of Emma's, Mrs Manfred, the one they hanged.'

'*You saw them murder him?*' A thin, cold shiver ran down Molly's spine. For some inexplicable reason, she felt so afraid that it was almost as though she herself might have been there. Now she also made a hasty sign of the cross on herself.

'Did we see them murder him?' repeated Tilly thoughtfully. 'You might well ask. What we saw that night was enough to put the fear of God into any decent soul.' Something in Tilly's voice reflected the turmoil that was going on inside her. There had been times over the long, hard years since that dreadful night when she had feared for her own soul. She feared for it now: if the truth ever came out, it would reveal that what she and her husband *actually* saw on that night was no more than a struggle between three people, when one of them was unfortunate enough to lose his balance and go hurtling down the stairs to his death. Oh, it was true that Mrs Manfred was fighting like a tiger to protect Emma, there was no doubt of *that*. But Emma herself had nothing to do with him tumbling down the stairs, Tilly was certain of it. Yet, because she was desperate and times were hard, she had told the authorities otherwise, therefore pointing the

finger at Emma in as final a way as her own worst enemy
might have done. She had lived to be ashamed of it, but
never to admit the truth to a living soul. Dear me no!
That would be a very foolish thing to do!

The reason for Tilly's betrayal of somebody who had
been a good and loyal friend to her was a tin box. A tin
box that she had secretly taken from the deathbed of
Gregory Denton's mother, soon after the latter had
witnessed her son lying in a heap at the foot of the stairs.
Tilly found the box to contain a few old documents that
she had no use for at all, and a deal of money that she
had a dire need of. So, she kept her mouth shut about
thieving the box, and opened the same mouth as wide as
she could, in order to see Emma arrested. That way her
own secret would be safe: there was no danger that
Emma might find out about the box and lay claim to it.

When Emma was transported, Tilly spent many a
sleepless night. Later though, she took a strange comfort
in making herself believe that Emma *was* guilty. Indeed,
she told Molly the very same now. 'She murdered the
poor unfortunate fellow. You have my word on it. Me
and Emma lived next door to each other. Soon after she
and Mr Denton were wed, and he brought her to live on
Montague Street, I was called in to look after the old
woman . . . bloody cantankerous old sod *she* were and
all. But now, do you see what I'm telling you, Molly?'
Molly shook her head and Tilly went on to explain,
'What I said earlier was that it's strange how life turns
full circle.'

'I see what you're getting at now.'

In her mind, Molly quickly ran through all that Tilly
had revealed. And it did seem like a horrible justice.
Somehow, she did not take the same pleasure in it as did

Tilly. 'You're saying that Emma Tanner's son was killed in a manner that was uncannily like the way in which she helped murder her husband?'

'Vengeance is mine, saith the Lord!' Tilly threw her arms in the air and, clapping her hands together, she cried jubilantly, 'Emma pushed her husband down the stairs to his death . . . and now, over twenty years on, her own son meets a sorry end, by falling down a cliff face in Corporation Park.' Puffing out her narrow, bony chest, she shook her head and, just for a second, seemed about to express some small sympathy. But then she remembered her own part in Emma's conviction all those years ago, and caution took over. She must always be careful to remind folk of what a callous woman Emma Tanner was. 'Like I said, Molly . . . it's the hand of justice, don't you think?'

'It's a cruel hand all the same . . . that takes an innocent child from its mammy,' Molly murmured. The news of young Bill Tanner's tragic accident had subdued her. Being a mother herself, she could understand how devastating it must be to have the child you adored snatched away. She thought of her own lasses, little Sal and Peggy; she thought of her newborn who, crippled though he was, had not lost his life. For a moment, that part of her that was a mother went out in sympathy to Emma and Marlow Tanner. But then she remembered how Emma had been convicted of helping to murder her own husband. She thought of how Marlow Tanner had betrayed his own darling sister, old Sal, who had brought him up after they had lost their parents in strange and mysterious circumstances. Molly was made to remember all of this. And more besides: how Emma Tanner was blood kin to Caleb Crowther, and how that fiend had set out to make Molly's life a misery from when she was a child – even now he was hell-bent on destroying her, should she give him the chance.

Molly's hackles were up. Caleb Crowther would *not* be given the chance to destroy her, because this very day she had vowed to tread more carefully in future. Since the other day, when she had come upon him in that carriage, Molly had been in a state of panic, even considering whether or not to move out of Dock Street. She had decided against that. Her reasons were twofold. Firstly, she was certain that she had not been followed, and secondly, should Jack ever come home again, it would be to this little house on Dock Street. So, for the time being at least, she had no plans to up sticks and take to the road.

She didn't tell Mick about her upset with Caleb Crowther. He might renew his pleas to get her and the lasses living aboard his barge. Her mind was as stubborn as ever on that particular issue. Mick Darcy was to keep his place where Jack's family were concerned. He knew that now, and that was the way Molly preferred it.

All the same, Molly was forced to admit to herself what a good and loyal friend Mick was to her and the young 'uns. In fact, of late she found herself comparing him more and more to Jack. *Jack!* A spiral of anger and disillusionment rose up in her. In all this time there had been no word. Soon, she promised herself, he'll come home. In spite of everything, she knew that she would be waiting.

Long after Tilly returned to her own brood next door, Molly's quiet thoughts strayed to Emma Tanner, who, according to Tilly, had lost a son. Though Molly's sympathy was tempered by her fear and loathing of that particular family, she hoped, with a mother's heart, that the Lord might ease the awful grief which Emma Tanner must now be suffering.

On the second of September, in the year of our Lord 1886, the son of Marlow and Emma Tanner was laid to rest. Afterwards the many mourners filed through the big wrought-iron gates, each one with heavy heart and bowed head. Each one to pause at the gate, where they took Emma's black-gloved hand into their own and murmured their genuine condolences at such a tragic waste. Throughout the whole, sad ordeal Emma stood upright and dignified, loyally supported by her dear friend Nelly on one side, and her beloved husband Marlow on the other. He also was grief-stricken at the loss of his adored son. But he had vowed to remain strong for Emma's sake. Emma was crippled beyond redemption at having lost her son, Bill. Her precious son. Her pride and joy. The one child with which the good Lord had blessed her, only to snatch him cruelly away. Just as he had robbed her of the girl-child all those years ago.

Of a sudden, Emma felt incredibly old. On that day only last week, which seemed a lifetime ago, a shining light had gone from her life. Oh, she loved Marlow as much as any woman could love a man. He was her rock, the strong anchor that had sustained her faith for all the years when she was alienated from her homeland. He was everything a man could be to a woman, and life without him was unthinkable. But there had been another part of him that she had cherished with all of her heart – his son and hers. Bill was the living creation made out of their deep, abiding love for each other. In his stalwart and gentle character, he was all that Emma could ever pray for in a son. Now that he was gone, how could she face another day without his eager, shining face to smile at her and his boyish ways to vex and try her?

'God! Oh, dear God,' she prayed inwardly now, 'if you really are there in your heaven, tell me why you've taken his young and innocent life? *Why?* WHY?' Only the muffled sound of shuffling feet answered her, as one by one the mourners gave their love and sympathy. 'There is no answer from God,' she thought bitterly, 'because there *is* no God. And for me, there never was!' All the trauma and tragedy of her life came rushing back to haunt her. So many mountains to climb. So much heartache. Would it never end? A tide of weariness surged through her and for the briefest moment her strength wavered. Leaning into Marlow's loving embrace she whispered, 'Take me home. Please, take me home.' But then she realized with a stab of pain that there would be no small welcoming face there to greet her. Never again. *Never again!* No laughing bundle of joy to come eagerly running at the sight of her. In her house there were no children. The cruel words seared into her mind. No children. *In her house there were no children.* Now, there could be no *grandchildren* either!

Softly, Emma allowed herself to be taken on Marlow's arm along the path towards where the long line of carriages waited. They made a splendid and sombre sight against a cloud-dappled sky, with their dark-curtained windows and magnificent black horses bedecked with grand funereal plumage, and seated atop, the serious-faced drivers in top hat and tails. Lost in her most inner thoughts, Emma could see nothing before her but a small boy's face. She would *always* see it. Always cherish it. Like the one before. The one before.

'Mr Tanner . . . Mrs Tanner.' The soft, lilting voice caused Marlow to pause and turn around. Emma did not look up. Instead she kept her gaze to the ground. The voice was an intrusion.

Marlow reached out to take the priest's proffered hand. 'I must get my wife home,' he said quietly, 'she needs to rest.'

'Of course, of course . . . I understand.'

Suddenly Emma raised her grey eyes to him, and he was astonished to see how they fastened on his face with naked accusation. He was visibly shaken when, in a stiff and remarkably calm voice, she told him, 'No. You do not "understand". How could you?' Emma's white, stricken face betrayed little of the heartbreak she was suffering. Nor did it reveal the extent to which her faith in God had been shattered. Her next words, however, were delivered with such contempt that even Marlow gasped. 'Although I respect your intention, Father Mason, I'm afraid you bring me no comfort. Nothing you can do or say will change what has happened. In your prayers you may ask your God why he should rob a young innocent of his life. You may pray . . . just as I have done. And, just as I have done, you will be greeted with silence. Go back to your church, Father Mason, and seek your own comfort. There is none for me . . . no sanctuary in your master's house. *No place for me here*.' Her words rained down on him relentlessly. 'You will never see me cross your threshold again in my lifetime!'

'No, no . . . Mrs Tanner . . . Emma, *please*,' he entreated, 'think long and hard about what you are saying!' The colour had drained from Father Mason's face. As he stepped forward, Emma recoiled from him.

'Good day,' she uttered quietly, with no hint of regret in either her voice or her countenance as she moved away. Devastated by Emma's cold outburst, an astonishing outburst in view of her extraordinary faith in the Almighty, Marlow gave his apologies to the priest and hurriedly took up his place beside his wife. Later, when she had recovered enough from her grief and was made to reflect on her bitter words, Emma would relent. He was certain of it.

Some short way behind, Nelly quietly followed her darling Emma. The anguish in Nelly's heart was unbearable, and as the tears flowed down her face, she asked, *Help her, Lord.* She hasn't stopped loving yer . . . she never could. But oh, yer bugger, Lord . . . yer have put Emma through the mill, ain't yer, eh? So don't cross her off yer books yet, will yer? . . . 'Cause she'll be sorry for what she said to Father Mason, soon as ever she teks the time ter think on it.' Her heartfelt prayer broke into a fit of sobbing and, for a moment, Nelly found shelter behind a broad oak tree. Here, she plucked up the corner of her cape and dried her eyes on it. Then, before emerging in a more composed manner, she asked one other thing of the Lord. 'Should I tell Emma what happened all them years ago at the prison gates, when she gave birth to that bonny lass? If yer remember, Lord, there were an old tramp who collected the child from the gutter and made off with it . . . and I swear I heard the cry of a newborn. Oh, dear Lord, what shall I do, eh? *Shall I tell her?* Will yer help me ter decide fer the best? You think on it, Lord, and let me know.'

When the flurry of clouds quickly shifted to reveal a bright, smiling sun, Nelly took it as a sign that the good

Lord had heard her, and was thinking on it. With a lighter heart, she followed the path to where Emma was being helped into the carriage. In that moment, it struck Nelly how slow and pained were Emma's movements; not only bowed with grief, but something else. 'Yer ain't no youngster no more, Emma, me old darling,' she murmured with affection, 'we none of us are.' Old age has a nasty way o' creeping up on a body, she mused, because here they were, her and Emma, well into their forties. It was right what they said . . . 'time and tide wait for no man'. 'Nor no *woman* neither,' she murmured with a sigh. It seemed like only yesterday when she and Emma first met, in a dingy prison cell. Ridiculously young, they were, and terrified of what life might have in store for them. Well, they had come through those terrible times and found some sort of peace here in Blackburn: she with Emma's stalwart friendship over the long hard years and Emma with Marlow and their son. 'Oh, Emma, *Emma!*' Nelly could only guess at Emma's heartache and, beside it, her own sorrow paled in comparison.

On the slow, respectful journey back to Park Street, Nelly glanced often at the stiff little figure of Emma, with its straight, narrow shoulders set against the world, and her pale, drawn features that were like cold marble. She dared not imagine the fire that raged beneath.

Nelly thought about the accident that had taken the life of Emma's son, and she still could not shake off the feeling of guilt that had haunted her since that awful day only a week ago. It was a day bursting with all the warmth and colour of a splendid summer. A day when Emma and young Bill had jumped at Nelly's suggestion that they should picnic in Corporation Park . . . 'go right to thc top where the Crimean guns were sited', and afterwards meander the long winding path down. It was on the way down that the accident happened.

Against Emma's light-hearted warnings to 'stay on the footpath', the excited boy had clambered on to the brink of a dangerously steep cliff-face, whose surface made a deep and sheer drop to the rockeries below.

Nelly thought she would hear Emma's unearthly scream for as long as she lived. When they rounded the corner to see him balancing on the jagged protrusions above the slate face, it was something she would never forget. The mischievous smile on his face as she and Emma dashed forward. Then, in an instant, the boyish smile turning to horror as he lost his balance and went crashing to his death. It was instantaneous, or so they said. But not to Emma, and not to Nelly, for those few fleeting seconds seemed like a lifetime. A nightmare that would go on.

Nelly had to make a decision. One of the most difficult she had ever encountered. Would it help Emma, in her grief, to believe that *somewhere* she might have a daughter? Oh, it was true that, if the newborn *had* lived on that fateful night, she was no longer an infant but a full-grown young woman in her twenties. And what kind of young woman was she, Nelly wondered. Why! She might turn out to be the worst kind of gold-digger, who cared nothing for who her real mammy might be, only how much she was worth. The idea frightened Nelly. Besides which, she reminded herself, after all these years it would be nigh on impossible to trace Emma's daughter. It might be as well then to leave it be. Let the past and its secrets lie buried where they couldn't do no harm. 'Who are *you* to decide on it?'

Nelly asked herself indignantly. 'It's fer Emma ter decide.'

But before Emma could decide, she had to be told, Nelly mused. If she were to be told now, after all this time, she might just want to know why she had not been told years before, why all that time ago Nelly had lied to her. Would she understand that Nelly had only kept the truth from her in order to make her exile that much easier? Or would she condemn Nelly for betraying her? Nelly was in a terrible dilemma, because Emma's friendship meant more to her than anything else in the world. Yet she knew in her heart that Emma had a right to know the truth, especially now, when she believed herself to be childless. But then Nelly asked herself another question: suppose Emma's grief were eased by the news only to discover that the young woman had disappeared off the face of the earth and couldn't be traced – wouldn't that only add to Emma's pain?

'Oh, dearie me, Lord,' Nelly murmured, peering out of the carriage window to the shifting clouds, 'you'd best tell me what to do soon . . . 'cause I ain't got no idea at all which way to turn!' She knew that, either way, it would not be easy for Emma. On top of which, in a few months' time there was this blessed court case involving Emma's uncle, Caleb Crowther. Nelly bristled with anger at the thought of that man. She believed beyond a shadow of doubt that all of Emma's troubles were securely rooted in his black heart. 'May the devil take you,' she muttered through clenched teeth, 'for it's with *him* that you belong.

Chapter Six

'You little sod!' Tilly Watson wrenched the boy from the cupboard, where he was on tiptoe in the process of secreting a freshly-baked jam tart into his trouser pocket. '*One each* . . . you know well enough what Joey said, my lad! And it's his hard-earned money that keeps us all from starving . . . so you'll do as he says, you greedy little bugger, you!' When he twisted his fat little body from her and attempted to stuff the whole tart in his mouth at one go, she snatched it from him and lashed out with a swipe of her left hand – as a consequence the tart was well and truly mangled in the tussle. When Tilly's random swipe caught him a good cuff round the ear, the boy was sent reeling sideways to fall in a heap on top of the two small onlookers, who were filled with glee at seeing their greedy brother well and truly chastised. When he landed on them and all three crumpled to the floor in a jumble of arms and legs, they collapsed into fits of hysterical laughter that had both Tilly and Molly laughing also. Peggy and little Sal hugged each other and quietly giggled; though they carefully hid behind Molly's skirts and seemed unsure as to whether Tilly's temper was safely spent.

'Get out and play, the lot of you!' Tilly yelled now, running at the heap of fighting, squirming bodies, until they began squealing in make-believe horror and

107

emerged upright to scamper out on quick little legs. 'Play in the yard till Joey gets home from work . . . then I'll call you for your teas,' she told them. After which, she fetched the big iron kettle from the hearth, part-filled it with water and returned it to the cheery coals, where it soon began to sing.

'Are you sure it's all right to leave Tom and Peggy with you?' Molly asked. 'You do seem to have your hands full.'

'*Of course* I'm sure, dearie.' Tilly Watson gestured for Molly to sit down at the big, square table in the centre of the room. 'I'd soon tell you if I didn't want the young 'uns,' she said, 'but, like I've said many a time, I might as well have *thirty* as three like my brood . . . little sods they are, every one!' She laughed to see Molly's two hiding behind their mammy's skirts. Her laughter subsided at the sight of the small bundle in the curve of Molly's arms. The boy was some eight months old, yet he was so small and thin-looking that he could have been mistaken for an infant much younger. He was a happy child though, in spite of that crippled leg. Handsome too, with the same black eyes as his mammy, and crisp dark curls that tumbled freely about his heart-shaped face. 'By! . . . That child is the outright image of you, Molly . . . uncanny it is . . . the very same hair and eyes, the same jaw-line, and even a temperament to match his mammy's!' Tilly shook her head sadly. 'Such a lovely, cheery little chap,' she said quietly. But then she noticed how deeply her words were affecting Molly, and she changed tack. 'He's a strong child . . . you mark my words, Molly . . . he won't be held back by no crippled leg, you'll see!'

'*No, he won't*,' declared Molly, turning the boy on her

knee and kissing the outstretched fingers that came up playfully to touch her face, 'because I intend to get his leg seen to, soon as ever I can!'

Tilly was in the process of pouring the boiled water on to the tea leaves in the two mugs when Molly's statement pulled her up short. 'Aw now, don't go living no pipe-dreams, dearie,' she warned in a firm, shocked voice. 'Such things as . . . well, fixing the boy's leg . . . it takes more money than you and me will see in a lifetime, I dare say.' She shook her head vigorously, before marching to the window, where she stared down into the yard. Knocking hard on the window she yelled to the marauding group below, 'Stop that screaming! . . . And *you*, Walter . . . leave your sister's ears alone!' The noise subsiding, she came back to the table and finished the task of brewing tea. When the kettle was put back in the hearth and both she and Molly were in possession of a mug of steaming liquid, she broached the delicate subject again. 'Like I say, don't lose yourself in impossible day-dreams, dearie . . . there's *nothing* to be done for the boy, and it's best that you accept it.'

Molly resented the older woman's complacency, although she realized that Tilly Watson could not be expected to understand her feelings in this matter, which was so close to Molly's heart. After all, she told herself, how *could* Tilly understand, when all of her own children were so vigorously healthy. All the same, Molly did not want to discuss the issue so openly in front of the girls. 'You two . . . would you like to go and play in the yard with the others?' she asked. When they both eagerly agreed and ran off towards the scullery, where the steps led down to the yard below, Molly was quiet for a while, holding the boy up in her arms and watching with pride when he pressed his feet to her knees and tried unsuccessfully to draw himself up. It disturbed her to see how unbalanced and difficult his stance was. She did not fool herself that he would ever be able to walk in a natural manner, because it was painfully obvious that whilst his right leg was developing normally, the left one remained both stunted in growth and twisted away from his body. The foot was perfect in shape, but bent at a peculiar angle, so that when he pushed it against her lap it was not with the sole but with the inner ankle. To see this delightful and happy child so deformed was a great source of distress to Molly. She refused to believe, as Tilly did, that 'there's nothing to be done'. She said as much now.

'Stop fooling yourself!' Tilly Watson regretted not having snuffed the child's miserable life out when she had the opportunity. '*Look at yourself* . . . you're a young woman with no fellow, and three children looking to you for all their needs! You've told me yourself that you're a two-week behind with paying the rent.' She wagged a finger at Molly and, scowling, said, 'You listen to me, dearie. That landlord of ours is a mean and moody old sod . . . what! 'E'd have you out on your ear soon as look at you! Come to your senses, Molly . . . don't be a bloody fool. There's more important things to think about than that there twisted limb.' She pointed an accusing finger at the boy, who was playfully turning somersaults in Molly's arms; she thought the sight of his deformed leg hideous. 'To my mind, it's more important to have food in your larder and coal on your fire of a winter's night.'

Molly gave no reply. There would be no use, because no one could understand how she felt. Not Tilly, not any one. She changed the subject. 'So you will keep an eye on Peggy and the boy? Just for a few hours, while I see if there's money to be made in town.'

As usual, Tilly Watson did not hesitate. '*Of course* . . . I don't even notice them amongst my own brats. I expect you're after a few flowers, or an odd job or two, eh?' She evidently approved. 'Every shilling keeps the roof over your head and fills the belly,' she said. 'That's what's important, dearie . . . not trying to change the body the good Lord sees fit to give us.' She collected the child from Molly's arms. She would not have been squeamish in pinching the breath from its body soon after it was born, but unfortunately, the opportunity had been short-lived. So, now the child was here, and claiming a place in the world, there was no point in harbouring regrets. 'They'll be fine with me, as well you know,' she told Molly, 'and you're very welcome to leave little Sal alongside them . . . that eldest of yours is a godsend. You'll not be surprised when I tell you that she organizes *my* lot, with the force of a sergeant-major!'

Molly was not surprised, and laughing at Tilly's observations, she explained, 'My Sal's a puzzle, right enough. She can be shy and wary of strangers, but put her in amongst them that she knows, and she'll take complete charge in a minute. There's no denying that she's a born madam.' Just like her mammy before her, thought Molly with nostalgia, and just like her darling, eccentric namesake, old Sal Tanner.

'Will you leave the lass, then?'

'Oh, I don't know about that.' Molly had grown accustomed to Sal tagging along with her everywhere she went. Of a sudden though, she was reminded of her true errand today. It was not in search of a few half-dead flowers from a market-barrow which the seller had flung to the cobbles, nor was it to land herself a few hours' labour for a shilling or two. *No!* She had more ambitious things on her mind today than selling a few flowers or toiling in the market, lifting and stacking crates until her back ached. The money earned from these ventures would never bring enough to pay the rent, fill the larder, and put aside a tidy bit towards getting Tom's leg seen to. Molly had despaired at Tilly's warnings in that quarter, because hadn't she already told herself that it would take years, perhaps for ever, to accumulate enough money to pay for an operation. On top of which, Molly didn't even know whether there was such an operation that would put Tom's leg to rights, nor that there was a surgeon in the whole of Lancashire who was capable of such a delicate thing. But she had to believe, for Tom's sake, because how could he be a man amongst men and labour alongside them if he were a cripple? Molly had therefore set herself an enormous task. Until Jack took up responsibility for the boy, Tom had no one but her to rely on. And, God forgive her, she would employ every means at her disposal in order to see Tom become a whole being.

Realizing the dangers in what she intended doing that day, and being herself somewhat nervous of the consequences, Molly thought long about Tilly Watson's suggestion. She came to the conclusion that it might be wisest, after all, to leave little Sal with Tilly on this particular occasion. After all, Tilly could be relied on to keep the children occupied and to see that they came to no harm. Her mind was made up.

* * *

'All right, Mammy . . .I'll stay here with the others and see they're not naughty.' Little Sal's blue eyes smiled up at Molly. 'I don't want you to leave me behind *all* the time,' she declared, 'but I'm a big girl now, aren't I? . . . So I'll stay, if I can be in charge.' She peeked at Tilly Watson, who was standing at the top of the stone steps that led up to the scullery. It was obvious to the two women that Sal was seeking reassurance, and, perhaps, in her own small way, issuing an ultimatum.

'Well, *of course* you must be in charge!' agreed Tilly, casting a wary glance at the other children, who had stopped their yelling and fighting to view the proceedings. 'Isn't that so, you lot?' Tilly asked them. 'Sal must be in charge.'

'Only if I can be a soldier!' replied the chubby, fair-haired boy.

'And me, too,' chirped the smaller boy, who had a definite crossover in his speckled green eyes. The baby of the group, who was not much younger than Peggy, said nothing. Instead, she stood slumped against the back wall, sucking her thumb and using her free hand to hitch up the pee-stained knickers that had slipped to her knees.

'There you are then, Sal. It's agreed,' confirmed Molly, bending down and taking the two girls into her arms. 'Give your mammy a kiss.' She almost lost her balance when they flung themselves tight into her and rained her with kisses and hugs.

As she climbed the stone steps, Molly was made to pause when Sal's voice called out, 'Promise you'll be quick as you can?'

'I promise, sweetheart.'

'And will you bring us something?' Peggy chipped in.

Molly smiled at the difference in the character of her two daughters. All Sal wanted was for her mammy to come back quickly. That was enough. Peggy wanted her mammy back also, but she preferred her to return with a present in her pocket. 'I'll see what I can do,' she told the eager, uplifted faces. When she saw that little Sal was not altogether satisfied, she added a message just for her, 'I promise I'll be back as quickly as possible.' She warmed at the child's smile, and watched as she happily returned to the others, quickly beginning to stand them up against the wall and issue orders to 'get into a straight line, and no fighting'.

Thinking how much she adored her children and how empty life would be without them, Molly left the house and went away down Dock Street with a determined heart. She hoped the good Lord would understand why she was about to go back on a promise she made to him soon after Peggy was born. At that time, Molly had thought long and hard about the responsibility of having two children, one of whom was old enough and quick enough to follow her mammy's example, whether it be good or bad. Pickpocketing and stealing at every given opportunity was a bad example for little Sal, Molly had decided. She knew well enough that her older daughter was already beginning to acquire certain traits that would lead her into a life of street crime; just as she herself had done while under the influence of old Sal Tanner, albeit a loving and protective influence.

So Molly had stopped her thieving and turned to more honest ways of earning a living. Such as selling flowers that were past their prime, and moving crates in the marketplace, or singing outside a public house on a Saturday night – that was the most lucrative of all. But none of these enterprises ever allowed Molly and her offspring more than just a meagre existence. In fact, as Tilly had rightly pointed out, Molly had fallen behind with the rent and was having to dodge the landlord for fear he would give her notice to quit.

The last time Molly had been two weeks in arrears with the rent, he had made a lewd and improper suggestion. Nauseated by his proposition, Molly had worn herself to a frazzle that week, humping and shifting crates from early morning to when the market shut down. By the time she had paid the arrears and given Tilly a small sum for minding the children, there had been precious little left for food and fuel. Sometimes Molly despaired. Now she had the added burden of Tom's awful handicap. It was a combination of all these things that had made up her mind. She wasn't proud of her plans, not at all, because she intended to rob the fattest wallets and steal the most handsome fob watches, in order to accumulate enough money so she could take Tom to see a doctor who could put his leg to rights. She was even prepared to sell her precious gold clasp if it proved to be necessary. That particular prospect was the most daunting of all.

As Molly passed the Church of All Saints, she quickened her step and averted her eyes, while murmuring softly, 'I know it's wrong, Lord, and I'm sorry . . . but it was *you* that gave my boy a crippled body! You've left it to me to put right. And, if you don't mind me saying so . . . it's better if I *steal* than to earn money the way my landlord would have me do!' To Molly's thinking, she was employing the lesser of two evils, and considered that there must be some small merit in that.

Hurrying along the cobbled alleys, by way of Hart Street and Cicely, Molly's thoughts were drawn to two men in her life: Jack, the husband she still foolishly adored, and the bargee, Mick, who foolishly adored *her*. How different they were, she mused. And isn't it cruel the way Fate stirs things up into such an unhappy muddle. Molly was unpleasantly aware how Mick kept creeping up in her mind of late. In fact there were times when he, *and not Jack*, figured prominently in her thoughts. It frightened and worried her. She might be presently deserted by her husband, but she had grown accustomed to that and as a rule he always came home after a while. And she might be a thief, but to tell the truth, Molly could see little alternative in the circumstances. She was poor, and often desperate. That could not be denied. But she was not the kind of woman to go cap in hand to anyone. Neither was she the kind of woman to go from man to man, in exchange for a degree of security. She was a very simple and straightforward being, with an equally uncomplicated view on life: although he lacked a certain strength of character, Jack was her *husband*, and she loved him. But that was not to say he wouldn't get the length of her tongue when he did come creeping back! Until then, it was up to her to do the best for the children that it was in her power to do. Thanks be to the Lord, she was young and healthy, with a strong enough back to carry the particular load he had placed on it. As for Mick, well he was just a friend. A very *special* friend, there was no arguing. But Molly had every intention that he must remain only that.

'Gorra penny ter spare, 'ave yer, darlin'?' The thin and pitiful plea caused Molly to glance down. What she saw almost stopped her heart. It was a young man of about fourteen years, although he might have been older. It was difficult to tell, because he was horribly hunched at the shoulders and beneath the flat peaked cap, his narrow face was gaunt, with huge pleading eyes that stared up at Molly and touched her deep inside. He was seated on a makeshift trolley, just large enough to carry the small pathetic figure with only stumps for legs. *In her horrified mind, Molly saw her own son, Tom.* 'Ain't yer gorra penny ter spare fer a poor soul?' he insisted.

At once, Molly reached beneath her shawl and drew out the purse there. 'It's all I have,' she said quietly, giving it into his outstretched hand, 'take it . . . and God bless.' As she hurried away, the tight painful lump in her throat suddenly broke, and the tears welled in her eyes. She could feel the young man's bulbous eyes staring after her, but she dared not look back. 'That could be Tom,' she whispered over and over. Her determination was resolved: it would *not* be Tom. *NEVER!* She wouldn't allow it.

Molly quickened her steps towards the railway station. There were always easy pickings to be had wherever folks congregated. It was a known fact.

'I wish you were coming with us, Nelly.' Emma took her old friend into a loving embrace, holding her close for a while and gently patting the trembling shoulders, while she herself fought against the emotion of their parting. 'But the time will fly . . . you'll see. We'll be back before you know it.'

Nelly drew away and began frantically fishing about inside her cape until, in a moment, she produced a bold, white handkerchief, with which she promptly dried her eyes and afterwards blew her nose. 'Oh, don't take no notice o' me Emma gal,' she said with deliberate flourish. 'I'm just an old mardie arse!'

Emma laughed, but it was a mirthless and sorry sound. 'Just look at yourself!' she gently chastised, smiling into Nelly's round, brown eyes that were pink at the edges from crying since early morning, and at the strong, straight nose that was bright red and sore from the constant friction of the handkerchief. 'You'll only make yourself ill if you go on like that!' There was genuine concern in her voice. It came to her, with a stab of astonishment, that since their first meeting in that prison cell more than twenty years ago, her impending trip to Australia would be the first and longest time that she and Nelly had been truly parted. 'I know how you feel, Nelly,' she murmured now, 'don't think I *wanted* to leave you behind . . . Oh, Nelly! Why did you insist on remaining behind, if you knew it was going to upset you so?'

'You know why!' Nelly exclaimed, hating the idea of Emma going all the way to Australia, but fearing even more the thought of going *herself*.

'Because she's a loyal friend.' Marlow stepped forward from his discreet vantage point some way beyond where the two ladies were saying their farewells. He had seen how Nelly's unfortunate outburst had affected Emma, and at once he was greatly concerned that even now, at this late moment in time, Emma might refuse to make the long journey to the other side of the world. As it was, he'd had the devil of a job convincing her to undertake this trip in the first place. It was both the doctor's sound warning with regard to her health and his own desperate pleas to Emma that had finally persuaded hcr of the need to get right away from all that reminded her of their son, and of what might have been. Since Bill's tragic accident, Emma had withdrawn deeper and deeper into a dangerous, twilight world, until Marlow lived in fear of losing her also. His own heart was empty and heavy with grief at the loss of the son he'd idolized. But, unlike Emma, he had made himself come to terms with that dreadful loss, if only to help Emma out of her own, crippling grief.

In these last few weeks since the boy's funeral, he had privately shed many a tear and, strangely enough, the shedding of those tears had somehow eased his heart-ache. But Emma's grief had turned inward. She had not spoken one word about their son: she would not be drawn into any conversation regarding him, nor had she cried a single tear on his behalf. It was as though she had locked his memory and his precious image into that secret part of her where he would be kept safe, intact and still alive. But in doing so, Emma had created for herself another place, another time, where she and the boy remained aloof from the world, where he lived out his life in her mind, and that mind was beginning to lose the boundaries between what was real, and what was not.

'*Must* we go, Marlow?' Emma pleaded now. 'You know I would much rather stay at home.'

Nelly was horrified! Filled with mortification at having betrayed her emotions in front of Emma, she resolved to make amends. 'Don't you talk such stuff and nonsense, Emma, my girl!' she chided in her most authoritative voice. '*What!* . . . And spoil my chance at being the "lady of the house"? You wouldn't do that to yer old friend, would you? No, you get off to Australia . . . say hello to that Silas Trent for me . . . and make sure the buggers take proper care o' the business you built up with your own sweat and blood!' She laughed and winked, casting a cheeky glance to where Marlow was silently thanking Nelly for her splendid efforts, when he knew it was tearing her apart to see Emma leave. 'You and Marlow . . . well, you know what I mean, Emma, gal . . . it's so romantic, ain't it, eh? Gazing over the ship's rail into the horizon, and watching the moon play on the water. Oh, and when you *get* there . . . to Australia, there'll be long, sultry nights . . . all that sun and gently strolling along the beach.' Of a sudden she laughed out loud, and clutching her cap tightly about her, she began shivering and chattering her teeth, 'While us poor mortals are left to suffer an English October!'

Emma saw through Nelly's ploy. And she loved her all the more for it. Reaching out her arms, she gripped Nelly's shoulders and, keeping her at arm's length, she gazed into her friend's twinkling brown eyes with a veil of nostalgia in her own strong, anxious gaze. Those merry eyes had carried her back to when she and Nelly were young. All the joy of that time, all the pain, all the defiance, it was still there, as if it were only yesterday.

Fleeting images paraded through Emma's turbulent mind, and paramount in these were the images of two children: one a newborn girl-child, and the other a boy already maturing towards manhood. Both children were hers and Marlow's. Both had been conceived out of wedlock, and worse, they had been conceived when she was married to other men! Both were now lost to her and Marlow for ever.

Now Emma asked herself the same question she had asked time and time again since the death of her son: *was she being punished for her sins?* In her terrible grief, she had denounced God. Now she wondered whether there really were an Almighty that was unforgiving, more cruel than any mere mortal could conceive, totally without mercy. If that were so, then she had been *right* to denounce a God in his heaven, for such an awful and powerful force could never be described as anything other than malicious. Therefore she regretted none of the harsh words which she had spoken in the churchyard on the day of her son's funeral. The only truth that now stayed with her was that she had sinned, and she was being punished. Beyond that, her reasoning refused to go.

'All right, Nelly . . . but take good care of yourself, won't you?'

'Don't I allus?' Nelly wrapped her two fists round Emma's gloved hands and tenderly lifting them from her shoulders, she squeezed them in a frantic gesture, saying in a dangerously trembling voice, 'Ooh, Emma, gal . . . let the good Lord smile on yer and bring yer both home safely.' She was not surprised when Emma quickly withdrew her hands. But her mention of the 'good Lord' had been *deliberate*, because she had prayed with all her might for Emma to return to the faith. And she would go on praying.

'Goodbye, Nelly.' Emma leaned forward to kiss the weatherworn and ageing face that she knew as well as her own. 'Just remember what I said . . . take good care of yourself.' Nelly clung to her for a moment, and then they were parted.

Having suppressed her tears for Emma's sake, Nelly's resolve melted as the train pulled away in a rising cloud of steam, and soon she could no longer see Emma's fluttering handkerchief for the blinding tears that tumbled down her face. 'God keep you both safe,' she murmured, in between rubbing at her eyes with the now soggy linen square.

After a few moments the train had gone from her sight. With a bowed head and heavy heart she turned away towards the ladies' cloakroom. Here, she regained her composure, straightened her bonnet and smoothed out her cape. Then, fearful of the long, empty days ahead without her Emma, she emerged on to the platform once again.

Only now had Nelly come to realize just how very long Emma would be gone. *Four months.* Four endless months that, to Nelly, would seem like a lifetime. Oh, she knew that Marlow had been right in applying for a postponement of the court hearing between Emma and the infamous Caleb Crowther. In her weakened and distressed condition, Emma could never have defended herself properly against her uncle. The authority had conceded to this and, in view of Marlow's request, together with the recent bereavement of their only son, the hearing was duly posponed to the thirty-first of March, in the year of Our Lord 1887. Marlow intended to keep Emma away until the month before, especially as the groundwork for the case was already prepared.

'Come on, Nelly gal . . . get yer pecker up and stop maudlin'!' Nelly told herself, in a loud whisper that drew a number of curious glances from passengers awaiting their respective trains. 'Oh, yer may well gawp and wonder,' she told them, unaffronted, 'but none o' *you* buggers have just seen yer darling off ter the other side o' the world, I'll be bound!' When all she received in return were haughty looks and a few disgruntled murmurs, she snorted aloud and stormed away, saying in a loud, firm voice, 'Miserable buggers!'

Lingering awhile by the flower-stand and debating to herself whether to purchase a posy, Nelly was interested to hear a conversation taking place nearby. The tall lady – with a head full of feathers and flowers that were tied beneath her chin with a wide extravagant bow – was relating to her smaller, plainer colleague a most detailed explanation of the 'disgusting affair . . . when a decent, respectable gentleman or lady could not attend their normal business without being robbed. And in broad daylight!' She was most indignant.

Amused by the manner of the two ladies who, in Nelly's opinion, were 'hoity toity and too blessed with their own importance', Nelly would have left the station there and then. But the woman, still speaking in loud and injured tones, drew her colleague's attention to the culprit. 'Oh, my dear!' she declared, sounding as though any minute she would fall down in a dead faint, 'What a *dirty*, despicable ruffian that young woman was . . . thin and undernourished of course. But I am quite certain to have nightmares about her, quite certain, my dear. Such large, piercing eyes she had . . . *black as the devil's*, and a look about her that quite unnerved me. Why, my dear! When the officer escorted her into the station-manager's quarters, I believe she was quite capable of putting a curse on him . . . fighting and spitting like a demon, she was!'

At once, Nelly was convinced that here was the very girl she had been seeking these many months: 'thin and undernourished . . . large black eyes', and by all accounts, possessed of a bit of fire in her character. Yes! It was the same thief, of that Nelly had no doubt. Putting on her sweetest smile, and sidling up to the two ladies, she imitated the tall one, saying 'Oh my dear . . . do excuse me, but I could not help overhearing. How *frightful* for you!' It was all she could do not to burst out laughing.

Both ladies seemed momentarily taken aback by the interruption, carefully regarding Nelly's expensive cape and bonnet, and seeing how altogether refined she did appear. Accepting that she was a woman of quality, they were soon spilling out the entire story of how a well-to-do gentleman had raised the alarm when 'this raga-muffin' dipped her hand into his pocket. The outcome was that he caught hold of her and was determined not to let her go until someone in authority was summoned. Upon the officer's arrival, the gentleman, together with the thief and a member of the public who was thought to have witnessed the unfortunate event, were quickly ushered into the station-manager's office. 'And, as far as I know . . . they are still in there,' remarked the tall lady. By this time, drawn by this particular lady's shrill, up-lifted voice, a small crowd had gathered to add its voice to the proceedings.

'Really!' Nelly was marvellous in her condemnation. 'Whatever is the world coming to, my dear?' Suitably shaking her head in disillusionment, she swung away and swept through the crowd of bodies, loudly tut-tutting as she went. A little smile crept into her heart as she made her way to the station-manager's office. At long last, here might be the opportunity to help this unfortunate creature. And wouldn't Emma be pleased?

Anxious to approach the 'injured' gentleman before he preferred charges, Nelly was mortified to discover that 'both the gentleman and the thief have been taken to the constabulary.' But being Nelly, a woman who was not easily thwarted, she promptly gathered up her skirts, ordered a cab, and instructed it to take her quickly to the police station. Once there, she had no intention of leaving without the young woman in question!

Chapter Seven

'Who *is* this woman, Molly? And why would she persuade the gent to drop charges against you?' Mick had been shocked when Molly told him what had happened, and he had made her promise never to go thieving again. He was also very hurt when he realized that she was prepared to resort to such methods rather than turn to him for help. He knew, however, that the limited help he could offer her would never be enough to get Tom's leg put right, and he could understand how desperation had driven her to go picking pockets. He knew what an awful thing it was, to be so desperate. Because didn't *he* feel the same way? And hadn't he lost many a night's sleep on account of his all-consuming love for Molly? And now, because of that same desperation, he had come to a decision. The hardest thing of all was how he might bring himself to tell Molly. Her visit to the barge on this chilly November Saturday had been a pleasant surprise, which he intended to enjoy to the very full, before breaking his news to her. He would have told her today anyway, because, if she hadn't turned up here, he would have gone along to Dock Street some time later that evening.

'She's an odd sort,' Molly replied in answer to his question. 'Her name's Nelly . . . and she's a sort of "companion" to Emma Tanner.'

'Tanner?' Mick was surprised. 'The same Emma Tanner who's wed to my boss?'

'The very same.'

'Well, I'm blowed . . . it's a small world when all's said and done!' A thought suddenly occurred to him. 'I remember you telling me that you had no time for the likes of Marlow Tanner . . . though you never said why? And here you are, working for his wife . . . or his wife's companion.'

'You're right, Mick . . . I *don't* have any time for the likes of Marlow Tanner.' Molly had never explained why she felt this way towards Mick's employer, and it was something she did not feel able to discuss with anyone. If the time ever came when she had to speak her mind about the way Marlow Tanner had deserted his own sister – the old dear who had raised her from a child – then it would be to the *man himself*. Oh yes, it would be interesting to see how Marlow Tanner reacted to her accusation. But she had no desire to exchange words with him, not on that shameful matter, nor on any other.

'He's always been a good employer to me,' Mick argued. 'Honestly, Molly, you're a strange little thing and no mistake. What in God's name has Marlow Tanner ever done to *you*, eh?'

'He's never done anything to me,' Molly said truthfully. It was old Sal Tanner whose heart had been broken by his callous disregard for her. 'And the reason I'm working for his wife's companion is because I've got no choice.' Molly's gaze reached beyond Mick's bulky frame in order to check that the children were not up to any mischief in the forward cabin. When she saw that they were happily playing with the small saucepans that Mick had given them, she relaxed into the seat and supped on the hot broth which Mick had dished up for all of them. The children had quickly finished theirs, before scampering off to lose themselves in the paraphernalia that cluttered the bulkhead quarters. Molly resumed her conversation. 'If I don't turn up every day at the big house on Park Street, this "Nelly" has threatened to persuade the gent to charge me after all . . . on top of which, the constable told her to let *him* know if I didn't behave, because he released me into her custody and he's taken her word that she'll keep me out of trouble.' There was anger and resentment in Molly's black eyes as she looked up into Mick's kind, handsome face. 'Bloody cheek!' she said. 'I'm a grown woman. I don't need no guard dog.'

Mick laughed. 'Well, *that's* a matter of opinion, me beauty,' he said. 'But how long does this Nelly expect to keep you working there?' He also did not like the thought of Molly being made to report there against her will.

'Three months, she said. We came to an understanding about it. I'm to work there as a general help for three months . . . after which time I'm free to leave, and nothing said.' Here, Molly chuckled. 'She thinks I'll stay on, of my own free will, when the three months is up.'

Mick was intrigued. 'And *will* you?'

'No!' Molly was adamant. But then she lapsed into deep thought: how she had actually come to *like* Nelly, and how, in spite of herself, she had begun to look forward to her mornings up at the big house. And there was something else as well. Something that was very precious to her, and for which she had grown exceedingly grateful. She explained to Mick. 'Though little Sal wasn't too pleased,' she said in a low voice. 'It weren't

fair to ask Tilly to mind all *three* children while I did my
duties at the house . . . so I told Nelly that I'd have to
fetch little Sal to work each day, because I'd nowhere to
leave her.' She chuckled. 'I was sure she'd refuse, and so
I couldn't come either . . . then she'd have no hold on
me. But she weren't a bit worried. Now she thinks the
world of Sal . . . and she's even *teaching* her things . . .
reading words, and writing. She tells her stories and she
plays in the garden with her.'

'Aren't you jealous?' Mick laughed.

'Oh, you might tease, Mick Darcy,' Molly chided, 'but
yes . . . I *was* jealous. But Nelly's not the sort to try and
steal a child's affection . . . she's really taken to Sal and
me. To tell you the truth, she's not a bad sort . . . rough
and ready she is . . . just like us.'

'No, Molly . . . not "like us",' Mick reminded her
quietly, 'she's rough and ready maybe, because she was
a convict with Emma. But now she lives the life of a lady,
in a fine house with fine things round her. And, like
as not, mixes with high, influential people.' Mick was
concerned that Molly was in danger of losing sight of the
real issues here. 'Don't forget *that*, me beauty, and don't
forget that she *forced* you to go and work there. Keep
your wits about you, Molly. These gentry have to be
watched . . . and they harbour some very strange ideas.
I don't know that you should let her take up so much of
little Sal's time. Remember, there's been a child lost in
that household . . . the Tanner's son. They're too old to
have any more children.' He glanced round to reassure
himself that Sal had not overheard, before looking into
Molly's uplifted face. 'You do know what I'm saying,
don't you, Molly?'

Molly knew right enough. The very same idea had

crossed her own mind and she had been made to recall her other fear, regarding Justice Crowther and the fact that he *was* kith and kin to the Tanner household, whatever the rumours said. She had broached the matter with Nelly, who had vehemently assured Molly 'that devil will not set foot in this household you have my word on it!' But then, she had gone on to ask awkward questions, such as why was Molly so intimidated by the Justice? . . . Had they ever locked horns? . . . Why should he be interested in a ragamuffin such as herself?

Afraid that she might reveal too much of her lawless past, including the fact that the Justice had hounded her badly, Molly cautioned herself, and from that point on, she remained vigilant and wary of letting her tongue run away with her. In spite of Nelly's assurances, Molly's suspicions were not altogether allayed. Yet, for all that, she still had a sneaking liking for Nelly, who had a straightforward and winning way about her. As for Emma Tanner though, and her husband Marlow, Molly was thankful that they were on the other side of the world. By the time they returned, she intended to be long gone. Three months, Nelly had said, and Molly was obliged to agree in the circumstances. Three months. And not a minute longer!

'Penny for them.' Mick clicked his fingers, and Molly instantly gathered her thoughts. 'All I'm saying is . . . be careful, Molly. Money and authority bring their own brand of law, and folks like you and me . . . well . . . be very careful, Molly lass. You never can tell what you're up against.'

'I'm nobody's fool,' Molly retorted, but not without a measure of gratitude in her voice; though Mick need not be so concerned. She was a survivor, and her instincts had always served her well. They would now. She would not relax her vigilance, not for a moment.

'Are you paid well?' Mick wanted to know, and was satisfied when Molly told him that yes, Nelly did pay her well. Fourteen shillings and sixpence a week; enough to keep the family fed and the rent up to date, besides giving Tilly a small payment for minding the two young ones.

'And did you buy *that* with your wages?' There was a softer, more intimate tone to Mick's voice as he pointed to the blouse that Molly had on. It was a high-necked garment in the warmest shade of burgundy, with full sleeves and pleated shoulders, and a row of tiny mother-of-pearl buttons from collar to waist. The deep, striking colour brought out the fire in Molly's dark eyes. Now, as she softly blushed beneath Mick's admiring gaze, he reached out and would have wrapped his strong hand over Molly's small fist.

Sensing his intention, she put her two hands into her lap and plucked at the grey serge skirt with its black hem. 'See this?' she said, cleverly drawing his loving eyes from her face. 'Nelly gave me this . . . and the blouse. She's got this chest in the attic . . . *stuffed* with clothes and things that don't fit her no more.' Molly smiled as she recalled how Nelly had explained: 'There was a time when I were thin as a pikestaff and fancied mesel' with the fellers . . . but now I'm lumpy as a cart-horse and the fellers would sooner strap a bag of oats ter me nose than put their arms round me!' Suddenly, in the wake of Mick's timely warning, Molly felt all the old suspicions rushing back. 'I'll give the blouse and skirt back . . . I should never have accepted them in the first place.'

'No, no . . . don't be foolish,' Mick said. 'Keep the

clothes. There's no reason why you shouldn't. If they don't fit her any more, then they're no use at all to her, are they?' His gaze mingled with hers, and Molly's heart turned over. 'Besides, me beauty, you look a picture of loveliness in 'em.' In that instant, the light of day caught his eye, and Molly was astonished to see her own image reflected in his strong, loving gaze. It frightened yet excited her at the same time.

When, somewhat shaken, she lowered her eyes, he stood up and touched her on the shoulder. 'Will you come up top with me, Molly? There's something that needs to be said . . . away from the children.' He collected her shawl from the nearby bunk and, taking it by two corners, he held it out. When Molly stepped forward, he wrapped it round her with great tenderness and, for a heart-stopping moment, she thought he intended to kiss the top of her head. Instead, he straightened his broad shoulders and gestured for her to go ahead.

On deck, Molly drew the shawl tightly about her. The mid-morning breeze had gained momentum, slicing the air with spite, and chilling her face. She shivered noisily. However, when Mick put his arm round her she instinctively drew away, although in truth Molly would have liked to snuggle into him. There was a feeling of great strength and protectiveness about this big, kind man.

'What is it you want to tell me, Mick?' Molly asked, looking up at him and thinking how ruggedly handsome he was. But he wasn't *Jack*, and he *wasn't* her husband. The three children inside the barge were not his either. He was a friend, a dear friend and that was all. Molly was disturbed to find that she was having to reassure herself of these facts more and more of late.

'Just listen, Molly . . . don't say *anything* until you've heard me out.' He paused, as though waiting for her to protest. When she did not, he went on in a quiet voice, all the while looking down at her lovely face, and fighting a terrible compulsion to grab her by the shoulders and force his lips on to hers. Dear God, how she haunted his every waking thought! His first words told Molly what she had long known, and been afraid of. '*I love you, Molly* . . . more than I've ever loved any woman. All I want in this life is to care for you and the children . . . to take you on as a family . . . *to belong*.' He raised his head and cried out softly as though in pain, '*Oh, Molly, Molly!*' Kicking his foot against the rail post he swung away from her, his two fists wrapped over the post and his tall, strong figure bent forward, the shoulders slumped wearily and his voice filled with despair as he told her, 'That husband of yours is a damned fool! I can't understand a man who could turn his back on a woman like you . . . leave his children . . . not giving a cuss whether they're cold or hungry.' Suddenly, he groaned aloud and came back to grip her by the shoulders. 'I know it hurts you to hear these things, Molly . . . but it's the truth, and I wouldn't be much of a man if I didn't say what was on my mind.' He sensed Molly's irritation and felt her shoulders stiffen beneath his hands. 'All right . . . all right.' He stepped away, keeping his eyes on her face, frantic that he was doing and saying all the wrong things, when he had spent these past few days planning how he could best win Molly over. He knew it would not be easy. She was fiercely loyal, worse, she loved her husband in spite of his roving ways.

'I'd best be going.' Molly took a step forward. She did not like the way things were developing.

'Don't do that, Molly,' he pleaded. 'Look, I've gone about this like a bull-headed fool. A minute . . . one minute more, and I promise I'll not mention him again.' His whole being relaxed when Molly stopped right beside him.

'It's simple enough,' he murmured in her ear, 'I love you and I'm asking you to come away with me. Let me take care of you, sweetheart . . . you and the young 'uns?'

In spite of herself, Molly was touched by the desperation in his voice. She knew he had not meant to slander Jack; in her heart she had to admit that he had spoken only the truth. It was strange that things had come to a head in this way, because she had intended telling him that, after today, she would not be coming to the barge anymore. Jack may be a coward, with the wandering heart of a gypsy, but he also had a vicious streak in him. It was wrong of her to see so much of Mick. It could lead to trouble. Besides which, she was not being fair to Mick by continuing these meetings, because, just as she had suspected, and in spite of his assurances to the contrary, they were encouraging Mick to believe that something more permanent might develop between them. Now she half-turned, her heart skipping a beat when she realized how close Mick's face was to hers. 'Please, Mick,' she said, her dark eyes melting beneath that intense, adoring gaze, 'you know you're asking the impossible.' He made no reply, but held her attention a moment longer until she became mesmerized by the softness of his gaze; there was something compelling about his whole countenance, keeping her there, trapped and helpless in the deep emotion that drew them together.

Molly could never remember exactly how it happened, but, suddenly, she was in his arms and he was pressing his mouth to hers. And she was willing him on, reaching up to wrap her arms round his neck, gently moaning as he rained frantic kisses on her face, her ears, her neck; all her resolve was was washed away in a tender and exquisite tide of ecstasy. 'Say you'll be mine,' he coaxed, 'just say the word, Molly.'

Suddenly Molly saw a movement out of the corner of her eye. It was little Sal! With a shock, Molly sprang from Mick's embrace, a wave of remorse sweeping through her when Sal said pointedly, 'I want to go home.'

It took Molly only a few moments to prepare the children, and soon they were clambering down the gangplank on to the wharf. As Molly passed by him, her gaze fixed ahead and a tinge of embarrassment warming her face, Mick reached out, to draw her tenderly to a halt. 'I can't go on this way,' he told her softly. 'I must *leave* this area. With or without you.'

Molly did not look back. There would be too much between them, too much pain in his eyes. So she told him as gently as she knew how, and not without regret, 'Then it must be without me.' She felt his fingers grip into her shoulder, and, for a moment, she was afraid that he meant to swing her round to face him. But then his hand slid away and she was free to go.

Without another word, Molly walked on, away from the barge where she had spent many happy hours, away from a man who was both good and sincere, and along the wharf until, at the far end, she turned. She had thought to see his strikingly handsome figure standing astride the deck, with his passionate brown eyes seeking her out. When there was no sign of him, it was as if a lead weight had filled her heart. 'God bless and keep you, Mick Darcy,' she murmured, 'wherever you go.'

As she turned away, realizing that she might never see him again, Molly wondered at the feelings she had experienced in his arms. Warm and wonderful feelings that left her still trembling. But she could not accept that it could be love. 'I'm lonely,' she told herself, 'that's all.' Then, with a surge of anger, she said through gritted teeth, *'Jack, you bugger! . . .* It's high time you came home.' In fact he had been gone so long that, if he were not home by the time she had served her three months up at the big house, she would make it her business to track him down.

Molly loved the clinging, flowery smell of beeswax; as she polished the lovely walnut dining table, its particular perfume filled the air and made her think of spring sunshine. Of a sudden she was softly humming a tune, every now and then peeping out of the window to stare across the lawns towards the summer-house. Little Sal was sitting there, browsing through a picture book that Nelly had lent her.

Seeing the deep and contented look on her daughter's face, Molly paused in her labours to gaze a while longer. Outside the sun was shining and there was no breeze at all. There on the sundial was perched a tiny robin redbreast, dipping his head this way and that, and occasionally letting out a thin, piercing chirp. There was a freshness about everything, and a wholesomeness that lent a deal of content to Molly, who was lost so deeply in the wonder of it all that, when the door was flung open, she gave a small cry and swung round with her black eyes big and fearful. 'Oh, Miss Nelly!' she cried, visibly sagging with relief.

'Heavens above, gal!' retorted Nelly. 'Yer nothing but

a bag of nerves.' She sauntered to the window where Molly had been standing until, upon Nelly's arrival, she had quickly resumed her polishing. 'It ain't like a *December* day, is it, eh?' she said, gazing at Sal who had caught sight of her and was frantically waving. 'More like spring, I reckon,' she said, cheerily waving back.

'That's just what I was thinking,' agreed Molly. She did not stop work, but began softly humming the pretty song again. However, when Nelly came to sit beside the table saying, 'Your Sal is a bright and quick little gal,' Molly was at once attentive. Putting her cloth on the table and straightening her back with a little groan, she looked directly at Nelly, a lovely smile on her face and a mother's pride in her voice. 'Oh, she is! She is! . . . Right from when she were so high.' Molly stretched out her hand to indicate a figure not much taller than Tom was now. 'She wanted to know *everything*. Whenever she found something to puzzle about, she'd ask "Why, mammy" . . . "Why" . . . all the time "*Why?*"' Molly laughed softly at her own private memories. 'Drove me nearly crazy with her questions.' Suddenly, she was regarding the older woman with a more serious expression. 'You've done wonders for little Sal,' she murmured, 'we'll never be able to thank you properly. If it weren't for you . . . little Sal would not have had any learning. Certainly not from *me*, because I'm a very poor scholar myself . . . though, thanks to my Jack, I can read a little.'

'Molly, please come and sit aside o' me for a minute . . . let the polishing wait. There ain't nothing important about putting a shine on a table. Come and set yersel' here.' Nelly pulled out the chair next to her. 'I want us to talk a while.'

Whenever anyone told Molly they wanted to 'talk', she always assumed the worst. 'There's lots more to be done yet,' she argued, remaining where she was, 'and it's almost midday . . . I've to be back home within the hour. Can't it wait, whatever it is?' Her heart sank when Nelly slowly shook her head. Reluctantly she walked round the table to the other side and seated herself on the standchair, her slim back as stiff as a rod and her dark eyes anxious as she asked, 'What is it you want to talk about, Miss Nelly?'

'Aw, fer goodness' sake, gal!' Nelly threw her hands into the air in an expression of frustration. 'Ain't I asked yer afore . . . time and again . . . *don't* call me Miss Nelly! Yer mek me sound like a bleedin' *gentry*!' She poked Molly's arm with a stiff, angry finger. 'How would *you* like it if I kept calling *you* Miss Molly, eh?' When she saw Molly's face break into a smile, she slapped her chubby hand to her knee and roared with laughter. 'There y'are then . . . it sounds bloody daft, don't it, eh? *Miss* Nelly this, and *Miss* Nelly that!' Here she gave a cheeky wink, saying in a furtive whisper, 'Mind you, gal . . . I don't complain when the *servants* call me by that title, 'cause my good friend Emma . . . well, she's told the buggers, "You must address my companion as Miss Nelly!" Oho, what a to-do there was, when Emma heard the housekeeper telling the scullery maid how "that Nelly woman is no better than we are" . . . well! My Emma were up in arms. Told 'em she did . . . not to refer to me in such an undignified way again.' Nelly chuckled. 'I would 'a loved ter see the face on that cook when Emma told her off . . . miserable, po-faced bleeder she is – I never have liked her.'

Molly really did have a soft spot in her heart for this

outspoken and unpredictable woman. Now, as Nelly ranted on about Miss Warburton, the cook, Molly quietly observed her. She wasn't certain how old Nelly was, although she thought it must be somewhere not far off fifty years; yet there was such life and enthusiasm about her that a body could be forgiven for thinking she was much younger. Only the deepening wrinkles etched into her face, and the streaks of grey that coloured her wispy brown hair belied the possibility. She had told Molly how 'I used ter be thin as a pikestaff in me younger days', but there was little evidence of that now, because the 'pikestaff' was thickly padded with round, bulging parts and a somewhat 'bouncy' bustle. Even in her pretty silk and taffeta dresses with their ribbons and frills, Nelly could never be taken for a 'lady'. But it took more than fancy clothes to make a 'lady', thought Molly now; if she were ever asked, she would say that this genuine, warm-hearted creature sitting here now was more of a 'lady' than any one of those living in their posh houses and riding in their coach-and-four.

'I said . . . why is it that yer never want ter talk about yersel'?'

Nelly's question surprised Molly, who straightaway was on her guard. She must never forget that Nelly was Emma Tanner's very best friend, and that this was the Tanners' house, where every wall had ears. And where there were ears there were mouths, and where there were mouths there was gossip. Gossip had hanged many an innocent creature before now!

'What do you mean?' Molly asked, feigning ignorance of the older woman's intention to draw her out.

'Don't you come *that* business with me!' Nelly chided good-naturedly. 'I've done it too often mesel' not to know what yer up to. What I said was . . . yer never talk about yersel', do yer? Keep yer secrets close ter yer chest, don't yer, eh?' She stared at Molly in a forthright manner, and when Molly stared back with a defiant look in her shining black eyes, Nelly laughed aloud and rocked in her chair. 'Yer little bugger!' she declared, wagging a finger. 'Yer don't intend giving much away, I can see that. But yer ain't gonna get the better of me.'

'I'm sure I wouldn't want to do any such thing,' Molly replied quietly. 'I don't talk about myself because . . . there's nothing to talk about. There aren't any "secrets" to "keep close to my chest",' she lied.

'All right then, me darlin' . . . don't get agitated.' Nelly was irritated with herself, because she had succeeded in frightening the lass . . . the very thing she'd wanted to avoid. Her old heart was touched by the way Molly was unthinkingly twisting her apron round and round her finger. And those eyes! Dark, handsome eyes that seemed to see right inside you. Of a sudden, Nelly was astonished to be thinking of *Marlow Tanner! He* had eyes like that, black eyes that spoke volumes. A funny little shiver ran down her spine as she slyly regarded Molly, with her thick, dark tousled hair and so exceptionally beautiful; even with black lead up her arms from doing the firegrate, and with that stiff, unattractive apron over her secondhand clothes. Nelly felt instinctively that there was something here, some strange, inexplicable quality – or secret – about this young woman that she hadn't yet fathomed. But she *would* get to the bottom of it, because she wouldn't rest until she did.

'Look, Molly, luv . . . yer'll have ter forgive a nosey old bugger like mesel', but . . . well, I've tekken a real liking ter you and the little 'un. At first, I just wanted ter do right by them as is less fortunate than mesel' . . . just as my Emma taught me. But since I fetched yer here agin yer will some six weeks back, like I say . . . I've come ter like yer a lot.' Nelly had Molly's attention now, so she went on, 'Yer don't need ter tell me anything that yer don't want to, but there's one thing I can see with my own eyes, gal . . . and it's this. Yer've had a hard life . . . it's written in yer face, and in that quick, defiant manner yer have . . . just the same as *me* when I were living rough an' ready after me parents died.' Here she was intrigued by something which had not until now occurred to her. In a gentler voice, she asked Molly, 'Ain't yer got no parents, child?' When Molly lowered her gaze and gave no answer, she thoughtfully nodded her head. 'I see,' she murmured although in truth she wasn't quite sure what she *did* see. 'Tell me one thing,' she asked now, 'do yer trust me? Answer me truthful, mind!'

Molly raised her head and looked directly into the older woman's eyes. What she saw there was real compassion, and more honesty than she had ever expected. Yet still she was not certain. So much had happened in her young life, so much to destroy her natural trust. So many things that warned her always to be wary, to suspect *everyone*, or suffer the consequences. She liked Nelly. Liked her a great deal. But she didn't *know* her. Not really.

Molly had been asked to answer truthfully, and she did. 'I don't know whether I trust you . . . or whether I don't. I *want* to. But I can't . . . not altogether.' Molly hated the sound of her own words. And yet they were straight from the heart, as 'truthful' an answer as she was able to give.

'Fair cnough, Molly gal, I can't say I'm surprised yer won't confide in me. Not when I fetched yer here agin yer will . . . threatening all kinds of retribution and punishment.' Nelly paused, looking into the troubled face of the young woman beside her, and a great surge of sympathy flooded her heart. She reached out and touched Molly's slender fingers. 'Aw, look here, darling,' she said softly, 'I would never have reported yer to the authorities like I threatened, should yer not turn up here . . . *Never!* That were just a ploy ter frighten yer . . . all I really wanted to do were to *help* yer, honest ter God.'

Impressed by Nelly's obvious sincerity, Molly looked at her searchingly, before asking, '*Why?* Why would you want to "help" me? . . . You don't know me.' She couldn't deny the suspicions that still persisted.

Nelly made a small noise, which sounded like a muffled laugh, or a groan of frustration. She took her hand away from Molly's fingers, and getting to her feet, she said, 'It's a long story, gal. It goes back ter when me and Emma were younger even than you are now . . . to a bad time, and a bad place.' Here she smiled and slowly shook her head. 'There are things in life that are best forgotten. But because life is by nature unpredictable, certain things that happen in the past have a direct and cruel influence on both the present and the future. Try as yer might, it's hard ter ever put the past completely behind yer.'

'I understand that,' Molly said now, being aware of certain parts of Nelly and Emma Tanner's past, such as them being sent as convicts to Australia. Molly couldn't help thinking that if the authorities still transported unfortunate wretches today, she would no doubt have been clapped in irons along with the rest of them. As it was, she could expect a sorry end if ever Justice Crowther had his way! Oh yes, she could understand how frightening and shocking were the circumstances in which Nelly and her Emma had been taken all those years ago. But what she could not understand was this: 'What has all that to do with me?'

'Well, it ain't got nothing ter do with you,' Nelly replied, 'but what I'm trying ter say is that when a body's been as low and sorry as it can be, then it gets ter thinking. Me and Emma came through all our trials and bad years.' She stopped, remembering how broken-hearted Emma was at the loss of her son, and how that same loss had shaken them all to their very roots; besides shaking Emma's faith in the good Lord who had given her the strength and determination to soar above her earlier hardships. 'Emma's done well for herself . . . all done by hard work and pure grit! And all through it, she's never lost sight of her own unhappy start, nor has she forgotten how cruel and unjust life can be for the poor wretches at the bottom of the layer, much like yourself if yer don't mind me saying. She's a good woman.' Nelly's love for Emma was obvious in her voice, and in the proud look on her face. 'We saw you once before, my gal . . . did yer know that . . . *winked* at Emma, yer did.'

Molly was intrigued. She could not remember doing anything so inexcusable. 'Winking' at the niece of her most dangerous enemy? *Never!* 'I'm sure I did no such thing!' she retorted. But then Nelly chortled and went on to describe how on the very day she and Emma had arrived back in England, they had seen with their own eyes how Molly had been 'collared' by a constable, for picking pockets at Liverpool Docks. *Molly remembered it all.* She had had the fear of God put in her on that particular day, some years back now. Nelly's tale unfolded; she explained how Molly went running past her and Emma, with the child tucked to her hip. 'And when yer came alongside us, why! . . . Yer cocked the cheekiest wink ter Emma, just like it were all a bloody game!'

Suddenly it was all coming back to Molly. She recalled how this smart and beautiful woman stared at her with astonished and admiring eyes and yes, she did recall winking! A ripple of fear went through her as she asked incredulously, '*That* was Emma Tanner?'

'It was! You made a big impression on her that day . . . she never stopped talking about the incident all the way to Blackburn.' Nelly explained, 'She kept saying as how she would have liked to help you . . . you and the young 'un. But nobody knew where you'd come from, or how yer might be found . . . or at least, they weren't telling if they did know. Honour among thieves, I suppose. Anyway, what with her boy and her new husband, Emma's thoughts were busily occupied elsewhere fer a while. But then, one day not too long back, I clapped eyes on yer agin. There were two bairns with yer on that particular day . . . well, I told Emma what a bag of bones you looked and, after that, she wouldn't take no for an answer. My orders was ter find yer. Emma was gonna help yer . . . whether yer liked it or not. So *that's* why I got yer released into my custody, y'see. It were an opportunity for me ter do what Emma would have done if she were here . . . see that yer had a shilling or two in yer pocket . . . and proper work ter keep yer out of mischief.'

'Does Emma Tanner know I'm here?' Molly believed Nelly. But for old reasons, she dared not trust Emma

Tanner; it was possible that, unbeknown to Nelly, Justice Crowther was *using* Emma to capture the urchin who, he was wrongly convinced, had snatched his grandson.

'No. I have written to Emma of course, but I've said nothing about our arrangement. Emma hasn't been well since her son's tragic death.' She smiled sadly and for a moment was lost in thoughts of a reunion that couldn't come too soon for her. 'It'll be a lovely surprise fer her when she gets back. But for the minute, she's got too much on her mind to worry about what's going on here.'

'You said she won't be back till March . . . I'll be *long* gone by then,' protested Molly.

Seeming somewhat surprised at Molly's outburst, Nelly eyed her curiously. 'So yer won't stay on, eh?' She seemed genuinely upset. 'Aw, that's a real shame, gal . . . I thought we were getting on right well and all. And what about little Sal? . . . She's coming on champion with her learning . . . yer ain't being fair ter the poor little soul, are yer, eh?' Her look was imploring. 'Yer *will* change yer mind, won't yer? . . . Aw, Molly gal . . . *say* ye'll change yer mind.'

To Molly's reckoning, what Nelly was doing now was nothing short of blackmail. Fancy trying to persuade her to stay by using little Sal. 'No, I won't be staying on.' Her basic, intuitive fears urged her to get to her feet and argue. 'Soon as ever I've served my time . . . I'll be going.' She was adamant.

'What d'yer mean . . . "served yer time" . . . yer make it sound like a prison sentence!' Nelly had taken umbrage at the younger woman's rigid attitude. When back came the reply that Molly saw her time here as being exactly that . . . a 'prison sentence', Nelly was made to realize how, if *she* were in Molly's shoes, she too might feel the same way. 'All right, gal,' she said in a softer, more understanding voice, 'I don't want it said that I'd ever hold a body against its will. So, yer can go whenever yer like. *Today*, if you've a mind.' She gazed for a moment longer at Molly's surprised expression, then swinging round, with her full, stiff, taffeta skirt making an angry swishing sound, she went to the door, pausing there to tell Molly in injured and clipped tones, 'I could have sworn you were content in yer work . . . and what with the young 'un making such great strides in her learning, I was sure you'd be with us fer a long time.' She was puzzled by Molly's attitude, and suddenly a thought crossed her mind. 'It ain't the wages I pay yer, is it? . . . Yer don't think the wages is mean, and yer can't manage on them, is *that* it?'

'No, no, it isn't that,' Molly told her. 'The wages are very generous and I manage well enough. No, it's nothing to do with wages. And as for the learning you've given little Sal, well, I really *am* grateful.' Molly hesitated. For one stupid, careless minute there, she had felt so guilty and hated herself for the way Nelly seemed so upset, that she had almost confided her fears. Thank God she had bitten her tongue in time, because how could she tell this woman who had been so kind to her that she suspected Emma of deceiving them both. How could she say that Emma's uncle, the hated Justice Crowther, was baying for her blood, and that he might have recruited Emma to find her?

With her justifiably narrow and prejudiced view of the gentry, Molly found it hard to believe that any one of them – even someone like Emma Tanner who had been reduced in fortune for a while – would actively seek out a pickpocket, in order to 'help' her. Oh, Molly had heard the rumours of a terrible rift between Emma Tanner and the Justice. But two things warned her not to be too easily fooled; firstly, the Justice was Emma Tanner's kith and kin, and it was a known fact that every family had its rows, and quickly made up again. Secondly, when it all came down to it, blood kin tended to stick together against outsiders; especially when that outsider was thought to have snatched one of their children, in order to demand money.

Molly had survived by following her instincts. She had to follow them now. So, with regret she told Nelly that yes, under the circumstances, it would be best if she and little Sal left straightaway. It suddenly occurred to her, however, that Emma Tanner and Justice Crowther might not give up so easily. She must be very careful to put them off the scent; there might be just one way. Quickly, she added in a convincing voice – even putting a little smile on her face – 'Anyway, I would have been leaving soon,' she lied, 'because my husband doesn't want me working no more.'

'Oh!' Nelly could not hide her astonishment. 'I was under the impression that yer fella had left home a long while since? . . . . Are yer saying he's back?'

Molly rebuked herself for having revealed that she was a woman on her own, although she had never told Nelly the circumstances of Jack's leaving. In fact, she had closely guarded all information concerning her life outside of these four walls, and had instructed little Sal that under no circumstances was she to talk to Nelly about where they lived, or tell her *anything* at all about the family. The girl appeared to have done as she was told, except on one occasion when she had mentioned how her sister Peggy had hid in Tilly Watson's cellar and 'frightened everybody to death, because they all thought she'd got lost'.

'He's been back some time,' Molly went on, desperate that Nelly should believe she was telling the truth, and sad that it was sometimes necessary to deceive people with a lie. 'He's brought good news too! My man's been offered a job down south . . . with a little house besides. So we'll be moving away in no time at all.' She painted a happy smile on her face, but her dark eyes remained troubled.

A great silence fell over the room and for what seemed an age Nelly showed little response to Molly's words, other than to look out of the window to where little Sal's fair head was bent over her picture book. As though sensing that someone was looking at her, she raised her head and, seeing that it was Nelly, she waved her hand again, before returning to the book which Nelly had given to her. 'I'll be so sorry to see the young 'un go,' Nelly murmured, looking at Molly with regret, 'and you too, Molly.' Suddenly, there was a smile on her face, and coming back into the room, she astonished Molly by grabbing hold of her in a rough embrace. 'But I'm glad at yer news, child,' she said in a curiously gruff voice. Suddenly, as though embarrassed, she thrust Molly from her, saying a little too loudly, 'O' course yer must go with yer fella . . . and find happiness where yer can. There ain't enough of it in this world, and *that's* a fact.'

Within the hour, Molly and little Sal were turning out of the long path from the big house; the girl unusually subdued by the unexpected and unhappy event, and her mammy wondering whether she had made the right decision; after all, Emma Tanner was not due back for some many weeks. On top of which, Molly dreaded losing the regular wage she had brought into the wretched little house on Dock Street. All the way down Park Street Molly agonized over her decision. Nelly had been such a help to her. She seemed such an honest and straightforward person, and wasn't it unlikely that such a person would love another woman like her sister if that woman were deceitful? Could it be possible that Emma Tanner was *not* doing Justice Crowther's dirty work after all, and therefore Molly's suspicions were totally unfounded?

For a moment, Molly's resolve began to falter. There was little Sal to be considered and the child's bewilderment was written clearly on her face. Had she done the right thing? Molly asked herself now. Had she acted too hastily? Couldn't she safely have stayed on, at least until just before the Tanners returned? Nelly's unhappy face came into her mind and now Molly stopped, her thoughts churning round in her mind. Surely a few more weeks wouldn't matter, she argued with herself, and she did need the money, there was no denying that.

Molly's mind was made up. Gripping the child's hand tightly in her own, she began walking back towards the big house, slowly at first, then more hurriedly. 'Where are we going, Mammy?' Sal asked, her little legs running to keep up with Molly's long strides. 'Are we going back to Nelly's house, are we, eh?' She was obviously delighted by the prospect.

'You'll have to wait and see, won't you?' Molly teased, a warm smile lighting up her lovely features as she looked down at the girl's eager face.

When Molly raised her eyes towards the grand iron

gates of the Tanner residence, the smile slid from her face, and in its place there came a look of fear and horror. There, climbing from a carriage which had stopped at the roadside right outside the big house was the unmistakable figure of Justice Caleb Crowther. Molly's heart missed a beat and she stopped in her tracks. All manner of emotions tore through her: shock, disbelief, fear and repugnance. So! She *had* been right about Emma Tanner all along! And what of Nelly? For it seemed as though she also had been deceitful, and was no better than the rest.

As he strode towards the gates, Caleb Crowther seemed to cast a glance in Molly's direction. Terrified, she pulled little Sal behind an overhanging laurel bush, warning her to 'stay very still and don't make a sound!' Sensing the fear in her mammy's voice, the girl did as she was told.

Not daring to show themselves, for fear that Justice Crowther might suddenly spring on them, the two stayed hidden, pressed deep into the shrubbery and hardly daring to breathe. From high up on his seat, the carriage driver could be easily seen. Molly's fear of discovery was heightened when suddenly he stretched his neck as though searching the very spot where they were secreted. Terribly afraid, Molly clutched the girl to her and pulled her down into an uncomfortable crouching position. Through an open patch in the laurel bush, she saw the driver relax in his seat, draw out his pipe, which he proceeded to fill with strings of tobacco from his pouch, and afterwards lean lazily into the seat, head back, eyes heavenwards as he took great sensuous pleasure in the puffing of his pipe.

The carriage driver's pleasure was short-lived, however, when suddenly there came the sound of slamming doors and angry voices, followed by the unsightly appearance of Justice Crowther as he rushed out of the gates and instructed the flustered driver, 'Breckleton House . . . and be quick about it!' As he climbed into the carriage he was clearly heard to say, 'So, she's gone, has she?' Then he laughed out loud. 'Well, she can take refuge where she likes, but she'll never get the better of Caleb Crowther! *Never!*' Yelling out another instruction to 'make haste, you fool . . . there's no time to lose', he flung himself into the seat and slammed shut the door.

In a moment the carriage was thundering past the very spot where Molly and the girl remained, not daring to move a limb. When little Sal glanced up at Caleb Crowther's stern, granite-like features, she instinctively cowered, clinging to her mammy's skirts and holding her breath until the carriage was out of sight.

After what Molly considered to be a safe passage of time, she and the girl emerged from their hiding place and went at hasty speed down Park Street and on into Blackburn town. Molly's dark thoughts were relentless in their condemnation of Nelly, who had very nearly tricked her into believing that she was a genuine friend. How cleverly Emma Tanner's companion had wormed her way into Molly's confidence. How despicable that the woman had used little Sal in such a way; plying her with books and 'learning' when all the time it was probably a way of trying to gain the child's confidence, loosening her tongue, hoping to pry valuable information out of her, with regard to where they lived and other useful snippets that would lead the Justice right to their front door. Oh, dear God above! What now? Molly's mind was in turmoil. *What now? What now?* The question had no sooner come into her mind than it was on her lips. 'Sal . . . did you ever speak of Dock Street to Nelly?' She drew the girl to a halt. 'Did she ask you questions? Did you tell her anything?'

Little Sal shook her head, her vivid blue eyes looking up at Molly, a deep frown etched into her forehead. 'I never told her about Tom,' she said, 'and I never said anything about Dock Street.' A look of guilt wrote itself across her face and she lowered her gaze.

'But you did say *something*, didn't you, Sal?' Molly had sensed her daughter's fear and was careful to speak more softly. 'What did you tell her? I need to know. Did she ask you questions, Sal? . . . What did you tell her?' Her voice was marbled with such anxiety that the girl lifted her gaze.

'I only said about that time when Peggy hid in the cellar and we all thought she was lost.'

'*What else?*'

'I told her it was *Tilly Watson's* cellar.' The girl hesitated, before adding quietly, 'and I said we sometimes go down Eanam Wharf and play on Mick's barge.' She smiled brightly, as though a weight had been taken off her small shoulders. 'I never said no more, honest, Mammy. I haven't got us in trouble, have I?'

'It's all right. It's not your fault, darling,' Molly assured her, although there was a crippling knot of fear in her stomach at hearing Sal's 'confession'. Oh, that Nelly had been cunning! She had not managed to worm the name of their street out of little Sal, but she might as well have done, because she knew the name Tilly Watson, and she had learned about Mick, living in a barge by Eanam Wharf. Molly suspected there was more than enough information there for her to be tracked down. By now, Mick was long gone, probably to southern parts where work was plentiful. He would not be so easily found, she supposed. Thinking of Mick brought a strange fleeting sadness to Molly.

But there was no time for dwelling on regrets. Molly realized that she was in great danger. Her *family* was in great danger. Her one thought now was to get them all to safety. But *where?* Where could they go, with only the week's wages given to her by the devious Nelly – Judas money! Molly called herself all kinds of a fool for having been so gullible! Still, she did have fourteen shillings all told, and it was better than nothing. Ah, but there was something else, she reminded herself. There was the gold petal-clasp that old Sal had entrusted to her. As she and the girl hurried towards Dock Street, Molly dipped her fingers into the neck of her blouse, feeling for the gold droplet. She would be loath to part with it, because it had been on her person ever since the day old Sal was buried. Besides which, she had promised the old darling that it would stay with her always. Up till now, Molly had managed to keep that promise. But here was a very bad and frightening thing that was happening now. She hoped old Sal would agree that pawning the clasp was preferable to being pounced on by the Justice, when she and the children would be horribly punished, she was certain. With the money got on the clasp, Molly might go further afield in order to escape his clutches. Suddenly, Molly drew the girl to a halt.

'What's the matter, Mammy?' Sal saw how Molly's face had drained of colour and she was frantically searching in the neck of her blouse. It was gone. *The clasp was gone!* For the first time in a long while Molly wanted to cry. She felt desolate. Unbeknown to Molly, the clasp had been plucked from the carpet by Nelly, who, not realizing it was Molly's, had assumed that it belonged to Emma, and had put it safely away. 'Mammy . . . what's the matter?' little Sal insisted, her bottom lip quivering. For a moment, Molly continued to forage for the clasp, but stopped at once when she saw little Sal's fearful face.

Realizing what a frightening experience the child had just endured, Molly got to one knee, and taking little Sal into her arms, she said, 'It's all right, sweetheart . . . it's all right. Nothing for you to worry about.' In a brighter voice, she added, 'Let's hurry home, eh? We've all kinds of exciting plans to make . . . and as you're the eldest, I'll be looking for some good advice from you. I know you won't let me down, will you?'

'I have to be growed up, don't I, Mammy . . . 'cause I'm older than Tom and Peggy, aren't I, eh?'

Getting to her feet, Molly nodded, and actually laughed aloud. What a little madam you are, my Sal, she thought proudly. But then, as they rounded the corner of Dock Street, Molly's 'pride' turned to shame. What would her daughter say when she discovered that her mammy meant to take her away from the only home she had ever known – miserable though it was – and that they had no other place to go? Molly had been heart-stricken at the loss of her precious clasp; now she was more frantic at the daunting future that lay ahead. Here she was, with only a few shillings to her name, three children – one of them a cripple – and being hounded by a Justice and his spies, who all wanted her blood. Hounded on to the streets; forced to find a safer place.

Molly's thoughts came back to Nelly, and for a moment she was saddened. But then her sadness quickly turned to anger. That woman had almost duped her.

Almost! But Molly thought she had her measure now all right! No wonder she was able to persuade the authorities to release a pickpocket into her custody. Why! She probably told them that she was acting on Justice Crowther's instructions. Right from the start it must have been a devious plan. Nelly had been playing with her all along; probably getting little Sal's confidence too, so that she could lay claim to her for the Tanners. Molly could not fathom out why the Justice was not summoned to move in on her before today. Perhaps he, like his niece, had been out of the country, or possibly he had been trying to discover where she lived, so they could take the whole family into custody. But here Molly had taken precautions because, being made by nature and circumstance a suspicious person, she had cleverly varied her path home, dodging this way and that, in case she was being followed.

When the front door of her small, dilapidated house was in sight, Molly breathed a sigh of relief and gave thanks to whoever had watched over them that day. She and her family were still free, in spite of the woman called Nelly. With a sense of disgust, Molly imagined the scene that had taken place in the Tanner household when the Justice had come to collect his quarry, only to find it had flown. The thought of his fury gave her a small rush of satisfaction.

As Molly went into Tilly Watson's home to collect the children, her feeling of satisfaction at having outwitted both Nelly and the Justice might have turned to regret if only she had been aware of what had *actually* taken place between Nelly and Caleb Crowther that morning.

Caleb Crowther was beside himself! Having heard nothing all these weeks, except notification that the court case was postponed he saw the delay as being another trick by Emma Tanner to unnerve him. When he could stand it no longer, and against the advice of his solicitor, he had gone to the house on Park Street with the intention of thrashing the whole thing out once and for all. How infuriated he had been to be told not only that Emma Tanner had gone blithely off for an indefinite period. On top of which the common and repulsive creature she had left behind had actually ordered him from the premises. *Him!* A distinguished Justice of the Peace, albeit retired. He would not have budged one inch were it not for the awful uproar she was making, and the threat he knew she would not hesitate to carry out – 'to shout and yell blue murder and fetch the bleeding authorities down on your head!'

All day long the thought of how Emma Tanner meant to ruin him ate into his thinking and filled him with fear, an emotion with which he had never been too familiar. Yet here he was, a man much older and worn with the passage of time, whose comfortable lifestyle was threatened because of what had taken place so many years before; a man who was always used to being the victor, yet in this instance could well be defeated and, consequently, reduced to poverty.

Everything he owned, every penny he had, could be forfeited if the courts found in favour of Emma Tanner. It was a possibility that he must face. Caleb Crowther had never fooled himself on that score. But he would fight that damned woman with every means at his disposal, legal or otherwise. Even though, in his deepest, darkest heart he was made to acknowledge his own guilt. He *had* betrayed a dying man's wish and married Emma off to a totally unsuitable young man, in order to cheat her out of the marriage settlement her father had bequeathed her. He *had* plotted to have her convicted of murder and afterwards transported to the far-off shores of Australia. When she was safely despatched there, he had lost no time in looting her entire inheritance, selling the assets and converting them into hard cash which was duly deposited in his own name. All of these things he had done, it was true. But no one would ever know the *full* extent of his corruption concerning Emma. Because it went much, much deeper. So awful, so terrible and damning were the deeds he had committed that, even now after long haunting years, he would relive those heinous crimes in his uneasy slumbers, waking in a cold sweat of fear and shame, and horrified for the sanctity of his very soul.

Suddenly that same horror and shame was on him now. Leaning forward in his chair, he dropped his grey, balding head to the desk-top, his small pink-rimmed eyes staring upwards at the ceiling and, for a moment, he seemed almost demented, his eyes beginning to roll and the chilling sound of soft laughter emanating from his loose, open mouth. In that moment, he saw how foul and murderous was his character. In that moment, he was made to relive every terrible act over again. Now, when he screamed aloud and tore his fingernails into the flesh on his face, there was madness in him.

When there came an urgent knock on the door, he snatched himself to an upright position in the chair, desperate to compose himself, for he was trembling uncontrollably, and still in the grip of his terrible thoughts.

'Grandfather . . . are you in there?' Edward Trent's anxious voice penetrated Caleb Crowther's troubled mind, and at once the change in him was astonishing.

Springing from his seat with a surge of energy, he hurried to the door, quickly unlocking it and, with a smile on his ungainly features and a brighter light in his eyes, he flung open the door to greet his beloved grandson. These two did not always see eye to eye, but underlying their many differences was a degree of love which was forged many years ago and which had somehow survived the numerous upheavals between them.

'Edward! . . . Oh, my boy, it's good to see you.' Caleb Crowther slapped one large hand on the young man's shoulder, and with the other he took Edward's hand into his own, gripping it hard and shaking it enthusiastically as, at the same time, he propelled his grandson into the study, kicking shut the door behind them. 'What's brought you here today? . . . Why aren't you at the infirmary? . . . Are you with your mother? . . . Is Martha here?' His questions tumbled out one after the other, until, realizing he had hardly given the young man time to draw breath, he laughed aloud. 'Forgive me,' he said, 'but I really am so very pleased to see you.' He gestured to the deep leather armchair on the near side of the desk opposite his own seat. 'Sit down . . . do sit down, Edward,' he urged. Then, when the young man had done so, he went quickly to the walnut cabinet by the fireplace, and here he part-filled two tumblers with whisky. 'Drink up, my boy,' he told the young man, who reluctantly took the glass. 'We'll drink a toast to *me* . . . your grandfather . . . who will soon show the Emma Tanners of this world that they take on too much when they take on Caleb Crowther!' He swung the glass up high in a gesture of salute, before putting it to his mouth and emptying the fiery liquid down his throat. A look of consternation crossed his features when he saw that, instead of following his grandfather's example, Edward had put his own glass to the desk. '*What?* . . . You won't drink to your grandfather's victory over a wretched creature who would see him paupered?' He stared penetratingly at his grandson, before drawing a hard, long breath that swelled his chest to enormous proportions. Noisily releasing the air through flared nostrils, he slammed his glass on to the desk. 'What ails you?' he demanded, suddenly realizing from the serious look on Edward's face that his grandson was here for a particular reason; one that was not too pleasant if his quiet and disapproving manner was anything to judge by. 'And what brings you to Breckleton House . . . if it isn't to console your old grandfather?'

He spoke with an injured tone as he sat heavily into his chair and continued to stare at the young man, grudgingly thinking how he would forgive him almost everything. Edward was his only grandson and, thankfully, had inherited none of his mother's petulant and selfish ways. Martha was a weak-willed, grasping and repulsive creature, who had alienated her father from a very early age.

From the day of Martha's birth – and for very secret reasons to do with Emma Tanner's lovely mother, Mary Crady, whom he had adored beyond reason – Caleb Crowther had taken a deep dislike to his daughter. Martha did not earn his love when she was a new-born in his wife's arms; she did not earn it when she was a child; and she had not earned his love when she became a woman. If anything, she had earned only his intense loathing. There were times when Caleb Crowther was forced to examine the unpleasant and shamefully weak traits in his daughter's character and to question himself about their origin. Certainly they were not inherited from her mother, for Agnes Crowther could never be described as weak, or petulant. Grasping perhaps. And devious on occasion. But by and large she was a strong-willed and determined woman, who was not afraid to show her claws, a characteristic that had greatly irritated him of late.

With deepening concern, Caleb Crowther regarded the young man who was his grandson; he let his anxious eyes rove over the familiar straight and strong features, the dark, well-groomed hair and those intense green eyes that gave Caleb Crowther the odd impression that his grandson was able to see right through him. 'There's something on your mind, isn't there?' he said now, keeping his gaze on the young man's face. 'Out with it, then . . . let's hear what you have to say!' He sensed an imminent battle. All the familiar signs were there. They had battled before on many issues, and no doubt they would battle again on many more. But there was one particular issue on which they could never agree, yet which would not go away. Caleb Crowther's instincts told him that the very same issue was about to raise its ugly head now.

'I had a letter from my father this morning,' Edward began.

'Oh, yes! . . . And no doubt he had some very damning things to say about me, *did* he?' Caleb Crowther had not expected his grandson to bring Silas Trent into the conversation, nor did he like it. The man was an upstart! Arrogant and obstinate in the matter of his wife, Martha who – encouraged by Caleb Crowther – adamantly refused to leave England in order to join her husband in

Australia. Since buying out the trading business which Emma had built up over many years and in which he had been generously offered a partnership, Caleb Crowther's son-in-law had taken it from strength to strength until now he had secured shipping contracts right around the globe. His only remaining ambition was that Martha, whom he adored in spite of her childish, obstinate ways, should join him in Australia, where they could enjoy the fruits of his labours together. Now that their son Edward had fulfilled his own lifelong desire to qualify as a doctor and had moved out of the family home to be nearer his work, Martha *might* have been persuaded to go to her husband and remain by his side, if it weren't for the strong influence exerted over her by her own father.

Caleb Crowther cared not whether Martha should disappear from the face of the earth, so obnoxious was she to him, but he saw her as a means by which he might make Silas Trent pay for having joined forces with his old enemy, Emma Tanner . . . or Emma Thomas as she had then been. Silas Trent's unbelievable success, and Emma's part in it, was a thorn in Caleb Crowther's side. He could not forgive his son-in-law for going against his advice to 'stay clear of that woman . . . there is no love between us, and I want no kin of mine kowtowing to a creature of that sort.'

It was true that Silas had asked Caleb Crowther for a loan in order to save his own dwindling fleet of merchant ships, long before Emma had put her own propositions to him, and it was also true that Caleb Crowther had callously refused his son-in-law's desperate plea out of hand. Yet he saw Silas's acceptance of Emma's offer as being both traitorous and rebellious. He had never forgiven him. He never would!

'My father made no mention of you . . . only of my mother, who refuses to answer his letters.'

Caleb Crowther impatiently waved his arm in a gesture of dismissal. '*Enough!* . . . I am not interested in your father's domestic squabbles. If Martha has turned her back on him, then it's no more than he deserves!' Secretly he was delighted, and if his constant interfering was worsening matters between his daughter and her husband, then so much the better.

'Did you know that Emma was in Australia? . . . And that she and Marlow Tanner have met up with my father?' Edward Trent eyed his grandfather closely, gauging his reaction and hoping against hope that the animosity between this man and his own beloved father might diminish with the passage of time. However, Caleb Crowther's next words dashed his hopes to the ground.

'Always the traitor, eh?' The news had been an unpleasant shock. That blasted woman at the Tanner house had not told him that Emma had sailed to Australia, only that she was 'out of town'. Damn and bugger it! What was Emma Tanner up to? . . . What devious little game was she playing at? He had been furious when the courts agreed to Marlow Tanner's request of a postponement of the hearing on the grounds that Emma had suffered a tragic bereavement. *He* stood to suffer more than that! And *would* if she had her way. He wanted this business over and done with, and to that end he had gone to a great deal of trouble and expense in falsifying certain 'evidence', some of which would show how Emma had systematically robbed her own father while he lay dying. *That* was the most difficult of all the manufactured documents, but a guinea or two extra had been enough to procure them. Now, when he had all these little surprises in store for her, she had upped and departed, leaving him floundering and frustrated. Oh, she was a wily one! Now here she was, hobnobbing with his traitor of a son-in-law. What were they up to? What in God's name were they up to? Not knowing her next move was more than he could bear. 'What else did your father have to say with regard to that creature?' he demanded to know. 'How long does she intend to rob me of my moment in court . . . when I mean to turn the tables on her!' He chuckled, but was quickly silenced by the condemning look on Edward's face. '*What* . . . you don't see the funny side of it? Oh, you will . . . believe me, *everyone* will! She may have been the one to instigate proceedings, but *I'll* be the one to finish them.' His smile was darkly unpleasant. 'I intend to see Emma Tanner regretting the day she ever locked horns with such a fellow as me.'

There followed an uncomfortable silence, during which time the two men regarded each other with a degree of hostility. 'I want you to end this dispute with both my father . . . and Emma,' Edward declared in a quiet and serious voice. 'She is a good woman . . . and have you forgotten that she has recently lost her only child?'

'What is that to me?' Caleb Crowther rose to his feet and, curving his fists round the desk edge, he leaned forward in an ominous posture. 'And don't you dare tell me that she is a "good" woman,' he thundered. 'To my mind, she is no better than a common criminal . . . an opportunist . . . of no more consequence than the wretched women who roam the streets in the dark hours!'

Now Edward also was on his feet, glaring at the older

man with stony, condemning eyes. 'It does not become you . . . a distinguished Justice . . . to be so prejudiced, so vindictive . . . *and to one of your own blood kin!*'

Edward Trent could not have known what terrible effect his last words would have on Caleb Crowther, for he was not aware of certain dark secrets that had lain heavy in his grandfather's guilty heart these many years. When Caleb Crowther reeled at Edward's accusation, his face growing distorted as though in crippling pain and his clumsy bulk falling backwards into the chair as though pushed by some unseen hand, Edward's medical training convinced him that his grandfather was suffering a heart attack. Rushing forward, he would have grabbed at the older man's stiffened collar and frantically tried to loosen it, but his efforts were angrily shrugged off. 'LEAVE ME BE!' Lashing out at the young man, Caleb Crowther sprang from his chair and breathing unnaturally hard, he snarled, '*You!* I thought at least you would stand by me in this. But it's plain to see that you're no better a man than is your father. Get out . . . *GO ON! Get out!* I don't care if I never see you again.'

Edward knew the futility of trying to reason with Caleb Crowther when he was in one of these terrible moods. He had hoped to convince his grandfather to make good the relationship between himself and Emma, who was after all his own niece. But as he might have expected, his words had fallen on deaf ears. Some time ago, before the death of her son, Edward had tried desperately to persuade Emma to think again about the case she was relentlessly pursuing against her uncle, Caleb Crowther. But she had been no more receptive to his pleas than had his grandfather.

Dejected, Edward left Caleb Crowther angrily storming to and fro across the room. He consoled himself with the thought that at least he had tried. Tried, and failed. It was painfully obvious that this vicious feud between Emma and his grandfather, in which his own father was caught up, had gone on too long and was too ingrained in both their lives to be so easily resolved. He prayed it would not end too harshly, although somewhere deep inside him Edward Trent had the uneasy feeling that it would all end in tragedy.

Martha Trent and her mother Agnes had been deep in conversation in the drawing-room when the furore between the two men disturbed them enough to send them rushing into the hall. Seeing her son striding towards them from the study, Martha hurried forward, her round face pink and flustered, and her chubby hand to her heart. 'Whatever is the matter, Edward?' she asked, as he came to a halt before the two women. Suddenly she gripped his arm as though to lead him into the drawing-room, her small brown speckled eyes boring into him with disapproval. 'I hope you haven't been upsetting your grandfather!' She added angrily, 'I trust you had the good sense to keep the contents of your father's letter to yourself. There is no one in this house who wishes to know that Emma Tanner and your father appear to be as thick as thieves.' She tugged at his arm, but was incensed when he remained rigid and unmoving. 'You *did* tell him, didn't you?'

'Yes, mother . . . I did.' Edward did not regret his actions. 'It's high time that Grandfather was made to see sense.' He took Martha's hand gently from his person. 'I hope I am never forced to take sides between them, because I honestly could not say where my sympathies would lie!'

'*Really, Edward!*' Martha's face had grown so red it seemed she might explode. 'You can't know what you are saying!'

'What I am "saying", mother, is that my father . . . *your husband* . . .' he felt the need to remind her '. . . is one of the few people who enjoys Emma's confidence. What I am *also* saying is that she has suffered a very tragic life . . . we *all* know that. It would be useless to deny it.' He had seen his mother open her mouth to intervene and at once he flashed her a warning glance. 'You *least of all* cannot deny the truth of it! . . . Only very recently she lost her son in a tragic accident. Yet still grandfather heaps loathing and retribution on her head. *One* of them must be made to see sense.' Seeing his mother's expression harden, he looked beyond her to the tall, dignified woman who had made no remark throughout, but who had listened with great interest. 'Grandmother . . . surely you agree? A family must not fight within itself.'

At this point Agnes Crowther stepped forward, a regal figure with greying hair bound tight to her head with expensive mother-of-pearl combs and, as always, her long slim hands held together in a posture of prayer. She made no answer to Edward's question. Instead she turned towards the dumpy, plain figure beside her and in a patronizing voice, instructed, 'Leave Edward to me, dear . . . you go and pacify your father.'

'Of course,' Martha replied, nodding her head in a serious manner and going quickly towards the study, her voluminous skirts swishing angrily against her ankle boots as she quickened her step.

Agnes Crowther watched her daughter disappear into the study and waited until the door was closed before addressing her grandson. 'Your grandfather is unlikely to heed your advice, I'm afraid,' she told him with a half-smile, which belied her delight in the fact that her husband did not always persuade this young man to his own thinking. 'He does not listen to anything *I* say . . . and as you should know, he will insist on doing things his own way . . . however unpleasant the outcome.'

'So you're of the same opinion?' Edward asked, glad to have at least one ally in this spiteful business. 'You believe the outcome *will* be unpleasant?'

Agnes Crowther gave a small, cynical laugh. 'Oh, my dear Edward . . . there is no doubt in my mind at all!' she told him. 'But *whom* will it be more "unpleasant" for, I wonder? After all, between you and me, Emma Tanner has a very good case. On the other hand, your grandfather has a number of excellent contacts . . . both in the legal world . . . *and* in the criminal world.' Here she smiled at the disbelief on his face. 'Don't feel too sorry for him, Edward, because he is not a man to be crossed lightly. Rather, he is a man who will employ *any* means in order to rout his enemies.'

'Are you saying he would resort to *criminal* means to answer Emma's charges?'

Agnes Crowther realized that she had said enough. She would have liked to have said more. She would have liked to have shattered Edward's image of his grandfather once and for all. Such a thing would not prove too difficult. All she had to do was reveal the *truth* of how Caleb had set about destroying Emma's life. But then she would have to confess *her own* part in it: how she was the one who kept Emma locked in her room while her dying father called out for her to come to him. She would have to explain why it was that she had stood idly by while Caleb submitted Emma to a catalogue of injustices. Agnes Crowther had since grown ashamed of her own complicity in these events. But she had also grown older, and her courage was not so strong that it would allow her to go to Emma and ask forgiveness. Such a humble act had never been in her nature. It was not in her nature now. Far better to let things lie, for they could not be undone. 'Come and keep me company, Edward.' Agnes Crowther's instincts warned her to change the subject, as the two of them made their way into the drawing-room. 'Tell me about your father's letter . . . how is he? . . . Does his business still flourish? . . . You do know how I feel about Martha refusing to join him out there, don't you? Silas is a good family man and has always been an excellent husband to my daughter . . . to my mind, she should at least make the journey to Australia . . . if only to spend a short time with him. I have said as much to Martha, but well . . . you know how disagreeably stubborn she can be.'

Edward knew only too well. He knew also that his grandmother had cleverly diverted the conversation from the more important issue that had brought him here, that of his grandfather's continued loathing towards both Emma and his father. A crippling and unreasonable loathing that touched on the whole family and lingered in the air like the poison it was. Though he did love his grandfather, Edward could not deny that there were times when he positively disliked him. His unbending and vindictive attitude was something Edward saw as being both frightful and dangerous.

Now, as he followed his grandmother into the

drawing-room, Edward was made to recall a time when he was but a boy and had foolishly run away from home, after his father had gone to sea. He had been set upon by ruffians and later safely returned by a small, ragged girl. He still carried the memory of the girl's face in his mind: small and heart-shaped with big black eyes, and unkempt hair as dark as midnight. He remembered how she took money from his grandmother, money which would be used to save some old 'friend' from a pauper's grave. He often thought of her, but for some inexplicable reason he could not bring himself to discuss her with anyone. Except of course when he felt obliged to defend her to his grandfather, who would have hunted the girl down and had her severely punished. That was the first time Edward had witnessed Caleb Crowther's terrible, almost insane obsession with his own sense of power. It was not something to be admired. Edward thought of the scene which had taken place between them just now. He thought of Emma, and of his father, who could do nothing right in Caleb Crowther's eyes. He thought of his mother, whose own behaviour towards her husband was somewhat callous. Edward thought of all these unfortunate people whose lives were, either directly or indirectly, influenced by his grandfather to some degree or another. He secretly acknowledged that all around him there seemed to be an air of conspiracy, and his loyalties were painfully divided.

Martha's loyalties, however, were not divided. She adored her father and though the affection had never been mutual, she had spent the whole of her life trying to please him. Caleb Crowther had preyed on this weakness in his daughter. He preyed on it now. 'Silas Trent deliberately went against my express wishes when he accepted Emma's offer of a partnership in the Australian trading company,' he told her in injured tones.

'I know that father . . . and I did my utmost to prevent it.' Martha was mortified for fear that he might hold *her* responsible. 'That is the sole reason I refuse to acknowledge his letters . . . nor will I ever be persuaded to leave these shores at his request!' She was desperate to pacify this man who, in her eyes, could do no wrong.

'Ah!' Caleb Crowther swung round from the window, where he had been looking out on a crisp, dry morning and churning over all manner of possibilities in his mind. One in particular, stimulated by Martha's declaration, brought a devious smile to his face. 'So . . . you will not leave these shores to please your husband, eh?' he asked coyly, coming towards her and pausing before her chair, where he stooped in order to look directly into her brown-speckled eyes. 'But will you leave these shores in order to please your old father, eh?' He smiled a wicked and intimate smile that seemed to unnerve her momentarily.

'What do you mean?' She was obviously perplexed by his remark. She began stuttering, a characteristic that betrayed Martha's insecurity where her father was concerned. 'I . . . I don't un . . . der . . . stand.'

'Oh, it's very clear, my dear. Apparently, *your husband* and *my niece* have once again joined forces . . . or so it would seem. It therefore follows that they must be up to something, don't you think?' When she appeared lost for words, but eagerly nodded, he went on, 'I strongly suspect that those two would not hesitate to conspire against me. Do you agree?'

'Yes, yes . . . they both would like to see you ruined, I'm certain of it.'

'Then don't you also agree that *someone* should be out there to keep an eye on them? . . . Someone who might *naturally* be amongst them without arousing suspicions, and therefore in a position to report everything back to me?'

'How clever. *Yes . . . yes*. With the court case raising its head in the not-too-distant future, you need to be aware of what that vixen, Emma, is plotting against you.' *Still* she did not suspect her father's intention.

Caleb Crowther was pleased with himself. Stretching noisily, he smiled down at her and, keeping his eyes on her keen upturned face, he seated himself on the edge of the desk. What a fool you are, Martha my dear, he thought with repugnance. What a naive, addle-brained little fool! But useful to him at times. Like now, when he would plant a spy on his two unsuspecting enemies. A pair of eyes and ears, and an observer who would duly report back to him without question. 'Have a sherry, my dear,' he offered sweetly, 'and then we must talk. I have a proposition to put to you, for I am sure that the last thing you would want to see is me and your poor mother in the debtors' prison.'

It was late evening when Caleb Crowther emerged from Breckleton House and climbed into the waiting carriage. He had succumbed to a driving need in him to visit old haunts where there were women who would be only too eager to satisfy the basic urges that had come on him. 'All the way to London my good man!' he called in a jocular voice as he climbed into the carriage. He felt good. Anger was an invigorating emotion that suited him well. Besides which, the gullible Martha had been like dough in his hands. Within the week she should be setting sail for foreign parts. He chuckled aloud at the thought of having manufactured yet another little plot that just might prove to be most rewarding to him. What was even *more* amusing was that the effort required on his part had been nothing at all. Let other fools use up their finances and their strength, he mused; the cost to him was only a little scheming. *That* was always a very gratifying pleasure.

As the carriage swiftly conveyed him out of Lancashire and along the highways to London town, Caleb Crowther was bloated with his own cleverness. It might have sadly deflated him to know that even at that moment he was not heading for pleasure or gratification, but was hurtling headlong towards catastrophe.

'It's too late, sir . . . we closed the doors at two o'clock this morning.' The young man's spotted face pushed itself closer to the small grille in the door. What he had first seen on looking out was a man too intoxicated for his own good, so intoxicated in fact, that it would be inadvisable to allow him into even this club, which was notorious for its inebriated membership. What he saw on closer inspection was a drunk who was well dressed and 'possessed of an air of authority'. He thought it wise to address the toff with more caution – after all, a body could never tell *who* were knocking on these doors! It could be royalty, millionaires from America, or even the law in disguise. 'I'm afraid I'm not allowed to let you in, sir . . . it could cost our licence if we opened these here doors after two in the morning.'

'Damn and bugger your licence, man!' Caleb Crowther rapped his cane into the grille, causing the poor fellow to snatch away his face for fear of losing an eye. '*Open* these doors, I tell you!' There then followed a loud and abusive exchange, which in turn alerted the proprietor of the establishment, who came rushing to the door and at once pushed his well-fed face to the door, instructing the offender to 'clear off . . . or I'll call the law.'

'Oh, you will, will you?' demanded Caleb Crowther, whilst swaying in his boots. 'You'll call the law . . . *to see off the law!*' He began laughing uproariously and clattering his cane up and down the door panels, until the sounds echoed in the dark early hours like an approaching army.

'Good lord! . . . It's *Justice Crowther*.' The proprietor now recognized the great bulky figure who, in his time, had spent many a long night and many a handsome fortune in these very same premises. 'Open the door, you fool,' he ordered the flustered fellow who was cringing behind him. 'Get this bloody door open this instant! Have you any idea who our guest is? . . . Well, I'll tell you . . . it's none other than the eminent Justice Crowther!' The door was quietly swung open and the dead weight of Caleb Crowther fell into the proprietor's arms. 'I might tell you also that this distinguished figure of the law was a regular client beneath this roof some years ago.' He also recalled that this same uncouth and spiteful character had caused them a deal of trouble on occasions, even scarring one of the girls when she had displeased him. That same girl was still employed here, though she was an embittered woman of more mature years, who had never been the same since her looks were so cruelly spoiled. She was not much in demand afterwards, and had been glad to accept an additional position in the kitchens. It crossed the proprietor's mind to keep these two well and truly apart. Yes indeed, the

Justice was a man who brought trouble with him. But he also brought enough guineas in his waistcoat pocket to compensate for such a curse. And as the proprietor's only concern was that these guineas should be suitably and properly transferred from the pocket of the Justice to his own, then a body must allow for a small upset now and then.

'I fancy one of your harlots! . . . No rubbish, mind!' Caleb Crowther steadied himself between the two men, addressing the fat, balding proprietor who was short enough to be looked down on. 'I prefer a whore with a bit of quality . . . I'm not after catching the pox, neither!' he warned.

'Now, now, Justice . . . sir . . . we don't keep that sort here, you should know that . . . you being familiar with this establishment.' The proprietor's hardened senses were surprisingly offended, both by Caleb Crowther's manner, and by the stench of stale booze that emanated from him. It was obvious that the Justice had been on a prolonged drinking spree, and had only happened here as a last resort, probably drawn by the smell of cheap perfume and the promise of willing, wide-open legs.

'A *redheaded* whore,' chuckled Caleb Crowther with an unseemly and lecherous expression, 'the redheaded ones give a bit more than their money's worth.' Somewhere in the back of his memory he recalled another redhead on another night, in this very same club. But it was long ago and the memory was no more than an irritating blur; besides which he was presently under the influence of too much whisky. 'Never mind what colour hair she has,' he ordered now, his temper darkening at his own inability to remember, 'just get on with it, man . . . like I said, make sure it's quality . . . don't want *any* old tramp!' He began giggling as the proprietor gave instructions to the clerk, 'Take the Justice up to the best room. If there's anybody in there . . . shift 'em down the corridor. Any trouble, and you fetch *me*, straight away. We want nothing but the best for the Justice.'

'Nothing but the best for the Justice,' repeated Caleb Crowther as he ambled drunkenly towards the staircase, 'nothing but the best.' He swore aloud when the clerk tripped beneath the heavy, lumbering weight that leaned against him. 'Get off, you damned fool!' he roared, staggering against a nearby table and drawing angry looks from the clients seated there. Infuriated by the manner in which the lady and gent were eyeing him up and down, he skimmed his arm across the table-top and sent every object crashing to the floor. At once there was uproar. The lady began screaming and the gent was all for launching himself at the drunken intruder; he *would* have done, were it not for the intervention of the frustrated proprietor, who calmly transferred the agitated couple to another table, where they were to be given 'anything they wanted on the house'.

As Caleb Crowther was discreetly ushered upstairs, the proprietor was made to ask himself whether the 'distinguished' client was worth all the trouble he had brought with him, yet again! Still, he consoled himself with the belief that, before the Justice finally left these premises, he would likely have paid handsomely by way of compensation. If his memory served him right, Justice Caleb Crowther was not only a big man, but a big sinner, and a big spender. After all, when it came right down to it, nothing else mattered but the size of a client's wallet. And they didn't come much bigger than this client's! Let him have his display of bad temper. The proprietor had seen many such displays but, as a rule, they were short-lived and made no lasting damage, at least not so far as the proprietor himself was concerned.

In the few hectic moments when Caleb Crowther had made his presence known, he had provoked both anger and amusement amongst the gathered clientele, who saw this great arrogant drunkard as something to be either spat at, or laughed at, but in any event soon forgotten.

There were two observers in particular, however, who had been deeply shaken by the sight of Caleb Crowther: one being filled with alarm, and the other shot through with a terrible loathing of him. From a safe distance, the two watched as Caleb Crowther was led away, swearing one minute and laughing the next.

The woman was tall and slim, wearing a crimson gown and black feather boa. In her late thirties she was still an attractive figure, her striking countenance marred only by the angry, jagged scar that ran down one side of her face. The scar was a legacy from over twenty years ago, inflicted on her in this very establishment, by the then much younger, but equally obnoxious, Caleb Crowther. Then, as now, the redhead had been employed in the capacity as 'hostess' to the many pursuers of pleasure who frequented this seedy London club. She had been young and tender when Caleb Crowther had disfigured her in one of his uncontrollable rages. At the time she had been highly desirable and extremely popular with the clients. Ever since that night her popularity had plummeted. Now she was called on only as a last resort, to serve those who were either half-blind, short of money or too drunk to know or care what they were paying for.

The proprietor had kept the redhead on, but not altogether out of the goodness of his heart. It was his business to cater for every kind of client, providing that client had enough money. There were a number of these more undesirables whom his other girls refused to 'serve'. The redhead, however, had no such choice; *Caleb Crowther had seen to that.* No other club would employ her, and she knew no other way of earning a living. Girls such as her often ended up on the streets and from there there was no place else to go but down.

The redhead survived, being used by the worst dregs in society, and filling her time in between by working in the club's kitchen. Life was hard, and degrading. Over the years she had grown more bitter, eaten up by her hatred of the man who had so drastically altered her life. She had always promised herself that one day her chance to settle the score would show itself. When that happened, she vowed to be ready. *She was ready now.* At the sight of Caleb Crowther, drunk, floundering and ravaged by the years, her mind was in a fever, planning the revenge for which she had waited so very long! For the moment, the redhead was not quite certain what form that revenge would take. But of one thing she was sure: that man, that monster who had scarred her, would not see the dawn without her having repaid him in full.

'Do you know him?' The young man kept his arm round the redhead. He would have preferred a much younger and prettier whore, but on this night she was all he could afford and besides, when they were abed with the lights out, it wasn't her face that interested him.

'I *did* know him . . . a long time ago,' she replied thoughtfully, forcing a smile and taking him slowly across the room. 'Let's not talk about him, eh? . . .

You're here for a good time, aren't you?' She tousled his hair and winked at his merry brown eyes which were suddenly troubled.

The redhead could not have known how the unexpected appearance of Caleb Crowther had also brought back fearful memories to her young colleague. Memories of being captured by the law one dark night when he was not yet a man. Memories that made him tremble when he recalled the Justice in charge that night; the same Justice whom he had just clapped eyes on and who, though more aged and sodden with booze, was every bit as formidable as he had been those many years before.

'Come on, let's see you get your "good time", darling,' the redhead urged. She wanted this one over quickly; after which she would be free to retire to her own bed. She needed to be alone; there were things to be sorted, things to be done. She grew excited at the prospect of revenge.

The young man followed. But the urge to gratify his ardour had diminished the moment Caleb Crowther had appeared, bringing back those unpleasant and unwelcome memories. Because with the memories had come the image of a small, ragged figure: a girl with eyes as black as coal, and a heart of gold. A girl he had saved from Justice Caleb Crowther's clutches, and whom he had grown to love, in a way he could love no other.

Suddenly Jack was swamped with guilt. A guilt that tore at him like so many claws. What kind of man was he, he asked himself, to treat Molly in the shabby way he had done, ever since the day he had taken her virginity? In all that time he had not been a proper provider; nor had he shown himself to be a good father. He recalled the last occasion when he had deserted Molly, and his shame was like a weight inside him. How could he have done such a thing, when only hours before she had given birth to his son? But then he reminded himself that the boy was a cripple. *A cripple!* He could not come to terms with anything so grotesque. He was too shocked by it. Too repulsed. Suddenly, his guilt and shame were smothered by the spiral of horror that rose up in him. He wanted *nothing* to do with that incomplete being. He could never belong to it; never truly acknowledge it. So, he had done right to leave, and it was likely that he would never go back. But what of Molly? Molly, whose strong black eyes had the power to melt him, what of her? How in God's name would she cope? His sorry heart was squeezed inside him at the thought of how Molly seemed born to suffer. Softly, the guilt began creeping back. *No!* He mustn't let it. It was no good, because he would never change, however much he adored her. He was a loner; a man born to wander.

As the redhead urged him onwards, turning to the small, cheaper rooms on the ground floor, Jack wrapped his arm round her, laughingly squeezing her narrow waist. 'Mind you cheer me up, sweetheart,' he told her, ''cause I'm feelin' a bit miserable, d'you see?' He quickened his step, propelling her along with him. He had not forgotten that the Justice was upstairs and, drunk or sober, he was a powerful enemy. Jack believed it was in his own interest to leave that place as soon as he could. Oh, but not before he'd tasted the delights of this here redhead. Not before then!

In the darkest hours before the dawn, the redhead saw Jack from the premises. 'Take care o' yourself, darling,' hc told her merrily. 'Keep yourself warm for the next time I'm feeling lonely.'

'Any time,' she replied with a suggestive wink, 'any time at all.' When the door was closed and bolted, she leaned against it for a moment, all manner of schemes running through her mind. The night was almost gone, and soon the various clients would begin to creep away under cover of darkness, to scurry home before the daylight fell on them. The Justice would be among them.

Stealthily the redhead made her way towards the kitchen. Once there, she paused for a while, gathering her thoughts. Uppermost in her mind was her intention to make the Justice pay for what he had done to her.

As she stood there in the vast, eerily silent room, its darkness penetrated only by the soft glow from the oil lamp she carried, it came to the redhead that she must demand payment *in full* from the Justice. SHE MUST KILL HIM! It was the only way. Having mulled over the alternatives – including blinding or crippling him – she always returned to the obvious. But she had no intention of swinging for the deed. Not her. Because no man was worth that. Not even scum like the Justice. So she must be very careful.

Quickly, the redhead crossed the kitchen, going silently towards the big, dark-wood dresser, where the longest, sharpest knives were kept. Here she positioned the lamp on top of the dresser, so that its light shone directly into the drawer. Taking malicious pleasure in thc choosing of the instrument, she spent a moment or two picking up the knives one by one and turning each one over in her hand, before deciding on a long, slender, meat-boning tool. The feel of it seemed right to her, and she was satisfied that, when it entered his heart, the Justice would have no time to struggle.

A wicked smile lifted her scarred features as she began her way upstairs. It had occurred to her that, if he had spent himself well in his night of debauchery, the Justice should, by now, be in a deep slumber, as would the whore who had been unfortunate enough to bear his weight on top of her. She would not disturb either of them, so quick and silent would she be. Better still if the Justice had sent the whore away when he had finished with her, she thought.

The redhead knew well enough which room the pro-prietor would have allocated to such a 'distinguished' client as the Justice. The best room was situated at the end of the long corridor. Tiptoeing on bare feet she went quickly there, pausing outside the door, her courage fast deserting her. She had never been more afraid! But *what* was that? Someone crying out? A muffled, frightened sound, like someone was choking!

'Get a hold of yourself, girl,' the redhead murmured. 'Do what you've come here to do . . . then show a clean pair of heels before some nosey bugger claps eyes on you!' She would have turned the door handle there and then, but her feet seemed fixed to the spot. *She couldn't do it!* Not kill somebody in cold blood. Disheartened, she turned away. But then she raised her hand to run the tip of her finger along the scar that had drawn itself deep into her cheekbone. *He had done that!* Oh, but murder? Could she really *murder*? With her luck, she would be bloody sure to be hanged for it, she argued with herself. Yet she wanted him to suffer, like she had suffered. Slicing his face would have given her great satisfaction, but even that could never be enough to compensate. Suddenly some slight noise drew her attention. What

was that? There . . . there it was again. A muffled
sound, and a whole flurry of noises, as though in a
struggle, 'or passion-starved bodies going at each other
like there were no bleedin' tomorrow!' she whispered,
making a small snigger.

The noises were coming from that room! The room
where, the redhead was convinced, lay the Justice and
his whore. Intrigued, she bent her ear to the door and,
on hearing the sound she had first recognized as a
'muffled, choking sound', she suddenly stiffened with
alarm. It *was* coming from inside. But it weren't no
sound made by pleasure . . . more like the sound of a
body having the life choked out of it! No, no. She was
letting her imagination run away with her. It were all
that fever in her mind, and the obsession with getting her
own revenge on the beast in that room. A terrible
sensation of fear took hold of her. The sounds had
stopped. All was silent from within. But it was a strange,
uneasy silence that put the fear of God into her. Yet
there was something else it put into her. Curiosity. She
had to see for herself what was going on in there.

Slowly, and with trembling fingers, the redhead tried
the door handle. It could well be locked from the inside,
she thought, but that was not always the case. Locking a
door bespoke shame, and many of the clients who
frequented a place such as this were without shame.

The door handle moved easily beneath her touch.
Trembling softly and with bated breath, she inched the
door open, until, in a moment that seemed like a
lifetime, she could see right into the room. And what she
saw there stopped her fast in her tracks, her mouth wide
open and her eyes narrowed into thin dark slits that
seemed to want to shut out the scene before them.

It was the Justice right enough, even more repulsive in his nakedness. The whore was with him, a slim, dark-haired thing with white thighs and crimson lipstick besmirching her face. But her face was stark white and her naked body was awkwardly spread-eagled over the edge of the four-poster bed, her legs stretched wide apart and there, lying between them, was the Justice. The two of them might have been ecstatic in the throes of lovemaking – were it not for three things which were immediately obvious. The room was in a shocking shambles, as though someone in a terrible fury had vented all their rage on it; there was not a single item that hadn't been broken, torn, or split asunder. The whore was too still, too limp. The Justice was raised above her, staring down in horror, his two hands still wrapped about her throat. Now, as he turned to see who had entered the room, he began whimpering like a baby.

'Christ Almighty! . . . *What have you done?*' The redhead's voice was hushed with shock. Coming quickly into the room, she instinctively let the knife fall to the carpet and dropping the lamp on to the dresser, she rushed to the bed, viciously pushing aside the mound of blubber that was shaking with terror. '*You bastard!* . . . You've done it this time!' Even as she spoke, she saw that it really *was* a night for revenge after all!

'She's not dead, is she? . . . She *can't* be dead!' Caleb Crowther still had the dulling effects of booze on him as he began frantically to pull on his clothes, all the while stumbling and crying. 'We had an argument . . . nothing really. She teased me . . . poked fun at me. Oh, but she can't be dead. Not *dead!*'

'Shut up, you fool!' The redhead put her finger and thumb to the whore's neck, feeling for any sign of life.

She had seen nakedness many times, and she had witnessed most things that were both shameful and corrupt. But she had never encountered murder before. It was not pleasant, nor was there any dignity in it. Part of her wanted to scream at the top of her voice and alert the whole house. Yet a deeper instinct made her hesitate. Suddenly it was there. A pulse beneath her fingers . . . hardly noticeable, but there all the same. 'My God!' she exclaimed, the cry of gratitude already rising in her throat. But in the same breath, she stopped herself from declaring that the whore was still alive. Instead, she twisted her face into an expression of disgust and loathing. 'You've killed her! *Murdered* her.' She deliberately began to raise her voice, but not so high that it would go beyond that room.

'I'll pay you! *Anything!*' Caleb Crowther was beside himself with fear as he sidled up to her. 'Keep quiet about this . . . we'll get rid of her. Name your price . . . *anything, I tell you!*'

Coolly, the redhead eyed him, making him wait. Making him suffer, and secretly revelling in the sight of it. Yet she dared not linger too long, for fear the whore on the bed might start recovering. That mustn't happen. Not yet, or the sweetness of her revenge would all too soon turn sour. 'I could see you *hanged* for this,' she said in a hoarse and terrible whisper. 'There'd be no wriggling out of it . . . "Justice" or no "Justice" . . . caught red-handed at it . . . you can't deny it. Oh, I know they wouldn't take *my* word . . . a *whore's* word . . . against yours,' she sneered at the fleeting and conniving look that spread over his ungainly features. 'But you'd do well to remember that I only have to raise me voice to bring all and sundry running to see what terrible mischief you've done . . . they'd see it written in your face like the guilty fellow you are.' She chuckled to see the light of fear heighten in his eyes. 'And I dare say there'd be a judge or two come a-running . . . and happen even a constable from the streets. Oh, and what would the world say, to see an upright and legal fellow like yourself in a place like this . . . with a *dead* whore in your bed?' Her confidence had grown. 'Anything, you say? . . . You'll pay me *anything?*'

'Just name your price. Only keep your mouth shut about what you've seen here tonight!' There was a touch of arrogance in his voice, and even the suggestion of a threat.

The redhead cocked her eye at him, taunting, 'Or *what?*' she demanded. 'Or you'll shut it for me? . . . Strangle me, like you strangled this poor sod, eh?' She cast a sideways glance to where the whore's body lay. And she was alarmed to see the eyelids momentarily flutter. 'I'm no fool!' she told him now, coming forward in order to block his view of the whore. 'The minute you've gone, matey, I intend to write out a detailed story of what took place here, in this room. Oh, I *can* write, sweetie! I ain't the complete fool you take me for. Then I shall put that story in a place where neither you nor anybody else could find it, unless I was to suddenly disappear, o'course! Try double-crossing me, matey,' she warned, her loathing of him evident in her every word, 'and you'll live to regret the day!'

Caleb Crowther knew that she had him at her mercy. He had been all kinds of a damned fool. He was under no illusions but that he would have to pay the price. For now at least! Later though, when he was in less of a torment and had recovered enough from the ordeal to contemplate it, there might be something he had overlooked. Some liltle thing that could alter the situation to his advantage.

For now, though, he had no option but to play along. The club was too full of prying eyes and, as this bitch had pointed out, there was a danger of betraying his compromising situation to those who were enemies of old. Enemies who would take great pleasure in seeing him charged with murder, even though their own reputation might be damaged by their presence in such an establishment. Such a one was Bartholomew Bent, a legal man of considerable influence who had once been brought under severe pressure by Caleb Crowther, and who had a particular dislike of the fellow. He was here! Caleb Crowther had seen him with his own eyes some hours ago, though he had managed to keep discreet his own presence here. 'You have my word,' he reluctantly conceded. 'What are we to do about . . . about . . .' He pointed to the bed, but was too cowardly to look at it.

'You just leave that to me,' she retorted, at the same time throwing the corner of a blanket over the 'body', yet being careful not to cover the face. 'Take your shoes up!' she told him. 'I'll see you off the premises. *Hurry! Hurry, you fool!*' She waited impatiently until he had flung his cape over his arm and gathered up his cravat, white silk scarf, and the black polished shoes that were stuffed with socks and suspenders.

Quietly opening the door, the redhead gestured for him to go before her, out into the corridor. As he did so, she caught sight of a fat wallet protruding from his back trouser pocket. The wallet itself was of secondary importance to her, as were the notes within, although she could certainly make good use of them. But what prompted her to snatch it away were the gold initials etched into it: his initials. A vital piece of evidence as far as she was concerned. And, if that in itself wasn't enough, she plucked out the contents of one of his shoes; it had struck her as being amusing that many a gent took pride in displaying his initials on the fastener of his sock suspenders. A quick glance told her that this 'gent' was no different .

'Damn your eyes. Give them back!' Her swift and unexpected move had taken him by surprise.

'Ssh! . . . We don't want to wake the others now, do we, eh?' she goaded maliciously. The two objects would serve her better than they would serve him, she thought. Where he might claim that his wallet had been stolen in some public place, he could hardly give the same explanation for how one of his *sock suspenders* came to be missing: 'Now you go on, m'lud,' she sniggered, 'softly to the front door, and away to your fancy home . . . before your "nanny" comes a-looking for you.' When he glowered at her, she suddenly changed mood, her expression becoming dark and nasty. '*Get out of my sight, Justice* . . . or I might change my mind and rouse the whole household after all!'

'All right, all right . . . you give me little choice,' he whispered gruffly, his piercing, hate-filled glare devouring her every feature.

There was such naked animosity in his eyes that for an uncomfortable moment the redhead secretly questioned the wisdom of what she was doing, for here was a powerful, mean man, who could also be a powerful and destructive enemy. Yet even that fear of future retribution was not enough to dissuade her from her ambitious scheme. Not only had she stumbled upon the opportunity for revenge, but by some quirk of fortune – or *mis*fortune – she had also been afforded the opportunity to make her miserable life more comfortable. The thought was unbearably pleasant, even thrilling, as she followed the nervous, sweating figure down the stairs and onward, through the foyer, where the desk clerk was fast asleep.

Before closing the front door on him, the redhead held the lamp high on Caleb Crowther's face. 'Don't forget . . . *you've done murder here this night!*' She smiled as he seemed to cringe beneath her words. 'Oh, but don't you worry . . . I'll take care of everything. And I'll be in touch. Oh, yes . . . I'll certainly be in touch. *You can depend on it!*'

As Caleb Crowther slunk into the night, the woman's words kept coming back to haunt him. '*You've done murder here this night!*' What on earth had driven him to such dreadful extremes? The night was cold, but the sweat ran down his face as he questioned whether that redhead could 'take care of everything'. *But she must!* She must or he was lost.

Hailing a carriage, he climbed in and hid in the darkest corner. There must be no newspapers allowed into Breckleton House. He couldn't bear to think of reports describing the discovery of a body. At this minute, with his every limb shaking uncontrollably, he could only think of his own precious skin.

Part Two

1887

Life is a thread;
So easily broken.
J.C.

Chapter Eight

'What d'you mean . . . "she's gone"?' Mick Darcy's face fell with disappointment. '*Where's* she gone? When will she be back?'

His heart sank inside him as the young man slowly and solemnly shook his curly head. 'I'm sorry, Darcy, but Molly *won't* be coming back . . . "not to these parts ever agin" was what she told me mam.' Joey Watson's tone softened when he saw what a devastating effect his words were having on the bargee. 'Didn't she let you know? I were given to understand that you an' Molly had a, well . . . a particular understanding?'

'No.' Mick smiled, but it was a sad and sorry expression. 'Not that *I* wouldn't have welcomed a closer understanding between us. But if you knew Molly at all, you must know how devoted she is to that husband of hers.' He suddenly realized that he was openly discussing Molly's private affairs and he was shamed. 'Me and Molly had *no* such understanding, young man. It was my privilege to be a good friend to her, that's all . . . as I know your mother, Tilly, was.' He paused, allowing his statement to sink in. 'So, you've no idea *where* Molly might have gone?'

'None at all, and if me mam were in, she'd tell you the very same . . . Molly was cagey about where she was headed.' He rubbed his thumb along the dark fuzzy stubble on his chin, at the same time scrutinizing the bargee. He knew well enough how this broad, handsome fellow idolized Molly from next door because hadn't his mam said time and again, 'that Mick Darcy thinks the world o' Molly . . . tek her and the three kids at the drop of a hat he would, and he's a fine catch by any woman's standards. By! If that Molly had any sense at all, she'd bar the bloody door agin that useless husband of hers . . . and snatch Mick Darcy's hand off with his offer! Oh, but she won't! Not while she's besotted with that waste o' timer, Jack-the-Lad. But mark my words, our Joey . . . she'll come to regret waiting for that bugger. Oh, yes, there's no doubt she'll come to regret it. Tuh! If *I* were in that gal's place, you wouldn't find me turning down a fella the likes o' Mick Darcy!'

'Taken all her belongings, has she?' Mick glanced towards the unkempt little house that had been Molly's pitiful abode.

'Well, she didn't have *much* to take, but yes, she went away pushing a cart piled up with bits o' this and that. The littlest o' the lasses were sat atop the jumble, with the cripple. The one called Sal trotted alongside her mammy, helping to push the cart.' He shook his head and pursed his lips, making a sucking sound. 'They made a sorry sight and no mistake.' He deliberately kept back one significant piece of information. It wasn't often that folks hung on his every word, and even though he felt a measure of sympathy for the bargee – who was obviously head over heels in love with Molly – he was enjoying being the centre of attention.

'Thank you for your trouble,' Mick told him now, beginning to turn away. 'If by any chance Molly *should* come back . . . you will tell her I was here?' When the young man nodded, he went on, 'Happen I'll wander about a bit . . . keep a look out for her. I'd hate to think she was in need, or trouble, or anything of that sort . . . what with three young 'uns looking to her.'

'Oh, I shouldn't bother yerself about any o' *that*, matey,' interrupted Tilly Watson's eldest. He thought it just the right moment to reveal his 'snippet of information'. 'Molly ain't on her own, d'yer see? Because, according to what she told me mam . . . she's given the house up fer the very good reason that her Jack's got himself a job some fifty mile away . . . and there's a *place ter live* goes with it. That's where Molly's taken herself and the brats. She's gone ter set up home with her wandering husband.' He felt pleased with himself, until he saw how the colour had drained from the bargee's face. Thinking himself a heartless bastard, he said, 'Molly seemed in good spirits when she left Dock Street, mate – happiest I've seen her in a long time. Look . . . she'll be all right now her fella's seen sense enough ter put down roots. Her and the young 'uns . . . they'll be well looked after. That's what you want, ain't it? You being a friend?'

'Oh, that's what I want, right enough,' Mick was hasty to reply. 'It's what Molly would want too. Her husband and young 'uns all under the same roof, and him set up with a steady job.' He was lying. It *wasn't* what he wanted at all! If he had his way, Molly and the bairns would be under his own roof, and it would be *him* looking after them, not that vagabond Jack-the-Lad. Still and all, it was Jack who was Molly's choice and not himself. He had lost her. Her undeserving husband had won her back. For Molly's sake, he must accept that and be glad for her. But it was a hard thing. A painful thing that beat him down inside.

195

All this time, Mick had hoped that Molly was missing him, and that she would come to realize how much better a man he was than the useless article she had married. He had deliberately stayed away, giving her time and distance, so she might be watching when he returned. Instead of which, he had come back to find her gone from these parts 'never again' to return, if this young man's account was anything to go by. Well, he'd left Molly with a question to consider. She had given her answer, and it was clear enough to him. She kept no place in her life for Mick Darcy. He was not one to force himself on a woman. Molly had shown him the door, and he would stay out, even though his heart was broken.

But before he took his leave of this well-informed young man, there was one thing that needed to be said. In a firm and condemning voice, Mick told Tilly Watson's son, 'By the way, fella-me-lad, you'd do well to remember that the "cripple" you mentioned has a name . . . just as you have! *His name is Tom.* Don't forget that in future, will you . . . "matey"?'

'O' course not . . . the name escaped me fer the minute, that's all.' The young man had detected the warning in Mick's voice. It was a warning he would heed, for who in his right mind would want to get on the wrong side of a bloke who was built like *this* one? Not him, and that were a fact. 'Tom, y'say? Nice, cheery little fella too.'

With a nod and a nervous smile, the young man quickly shut the door, leaving Mick Darcy to gaze longingly at the sorry little house nearby, with its partly boarded-up window and peeling paintwork, and the smudged whitestoned step where Molly had spent many an hour bent to her knees. In his mind's eye he could see her there, scraping away with the whitestone and carefully marking the edges. She didn't have much, he thought, but she had worked hard to maintain at least a degree of dignity. Stubborn, independent and proud, she was a woman of rare breed. To his mind, the lovely Molly had only one fault: she loved the wrong man. Still and all, he reminded himself now, Jack *was* her husband, and the father of her children; while *he* was an intruder. Oh, yes, he thought the world of her and would lay down his life for her if she wanted him to. But she didn't. Nor did she love him.

He stood outside Molly's house on Dock Street, watching the door and willing her to appear. When she did not, he walked away, an unhappy figure with bowed shoulders and reluctant step. For him – without any hope of winning Molly – life had suddenly lost its meaning.

However, life must go on. There was always work to compensate a man. Now that he was back in the area, he would go to the mill on Eanam Wharf. When Marlow Tanner had taken his wife Emma on a long sea voyage after the tragic loss of their only son, he had left a good and loyal man in charge during his absence.

Mick Darcy quickened his step. That was where he was headed: to ask this 'good and loyal' man for work. Molly had gone to Jack, and, according to Tilly Watson's eldest, she was 'happiest I've seen her in a long while'. It was poor compensation for his own unhappiness. At least she had gone to Jack of her own accord and, at long last, it did seem as though she'd got her heart's desire. There was little he could do but to wish her well, and pray that the Good Lord would watch over her.

* * *

'Why can't we stay here, Mammy?' Little Sal was close to tears as she helped Molly to pile their pitiful bits and pieces on to the cart.

'Because we're going to find somewhere *better*!' Molly was at her wit's end. Since fleeing Dock Street and not even daring to confide her reasons to Tilly for fear that the Justice was closing in on her, Molly and her bairns had traipsed all over the north west, sleeping in derelict houses, rat-infested warehouses and even setting up home in a shed behind a laundry. Each time something had driven them on: either a curious constable or taunting children, and in the case of the shed at the rear of the laundry, an official who threatened to call higher authorities. The most recent abode was a condemned property in the centre of Liverpool, a good spot because the people there minded their own business.

Recently though, this block of condemned houses had begun to attract all manner of undesirables, layabouts and loud-mouthed drunks who had come to take an unhealthy interest in Molly and the young ones, particularly in little Sal, with her wide blue eyes and yellow hair. Only last night two men, the worse for drink, had come stumbling into the room which Molly had made surprisingly cosy. They made it clear to Molly that it was Sal they wanted. They offered money, promising to 'fetch the little angel back when we've done'.

Terrified, Molly had yelled and screamed at them, flinging every missile she could lay her hands to, until being the cowardly fellows they were, the two intruders took to their heels.

Molly suspected these fornicators would be back. Such foul creatures were not easily deterred. So, weary of heart, yet ever strong in spirit and determination where the safety of her bairns was concerned, at the first light Molly began gathering their belongings together.

Before the dawn lit up the sky on another cold January day, Molly could be seen pushing the cart along the alleys of Liverpool. When Peggy echoed little Sal's remark, 'Where we going, Mam?' Molly reassured them both. However, in her heart, she could see no comfort for any of them. She had to make plans, this much she knew; for now, her only aim was to keep her bairns safe.

With that in mind, Molly kept her eyes on the road ahead. She had no idea where it led; only that she must follow it, and hope against hope that, at the end of it, she would find her Jack.

Chapter Nine

On the fourth of March, in the year of our Lord 1887, Emma stood on the highest point in Corporation Park, thoughtfully surveying the scene below. It was a strange sort of day, with a keen breeze cutting the high ground, and the sun shining brilliantly from a spiteful, shifting sky. It was neither warm nor cold, and at half-past two in the afternoon neither light nor dark. The sharp, bitter wind was erratic, dying down in one instant and whipping up to a frenzy in the next. The sun's brilliant bright rays were piercing to the eye, but they held no warmth. There was a peculiar agitated mood about the wind, and a disturbing unpredictability about the weather in general. Emma thought it matched her own mood.

Against the drifting patchwork of grey and white clouds and surrounded by vast unbroken stretches of grassland, Emma made a lonely figure high up on the pinnacle beside the Crimean guns. She was impeccably dressed as ever: in a burgundy coat nipped in at the waist and chased with dark lace at the hem. On her feet were the daintiest black pearl-button shoes, and showing at her throat was the exquisite silken collar of her ivory-cream blouse. On her shining chestnut hair, which was loosely curled into the nape of her neck, she wore a large, soft tammy of the same striking colour as her strong grey eyes, which now were roving the streets and by-ways below, drawing in the years and reliving precious moments of long ago.

Even in her mid-forties, Emma was still an astonishingly attractive woman. She possessed a unique blend of dignity, grace and loveliness that would compliment any woman half her age. Yet she was never proud nor vain, and it was always others who acclaimed her beauty, while Emma saw nothing special or admirable about the way Nature had fashioned her. If she consciously strove to preserve any part of her character, it was that strength of spirit with which she had been blessed, and which had brought her through so many traumas in her eventful life.

So often, when life had sought to bring her to her knees, that special strength within her had helped her through. Always there for her to call on, never once had it failed to sustain her. *Until now.*

Since her return from Australia, Emma had made every effort to accept the loss of her son. But somehow she could not come to terms with it. Angry, bitter and confused, she fought against a natural grieving process. There were no tears to ease the awful pain inside her. Instead, there was only a hard core of resentment in her heart. She had built a wall of destructive emotion around her memories, which no one, not even Marlow, could penetrate.

In these past weeks, Emma had taken to frequenting Corporation Park, where she, Nelly and the boy had spent many happy hours. Always she came alone, staying sometimes the whole afternoon, when she would wander the meandering walkways, avoiding the spot where young Bill had tumbled to his death. Marlow had remarked so often how, if only Emma could bring herself to look again on that place, she might realize how final was the parting between herself and the boy she adored. But nothing would persuade her in that direction. Nor would she be drawn into any conversation regarding either the tragic incident or her own thoughts on it. Even now, after all these months, she refused to visit that corner of the churchyard where he had been laid to rest. The priest's well-intended visits to the house on Park Street had been greeted with such hostility that, at Marlow's request, he had ceased to call, entreating both Marlow and Nelly to 'do what you can to persuade Emma into the House of God where she must surely find a measure of peace'.

Emma had resisted all efforts to restore her faith in the Almighty. In her bitterness she could not forgive him; though outwardly she showed little sign of her turbulent feelings. Instead she appeared cool, reasonable to a fault, and stalwart in her support of Marlow's continued success in the transporting business. But, as Nelly had pointed out to Marlow only the other day, 'The *spark* seems to have gone out of our Emma . . . and it breaks my heart ter see how she's quietly torturing herself.'

Marlow had reassured the anxious Nelly; in truth he also was deeply concerned for Emma's state of health. She adamantly refused to see a doctor. To Marlow's heartfelt plea that Emma must 'reconsider this awful business between you and your uncle, Caleb Crowther . . . raking up so much bitterness and pain from the past with which to further torment yourself', she would only concede with great reluctance to 'delay the setting of a new date for the hearing'. Because, to Emma's mind, the very *root* of her pain was Caleb Crowther himself, and when a root was so rotten that it contaminated all it touched, then that same root must be mercilessly chopped out and destroyed.

All the same, Emma was in no great hurry to bring her despicable uncle to task, for to her way of thinking, the longer the delay, the more he would be made to suffer. Let him believe that she was having second thoughts about the charges she was bringing against him. Let him wallow in a false sense of security. The shock to his conniving heart would be all the greater when he was eventually made to answer her allegations.

After a while, when the clouds began to grow dark and threatening overhead, and a few isolated spots of rain warned of the deluge to come, Emma began her way down the steep incline towards the exit.

For the past twenty minutes and more, Nelly had been nervously pacing back and forth to the side window in the drawing-room. From there, the side gate leading out of Corporation Park was just visible, and now, when she saw the small familiar figure of Emma approaching, Nelly went rushing into the hallway to greet her, pausing only to poke her head in through the kitchen door with the instructions, 'Mrs Tanner's back. Be so good as to fetch a pot o' tea to the drawing-room. And a plate o' sandwiches . . . *proper* sandwiches, mind! We don't want none o' them silly little things as disappear with one bite!'

When Nelly's homely face had gone from the doorway, impatient glances were exchanged between the plump, round-eyed maid and the cook – who appeared a most unlikely candidate for the position of 'cook', being thin as a barge-pole and so tall that she had to bend from a great height when attending to her tasks at the big pine table. She had a gaunt, sour face and an equally sour disposition. But her culinary skills were second to none, and she had never been known to panic. Her name was Miss Warburton. Nelly disliked her intensely, and much to Emma's consternation, there was a great deal of friction between them, each one constantly looking to put the other in a bad light with the master and mistress of the house. Miss Warburton had been reduced to tears on more than one occasion, when Nelly had told her quite categorically to '*piss orf!*'

Just now there were other, more important things on Nelly's mind. 'Where've yer been all this time?' she demanded of Emma, who took off her coat and tammy, and at once had them snatched from her hands by the anxious Nelly. '*Two hours* you've been gone, yer bugger!' she chastized, hanging up Emma's outdoor clothes while still keeping a disapproving eye on her. 'I don't like yer going off on yer own fer hours at a time! . . . Wandering about in the park. Why! There could be *anybody* just waiting ter jump out at yer.' She frightened herself with such a terrible thought, 'Robbers an' murderers . . . them buggars are *everywhere.*'

'Don't exaggerate, Nelly,' Emma smiled at the wide-eyed face that glared at her so disapprovingly. 'I'm perfectly safe. You know as well as I do that there are *no* "robbers and murderers" in Corporation Park.'

'I don't know any such thing, my gal,' Nelly declared firmly, 'and neither do *you.*' She touched Emma lightly on the arm. 'There's tea an' sandwiches on their way,' she said, 'let's you an' me set in the drawing-room, eh?' She swung away, swerving towards the kitchen door where she screeched, 'Ain't that tray ready yet, Miss Warburton? *Be so kind as to get a move on!*' When

Emma cautioned her, she turned round and, squeezing her head down into her neck, she made a wicked and mischievous face. 'It's allus best ter keep the buggers on their toes,' she said in a loud whisper. ''*Er* type especially needs ter be reminded who's boss!'

When, some ten minutes later, Emma and Nelly were seated in the pleasant comfort of the drawing-room, with the tray duly placed on the table between them and the door closed against intrusion, Nelly picked up on the argument of Emma wandering Corporation Park alone. 'Why ever don't yer let me come with yer, darlin'?' she asked in between long, noisy gulps of her tea. 'Yer really *shouldn't* be going about them narrow little walkways all on yer own.'

Emma considered Nelly's argument for a while, before explaining in a firm and serious voice how she needed to be on her own occasionally, and how these frequent walks through the park were as good as a tonic to her. Although she dearly valued Nelly's companionship, there were times when she craved solitude and peace. 'Times when I can quietly contemplate and assess the way of things,' she said to the anxious Nelly.

Nelly put down her cup, at the same time closely regarding Emma. 'Did you go to the cliff face, Emma gal?' It was a delicate and daring question, but one she needed to ask.

At once, Emma was on the defensive, deliberately ignoring Nelly's pointed question. 'I think we're in for a storm,' she said, replacing her own cup on the table and getting to her feet. 'I'm going to my room for a while, Nelly. Marlow should be home within the hour . . . we can talk then, if you like?' She despised herself for walking out on Nelly's company. But she despised even more the prospect of being 'interrogated' by a persistent Nelly, who meant well, but whose questions were painful to Emma.

'Go on then, darlin'. . . you go and put yer head down fer a while.' Nelly realized she had frightened Emma away, and she was angry with herself. 'I might even do the same meself,' she chuckled.

'Bless you, Nelly . . . you're a good friend.' Emma reached out to take Nelly's hand in her own. There were so many things she wanted to say. So much that she needed to confide to this dear woman who had been like a sister to her. Oh, they had often talked for hours, of the past and their many adventures. They reminisced about years ago and the people who had crossed their eventful lives. She and Nelly had laughed and cried together; they had despaired and hoped together. There had *never* been anything between them that was awkward, or secret, or forbidden. Until now.

Nelly clung to Emma's small, slim fingers. She had seen the pain in her beloved Emma's eyes and she hated this terrible thing that was splitting them asunder. Like Marlow, she feared for Emma's peace of heart. Now, as she looked up with bright, tearful eyes she asked softly, 'Will yer not talk ter me, darlin'? . . . Stay and talk ter me, eh?'

'Oh, Nelly, Nelly!' Emma gazed down at the round brown eyes that were now encased in soft, wrinkly folds of flesh. She remembered them when they were young and vivacious, rudely alive with mischief and following everything that wore a pair of trousers; always shining with that very special love that had grown between her and Emma over the years.

Looking at her now, Emma realized with a rush of

compassion that little had changed with regard to the incorrigible Nelly. The eyes still held a measure of mischief, and few handsome men were safe in her company. There was no denying the affection with which she gazed on Emma now. No, Emma thought warmly, Nelly had not changed, she probably never would. Not even the ravages of time would change her except to broaden the already dumpy figure, or to couch those bright, honest eyes in fleshy cushions. Nelly was just Nelly. And you either loved or loathed her. Emma *loved* her.

'Stay with me, Emma gal,' Nelly pleaded now, 'and I promise not to chastize you no more.' In truth, although she didn't come right out and say it, she was pledging not to question Emma about things that were painful. They both knew what she was really promising. For Emma, it was enough. Sighing, but with a smile that warmed Nelly's heart, Emma sat down again. 'Oh, there's a good 'un!' Nelly cried. 'You can tell me again about your trip to Australia . . . about how that cousin of yours turned up unexpected . . . that dreadful Martha! Oh, and d'yer *really* believe as how her husband, Silas, has struck up a close relationship with Rita Hughes? By! I'll bet that mard arse Martha didn't like her nose being put out of joint, did she, eh? Oh, but she's only herself to blame . . . leaving a reg'lar fella like Silas on his own out there. Go on,' she urged, 'tell me *everything*. Don't leave nothing out.'

'I must have told you at least *four* times,' Emma protested. But then, seeing that Nelly was perched on the edge of her seat, all agog with excitement, she sighed and smiled, and outlined the highlights of her long journey yet again: the seemingly never-ending but peaceful sea voyage; the joy of having Marlow all to herself when business was so far away that it could not part them; the strange feelings of both excitement and regret at setting foot on those same shores where she and Nelly had been delivered as prisoners too many years before.

'Y'know, Emma gal . . . I've made me mind up good an' proper . . .' Nelly had grown thoughtful all the while Emma was describing how 'it was strangely unsettling to be walking the streets of Fremantle . . . seeing the prison where we were kept and the house where we later enjoyed our freedom; little has changed, although the convict system will shortly be a thing of history'. Now, Nelly was made to cry out, '*I never ever want to go back there* . . . wild horses wouldn't drag me, I'm telling yer!' Nelly was adamant, shaking her head and looking altogether terrified at the very idea.

'We did have awful experiences there, didn't we, Nelly?' conceded Emma. 'And I can understand why you would not want to go back. But we came out of it all very well, you can't deny that. And Australia is very beautiful.'

'Oh, I ain't denying *that*, gal. But they say Paradise is beautiful too, don't they? And I ain't ready to go there *neither*!' Nelly's face was deadly serious and to Emma, who understood her friend's horror of what she had endured, it was obvious that she would rather die than ever again leave the shores of her motherland. 'But go on, go on, darlin',' Nelly urged now, 'what about this here business between Silas and Rita Hughes . . . her that manages the trading post? . . . Y'say they fancy each other, eh? And that the sour-faced Martha walked right in on it, eh? Oho! . . . I'll bet *that* shook the bugger up, what!' Nelly was positively beside herself with excitement at the thought.

Emma couldn't help but laugh. 'Really, Nelly, you are incorrigible!' she chastized. 'That was *not* how I told the tale . . . well, not exactly,' she had to admit. 'What I said was soon after our arrival in Fremantle, both Marlow and I noticed how dependent Rita Hughes was on Silas . . . and how he seemed always unusually attentive to her. It was very clear to me that the two of them had grown close, enjoying each other's company.'

'Right! That's what I said . . . They were sweet on each other. Then what? Martha caught them at it?'

'Oh, Nelly, you do have a blunt way with words, and you mustn't let your imagination run riot,' Emma told her firmly. 'It was all very unfortunate. Silas planned a lovely farewell evening in Marlow's and my honour . . . a dinner dance for about a dozen people or so. Now, I'm not quite sure what actually took place, but it seems Martha had not informed Silas she was on her way to Australia. No one knew that she had arrived that very evening. It was quite a shock, I can tell you, when she appeared . . . then disappeared in search of Silas. Apparently, she found him out on the back porch . . . with Rita.'

'Kissing and cuddling, eh?'

'Yes, Nelly . . . "kissing and cuddling".'

'Oho! Then all hell was let loose, eh?' Nelly sat, wide-eyed and thrilled, while Emma described how there had been a shrill cry and the sound of an argument coming from the porch. Then, after a few seconds, Martha had flounced into the room and out of the front door, her face a bright red study in rage and embarrassment. Soon after, Silas had followed her, and Rita Hughes made her excuses to leave. Before she and Marlow had boarded their ship the next day, Silas had confided that he had been deeply attracted to Rita, and now he was caught in the dilemma of having divided affections. He was genuinely very fond of Rita – a hard-working and unusually loyal woman who had been lonely most of her adult life – but now that Martha had answered his more fervent plea, to join him in Australia, he was a man torn in two.

'Poor sod,' Nelly exclaimed, but with a cheeky twinkle in her brown eyes.

'He's a good man, Nelly, you know that. I can't help but feel for him.'

'He is a good man,' Nelly readily agreed, 'too bloody good fer a miserable sorry thing the likes o' Martha Crowther. Rita Hughes is worth *ten* o' that one! If Silas Trent had any sense at all he'd give that troublesome woman her marching orders and set up home with Rita. That's what *I* say!' Not being able to remain in serious mood for too long at a time, Nelly began chuckling, 'Oh, but I would a' loved ter see that Martha's face when she caught 'em at it.'

'We don't really know *what* they were "at" on the porch, Nelly, and like I said, it doesn't pay to let your imagination run away with you.' Emma picked at one of the sandwiches, but soon replaced it on to the plate, her appetite not being what it was. 'But what about *you*, Nelly . . . we've had no real opportunity to talk since I've been back. How did you cope, being left here in charge? Did you enjoy the experience?' Emma realized with a pang of guilt that it was *her* fault and not Nelly's that they had found no opportunity to talk. In truth, she had actually avoided discussions of any kind since her first day back. She had been too preoccupied with thoughts of her son, and when the weather permitted, she had spent most of her time wandering about Corporation Park and losing herself in memories.

''Course I enjoyed it; did a good job too, I did . . . kept that bloody cook in order an' all.' Nelly went on in great detail about how things had 'run very smoothly', assuring Emma that she need never fear about leaving her in charge ever again. But the one matter she did not discuss was that of Molly having worked here for a while. Nelly had already confided the whole story to Marlow, who had confirmed Nelly's belief that it was better not to trouble Emma with the details of that particular episode, on account of Emma's present unreceptive mood, together with the fact that there was a child involved. To know that Molly's young daughter had played and laughed in this house and had used the very picture books that belonged to her son might have proved to be too painful a reminder for Emma. It was therefore decided *not* to acquaint Emma with the facts at all. Indeed, Nelly had been surprised at how intrigued and upset *Marlow* had been on learning about the dark-eyed Molly and her daughter, Sal, though he made little actual comment on the two.

'But just 'cause I looked after things so well in yer absence, don't go thinking yer can swan off an' leave me agin, my gal,' Nelly rebuked Emma with a stern wag of her finger, ''cause *next time* I'm coming with yer . . . so long as it ain't to the other side o' the world.'

'You needn't worry, Nelly,' Emma suddenly felt very weary, 'I have no plans for travelling anywhere.'

'That's all right then.' Nelly settled back in her chair to sip leisurely at her tea. She felt pleased with herself at having cajoled the reluctant Emma into a long conversation. All the same though, she would have liked to tell

Emma about Molly and the child. Yet she dared not; her instincts warned her that Marlow was right. Young Bill was too fresh in Emma's heart for her to accept that a strange child had been enjoying his things. Nelly dared not take a chance in telling her. Perhaps later, sometime in the not-too-distant future.

'I think I will go to my room for a while, Nelly . . . until Marlow comes home.'

'Aye, well . . . yer do look worn out. It's all that trudging about in the park. I've telled yer afore, my gal . . . *we none of us* ain't as young as we were!' She watched as Emma began her way across the room. Suddenly she was on her feet, calling her back. 'You'd best tek this bit o' jewellery up with yer,' she told Emma, who paused by the door at Nelly's words and was looking at her in a curious way: Emma was never a lover of jewellery, and she was intrigued by Nelly's remark. 'Yer must 'ave dropped it afore yer left fer Australia, gal,' Nelly said, coming towards Emma with out-stretched palm that displayed a tiny gold clasp which she had retrieved from the drawer. 'Yer lucky it weren't lost, my gal . . . or trod on. I found it on the carpet soon after you'd gone, so I picked it up and kept it safe in the sideboard . . . though I can't see how yer could 'ave worn the necklace that it come from . . . not with its clasp missing.' She placed the clasp into Emma's hand. 'D'yer know, gal, I've scratched me brain ter think which piece o' jewellery it came from. Yer don't have that much, do yer? And I swear *I* can't recall seeing it afore. But it must be yours, Emma, gal . . . 'cause it ain't *mine*. And I'm sure it can't belong ter none o' the staff, 'cause by the look o' the markings on it, that there clasp is worth a tidy sum.'

Nelly's voice ranted on. But Emma had stopped listening. At first, when Nelly had put the tiny clasp into her hand, Emma's instinct had been to give it back, saying that it was definitely not hers. Now, as she turned it over and over in the palm of her hand, *her blood ran cold*. The feel of the gold clasp against her skin was like a series of shocks going through her. She was confused and trembling, afraid and hopeful all at once. THE CLASP WAS HERS.

On close examination of it, Emma soon realized that it belonged to the tiny timepiece that her father had entrusted to her many years ago, just before he passed on. Her feverish thoughts sped back over the years. She recalled the twilight hours when she and Nelly were hurriedly bundled into the wagon which would take them to the convict ship. In her mind's eye, she could see it all. The same sensations that she suffered then rampaged through her now: terror, pain and anger. She could almost *feel* the prison warder dragging her towards the waiting wagon, merciless in his duty, even though she was already in the throes of giving birth. She remembered how Nelly had pleaded on her behalf, and how, in that cold, darkened alley, she had given birth to a most beautiful baby girl, whose dark eyes haunted her still.

It was only later that Emma had realized how she must have lost her precious timepiece in that same alley. For years she had bitterly blamed herself for losing the one thing that had meant more to her father than anything else in the whole world – and consequently was dearer to Emma than the greater fortune her father had left to her. Fortunes could be made and lost and made again, but the timepiece held so many memories and so much love that it was irreplaceable. Emma had cherished it, for it had belonged to her mother, Mary, given to her by Emma's father, Thadius, when they were young and he idolized her so. Now, by some inexplicable quirk of fate, *here in her trembling hand* was part of that same timepiece.

'Good grief, Emma darlin' . . . whatever's the matter?' Nelly had seen how shocked and white Emma's face was.

'This gold clasp . . . tell me again, *where did you find it?*' Emma's voice was soft, but strange and fearful to the listening Nelly. When she shook her head and was about to remind Emma that she had only just this minute explained how she found the gold-piece on the carpet, Emma reached out and actually shook Nelly by the arm. 'Nelly! Where *exactly* did you find it?'

'Well, like I said . . . I found the blessed thing on the carpet.' Nelly was completely taken aback by Emma's attitude. She couldn't ever remember Emma shaking her like that; not in all the years they had known each other. Not even when they were in Australia, and Nelly was constantly getting them both in trouble with the authorities. 'There . . . on the carpet . . . not far from the spot where we're standing at this minute! It were just lying there, I tell yer.' A thought suddenly occurred to Nelly, and it was decidedly unpleasant. 'Hey! You never think I *stole* the bugger, d'yer?' She was deeply hurt at the prospect of Emma believing that she had reverted to her old bad ways.

'No, no . . . I don't think that, Nelly,' Emma reassured her, 'but I can't understand . . . how this clasp came to be in this house.' Her voice trailed off as she lowered her confused gaze to the carpet; after a while she went to the nearest chair, where she sat stiffly, staring at the spot where, a moment before, she had been standing. Her forehead was creased into a deep frown, and even from a distance away, Nelly could clearly see that Emma was trembling.

'It is *yours*, ain't it, gal?' Nelly didn't know what to make of it at all. She sauntered to where Emma sat, her own face twisted into a frown as she looked down on Emma. 'Like I said . . . it ain't mine. So, does it belong ter yer, or don't it?' When Emma gently nodded in response to the direct question, Nelly was still not satisfied, insisting, 'Then if it's yourn . . . whatever's the matter? Ain't yer glad ter gerrit back? By! The way yer paled at the sight o' that gold-piece, anybody'd think you'd seen a *ghost*!'

'A ghost?' Emma repeated in a wondrous shocked voice. 'Yes, Nelly, that is what I've just seen . . . a ghost.' Suddenly, Emma was on her feet and confronting the anxious Nelly. In quiet and intimate mood, she asked Nelly to cast her mind back to the day of their transportation, to the very moment when Emma had been delivered of a girl-child and afterwards been bundled into the wagon, leaving the newborn for dead in the gutter. Nelly remembered it all, and for more reason than did Emma – for it was she who had misled Emma into believing that the infant had been stillborn, when in truth Nelly had long suspected that the child had lived.

'Go on, Emma gal,' she urged now, being caught up in Emma's growing excitement.

'You may or may not recall the delicate timepiece that I kept hidden in my boot?' When Nelly lapsed into deep thought, then vigorously shook her head, Emma went on, 'It was the only thing I had of my father's, Nelly . . .

216

and it was my secret. I was mortally afraid that it might be discovered and confiscated.' Emma clutched her small fist about the gold clasp and raised her eyes heavenwards. When she looked again into Nelly's puzzled face, her lovely grey eyes were swimming with tears. 'On that unforgettable day when I lost my girl-child . . . I also lost the timepiece.' She opened her hand to disclose the tiny clasp. 'This was part of it, Nelly and *I have not seen it from that day to this*.'

'*That can't be!*' Nelly gasped. 'Yer must be wrong, darling . . . somehow, yer must be wrong!'

Emma slowly shook her head, saying in hushed tones, 'I can't understand it, Nelly. How on earth has it come to be here . . . in this house . . . so many years later?' She was greatly puzzled. 'You found it on the carpet, you say . . . soon after Marlow and I left for Australia?'

'That's right.' Nelly pointed again to the very spot. 'Just there, like I said. So if it is the same as yer lost that night . . . what's it doing back here? . . . And who fetched it, that's what I can't understand. *Who* fetched it into this house?' She shook her head, telling Emma, 'Naw, gal . . . it *can't* be the same trinket. There must be hundreds like it . . . thousands, I dare say.'

'Not like this one, Nelly,' Emma told her, 'my father had the timepiece and the chain especially made for my mother. He told me himself . . . it was his own design.' She raised the clasp between her finger and thumb. 'See the shape and curl of the petals, Nelly? *It is the very same*. I would stake my life on it.' Suddenly she was entreating Nelly. 'Oh, Nelly, Nelly . . . *think hard*; how could it come to be here? Did you entertain any visitors? Did any gypsies call? . . . It is possible that some wandering vagabond found the timepiece and sold it on.

Oh, Nelly . . . I must know. I must recover it if it is humanly possible.' She was frantic. '*Think, Nelly! Who* did you bring into this house?'

'There weren't no gypsies nor vagabonds, I can tell you that . . . what! Some o' them buggers would slit yer throat fer a shilling.' Nelly was filled with confusion. 'Aw, look darling . . . I don't know *how* that there came ter be in this house, I really . . . don't.' Her voice tailed off and her heart-beat quickened. She felt the colour drain from her face. *Molly! Of course.* Molly and the lass, little Sal. But no! If Molly had come across a gold-piece like that, she would have quickly sold it! Nelly's thoughts raced ahead. But Molly was a pickpocket all the same, there was no denying that! Happen she'd raided some gentlewoman's purse and was holding on to the clasp until it might seem safe to sell it on.

'What is it, Nelly?' Emma had seen the look of astonishment creep over Nelly's face and she saw it as a sign that Nelly had remembered something, or *some-body*. Now, as Nelly glanced up, Emma saw the rush of guilt in her homely face. 'Out with it, Nelly. Who was it? WHO DID YOU BRING INTO THIS HOUSE? . . . Was it a ruffian? A thief? *Who*, Nelly? WHO?'

Nelly was beside herself. Marlow had agreed that Emma should not be told about the young woman and her child. But oh dear, dear! What to do? Nelly was made to recall how, years before, she had kept certain things from Emma; how she thought the girl-child had cried out and was plucked from the gutter by a passing vagabond. She had lived to regret keeping that informa-tion from Emma and then as the years passed, it was too late to do anything else. Now here she was, faced with *another* dilemma! Should she tell Emma about the young woman and the child who had used her son's belongings like they were her own, or should she confess to Emma only a part of what took place . . . how she had tried to help Molly – just as she believed Emma herself would have done? *What to do?* Being afraid of hurting Emma in even the smallest way, and realizing that in revealing the truth to Emma, she would be going against Marlow's sound advice, Nelly blurted out the first excuse that came into her head. 'There was a ruffian here! *And a thief too*: Justice Caleb Crowther!'

Emma was shocked. '*He* was here?'

'Came banging at the door, demanding ter see yer . . . ranting and raving he were, but I told him to sod orf out of it!' A tide of relief washed through Nelly on having given Emma enough to occupy her mind, while at the same time not having actually lied to her.

'Caleb Crowther came here?' Emma was quietly digesting this information; yet she could see no real link between her uncle, and how the clasp came to be here. 'Did he come inside the house, Nelly?' she asked.

'Tuh! . . . A likely chance! Oh, he *would* have done if I hadn't kept the bugger where he belonged . . . *on the doorstep.*' Nelly thought the danger regarding Molly and little Sal had passed. But she made the mistake of looking too pleased with herself, too relieved, and too guilty – especially when she now saw Emma observing her with curious eyes. 'I sent him packing, Emma gal,' she finished lamely, visibly squirming beneath Emma's scrutinizing gaze.

There followed an endless and uncomfortable moment, during which Emma looked directly into Nelly's reddening face, and Nelly nervously fidgeted with her podgy fingers – a sure sign that she was feeling guilty.

'You're not telling me everything, are you?' Emma asked softly. Again, the ensuing silence was awkward.

'Don't know what yer mean . . . I've just telled yer what happened.' Nelly was on the defensive, and to Emma, who knew her only too well, Nelly was displaying all the old familiar signs of guilt. Emma had lost count of the times in Australia when Nelly had committed some misdemeanour or other, and had always managed to worm her way out of it. Not *this* time though, vowed Emma, 'I shan't budge until you tell me what it is you're keeping back,' she told Nelly now. 'You *did* have somebody in this house. Look . . . all I have to do is go and ask Miss Warburton . . . or the maid. They're not blind . . . there isn't much that goes on in this house they're not aware of,' she warned, 'but I know you'd prefer me not to give your "friend" Miss Warburton the chance to gloat. Am I right?'

'Yer a bugger o' the worst order, that's what *you* are!' retorted Nelly, but she knew how stubborn Emma could be if the mood took her. Her idea of going to the servants for information though would not bear fruit, because Marlow had given instructions that they were not to admit to the woman and child being in the house.

'*Please*, Nelly.' Emma's voice was pleading. 'You can't have any idea how important it is to me that I find out how this part of my father's timepiece came to be here. If there is the slightest chance that I can recover it all, it would mean so very much to me.'

Nelly couldn't bear to see Emma so desperate. She should tell her everything and suffer the consequences, she thought. Or live to regret deceiving this darling woman for the second time. But what about Marlow's instructions? Oh, she would deal with that when the time came, she told herself. For now, Emma was asking for the truth, and she deserved nothing less.

Nelly told her everything, reminding her about the little thief who had winked at Emma on the day when they had arrived in England some years back, and how Nelly had saved her from being flung in a cell during Emma's absence. She explained how Molly had come to work at the house, and she confessed that little Sal read young Bill's picture books and spent many happy hours playing with those toys which Emma herself had bought for her beloved son. Nelly left nothing out, and at the end of it all, she felt greatly relieved and hopeful that she had done the right thing. 'I don't know how, gal, and I'm blessed if I can believe it, but it is possible that Molly might have owned that there gold-piece. There was nobody else admitted to this here room, except me, the servants . . . and Molly.' There! It was all off her chest, and she felt better for it.

There was relief in Emma's voice too. 'Thank you, Nelly,' she said, adding firmly, 'and though I know that you and Marlow meant well, you had no right to keep this from me.' Her emotions were in a turmoil. The thought of another woman's child in her home created a murmur of resentment in her. Yet there was also a warm glow and a feeling of comfort that gladdened her heart; amidst all of that was so much pain and bitterness, so much love for the boy she had lost.

Now though Emma had a purpose. It was to speak to this 'Molly'. She needed to know how the young woman had come by the clasp. And she needed to know *now*. 'Where does she live?' Emma asked, hurrying from the room.

Nelly ran after her. 'I don't know. Not the name o' the

street . . . nor even the area. She never gave none of her business away. But I do recall the child talking about a neighbour by the name o' Watson. And a fella, by the name o' Mick . . . lives on a barge down Eanam Wharf!' She was astounded to see Emma put on her overcoat and tammy. 'Where yer going, Emma gal?' she asked, at the same time grabbing her own outdoor clothes.

'Eanam Wharf. *That's* where I'm going, Nelly,' Emma replied stoutly, and it occurred to the astonished Nelly that she had not seen Emma in such a determined and purposeful mood for many a long day. 'We're going to talk to Marlow,' declared Emma now. 'He knows all the bargees out of the wharf . . . and so he surely must know the one called Mick.'

Emma spent a moment eyeing herself in the long arched mirror of the ornate hallstand, tipping her tammy this way, then that, until, having secured it with a hatpin at just the right angle, she went smartly out of the front door, with the frustrated Nelly chasing after her, shouting abuse at all and sundry as she struggled to fasten the dark cape about her shoulders. 'Cor, bugger me, gal . . . when yer make yer mind up, there ain't no stopping yer, is there, eh?' she shouted, going down the path with a curious half-running, half-skipping gait. 'Wait on, wait on. I ain't got me bleedin' breath yet!'

From the window of his office, Marlow looked down into the mill yard. He had only just finished going through the ledgers with Joe Turney, the manager. Things were looking good and business was prospering. Cotton shipments were on the up and up, and the Tanner Transporting Concern was positively flourishing. Life had been good to him in so many ways. He had worked his way up from being a bargee who struggled for a living, going cap-in-hand to such men as Caleb Crowther who once owned most of the mills along the wharf – property that, by rights, had belonged to Emma. He had been broken-hearted when he could not have Emma all those years ago, afterwards sailing the world as a deckhand in order to find his fortune. He had not found that fortune in foreign parts though, but right here in his own backyard, doing what he knew best. In addition, he had the love of Emma. Here he was master of all he surveyed, while Caleb Crowther, by all accounts, was on a downward slide. Yes indeed, it was strange how fate and fortune swung its pendulum from one man to another.

There was an uneasy mood on Marlow this day: a disturbing and melancholy mood that would not let him rest. Part of it was the deep and lingering grief at the death of his boy, and part was because of something Nelly had told him.

For days now he had reflected on the news which Nelly had rightly confided in him, and which concerned the young woman and the child who had come to the house on Park Street in his and Emma's absence. When Nelly had first brought the news to him, wondering whether she ought to keep it from Emma, he had quickly instructed that Emma should not yet be told of the incident, especially as there was a child involved and Emma's grief was such that he dare not risk causing her any more pain. Once he and Nelly were agreed on that particular issue, he had seen no reason to pursue the matter any further.

But certain facets of Nelly's story had stayed with him, to tease and torment him, and now he could not put them out of his mind. Nelly had described Molly as being 'thin as a sparrer . . . with big black eyes and hair the colour of wet coal. The poor creature's had a hard life, I reckon . . . having ter pick pockets and forage for a living since she were growed enough ter outrun a constable.' Marlow reflected on Nelly's words, and the more he did so, the more he was made to recall other descriptions, of the waif who had been found and raised by his own sister, Sal, when he himself was forced to take to the high seas. One of the greatest and most painful regrets was discovering on his return that old Sal had passed away.

Over the ensuing months, Marlow had learned of the small girl who had seen to it that Sal had been given a proper and Christian burial. A girl who, according to various sources, was 'thin as a reed and dark in features . . . possessed of big black eyes, and a rare talent fer picking the gents' pockets'. All of Marlow's efforts to find the girl had been in vain.

Now, because of Nelly's tale regarding the one called Molly, the yearning to find that particular waif was once more raised in him. There was something else too, though he was not convinced enough to discuss it with anyone else – it had occurred to him that maybe, *just maybe*, this 'Molly' and the waif raised by his sister might be one and the same.

Marlow was not entirely satisfied though, because in this town, as in all other industrial areas, there were any number of vagabonds and pickpockets. It was sad but true. All the same, there was one other reason why Marlow had become more and more persuaded that he should go and talk to this 'Molly'. Her description tallied so closely with that of the waif's, it was true, yet more importantly, it was the name by which that young woman called her own child that intrigued him. Oh, Sal was a common enough name, to be sure. And yet. *And yet*.

Marlow's curiosity and his deep instinct determined that he would talk to the young woman. After all, what was there to lose by it? If his suspicions were wrong, then he would simply apologize and that would be an end to it. If he were right however, and this Molly *was* the child who had ensured that old Sal was not buried in a pauper's grave, then he owed her a great deal. But he must be careful, he reminded himself, because according to Nelly, the young woman had been caught picking pockets on that day when Nelly came to her rescue. She was obviously in poor straits and desperate enough to lie, cheat and steal in order to better her station. While he had every sympathy and was not averse to helping the more deserving amongst the unfortunates of this world, he had no desire to be made a fool of, nor to be misled by the quick tongue of a conniving thief, who saw him as an opportunity to be exploited. He must not rule out the possibility that the unfortunate creature whom Nelly took in was *not* the one who had been raised by old Sal, nor that, given enough information, she would not hesitate to claim otherwise, in order to pick his pocket in much the same fashion as she had picked many another.

The first thing he must do, though, was to talk again to Nelly, and see whether she knew anything at all of the young woman's upbringing. Besides which, he would need to find out where she lived, and whether Nelly would accompany him to that place. Now that he had made up his mind to talk with the young woman, and was determined to be cautious in his approach, Marlow felt easier than he had done for days.

* * *

From the mill yard below, Mick Darcy had seen the solitary and thoughtful figure of Marlow standing behind the office window and surveying all below. He thought for a moment of the troubles that might haunt a man in Marlow Tanner's position – a wealthy and successful businessman, yes, but at the same time just a man, a father who had recently lost his only son, and a husband whose wife was so stricken with grief that it was rumoured she hardly set foot outside the grand house on Park Street.

Bending his back to the stack of bales that needed loading on to his barge, Mick sighed and shook his head, thinking how, even for all the lands and fortunes that Britain was presently adding to its vast empire, he would not want to be in Marlow Tanner's shoes.

Mick Darcy would be the first to admit that he had never worked under a better man than Marlow Tanner. It occurred to him in that moment how, if the opportunity were ever to present itself, he would be quick to help his employer in any way he could, though for the life of him he could not see how such a situation would ever arise.

Thinking how he had better get a move on if he were to finish and have his load secured for the morrow. Mick concentrated his efforts and brought his thoughts back to his own heartache: the woman he adored and whom he was hardly likely ever to see again. Every night since Molly's going, he had dreamed of her. And every morning when he woke, she was the first thought in his mind. All the day long he carried her lovely image in his heart. The longing hadn't lessened with the passage of time; if anything, the pain of losing her was even sharper. Yet, for all that, Mick had to remind himself how Molly had freely made her choice between him and that waster, Jack-the-Lad. She had chosen her wayward husband and there was nothing else to be done. He had to resign himself to that fact, together with the belief that Molly had found happiness in her choice. All that remained now was for Mick to pray that her happiness was of the lasting kind.

Mick Darcy paused in his labours to glance at the carriage that now drew into the yard. He was surprised to see two women alight: one a dumpy, homely person with a quick, busy manner, and the other a more refined yet equally pleasant creature who had the kind of mature beauty that was both gentle and strong. When the grey eyes fleetingly smiled at him, Mick believed the woman to be the one and only Emma Tanner – no other woman could possibly answer the description by which he had come to recognize her. There was something admirable and especially lovely in her countenance.

As the two women made their way into the mill, Mick glanced up to where his employer had been standing a short while ago. Now he had gone from the window, and in a moment could be seen in the darker interior of the mill, his familiar figure rushing down the stairs that led from the office; a figure still tall and handsome in spite of the fact that he was no longer a young man. From where he stood, Mick heard Marlow Tanner call out Emma's name, and in such a way that betrayed both his shock and delight at seeing her here. Together, Marlow and Emma climbed the stairs, with the ever-attentive Nelly only two steps behind, and eager to add her own chatter to the conversation.

Suddenly Mick's attention was drawn by the comment

of a mill labourer, who had been transporting the bales to the mouth of the warehouse. 'Well, I'll be buggered, mate. It ain't often yer see *Emma* Tanner down here. Must be some'at important, I'll be bound. Did you see the look on 'er face, eh? Like as not, that bloody uncle of hers has been up to his mischief again. By! He's a bad 'un, if ever there were.' He tipped his flat cap back and wiped the sweat from his eyes, glancing again to where Emma had disappeared into the office with Marlow. 'I'll tell you what, mate . . . I wouldn't mind being a fly on the wall o' that there office. Oh, aye! . . . It's some'at urgent that's fetched Mrs Tanner down ter these quarters . . . some'at terrible important, if it couldn't wait till her husband got home!'

In spite of himself, Mick's curiosity was also aroused. The fellow was right. It *had* to be something of great urgency that brought Emma Tanner to the wharf. He hoped it wasn't bad news.

Mick's curiosity was heightened when, much to his astonishment, he was quickly summoned to the office. As he made his way upstairs, how much *more* astonished Mick would have been to learn that the 'terribly important' matter to be discussed was none other than his own, precious Molly!

Chapter Ten

Molly scanned the faces at the table, just as she had done night after night, week after week, hoping to catch a glimpse of Jack. But he was not there. He was never there. Now she had begun to despair of ever seeing him again. She felt weary and heavy of heart, not certain what she should do next, or where she should search.

Since coming to Liverpool and taking the waitress job in a dockland café, Molly had worked like a slave; but she didn't mind the work, because she considered herself fortunate to have found an employer who had given her and the children an outhouse which Molly had made into a little makeshift home for the four of them. All the same, life was far from comfortable. The outhouse was crammed with piles of books, tools and crates at one end, and the wind whistled in through the many chinks in the wooden walls. At night, the mice could be heard scampering over the flour sacks, and all in all, there was little privacy to be had.

Her employer's self-righteous and interfering wife constantly harped on about 'your eldest daughter should be learning the Bible and how to sew . . . not gallivanting about like a common vagabond.' She even thrust a book into little Sal's hands, saying, 'Study that, my girl, or you'll end up useless.' The book was a fount of knowledge, entitled *Magnall's Questions*. To Sal it was a fearsome, daunting thing, to be promptly wedged in one of the draught holes, where it would serve a better purpose. But for all that, Molly was saddened by the incident.

She recalled how much little Sal had enjoyed being schooled by Nelly, and she wondered what in God's name would become of them all.

'You're not dreaming of that husband of yours again, are you, Molly?' The large, friendly fellow with the weather-worn face and huge appetite shook his head at Molly before hurriedly tucking into the meal of steak pie and vegetables that Molly had put before him.

'You haven't come across him on your travels, then?' Molly had made the mistake of confiding in the old bargee, who ran a regular route between Liverpool and Manchester. He had not betrayed her confidence, but the mere fact that she had revealed her purpose here made her uneasy. Not a day or night passed when she wasn't reminded how there were certain people who would give *anything* to know her whereabouts.

'I ain't seen hide nor hair of the fellow answering this Jack's description,' the big man told her in hushed, fatherly tones, 'but I reckon a man who could leave a pretty little thing such as yourself ain't worth salt.' He rammed a forkful of red meat into his mouth, before adding kindly, 'Go home and wait for him there, why don't you? It ain't right that you should be working in a place where fellows congregate . . . not a young, good-looking girl like you.' He indicated a nearby table, where a group of young seamen appeared to be taking a little too much interest in Molly's slim, shapely figure. 'This is dockland, Molly. I've got a daughter myself . . . not much younger than you, and I wouldn't want her within ten miles of this place.' He smiled and nodded his greying head. 'Look . . . you take yourself off home and I promise you . . . if I *do* clap eyes on that husband of yours, I'll send him back to you with a swift kick in the breeches. Molly gave no answer, other than to smile at him and turn away. 'You think on what I said, Molly girl,' he urged, 'think on it real good.' His warning duly given, the man returned his noisy attention to the food on his plate.

For the rest of the day, Molly continued to search the faces that frequented Bill Craig's café; there were faces that had grown familiar to her, new faces both hostile and friendly, old faces and young ones. But none of them belonged to Jack. For all Molly knew, he could be miles away and she had been looking in the wrong direction. 'Go home and wait for him there,' the big man had told her. Molly smiled at the irony of his remark. She could have explained that she had no home. She could have told him that in the outhouse behind the café were three children belonging to her and Jack – whom the big man had said was 'not worth salt'. Three adorable bairns who deserved something better: a crippled boy aged one year and a half, a mischievous girl going on three, and little Sal, not yet seven years old, but made to grow up before her time.

Here, Molly paused to think how very much she had come to rely on Sal, a darling little creature who took care of her brother and sister during the hours when Molly worked in the café. At first, Mr Craig, the owner, had insisted that Molly work both mornings and evenings, to cover the busiest times serving breakfasts and suppers. When she protested that she would have to leave, he relented, getting someone else in to do the breakfasts. His motive was purely selfish.

231

Molly was one of the best workers Bill Craig had ever employed at the café; the pay was not so handsome and most waitresses spent too much time chatting up the customers. Molly, however, preferred to just serve their meals and get on with her duties. He considered Molly to be well worth keeping for as long as possible – in spite of the fact that she came with three brats on her coat-tail and was not as friendly to *himself* as he would have liked. When all was said and done, she was a tasty little article, and in view of the fact that she had no man to satisfy her needs, Bill Craig fancied she might come to enjoy his company between the sheets.

So far, the opportunity had not presented itself. To-morrow, though, his good wife was making her monthly visit to her ageing mother in Yorkshire, and he did not intend to let his chance slip by. The thought of taking Molly's naked body in his arms caused him such great excitement that he had hardly been able to contain himself these past few days.

Whenever Molly had a minute to breathe between the rush of customers, she used that minute to dash back to the outhouse and check that the children were soundly sleeping. Now, when there came a suitable lull, she looked into the kitchen to tell Bill Craig that she was 'just making sure the bairns were all right'.

'Sure, Molly,' he told her altogether too sweetly, 'quick as you can, mind . . . we don't want a riot in here.' He was a long, thin man with a pencil-trim moustache and ang-ular features. His dark eyes were disturbingly penetrating and constantly darted about so as not to miss anything. Molly kept her distance. He was her employer. His wife had not begrudged her and the children using the outhouse. For that Molly was grateful, but, for reasons she found difficult to define, she did not like this odd couple.

Opening the door softly, so as not to disturb the sleeping children, Molly crept forward towards the makeshift beds. Outside the keen April wind teased and rattled at the walls of the outhouse, whistling eerily down the chimney and wailing like a lost soul in torment. At once, the gentle sound of children slumbering comforted Molly. In the soft glow of moonlight which filtered in through the four small panes of the room's only window, Molly could easily recognize the familiar shapes of the three small figures all huddled together in the bed: there was Sal, her fine golden hair making a gossamer cloud on the bolster; to the right of her was Peggy, a sturdy little frame tucked into the protective crook of her sister's arm, her mouth wide open and emitting a strange whimpering sound, which was something between a whistle and a snore.

The only lad was on the other side of Sal. Molly had always believed Tom to be an unusually handsome baby, with his thick black hair and dark laughing eyes. Tilly Watson likened him to Molly herself, and now Molly wondered about their distinguished dark features. It was true that Tom had her looks. But where had they come from? Not from old Sal, because Molly knew that the old dear was *not* blood kin to her. Again, she was made to think on her true parentage. It was obvious that her own dark hair and eyes, and those of Tom, were inherited from one or both of her real parents: Tom's grand-parents. Certainly, Tom did not get his own dark features from his daddy, because Jack's hair was fair, and his eyes a pale brown colour. Peggy was the nearest to Jack's colouring. As for little Sal, well, Molly had often been puzzled by her blue eyes and golden hair. It was a funny thing but little Sal so often reminded Molly of that *other* Sal, the old lovable and eccentric tramp who had been everything to Molly in her formative years. There was something about her older daughter that really did put Molly in mind of old Sal Tanner. It was a curious thing, especially when Molly knew that old Sal had been no blood relation to her at all, a very strange and inexplicable thing to be sure.

As always, Tom was restless, tossing this way and that, throwing his little arms in and out of the coarse grey blanket and rolling from one side of his body to the other. Molly's heart went out to him. She wondered at his restlessness, suspecting that it stemmed from the discomfort which his deformed leg caused him. She had discovered that, if he laid for too long on that grotesque little stump, the feeling would go from it. On other occasions, he would be gripped by a cruel and vicious fit of cramp, which only his mammy's loving fingers could massage away. It pained Molly's heart to know that here he was, only a few months away from his second birthday, and she was no closer to getting Tom's crippled leg mended than she had been on the day of his birth; when his own daddy had run away at the sight of his son. When his daddy had run away! *When Jack had run away*.

Of a sudden, Molly was filled with disgust and dread. Spiralling up in the midst of all these painful emotions was a surge of guilt. *Guilt* because she had somehow failed not only Tom, but all of her precious children. It was because of her and the misdemeanours in her past that she was now forced to drag these little innocents from place to place. And what of their daddy? What of Jack? Jack, who had never grown up. Jack, whom she had fallen in love with on the night of their escape from Caleb Crowther's clutches, and whose children she had lovingly conceived and born. *Where was he now?*

Lately, Molly had come to ask herself why she was driven to search for him. Just as often, she had come to wonder whether or not she really wanted to find him. If, one day, he walked into that café, what would she do? What would she say to him? And – more importantly – would he be pleased to see her? All of these questions Molly tormented herself with. But there was one in particular which would not go away, and which caused her the greatest torment of all. Did she still love Jack? It was as though, in her desperate longing to find him, Molly had lost the real reason as to why she scanned every face in every crowd. Somewhere along the way she had begun to lose faith in her children's daddy. Little by little, that feeling she had for him, and which she called 'love', began to dwindle, until there was only shame and anger left.

If Jack's memory was shrinking in Molly's tired heart, there was another whose image was becoming more and more cherished. These days Mick Darcy was closer to Molly than he had ever been. In the late, dark hours when her duties were over and she lay in the narrow bunk some way from her children, Molly would remember the many happy times she and Mick had shared with those infants. All of her instincts told her that were she to search the world over, she would never find a better man; a man who had never wanted anything more than to take care of her and her babies. A good and loyal fellow. Certainly no other man could love her more deeply than Mick had loved her.

Molly derived great comfort from the knowledge that, though one man had shamefully deserted her, there was another who had offered her everything he owned. *Did she love Mick Darcy?* Molly dared not dwell too deeply on it. She could not deny that his memory was precious to her, nor could she deny those long, lonely nights when she imagined how wonderful it would be to feel his strong arms secure about her. Occasionally, she would recall their last meeting, when he had kissed her. The thought of his lips against hers brought a warm glow to her, and made her pleasantly embarrassed at the very real memory of it all. So real in fact did it seem in that moment when she gazed lovingly at her slumbering brood that Molly instinctively put the tips of her fingers to the outline of her lips. Mick's kiss had been so gentle, yet angry and possessive at the same time. Suddenly she was swamped with a terrible sensation of loneliness and regret until, impatient with herself, she turned about, going on tiptoe across the room. She was on the point of opening the door to leave when a small tired voice whispered into the darkness, 'Will you be long, Mammy?'

Checking the persistent feeling of guilt that pulled her down, Molly came back to where little Sal was raised up in the bed, leaning on one skinny elbow and peering at Molly through sleepy eyes. 'Ssh . . . go back to sleep, sweetheart,' Molly said in a whisper, bending forwards to kiss the child and tuck her back beneath the blankets. 'I'll be back in no time . . . no time at all,' she promised.

Molly's promise was enough. In a moment, Sal was snuggled up once more, and contentedly drifting off to her slumbers.

At the door, Molly whispered, 'Goodnight, God bless,' and was surprised to hear Sal reply dreamily, 'Night, Mammy . . . don't be long.'

For the remainder of the long, demanding evening,

Molly was rushed off her feet. Saturday night was always a busy time, but for some reason, on this particular Saturday the café was bursting at the seams, with loud groups of men who found Bill Craig's establishment a good stopping-off place before congregating at the public house. Here they could fill their bellies with food at a reasonable price, whilst exchanging snippets of gossip, and generally putting right the world at large. The more they swilled down the food with the cheap booze illegally supplied by the ever-enterprising Bill Craig, the noisier became their discussions, and the sooner they developed into aggressive arguments.

All manner of subjects were put forward, to be shaken, bandied about, denied or confirmed, but never resolved in any way whatsoever. Molly had witnessed them all – how industry was suffering a terrible depression and 'times can only get worse'. There were those who firmly supported Sir Randolph Churchill's claims that the iron industry was 'dead as mutton'; the silk industry had been 'assassinated' by foreigners; the cotton industry was 'sick'; the shipbuilding had 'come to a standstill' and that in every branch of British industry there could be found 'signs of mortal disease'.

The arguments raged and tempers became hotter. 'Not bloody true,' cried one; 'Churchill wants ter get his facts right afore he goes shouting fro' the rooftops,' said another, this one pledging allegiance to another public figure by the name of Alfred Marshall, a Cambridge economist. This 'educated' fellow claimed that while there had been in the previous ten years 'a gradual depression in prices, a depression of interest and a depression of profits' for those above working-class status, there had been 'no considerable depression in any other respect'. In fact, it was becoming widely accepted that the working-class were beginning to enjoy a 'much better quality of life'.

'Oh, aye?' interrupted a somewhat irate and weary man, dressed in a threadbare jacket that was too small, trousers that shone with wear and a cap whose peak was limp with age. 'It's all very well tekking notice o' those plump, well-to-do fellas with their airs an' graces, an' the smell o' money up their noses . . . but let the buggers do what us dockers 'ave to do day in an' day out! They'd have quite *another* smell ter contend with . . . an' it wouldn't be half so bloody pleasant neither. I wonder how long the sods would last if *they* had ter turn up at these 'ere docks in all weathers, four times a day ter the call-on, eh? . . . An' there may be work, an' there may not! Oh, aye, they'd change their tune then, I'll be bound . . . hanging about at the docks, begging an' hoping fer a bit o' work an' thinking usself bloody lucky if we get six hours' work in a week!' The cry was quickly taken up, and so the heated arguments continued.

Molly was often used to bounce grievances off, but she was always very careful not to get involved. She had enough of her own problems to contend with, and anyway, she thought, it wouldn't matter whether she agreed or disagreed, *her* opinion was unlikely to alter the dockers' grievances; in truth she did believe their arguments were not without foundation.

'That geezer's had his eye on you all night long. You ain't been encouraging him, have you? . . . You know how Bill frowns on that sort o' thing!' The accusing voice belonged to Nell Casey, the fair-haired girl who came in of a Saturday tea-time, waiting-on for three hours, when the crush of customers was at its worst. Molly had taken an instant dislike to the brazen, sour-tempered creature. She in turn made every attempt to belittle Molly in front of the customers, and she particularly resented the way Bill Craig ogled the beautiful Molly when he thought no one was looking.

Nell Casey had almost collided with Molly when the two of them had returned to the counter to collect their respective orders. Molly felt uncomfortable beneath the other girl's hostile stare. 'I don't encourage *no one*!' Molly told her quietly. 'You know that.'

'Well, what the 'ell's he staring at you for then, eh? . . . I'm telling you, he ain't took his eyes off you all night!'

Molly shrugged her shoulders, collected her order and began weaving her way in and out of the tables. From the corner of her eye she saw the man that Nell Casey referred to. He was obviously a seaman, young, bold-looking, and just as the other girl had described, he was deliberately watching Molly, following her every move with sly, calculating eyes.

Molly was suddenly gripped with fear. The way he was staring after her was not the usual flirtatious way in which a man might hanker after a woman. His manner was too furtive, too curious. Beneath those sly, narrowed eyes, Molly felt her heart shrink inside her. Who was he? Why did he seem so interested in her? And what devious game was he up to?

'Hey! Watch what you're doing, me beauty.' The laughing, surprised face peered up at Molly as she disentangled her feet from the chair leg that had protruded across her path and nearly brought her tumbling to the man's lap. As it was, the bowl of soup on her tray slid dangerously to the edge and would have spilled over the protester's ginger curls, if he had not been quick enough to steady Molly by the arm. 'Are ye trying to ruin me love life, or what?' he chortled, much to the delight of every manjack there. 'By God . . . there's no telling *what* dreadful damage a bowl o' hot soup can do to a fella's pride.' When Molly mumbled her apologies and hurried away, he huddled towards the group of men close by and began whispering. Molly heard their lewd laughter echo across the café, and her lovely face burned with shame.

It was some time before Molly had time to glance again towards where the seaman had been sitting. When she did look across, it was to see his seat empty. He was gone, and she should have felt relieved. Somehow, she did not. In fact, his abrupt disappearance unnerved her almost as much as the knowledge that he had been watching her so intensely.

Molly tried to console herself with the knowledge that she had never seen him before and, so far as she could recall, he had never seen her. Besides which, her enemies were not here in Liverpool, but some miles away in Blackburn town. 'You're being foolish,' she told herself, 'letting your fear and imagination run riot.' All the same, she could not shake off that insistent little warning voice – the same voice that told her how one waterway led to another, and how waterways carried vessels, vessels carried men, and men carried all manner of talk. How was she to tell whether the Justice had not put spies out after her? . . . Or offered a substantial reward? It was the kind of thing such men might stoop to. So the whisper might have been put out, and that whisper carried far and wide. Molly's terrible fear was heightened. Dear God, was there no safe hiding hole?

From his place behind the counter, Bill Craig also watched Molly. He saw how suddenly nervous she was, and how her anxious dark eyes kept flitting towards the spot where the young seaman had been. Mistaking Molly's anxiety for interest, his own appetite was teased. He thought she looked especially bewitching tonight, with that blush on her face and those exquisite black eyes so filled with secrecy. Her short coal-black hair was thick and incredibly rich . . . the kind a man was tempted to run his hands over. Unashamedly, he feasted his eyes on Molly's trim little figure, thinking how it should be dressed in silks and furs, instead of a worn-out dress of brown calico that covered her ankles and stole the colour from her face. Even the apron she wore was ill-fitting – having belonged to his own rather too ample wife. But when Molly leaned forward to serve at table, the glimpse of her slim and shapely ankles more than compensated for the ungainly manner of her dress. Even in the calico smock and the small, worn boots, he thought Molly to be the loveliest creature he had ever set eyes on.

Bill Craig was greatly excited. He could hardly wait for the morrow, when his wife took off on her travels. Deep inside him, there was a great longing, a burning that had to be satisfied. The only one to satisfy it was Molly!

The young seaman went along the docks in a jaunty manner, a merry tune on his lips, and a crafty gleam in his eye. He felt good. The money put up by Marlow Tanner would shortly be sitting in the pocket of this here seaman. Rightly so, he prided himself, rightly so! Because wasn't he the most diligent and observant fellow? Hadn't he just seen with his own eyes the very merchandise that Marlow Tanner wanted? Oh, yes! At first light, he would be on

241

his way to carry the good news and to lay his claim to that there money. But for now, he had a crippling thirst on him, and a need to celebrate. A few jugs of ale and a floozy for the night seemed like a just reward for the minute. Tomorrow would be here all too soon, but tonight was Saturday. A night for making merry, and letting tomorrow look after itself!

Molly sat on the edge of her bunk. Through the grimy window panes she watched the dark, lazy clouds against a silver-shot sky. Every bone in her body ached and she longed for sleep. But sleep would not come. Her mind was in turmoil. So many things came to haunt her. Disturbing images had kept her wide awake when she might have enjoyed the rest which she had honestly earned.

All the night long, Molly had softly paced the room, pausing only to gaze at her sleeping children and occasionally to glance out of the window. Dawn would soon be breaking. Outside, there was no breeze nor movement of any kind. It was as though life had run out of time and the earth had died. There was a terrible, sad atmosphere that shocked Molly, and made her wonder at it.

But then she was made to look closer. It was not the night, nor was it the earth that had died; they were merely slumbering. No. The sadness and the awful loneliness were not out there beyond this room. They were in here, in the room itself, and in Molly's own unhappy heart. All that had died was the hope she had fought to keep alive: that faint hope which had kept her going, kept her searching for her man. It had always been a delicate thing, but now, that tiny flame of hope had fluttered its last. *Jack was not here.* He was no place where she had been, and now a cruel and shattering reality came to her like a savage blow. It sent her heart reeling, for after all this time Molly finally admitted to herself that, somehow, somewhere along the way she had lost that which had been very precious to her. The awful realization had crept up on her without her knowing, and now it shone through her thoughts like a blazing beacon. She did not love Jack any more. *She did not love Jack any more!*

'Mammy . . . I'm cold.' In the half-darkness, little Sal had seen the familiar outline of her mammy, bent forward on the edge of the bunk, with her head resting on up-turned palms and a look of dejection about her weary frame. Now, when Molly raised her eyes to glance at the small figure climbing from the bed, the child faintly perceived the tears rolling down her mammy's face. 'Don't cry, Mammy . . . please don't cry,' came the little voice.

'Cry?' At once Molly was on her feet and surreptitiously wiping away the tears. Opening wide her arms, she caught the child lovingly to her breast. 'Whatever makes you think I'm crying, sweetheart?' she asked softly.

'You *are* crying,' little Sal insisted, twisting her body round in Molly's arms and peering into the dark luscious eyes. '*I saw you!*'

'No,' Molly lied. 'Why should I be crying . . . when I've got the three loveliest children in all the world?'

For a long, brooding moment the girl pondered deeply, then in that open innocent way that children do, she said, 'You haven't got Daddy, though, have you, Mammy? . . . and I know you miss him.' Her two skinny arms wound themselves tightly round Molly's neck, as she asked in a small tearful voice, 'When is he coming, Mammy? . . . *When* is Daddy coming to find us?'

Molly was mortified! This was the very first time that

Sal had mentioned Jack in that way. Suddenly it was painfully obvious to Molly that she had been greatly unfair to little Sal – taking her for granted, making her grow up before her time, leaning on her as though she was another woman, instead of a small child who missed her daddy. She wondered now how often little Sal had woken up during the long dark hours when she herself was earning the money that fed and sheltered them. Had her daughter been afraid and lonely without her mammy close by? Was Molly placing too much of a burden on those narrow shoulders, by depending on Sal to mind her brother and sister? Had there been times when either of them had woken in a nightmare, looking for their mammy and, finding her gone, then turned to their elder sister for comfort? Every painful question stabbed at Molly's heart and made her desperate. In that moment, she came to a crucial decision.

'I don't know when Daddy is coming to find us, sunshine,' she told the clinging child, 'but, somehow, I don't think we'll find him here in Liverpool.' She put the girl to the floor and, keeping her voice soft so as not to disturb the sleeping babes, she asked, 'Do *you* miss him, too?' When little Sal slowly nodded, Molly smiled and went on, 'Well then . . . where do you think we should look for him, eh?'

'In *Dock Street*, because if he goes there . . . looking for us, he won't know where we are.'

Molly smiled at the simple logic. 'You're right, sweetheart,' she agreed. But her heart sank to her boots. If she *were* to return to Dock Street, it might not just be Jack that found them! She should have been elated at the thought of Jack being reunited with them. Instead, she felt cold and confused at the prospect. Yet she could not go on as she had done since fleeing the house on Dock Street, especially not now, having seen the true depth of her daughter's feelings. It was possible that Jack might return to Dock Street looking for them – although, somehow, Molly thought it highly unlikely. With the thought came a spiral of disgust.

Thrusting aside her better instincts, Molly promised the girl, 'We *will* go back to Blackburn, Sal. But maybe not to the house on Dock Street.'

'Why not?'

Molly had to think fast. She didn't want to frighten the child by explaining how there were certain people, bad people, who meant to harm them. Instead she told her, 'There'll be new tenants living in the house now . . . the landlord wouldn't let it stay empty, not when there are plenty of people willing to pay for a roof over their heads.'

'Can we lodge with Tilly Watson then? She will let us . . . I *know* she will, Mammy!'

'No, sweetheart. You're quite right, though. Tilly would not refuse to take us in, but it wouldn't be fair . . . she already has a house full of her own brood.'

'Can we ask Nelly then? She's got a big house.'

'No. We can't do that either . . . you *know* we can't!' In spite of deliberately trying to sound matter-of-fact, Molly couldn't disguise the sharp edge to her voice. She saw the girl's blue eyes grow bigger and knew instinctively that the flicker of pain in them was an unpleasant memory: a particular memory, of the day when the two of them were forced to hide in the shrubbery outside the Tanners' house in Park Street.

'Was that man Nelly's friend?' Sal had asked the same question many times during the weeks following the frightful incident. 'I don't like that man,' she uttered now, her voice hushed and cautious, as though she were afraid he might suddenly appear.

'I think he must have been.' Molly wondered whether her own fear of Caleb Crowther had transmitted itself to little Sal, or whether the girl's horror of him was a virgin horror, impressed on her mind by that one, close sighting of him. Certainly he was a fearsome figure, not only grotesque to look at, but sending before him an atmosphere of terror. 'Yes, darling, I think he *must* be a friend of Nelly's . . . or she would never have let such a man cross her doorstep. No, we can't go to the house on Park Street either.'

'Where will we go then?'

'Ssh, darling. Don't you worry your pretty little head about that. You just go back to sleep now, and leave all the worrying to your mammy.' Easy words, thought Molly, but words would not feed them nor put a roof over their heads. Thoughts of Mick came over her. She smiled inwardly at the pleasure his company had brought her; images of the cosy barge insisted their way into the upheaval of her mind, of his tall, manly frame bent over the stove, warming up the stew he had made, or brewing a strong measure of tea. Whatever he did for her and Jack's children was always done graciously and with a loving smile. With the warm, contented memories came a flurry of pain and regret to Molly's young, lonely heart.

How many times had she lain awake in that hard, uncomfortable and lonely bed, reliving that last tender scene aboard Mick's barge, when he had taken her in his arms and murmured, '*I love you, Molly*'? How often had Molly questioned the wisdom of her decision to turn her back on that fine man? So often that she could not count the times.

Now, when little Sal put the question, 'Well, can we go

to Mick, then? I *like* Mick, Mammy,' Molly could find no words to answer. Instead, she gently put her finger to the child's lips. 'Ssh, sweetheart,' she whispered, taking her by the hand and leading her to the bed, where she coaxed the child in and tucked her up. The other two were sleeping so soundly that they were not disturbed; only Tom fidgeted, making a strange little noise as he struggled to roll himself over.

In a while, when she was satisfied that Sal was sleeping, Molly took off her boots and dress, and the cotton undergarments that were more practical than comfortable. In a moment, she also had climbed into the bunk and was heavy with sleep. She wasn't altogether surprised when a stocky little figure climbed in alongside her and nestled close to her heart. It was strange how Peggy seemed to know instinctively when her mammy was ready for sleep. Molly closed her arms about the child, and, in no time at all, the room was quiet, save for the soft, rhythmic breathing of slumbering souls.

Outside, the wind gained momentum, shivering against the walls of the outhouse and pushing in through the many cracks in its aged walls. Soon the rain was spilling down with a vengeance and the night was quickly lifting into daylight. Molly, though, was oblivious to it all. The sleep she had denied herself was upon her at last, refreshing her, and preparing her for the upheavals to come. Upheavals that would try her courage and strength to the full, and of a kind that not even Molly in her worst nightmare could have envisaged.

'But I want to leave *today*, Mr Craig!' Molly protested. 'I was hoping you would pay me my week in hand, and let me go right away.'

'I'm sorry, girlie. I can't do that.' Bill Craig had been up since early light this Sunday morning; first to accompany his wife to her regular service at nearby St Mary's Church, and afterwards to see her safely to the station. It was ten in the morning when he was summoned to the door by Molly's insistent knocking. The sight of her standing there with a freshly scrubbed face and her pretty figure looking especially desirable in that brown, swinging skirt and grey shawl, beneath which was her best ivory-coloured blouse, sent a delicious thrill right through him.

'I've made up my mind to go, Mr Craig,' Molly told him, with a defiant gleam in her dark eyes. 'Please be so kind as to pay what you owe me, and I'll be on my way.'

Unfortunately, the man was equally adamant. He had particular reasons for refusing Molly's demands. And they were very different from the ones he stated now. 'Look, Molly, I don't mean to be harsh. You know I'd pay you up and wish you a safe journey, wherever you mean to go.' He waited, as though for Molly to explain her destination. When it became plain that she had no intention of doing any such thing, he went on, 'But y'see, if you was to up sticks and leave me in a minute's notice like this . . . you'd have to go *without* your pay, I'm afeared. First of all, it's the wife who sees to the wages and such like. And, I'm telling you, girlie, if I was to interfere in her cash-box, you wouldn't be the only one travelling down the road, 'cause she'd throw a blue fit when she got home a Tuesday, and with the black temper she's got, I'd be kicked out that door in no time!' He smiled sweetly and scratched his head, feigning to think of a way out of his dilemma for Molly's sake. 'Naw. Like I say, I'm sorry, but I daren't open that there cash-box . . . it's more than me life's worth, an' that's the very truth.'

Molly was no fool. She knew that he was deliberately
lying. Yet if she were to insist on leaving today, it would
have to be without her wages for the week she had
worked in hand. She could not afford to do anything so
irresponsible. And yet, she had promised Sal that they
would be leaving just as soon as she had told Mr Craig
and collected her wages. 'You *must* have money of your
own!' she said now, ignoring his smile and thinking it too
greasy by half. 'My wages aren't so great that you need
to raid the cash-box.'

'Oh, but they *are*, because, y'see, the wife keeps *every
penny* under lock and key.' He shrugged his narrow
shoulders. 'I'm no good with money. It's *her* that takes
care of all that, and you know yourself how sharp she is.'

Molly couldn't deny the truth of that, because Mrs
Craig might be small and wiry, but her tongue was spiteful at times and she did have a very domineering way
with her. All the same, Molly could not bring herself to
believe that Mr Craig bent entirely to his wife's demands. She had seen him defy her too often in the café
for that to be so. But, be that as it may, Molly was *not*
leaving without her wages, and she told him so in no
uncertain terms.

'And I don't blame you, girlie,' he said in a mock
serious voice. 'I'd be the very same meself. But you'll
have to wait till the wife gets back.' Suddenly, his mood
changed and he eyed Molly in a resentful manner.
'Y'know I'd be within me rights to send you packing
without a penny don't you?'

'How's that?'

'Huh! It's easy to see that you don't often take up an
honest day's work, ain't it?' he sneered. 'Else you'd know
that it's quite in order for me to insist on a week's notice.'

'I've only got your word for that,' retorted Molly, thinking how soon he had betrayed his true, obnoxious character.

'Oh, it's right enough! Just ask around . . . you'll see I'm telling the truth. And besides that, don't you realize what a terrible problem you're setting me, by clearing off without giving proper notice, eh? Where am I gonna find somebody to replace you in a matter o' twenty-four hours?'

'That's your problem.' Molly resented the way he had begun to make her feel guilty. 'The plain fact is, I can't stay on. Me and my young 'uns have a particular place to go.' Suddenly she remembered how kind Mr Craig and his wife had been when she and the children turned up here, cold, hungry and homeless. It wasn't in her nature to be thankless. 'I *am* grateful for you giving me a job and a roof over our heads,' she said in a softer voice, 'really I am, Mr Craig. But I have to move on . . . my children aren't all that happy here, and I dread leaving them on their own when I need to work. You do understand how I can't go though – not without my wages. I've no other money, except the twenty shillings you paid me for *this* week's work. And that won't last long, as well you know.'

'Look, Molly.' He stepped aside and beckoned her with a thin, heavily veined arm. 'Come inside where we can talk things over,' he suggested in a fawning voice. 'I'm sure we can come to an agreement of sorts.' He touched her on the shoulder, appearing astonished when she shrank from him.

'*Can I have my money?*'

He stared at her, dropped his arm and inhaled an almighty breath which he noisily exhaled through his nose. 'You're a stubborn little bugger, an' that's a fact!' he said, with a small chuckle. He stared a while longer, drinking in Molly's dark beauty and calculating how he could take it to himself. Presently, his bony face split into a grim smile. 'All right, girlie,' he said, at the same time stepping aside. 'You'd best come in. I can see you'll not budge till you've got what's due to you.' When she looked both surprised and suspicious, he quickly urged, 'Come in, I tell you . . . it'll take me a minute or two to get the box open.'

'All right, Mr Craig, but I can't stay no longer on account of the children being on their own.' Something about him made her feel uncomfortable. 'Happen it might be better if I were to come back when we're all packed and ready to go.'

'You'll do no such thing! I'm not dithering about waiting for you to knock on the door when it suits you! You'll come inside now, and wait while I get your wages, or you can be off and leave me to think on how I'm gonna find a replacement for you at such short notice.' The smile had gone from his face as he proceeded to close the door.

'A minute or two, then,' Molly reluctantly agreed, 'but no longer.'

It was the first time Molly had set foot in her employer's house. It was a big old house, with stained-glass windows, a regal air, and a sense of desolation about it. There was something especially forbidding about the outside – as though it was brooding for the grander age to which it belonged. It was rumoured that, at one time, the house had been the home of an industrialist who came on hard times and was forced to sell. That was the beginning of its descent. Over the years the house and its land were separated; the land was quickly developed, afterwards leaving only a narrow stretch behind where the outhouses stood, and a wider area to the side where the diner was erected, to serve the dockers and other passing trade.

Molly felt like a trespasser. The house was deep inside, with a long narrow passage going down to the sitting-room. She felt on edge, reluctant to stay for even one minute. But she so desperately needed her wages, and after all, she and the young 'uns would soon be on their way. 'A few minutes' – that's how long he said it would take to get her wages together; a few minutes, and she would be gone from this house into the fresh air again. Quietly, she followed his long, thin figure, listening to his meaningless chatter and hoping that Sal would be all right with her brother and sister for the little while she would be gone.

'You sit there . . . I'll not be long.' The man gestured towards a sprawling black horse-hair chair beside the fireplace. 'The cash-box is kept upstairs. I'll fetch it.'

Shivering from the damp atmosphere, Molly made no move to do as he bid. 'I'll wait here,' she said.

His eyes raked her face, then, shrugging his shoulders, he muttered, 'Suit yourself.' Afterwards, he turned away and hurried from the room, leaving Molly with a bad feeling. She was tempted to run from the house before he returned, but the thought of heading for the open road without her wages kept her there. 'They're *my wages*,' she whispered into the room, as though justifying her intrusion. 'I worked myself ragged for them . . . and I'm not leaving here without 'em, no sir!'

As good as his word, Bill Craig was back downstairs wihin a very short time, the cash-box tucked under his arm. 'Can't find the key,' he told Molly; 'Like I said, the wife's a canny bugger . . . keeps it on her person, she does.' He put the cash-box on the table and opened the cutlery drawer beneath. When he had drawn out a small, bone-handled knife, he smiled at Molly, telling her, 'You'll have to grip the box tight, while I prise the lock open.' He clasped his long fingers around the box, pinning it to the table. 'Like this,' he said, 'you keep it still, mind. I don't relish the idea of slicing a finger off !'

Against her better instincts, Molly felt compelled to do as he said. After all, it was true that he could not hold the box and lever the lock open at the same time because the box was secured by a large, free-hanging padlock. He would therefore need one hand to hold the padlock, and the other to prise it apart. All the same, when she came to his side and took hold of the box between her hands, it was with growing trepidation.

'That's right, girlie. You just keep it from dancing about, while I get to grips with this bloody lock.' He chuckled, and to Molly – who was decidedly nervous at being in such close proximity to him – it was a disturbing sound.

As he worked on the lock, grunting and quietly swearing, Molly could feel the warm stench of his breath on her face. Disgusted, she turned her head to one side, all the while telling herself that at no time in all the weeks she had worked for him had Mr Craig made any unseemly suggestions, or been anything other than polite and impersonal. Somehow, she was reassured.

In a moment, though, the reassurance was shattered when Molly inadvertently glanced into the mirror which hung on the wall opposite. *What she saw there made her tremble!* It was his face. A face filled with longing, a face supposedly bent to its task, but instead gazing at Molly, the narrowed eyes intent on her hair, then lowered to her breast where they lingered a while. In that split second when Molly saw the terrible danger, there came a sharp click, and the lid of the cash-box sprang open. Instinctively, Molly pulled away, already backing towards the door, her dark eyes accusing and bright with fury. When he came forward, smiling down at her, his two arms outstretched and a certain look in his eye, her one thought was to get out of there, get away from him! Turning, she made a run for the door.

'Oh no you don't, girlie!' With astonishing speed he was on her and slamming shut the door. When Molly began struggling and biting into the hand that was over her mouth he laughed aloud. 'Struggle an' shout all you like, Molly darling. There ain't a soul to hear you. Unless o' course you want to frighten your brats? But then, what could three young 'uns do, eh? Except cry for their mammy an' wonder what she were screaming at.' He shoved her towards the table, putting her back to it, and thrusting his body against her. 'Naw! . . . I'm willing to gamble that you won't scream an' carry on, girlie. I reckon you ain't the type to frighten three little innocents that way.' He saw the horror in Molly's eyes and, pushing his face close to hers, he laughed in a low, sinister voice. 'I won't hurt you, girlie. But, y'see . . . I won't rest either . . . not till I feel you naked against me.' He began unbuttoning her blouse, pausing only to hold out his unsteady hand in front of Molly's eyes. 'Look there, I'm that excited I can't stop trembling. You're a real beauty, y'know that? The kind a man hankers after in the dark, early hours. Oh, I bet your skin's got the touch o' velvet, ain't it? . . . An' you know how to treat a man, I reckon; know how to pull him into them slim thighs an' allow him a deal o' pleasure he'll not likely forget in a hurry.' His eyes were heavy with longing, his lips partly open, moist and reaching for her. He groaned when Molly struggled against him. 'No, no. Don't spoil it, girlie,' he murmured, pinning her tight in his strong, thin arms. 'Look, see this?' He dragged her to where the open cash-box lay, its contents bulging. 'Bank notes, an' silver coins,' he said. 'You cooperate with me . . . make it worth me while, and I swear I'll give you *three* times your wages. What d'you say to that, eh?'

Molly's reply was swift and painful. With fierce determination that took him by surprise, she twisted herself far enough out of his grip to reach the cash-box. With her fingers locked round it, she brought it upwards in a straight line towards his head. There was a brief instant when his eyes opened wide with surprise at the bank notes fluttering to the carpet. Then, as the sharp edges of the tin box came crashing to the side of his head, the eyes darkened with fury. Molly felt his grip tighten round her throat, and she knew that it was either him or her! She felt herself choking, the room was spinning round and her senses were failing fast. But she found within her a mighty strength born of desperation. Again and again she brought the tin box against his temple, until at last his grip was relaxed. Yet still she could not move, because his whole weight had her trapped beneath him and the table. Slowly, she inched her way from beneath him, and when he slid silently to the floor, the awful horror of what she had done came over her. As she stared down, wide-eyed and disbelieving, her every limb was shaking uncontrollably, and a tide of nausea flooded her senses. Was he dead? Dear God, she hoped not! Her shocked eyes followed the trail of blood, crimson splashes everywhere; on the tablecloth, on the carpet, on the bank notes littered there, on her. *On her!*

Terrified, Molly threw down the bloodstained cash-box and ran into the passage. From there, she found the scullery, where in a frenzy, she dabbed at the blood spots on her blouse with a wet flannel, until the spots became large, shapeless dark patches. After she had splashed clean her face and hands, she would have run from the house with never a glance back. But she could not. In spite of the fact that he had meant to ravage her, how could she leave him, not knowing whether he were alive or dead? Molly knew that if she was to leave now, her conscience would never let her rest.

Shivering with fear, she went out of the scullery, down the passage and back into the sitting-room. On hesitant feet, she came to where the figure of Mr Craig lay sprawled beside the table, the open cash-box only a short way away where she had dropped it, and its contents spilled over a wide area. Even though she was in desperate need of those silver coins that were strewn about, Molly could not bring herself to touch them. 'Mr Craig.' Her voice trembled in the terrible silence. She came closer, peering down at his face to see whether there was any sign of movement. There was none. Panic took hold of her. 'Dear God, what have I done?' she whispered into the eerie silence, and back came her own horror-stricken answer, 'I've killed him. *God above, I've killed him!*'

For a long and seemingly endless moment, Molly stood there loudly sobbing, her hands spread against her throbbing temples and her disbelieving gaze fixed to the man's pale, upturned face, with all manner of terrible thoughts raging through her. She had committed *murder*! There was no doubt in her own mind that she would surely hang for it. Suddenly, above all else came the thought of her children. And it was this thought that quickly sobered her. She must protect them at all cost, for they had no one but her. No one at all.

Quickly, Molly dried her eyes and composed herself. Sal was quick to notice when anything was wrong, and Molly did not want the child to suspect. She took one last look at the man who had so viciously attacked her, and still seeing no signs of life, she went quickly from the house, consoling herself with the facts that no one had seen her go there, and no one had seen her come out. He would not be found until the next day, by which time she would be long gone. But Molly knew that the awful memory of it all would never leave her, neither would the fear. These she would carry with her, wherever she went, always hiding, always the hunted.

The sound of the front door closing echoed through the house. There was no other sound. No movement – only the signs of a bitter and fierce struggle having taken place. But then, after a while, there did come a small sound, a pitiful and weak cry that became a groan. The groan subsided, and in its place emerged the sound of laughter, wicked, spiteful laughter, and amidst it, the softest of murmurs. 'So, you reckon you've done for me, d'you, girlie? . . . Well, you just take that thought with you. *And may it haunt your every waking hour, you little vixen!*'

Bill Craig stood unsteadily before the mirror, ill and dazed, angrily beholding the deep, uneven tear along his temple. 'Little bastard,' he muttered. 'I hope the divil don't give you a minute's peace.' He might have deserved it, but that was no comfort. He might have saved a whole week's wages that belonged to her. Even so, there were only two things on his mind right now.

Firstly, he wished every curse on earth might pursue the bitch. And much more importantly, he had his work cut out to clean this place up before Mrs Craig returned. She was a clever, shrewd woman, who'd already accused him of hankering after Molly. As it was, he had to explain why she'd gone so sudden. Damn her eyes! Women were a curse, and that was a fact!

It was some weeks later when Mick came into Bill Craig's café, asking after the one called Molly. He spoke to the surly proprietor at great length, but was made to depart heavy hearted when he learned that Molly had left some time ago. And no, there was no man with her. Just three young 'uns.

He had thought to find her here, after the seaman had so vividly described her. The unfortunate thing was that the seaman had carried the information too long, having 'met this lovely little floozy and spent a while drinking to me good fortune'.

Mick, though, was undeterred as ever. He would find his lovely Molly: for his love of her, for the Tanners who seemed so very anxious to talk to her and who had launched their own enquiries, and not least, for Molly's own sake.

Chapter Eleven

The children's laughter was a tonic to Molly's heart. She had watched their playful antics and enjoyed their squeals of delight these past twenty minutes and more; minutes that had gone all too quickly, each one ingrained on her memory for all time. If she had nothing else in this world, she had her children and she thanked the Good Lord for them.

Seated at the top of the stone steps that led down from Tilly Watson's scullery to the enclosed yard below, Molly looked a sorry little figure. After those long weeks of hiding and scraping a living any way she could, her already slim figure was now pathetically thin, with the threadbare clothes hanging on her like a shapeless sack. Even the long, respectable shawl given to her by Tilly could not disguise the undernourished form beneath. But for all that, there was a unique strength about Molly's pale, almost gaunt face, and a particular beauty that drew a body's attention; especially the black eyes which were now drawn up towards the radiant sky of a lovely May evening. Certainly, to the young man who was closely regarding her from the parlour doorway, Molly's special beauty outshone even the dazzling sunshine that spilled over her upturned features highlighting the exquisite loveliness of that familiar face and awakening in him a deep aching desire that he could no longer suppress.

For a moment longer, Joe Watson let his eyes rove over Molly's unsuspecting countenance. The more his gaze lingered on her, the sharper became his need for her. At last, he thrust his two hands into his jacket pocket and turned away sharply, consoling himself with the pleasing thought that there would be time enough to show Molly how strong were his feelings towards her. Time enough, *later*, when the Watson brood were all abed and Molly's three were also tucked up for the night.

In the short time that Molly had stayed under his mother's roof, Joe Watson had come to know her routine like the lines on his own hand. After she had made sure her offspring were quietly sleeping, Molly would creep through the silent house to the back steps, to the very spot where she sat even at this minute – there she would stay until the night grew darker and colder, wistfully looking up to the shifting sky and its scurrying shadows, searching for some elusive distant thing that was known only to herself.

During these dark, quiet hours, Joe Watson had stayed hunched against his bedroom window above, watching, needing, and wonderfully intrigued by the lovely secret creature that was Molly. Of late his longing for her had become an obsession that he could no longer control. Any feelings of decency and respect that he might have had towards his mother's unlikely lodger were in danger of being hopelessly smothered by other, more urgent feelings: of greed and lust, of selfish appeasement and the driving desire to take Molly to himself, even against her will if needs be. The ugly strength of his feelings were a disturbing revelation to him.

Now, as he left the house to make his way to the

nearest public bar, Joe Watson smiled to himself. 'Oh, yes, Molly me beauty . . . there'll be time enough for me to tell you how much I want you, when there's only you and me . . . and the dark to hide in, eh?' He chuckled aloud and went on his way with a livelier step at the thought of Molly, naked, leaning into his arms and gazing up at him with big dark eyes ablaze with a desire to match his own.

By the time he strode into the bar, Joe Watson had convinced himself that the lovely Molly wanted him every bit as much as he wanted her. Oh, that wasn't to say that she had ever given him any encouragement, because she had *not*, other than to indulge in a friendly conversation and to express her gratitude at his willingness to 'put up with me and the young 'uns for a while'. No, he could not claim that Molly had ever betrayed her deeper emotions to him. But then, she was one of those rare women who possessed a quiet tongue and kept her innermost secrets to herself. And wasn't it a known fact that often, when a woman said no, she was only being coy and meant yes all along?

Deep down, Joe Watson knew that Molly felt the same way he did. Knowing it made him bolder, filled him with arrogance and caused him to be so impatient that the hours before darkness seemed to stretch before him like never-ending years. But he comforted himself with the belief that the waiting would be worth it when he had Molly close in his arms. Oh yes, the waiting would be well worth it! And who knows? He might even be so foolish as to take her for his wife. Oh, but that might be going a bit *too* fast, he cautioned himself. After all, she had three young 'uns from her estranged husband. And tying yourself up for life to one woman wasn't all that wise. Especially if you could take that woman to your bed whenever the fancy came on you. *No*. First things first. In these past weeks, Joe Watson had cursed the fact that Molly already had a husband and he himself might be made to wait for her hand in marriage. Now, though, he was quietly grateful for it.

'Mammy, tell Tom to behave himself!' little Sal moaned. 'He won't let us play nicely.' With a loud sigh, she put down her side of the makeshift skipping rope and ran to where Tom was mischievously wrenching the other end from Peggy's determined grasp. 'I've showed you how to skip in the middle of the rope, you bad boy!' she scolded him. 'And you have to take your proper turn. If you don't want to play, then go and sit on the steps with our mam!'

'*Bad boy*,' echoed Peggy, stubbornly refusing to let go of the rope, '*not* your turn!' There then followed a bevy of jeers and calls from Tilly Watson's assorted offspring, who were dutifully lined up to wait their turn at running into the gyrating rope, where they might manage a few quick skips before getting their little legs hopelessly entangled, at which point they were promptly banished by Sal to hold the rope while others took their place at the end of the line.

'Do as Sal tells you, Tom,' Molly instructed, beginning to come down the steps, stopping only when she saw him turn from the indignant Peggy and scurry in that dipping, lopsided fashion to the back of the queue, his face spread wide in a happy, mischievous grin. Flattening himself against the wall, he looked up at Molly with such laughing eyes that she didn't have the heart to chastize him further. Instead she smiled back at him, shook her head in exasperation and began her way back up the steps, resuming her cold seat at the top and thinking how it would soon be getting dark.

'Little sods!' Tilly Watson had come to the scullery door to see what all the shouting was about. '*You lot buck yer ideas up!*' she yelled, wagging a finger to the upturned faces. 'Any more arguing an' you'll be put to bed afore yer time . . . d'yer hear me?' When the colourful assortment of heads – including those of Molly's three – all frantically nodded, she mumbled quietly to herself, before yelling again, 'Yer soon coming in anyroad, yer buggers . . . it's not long to yer bedtime as it is!' This observation produced a trail of loud moans and groans, which she stopped short by threatening, 'Yer can give over belly-aching . . . else I'll march the bloody lot of yer up these steps this very minute!' Silence descended. 'Huh! So think on!' she finished, cunningly winking at the amused Molly, who dared not look down at the small, fearful faces in the yard, for fear they might see how much she was enjoying Tilly's 'fierce' banter.

It was little over an hour later when the children were all herded in, moaning and pleading to stay out 'just a bit longer'. They whined all the way up the steps in the fading daylight; they argued round the big old table when Molly and Tilly dished out the last of the bread and preserve; they cajoled and cried when their hands and faces were being washed, and en route from the parlour to their beds they blamed each other for their curtailed enjoyment. 'It's all *your* fault, Tom!' Tilly's eldest complained, glaring at the unconcerned and misleadingly 'innocent' face of Molly's crippled lad. '*You* started all the trouble!'

'*Weren't* Tom's fault!' defended Peggy, furiously scratching at her arm, then beginning to bawl when she saw how red and sore it was.

'*Now* see what you've done!' accused little Sal, taking her small sister into her embrace, her vivid blue eyes drilling into Tilly Watson's eldest.

'She did it *herself*!' came the retort. 'Serves her right, an' all.'

Suddenly it was a free-for-all, with everyone squaring up to each other and heated threats of 'I'll smash yer in the gob', and 'Oh yea? Just try it on, matey!' being flung about.

'Whoa!' Molly quickly intervened, putting herself in the midst of pushing, squirming bodies. In a surprisingly short time, she had them despatched to their respective bedrooms and peace was restored – for another day at least.

'How much longer will we have to stay here, Mammy?' Little Sal leaned up in bed on one elbow, a troubled look in her eyes. 'Why can't we find our *own* house, eh?'

Molly smiled and after putting her fingers to her lips, she murmured, 'Ssh, sweetheart . . . don't wake the young 'uns.'

'But I want us to have our own house,' Sal insisted in a harsh whisper.

'We will,' promised Molly.

'When?'

Molly was always surprised by her daughter's direct-ness. She seemed never to be prepared for it. 'When your father comes back,' she told the attentive child.

'*He's not coming back!*' In the flickering candlelight Molly saw the tears in Sal's eyes and her heart turned over. For a long, painful moment, she searched for a suitable answer, but she could find none. Her own unhappy gaze mingled with that of the girl's, who, throwing her small thin arms round Molly's neck, told her gently, 'I do love you, Mammy.'

Hardly able to talk for the painful lump that leapt into her throat, Molly held her daughter very close, very tight, gathering strength from that slim, seemingly fragile frame and knowing in her own heart that between the two of them in that precious minute, *Sal* was the stronger. 'I love you, too,' she whispered now, gently releasing the clinging child and easing her back into the bolster. 'Go to sleep, sweetheart,' she urged, stroking the girl's forehead until the tired blue eyes closed and it seemed that, at long last, Sal was ready for slumber.

'Good night, God bless, Mam,' came the weary, unhappy little voice.

'Good night, God bless, sunshine,' Molly replied, bending to place a kiss on the smooth, tear-stained face. After satisfying herself that Peggy and Tom were sound asleep, she went to the window and looked out at the gathering darkness. The gas-lamps in the street below threw out eerie yellow haloes, whose lights flickered in the shadows and brought the darkening corners to life.

For a while, Molly was held entranced, her face pressed hard against the cold, stiff window and the glow from the candle in her hand creating a strange image of herself in the window-pane. She gazed at the reflection for a long, curious moment, being both shocked and comforted by what she saw there. *Shocked* because of the gauntness of her features and the weariness in those dark eyes that stared back at her; *comforted* because, in spite of the gaunt features and the weariness, the image was *her*! It was her face, her eyes, *herself*. None of that had changed, only the outside. Inside she was still Molly. She had her wits and her strength. She had her children. With God's help she could go on.

Up to this point, Molly had been deluding herself that perhaps Jack might come along looking for them. Maybe, wherever he was, he might wake up one morning and remember that he had a wife and children who needed him. Now though, Molly had stopped deluding herself. Jack was not coming in search of them. *He never would.* Stranger still to Molly was the realization that she was glad; she never again wanted to set eyes on him! But her love had not turned to hate. Worse still, it had become a cold indifference.

Just now Molly had told little Sal they would have their own place when Jack came home. It was a lie. Molly hoped the good Lord would forgive her. She had known for some long time now that, if she and the young 'uns were ever again to have a place of their own, it would be by her own efforts. There was no other way. But how? *How?* She had lost count of the long, lonely nights when she had sat on the scullery steps, searching for a way, agonizing over what to do, which way to go, or how she might earn enough money to secure and keep a roof over their heads. As it was, life was difficult enough. Tilly had been good enough to take them in when they had arrived here, tired and afraid. But it was a situation that could not last for much longer – 'Only temporary, mind . . . just till yer get fixed up. Two weeks at the most,' Tilly had said.

Tilly had already extended that 'two weeks' to four. Though she never made an issue of it, it was clear that her patience was wearing thin. After all, she had her own troubles, and this little house was bursting at the seams.

Molly suspected also that Joe was impatient to see the back of them. He hadn't said as much, but now and then she would catch him staring at her with a strange look on his face. It made her feel uncomfortable. Oh, she didn't blame him! He was a hard-working man who had tended to the family when his father died. He had every right to come home to a house free of lodgers. Molly understood that. If the house next door – which had been hers and Jack's – had not already been let to an elderly couple, she might have been very tempted to climb in through the back window and lay claim to it. Silly thoughts though, she now reminded herself, because if she wasn't able to pay a proper rent, the landlord would soon fetch in the strong-arms to put her on the streets. No, she had a lot to thank Tilly for, and she was very grateful. Molly hadn't forgotten how desperately ill she was that night when she and the young 'uns arrived at Tilly Watson's door. No sooner had little Sal rattled on the door than her mammy slumped to the ground, wasted and ill, swamped with relief at having safely delivered her babies to a familiar place, and not caring anymore whether she lived or died.

After two weeks of Tilly's care and attention – and the good-natured observation that Molly had better get well for 'I ain't being lumbered with *another* brood o' brats!' – Molly was well enough to get from the bed she shared with Tilly. A few days after that, she was pottering about and gaining strength by the day.

'You still look like a bag o' bones, gal,' Molly told her reflection in the window. The black eyes had begun to twinkle though, and the strong lines of her lovely features were not quite so sharp. Her hair, however, was a pitiful sight – still thick and black as midnight, but hacked short by Tilly who believed 'hair harbours lice, my gal . . . an' I ain't got no time for picking 'em out.' So she had brought the meat knife from the scullery and while Joe held out the rich thick hanks of Molly's hair, Tilly had chopped away at it. At the time, Molly hadn't minded. Now though she winced to look at it. It had cheered her when Joe told her, only the other day, how he thought it suited her short like that and 'fetches the beauty of yer eyes out'. Tilly had laughed out loud, saying how comical it was that Molly had been at death's door, and 'here yer are, worried about yer crowning glory!' Molly had laughed too, feeling vain and foolish. Since Jack wouldn't be coming back, and she had thoughtlessly sent Mick away, what did it matter whether she had shining black hair to be proud of, or a tangled shocking mess? It didn't matter. Not one little bit.

All that really mattered to Molly now was how soon she could be on her way with the children, so as not to be a burden on Tilly any longer? This was her dilemma. There was no one she could turn to for help. Two things she did know though: she had to find a way of making money and she had to leave this house. And it must be soon! For Molly was indeed convinced that she and the young 'uns had out-stayed their welcome. All the same, she wished she felt a great deal stronger and able to easily shoulder the load that was about to fall on her.

On tiptoe, Molly went across the bare floorboards to the big brass bed where her three children were fast asleep. The bed was really Joe Watson's but he had given it up to Molly's three and was content to sleep downstairs on the couch in the front parlour. Molly thought him a fine young man. Somehow, though, she always thought of him as being much younger than herself, when in fact he was a little older. She supposed it must be because of his laughing, wayward manner, which put her in mind of young Tom.

Before leaving the room, Molly took a moment to glance round, holding the candle high, and wrapping her shawl tighter about her when the air struck damp and chilly. This house was the same as the one next door – small rooms with high ceilings and crooked floors; upstairs were three bedrooms, each with a long walk-in cupboard and tiny fire-grate. Downstairs were the front parlour, always a cold, empty space, and the back parlour with its huge, black oven range and steps leading down to the coal-hole. Following on from that was the scullery, with its stone-flagged floor, big pot-sink and outside door to steps leading into the yard below.

Molly closed the bedroom door behind her, thinking how Joe Watson's room was nicely furnished in comparison with the same room next door; at least when she and Jack lived there with the children. All *they* had in that same room was a bed and a chest of drawers, while this room had a wardrobe besides, and a comfortable arm-chair with a square matting covering the floorboards beside the bed. Tilly's bedroom was the same, but with a row of nails along the picture rail on which to hang her clothes. To Molly, it was all sheer luxury, and her respect for Joe had grown when Tilly claimed, 'My lad's looked after us well since his father died'. Molly thought how grand it would be if she were to have somebody to look after her in the same way. Yet she knew there was no one but herself. And wasn't likely to be.

* * *

'Where've yer been, Molly gal? I thought ye'd fallen asleep on the bed, trying to get the young 'uns off.' Tilly Watson had been rocking herself back and forth in the wooden rocking-chair by the fire-grate. When she saw Molly coming through the door from the passage, she slowed the rocker to a halt and reached down for the pint-pot which had been standing on the fender. Holding it out to Molly, she said, 'Make us a fresh brew, there's a good 'un . . . we've time for a sup or two before our Joe gets back.' Here she chuckled, 'I expect he's got caught up in a game o' cards. Oh, he's a bugger for the gambling, but he'll never go beyond the coppers in his pocket,' she added quickly, with a firm shake of her head. 'Sticks well within his limits, does our Joe. Oh aye! I know that, because old Bill the knocker-up goes there reg'lar . . . *he* likes a game o' cards too. And he has nowt but good ter say about our Joe. First and foremost, Joe looks out for his family. *Then* he enjoys what few coppers he has left!' A self-satisfied smile spread over her features, as she reminded Molly, 'It's a pity your Jack weren't as responsible, the bugger! He wants his arse kicking, and no mistake!'

'Do you want milk in your tea, Tilly?' Molly had been deeply wounded by the other woman's thoughtless observation and was deliberately making no response to it. She knew Tilly meant no real harm. She was not by nature a spiteful person. Besides, Molly reminded herself, Tilly's comments were only the truth, and she herself had come to recognize that more and more. Jack had been her whole world and she would have lain down her life for him. Now he had deserted her, and the children were all she had left. *They* were now her world, and these little innocents had no one else to look to but her. She would not let them down.

When Molly returned from the scullery with Tilly's tea, she was told in a kindly voice to 'sit down. There's things we need to talk over'. Molly's heart sank to her boots. It's time, she thought, time for me to be sent on my way, for Tilly's patience is at an end.

'I know what you're going to say, Tilly,' Molly ventured, doing as she was bidden and seating herself in the upright standchair by the table, 'and I can't blame you. Me and the children have put on you long enough, but I've got plans in hand and we'll be on our way soon.' She hoped that Tilly would be kind enough to give her at least a couple more days, because she still felt incredibly weary and bone tired. Besides which, she had been exaggerating when she told the other woman that she had 'plans in hand'. She had plans to leave, yes. But she had not the slightest idea of where she and the children would go. Somehow the thought of roughing it yet again in a derelict house or a disused factory was terrifying to her. But happen she would have no choice in the matter, for the truth was that she and the young 'uns were beggars. Beggars could not be choosers. Oh, if only she were strong again! If only she could shake off this feeling of tiredness, when every bone in her body hurt and there were times when it was a terrible effort just to put one foot before the other. 'You've been good to us,' Molly said now, 'and I'm grateful for that.'

'That's as may be.' Tilly Watson peered at Molly through quizzical eyes. 'But if I was to tell you the truth . . . I'd say as how I've really enjoyed having another woman in the house.' Here she chuckled and fell back in the chair. 'Even if I'm a good twenty year older than you,' she reluctantly admitted. Her gaze remained

271

intent on Molly's face, and when Molly smiled, it came to her not for the first time how astonishingly lovely this young woman was. Wasn't it strange, she asked herself, how the most gentle and beautiful of souls were always the most vulnerable and how they were ill-used by others. But then, she reminded herself, wasn't it always the very same? The fiercest and most cunning would survive on the blood of those meeker, gentler creatures. Yet wasn't it also true that the Lord himself promised, 'The meek will inherit the earth'.

For a moment longer the older woman took quiet stock of Molly: the roughly shorn hair, the thin figure that was still very seemly even wrapped in a threadbare shawl which Tilly had intended throwing out, and that hauntingly lovely face with its strong lines and big, expressive eyes. There was something very special about Molly. In spite of everything – the many weeks on the road, the suffering she had been through and the illness that had taken its toll – there was still something at the core of Molly's being that was strong, determined and most admirable.

While musing to herself and thinking on Molly's particular character, it came to Tilly how she was reminded of another such creature; one who had been 'used' by others and thrown to the wolves, as it were. One who had suffered more than any other woman she had ever known, and yet had risen above it all to emerge even stronger and wiser. That woman was *Emma Grady* – now Emma Tanner. That one, and this one, known as Molly. They were two of a kind. Like peas out of the same pod!

Tilly Watson's conscience had long since bothered her where Emma Grady was concerned, for she knew beyond a doubt that it was *her* own testimony that had helped to convict Emma Grady and consequently get her transported to the far side of the world. And all for shameful greed. For the taking of a cash-box belonging to Emma's ma-in-law on the night her son was killed – 'murdered' by Emma and the woman who was Emma's only friend. O' course, it were more of an accident than murder. But at the time, it suited Tilly Watson to claim how she had 'seen it all! . . . He were pushed, your Honour. *Murdered* right before me eyes!'

The bank notes which Tilly had taken secretly from the tin-box were long ago spent; most of them on furnishing this very house and affording a set of nice clothes for her and her entire brood. Because of them bank notes, the pantry had never been bare. Oh, the money was long gone now, but it had set the Watson family up well enough, and buried the old man in a decent fashion. Now, what with Joe fetching home a good wage, they managed well enough and, compared to other unfortunates, they had few worries.

The only worry that plagued Tilly was her conscience. She was beset by nightmares about having helped to convict a young, innocent creature who had no parents and was cursed with more enemies than friends. Yet it was a long, long time ago. Too many years had fled, and too much water had passed under the bridge for her to make amends.

All the same, it had eased Tilly's mind when Emma had returned home, a wealthy and influential woman. She might have gone to her there and then and confessed her wickedness. But what good would it have done? It was too late. Emma had endured her ordeal with courage and had done well. Tilly accepted that she too must endure her own particular ordeal of guilt, for it was self-imposed. Apart from which, she had come to believe that it was wiser to keep her own counsel than to foolishly reveal how she had deliberately lied to the courts. Emma's own uncle was a Justice! You had to be very careful with the likes o' them, because they'd clap you in jail soon as wink at you! On top of which, that Marlow Tanner adored Emma, and though he was well known as a likeable and fair-minded fellow, there was no doubt he'd be up in arms at how Tilly Watson had put the finger on his Emma. No. It were always wisest to keep your own counsel in such cases.

All these years, Tilly had wanted to make amends for her terrible deed, yet was unable to. Helping Molly – who to her mind was another Emma in the making – had done a great deal to banish the nightmares that had haunted Tilly Watson.

Now Tilly revealed as much as she dared when she said, 'It's been grand having you here . . . hand on my heart, Molly, you've done me more good than you know.'

'Bless you for that, Tilly,' Molly leaned forward to squeeze the older woman's shoulder, 'but I know what a strain it's been . . . all these little bodies underfoot and more mouths to feed. I don't fool myself that the few shillings I earn here and there are anywhere near enough to fill their bellies.'

'I won't deny that there have been days when I'd be glad to see the back of you . . . when the buggers have been scrapping and my head's felt like it's been jumped on! But I'm not chucking you out on the streets. I'd rest easier in my bed of a night if I knew you had somewheres to go.' She felt Molly move her hand away and she saw the forlorn look in her face. Eyeing her severely, she asked point-blank, '*Have you?* . . . Have you somewhere to go? Come on, the truth, now!'

'No.'

'So, you intend to leave here and take to the roads, is that it?'

'We'll be fine, Tilly. I'll find a place for us now that I've got my strength back.'

'Be buggered!' Tilly snorted. 'Have you looked at yourself lately, eh? . . . Thin as a poker and weak as a kitten! Oh, I've watched you . . . trying to put on an act. But the truth is you're nowhere near fit . . . certainly not fit enough to be trudging about the streets in all weathers.'

Molly could see the other woman's dilemma. On the one hand, she was obviously concerned that Molly and the children should be all right. On the other, she was secretly relieved at the thought of having her little house returned to the bosom of her own considerable brood. All Tilly wanted was a reassurance from Molly that there was nothing at all for her to reproach herself for. Without hesitation, Molly gave her that assurance. 'You are *not* to worry yourself over us, Tilly!' she told her firmly. 'In spite of the fact that I'm still a little thin, I feel better than I've felt for a long time. You remember I was talking to the chimney sweep when he came to clean the flue last week?'

'Aye . . . I thought the pair of you had a lot to say to each other. It took the bugger long enough to do a simple job and *that's* a fact!' replied Tilly good-naturedly.

'Well, he told me how he'd heard there were these big hotels in London . . . crying out for chambermaids and kitchen hands.'

'*London!*' Tilly was horrified.

'It's a chance, don't you see, Tilly? A chance for me and the young 'uns to make a fresh start.' Molly had been quietly churning the idea over in her mind and now that it was out in the open, she was greatly enthused by the idea. Though she would not easily admit it, somewhere in the back of her mind were the last words spoken to her by Mick, before they parted. He had expressed his intention to leave these parts and, as far as she knew, he also had gone south. Perhaps as far as London. Who knows, she might even come across him there?

In these past weeks, when Molly had at first been too ill to leave the house, then later, when she had hesitantly ventured out, she had been most careful to stay well away from the wharf. Her reasons were twofold – firstly, knowing that Mick had left the area some time back, she felt it would be a sad, lonely place without him there; secondly, she had to be most careful not to show her face in places where she might be seen and recognized. Certainly she had to avoid the wharf, if only because of the fact that Marlow Tanner was a regular figure there; Marlow Tanner meant *Emma* Tanner, and Emma Tanner meant the *Justice Crowther*! Her blood ran cold at the very thought of him. Especially now, since she had been forced to flee Liverpool. She had not forgotten (how could she?) that man in the café left for dead. And she had killed him! She was more of a fugitive now than ever. There could never again be a moment's peace.

Molly was not so much concerned with her own safety as with that of the children. So now, when Tilly made a suggestion, she was instantly tempted to reject it out of hand, but then felt compelled to consider it more carefully. 'Oh, but Tilly . . . how could I leave my children behind? It's unthinkable!' The very idea shrank the heart inside her.

'If you ask me, my girl, it's the most sensible thing you can do!' Once Tilly had made her mind up, there was little shifting her. 'You go to London and find that job you were talking about. Get yourself a place where you can all stay together. *Then* come back and collect the young 'uns. They'll be content enough here, I promise . . . no harm will come to them.'

Molly was mortified at the thought of what little Sal would have to say to such a suggestion. 'Oh, I don't know that I could leave them behind, I really don't.'

'Then *don't* go to London . . . or anywhere else. Look for some'at round these parts . . . and I'll help you.' She was curious as to why Molly would even *think* of going to such a fearful place as London, so far away, and full o' strangers.

'I can't stay round these parts, Tilly . . . I *must* get away.' Molly's desperation and fear betrayed itself in her voice.

'What is it, Molly?' Tilly had suspected for some time that Molly was hiding something, afraid, maybe even running from someone. Certainly, when she arrived here at this door some four weeks since, she had the look of a haunted soul.

If ever Tilly Watson saw real fear and desolation in a body's eyes, she saw it when Molly first recovered after being close to death's door for nigh on a week. She felt *then* that Molly was driven by a dark secret. *She felt it now.* Her curiosity got the better of her. 'I weren't born yesterday,' she said in a chastizing voice, 'and I ain't so stupid not to know when somebody's on the run. What have you been up to? What are you afraid of, eh? Who's after you?' Encouraged by Molly's astonished look, she insisted, 'A trouble shared is a trouble halved, they say. You can trust me . . . I took a liking to you the same day you moved in next door with your family . . . though I never did think much to that bloody fellow o' yourn! Strange though, how I don't know all that much about you. As a rule, I like to know all about them as live next door. But you, you little sod! . . . You're a right secretive bugger an' no mistake!' Suddenly, she was deadly serious, telling Molly, 'But you're in trouble. I can tell. There is something badly wrong. What is it? Somebody on your tail, is it? After money, are they? Or have you done something unlawful . . . is *that* it, eh?' When Molly remained silent, she threw her arms out wide and shook her head. 'All right. It's none o' my business, I suppose. I've got no right prying.' She began to get from the chair, looking surprised and relieved when Molly put out a hand to press her back.

'Please, Tilly, don't take offence,' entreated Molly, feeling ashamed that it might appear she had thrown the older woman's genuine concern back in her face.

'I was only trying to help . . . in my own clumsy fashion,' Tilly told her, at the same time settling back into the horse-hair armchair and looking up at Molly with a slightly wounded expression.

'I know,' conceded Molly gently, 'and you're right . . . I *do* owe you an explanation.' After all, Molly told herself, she *had* turned up here with three young 'uns and taken every advantage of Tilly's kindness. 'No doubt you've been wondering where I *really* went when I left next door?'

'Ah, well now . . . it *did* cross my mind that you hadn't altogether told the truth when you said you were making a new life with your Jack . . . that he'd got himself a job an' a place for you all to stay. The bugger never did strike me as a suitable provider. And what with you clearing off so quickly . . . like you were running away . . . well, it did set me wondering, I must admit. Oh, I were right glad for you, dearie . . . and nobody wanted you properly settled more than me, honest to God! But, well . . . I had my doubts if you must know. Then, when you turned up on the doorstep four weeks ago looking like you were on your last . . . riddled with a fever and half-starved, well!' She pursed her lips and seemed to sink into the memory of that particular day. Suddenly she was accusing, looking at Molly sternly and wagging a finger. 'I expect you let yourself go hungry in order to keep the children fed, didn't you, eh?' Without waiting for an answer she went on, '*Don't deny it!* And, if I were to tell the truth, I'd say as how I would do the very same. Us mothers . . . we're all alike, and that's a fact.' Without warning she fell silent, and folded her arms while keeping her attention on Molly's thoughtful face. She was obviously awaiting an explanation of what had taken place between the day Molly left the street and the day when she came to Tilly's door seeking refuge.

Molly felt obliged to give that explanation. Besides which, it was all a great burden on her sorry heart and maybe what Tilly had said was the truth – 'a trouble shared is a trouble halved'. And so, with no small reluctance and a deal of trepidation, Molly opened up her heart to this kindly woman. She described how she had in fact fled the area because 'someone meant harm to me and the children'. She went on to explain how she lied about going to Jack, for fear that Mick might be tempted to follow her, 'and because there were *others*, more sinister, who might also make it their business to track me down'.

'But surely Mick the bargee would never hurt a hair on your head, child?' Tilly was astounded. 'You're right, though. He *did* come a-looking for you . . . but I could have sworn it were only because the fellow thought the world of you. I've *always* been given to understand that he wanted nothing more than to look after you and the children . . . *adored you* . . . that's what *I* thought!'

'You're right, Tilly. Mick wanted me to go south with him. He told me how much he loved me and the young 'uns.'

'What then? . . . You didn't love *him*, is that it?'

'Oh, no. I *did* love him . . . I *do* love him! Only at the time I was too blinded by my feelings and loyalty for Jack.' A sadness came into Molly's dark eyes. 'I had an idea that I could find Jack and when I did, everything would be all right. But I was wrong.'

'Then it *weren't* the bargee who meant you harm?' When Molly shook her head, the older woman nodded, as though satisfied that she had not misread that man's character. 'Who were it then? Who frightened you enough to make you up sticks and take to the road with three children . . . one a cripple!' she loudly demanded. It was obvious that she was ready to do battle.

Engrossed in their conversation, neither Tilly Watson nor Molly heard the front door latch being lifted and the door opening to admit a certain young man whose head was light from the booze he had tasted, and whose heart was pining for want of a woman. That woman was Molly. The young man was Tilly's eldest son, Joe. Being suddenly intrigued by his mother's emotional outburst, he came on unsteady tip-toes to the parlour door, where he pressed himself against the wall and strained his neck so as not to miss a single word. What he heard held him rigid and astonished.

In the space of a few minutes, Molly had confided everything to this woman whom she instinctively felt she could trust. She told how Justice Crowther had hounded her over the years and of the manner in which Jack had saved her from that man's clutches when Crowther had snatched her from the hut which had been home to her and old Sal, the lovable tramp who had found her as an infant. She revealed her terrible fear of that man and the awful consequences were he ever to ensnare her again.

The more Molly confided in Tilly Watson, the more she felt a great burden being lifted from her shoulders. It was true that 'a trouble shared is a trouble halved'. Only Molly had more than *one* trouble. She had a whole batch of them, and each one had bred another, until now – try as she might – she could see no way out of the cage they had made for her!

'Ah, you poor little sod!' exclaimed Tilly, her eyes popping out like bright buttons at the awful tale. 'And you've kept all this to yourself this long time? Why! It's a wonder you've not gone crazy with it all.' She patted Molly's hand affectionately. 'You poor little sod,' she repeated, gawping at Molly in wonderment. 'Mind you . . . I'd rather it were *you* than me who's made an enemy of that Justice Crowther. By! He's a right evil bastard and no mistake!' A look of horror crossed her features, until in a tick, she was staring at Molly again, urging her, 'Go on then, Molly . . . so where did you go from here? What adventures befell you? Oh, and *what* in God's name made you come back . . . when you knew that the Justice might still be looking for you? No wonder the first thing you did when you came out of that fever was to beg me not to tell anybody you were here!' She felt herself break out in a cold sweat and began feverishly dabbing at her forehead and face with a grubby hankie snatched from her pinnie pocket. 'Oh, dear Lord! . . . To think what might have happened if he'd found out! *What!* . . . the bugger might have even come bursting into this very parlour!'

'Now can you understand why I have to leave your house, Tilly? The last thing I want is that you should get involved.'

'I see.' Tilly Watson was never one to be intimidated and, as suddenly as she had broken out in a fearful sweat, she was calm again, and outraged that Molly should have been so persecuted by that fiend of the law that she had been forced to flee her own home. She said as much to Molly, and was reluctantly understanding when it was then explained to her that 'I wouldn't have been able to keep the house anyway, Tilly, because I couldn't afford the rent after Jack went off . . . leaving me with yet another mouth to feed.'

As Molly finished her story, she held nothing back. In complete and utter trust of this sympathetic woman, she told everything; describing the weeks of living rough, her constant fear that the law was waiting round every corner; her hopeless search for Jack and, last of all, with heavy heart and in such a small, fearful whisper that even the silent listener in the passage could not hear this awful confession, she described how Bill Craig, the café proprietor, had attacked her . . . how they had struggled and she had struck out. 'He fell to the floor . . . lifeless.

Oh Tilly, I killed him! When they catch me, *I'll hang for sure.*' The tears flowed down Molly's face as she thought of the three innocents sleeping upstairs. 'What of them?' she asked. 'What of the children?'

Tilly Watson was shocked. In her time she had cheated, lied and stolen in order to keep a roof above their heads. But Molly! *Molly had done murder!* No wonder she had to keep on the move. No wonder there were times when she seemed afraid of her own shadow. She glanced at Molly's dark untidy head bent into the long, slender fingers; she saw how distressed and desperate the unfortunate creature was, and to her mind there was only one solution.

Getting to her feet, she put her two arms around Molly's trembling shoulders, saying stoutly, 'They'll not harm you while you're in Tilly Watson's house, I can tell you that! From what I can see, my girl, you've already decided right . . . get to the big city and make a new life . . . change your name. Do what you have to do. But like I said before, Molly . . . the young 'uns will be best off left with me until you've got work and found a place to stay.' She sensed that Molly was about to resist that particular idea and was quick to intervene. 'All right, I'll tell you what. Let's call it a day and get a good night's sleep on it, eh? Tomorrow, you can tell me what you want to do.'

'You're a good woman,' Molly said now, gently kissing Tilly on the cheek and smiling when it blushed fiercely. 'Like you say . . . I'll sleep on it.' She turned away. 'Good night. God bless. We'll talk in the morning.' Going to one of the brass candleholders on the sideboard, she took up a match from the tray close by, struck it alight on the rough-edged side, and put the flame to the candle-wick.

With Tilly Watson only a few steps behind, carrying the oil-lamp, Molly went up the stairs to where the children were soundly sleeping, calling back softly when Tilly bade her, 'If yer gonna be a while afore you come to bed . . . mind you creep softly in beside me. I don't want you waking me up once I've gone off!'

After a while the house was quiet, the deep silence perforated only by the soft, distant snoring coming from Tilly Watson's room.

As a rule, Molly would sit a while with the children before tiptoeing out of the room and down the stairs to the back steps, where she would enjoy the cool solitude of the evening, indulging in thoughts of the past and all that might have been. It was at times like these when she sorely missed the eccentric old woman who had raised her from a babe-in-arms.

Old Sal had been Molly's heroine, her mammy and her world. Yet for all that, she had never given Molly the one thing she had always longed for – the truth of her origins. *Who was she? To whom did she belong?* How many times had she asked those questions? Old Sal had not been able to tell Molly the truth – simply because she herself never knew, always believing that the girl-child she found in the gutter had been left by the little people. '*Now I'll never know*,' sighed Molly, gazing fondly at her own three babies. 'But, if I don't belong to anybody else, *I belong to you*,' she told them. The tears sprang to her eyes as she leaned forward to kiss each tiny face in turn: little Sal, her first-born, named after the old dear whom Molly had adored, little Sal, with her vivid blue eyes and bold, forthright manner. Then came Peggy: sturdy, stocky little thing, blessed with thick, rich hair the colour of midnight and dark eyes so like her mammy's. And young Tom, possessed of a happy mischievous nature, lovable and infuriating all at the same time, yet cursed with a pitiful deformity that must hamper him for all his life.

Molly's children were uniquely different, each with their own special personalities and physical traits. She loved them all with fierce protectiveness. They were her life. Her reason for living. Because of these three help-less innocents, she had to stay free, and shrug off the weariness that had settled on her.

On this night, when Molly could so easily have climbed into bed and let the welcoming waves of slumber ebb over her, she found herself going back down the stairs. There was too much on her mind, and important things to be decided. Tomorrow she must answer Tilly's suggestion that she leave the children in her care for as long as it took Molly 'to find a place'.

In her heart, Molly had already decided. She could not leave the children behind. But wasn't that a selfish decision, she argued with herself. Wouldn't the children be safer and happier here, with Tilly and her brood, at least until Molly could fetch them? And, if Molly had her way, that would be sooner rather than later. So her heart led her one way, and her reason another.

There were other things to be carefully considered also: in particular, where did she intend going? London, she had said. But why not further *north*, instead of south? Did it matter, so long as she could isolate herself and the young 'uns? Where the Justice Crowthers and Emma Tanners of this world could not pluck her out? Ah, but remember what the chimney sweep had said: 'The big hotels in London are crying out for chamber-maids and kitchen hands'. He'd also said that they had attic rooms and such like, where a body could make its own little nest. And a nest for four needn't be much bigger than a nest for one, isn't that right, Molly asked herself, as she placed a candle on the scullery window-ledge.

It was a beautiful night. The sky was a dark, velvet ocean pitted with dancing stars and lit by a crescent-shaped moon. All round were strange and familiar sounds; the scurrying of little feet in the cellar below, the whistling of a cool breeze squeezing through the many chinks in the high stone wall that skirted the yard. And the gentle rush of the nearby canal was like a soft lullaby on the night air. Molly cherished these snatched moments of an evening; it was so peaceful here, so private and sheltered. For a moment, she pushed all the worrying and urgent thought to the back of her mind, and opened her soul to let in all things lovely.

Strange, how the first emotion that filled her with joy was the memory of a tall, handsome fellow standing proud and straight aboard the barge that was his home and could have been hers also – Mick. His name murmured itself on her lips and the memory was sweet. 'Oh, Mick, whatever will become of us?'

While at the back of the house Molly's thoughts were engaged in memories both bad and pleasant, there was another who also indulged in deep thought.

Joe Watson feverishly paced the pavement at the front of his mother's house, now and again leaning on the street lamp and allowing his senses to imagine all manner of secret fancies. Only a short while ago he had returned home delightfully intoxicated and boldly entertaining the prospect that not only would he make a play for Molly, but that when he did, that young woman would be so flattered she would eagerly fall into his arms, ready and willing to please him in any way he chose.

Now though the excited fellow had been shocked almost into sobriety, and made to see that there was more to Molly than he had at first imagined. The conversation he had secretly 'overheard' between his mother and her young lodger had certainly given him food for thought. From all that had been disclosed, one article in particular stood out bold in his mind – for some reason which he had not quite grasped, *Molly was a fugitive!* And worse still, it was the Justice Crowther whom she'd come up against!

'God Almighty,' Joe uttered, 'of all the enemies she could have been dealt, it seems she's drawn the worst.' Suddenly he was made to weigh his fancy for Molly against his fear of the most hated and reviled fiend ever set on this earth. 'Do I want Molly so much that I'd take on her enemies an' all?' he asked himself. And back came his own answer – '*Do I bloody hell as like!*'

There was no doubting that Joe Watson had a very real and very urgent hankering for the lovely, desirable Molly, who – though presently a bit too thin and scruffy for his usual liking – had a certain presence and grace that only made her loveliness more magnificent. Yes, he wanted her right enough, he decided. But whereas just over an hour ago he would have taken her with all her needs and troubles – three kids an' all – now it was a different tale altogether. There wasn't a woman alive who could be worth getting tangled up with the Justice for? *Not even the lovely Molly!* Oh, but that wasn't to say that he couldn't strike up a little fun and frolics with her, now was it, eh? he asked himself. And again, back came his own answer. 'O' course not! It's obvious the wandering Jack ain't fulfilling his manly duties, so like as not Molly would welcome this fine fellow as a substitute.'

Joe Watson had always prided himself on being a quiet favourite with the women. It was very plain to him that Molly was first and foremost a woman. Therefore, like all women, she had natural desires. That's where *he* came in – to satisfy those desires, and in the process, to fulfil his own deep-down needs. Needs that were getting more urgent by the minute, and which, even with the name of Justice Crowther still buzzing in his mind, gave him the courage to softly push home his key in the front-door lock, quietly let himself in and, on tiptoe, creep along the passage, then through the living quarters out to the scullery steps . . . where he knew instinctively Molly would be sitting alone, counting the stars and thinking about things that were private and precious to her.

The night had grown chilly. Shivering, Molly drew the shawl close about her shoulders. She had sat there on the hard steps, their marble coldness striking into her and penetrating her very bones.

It seemed like an age that she had stayed there, thinking and worrying, searching for so many answers that would not come. Only one thing was certain to her. She had no choice but to make a new life for herself and the children, and in a place so big and which teemed with so many people that she and the children would be as difficult to find as a raven up a chimney.

London Town! The decision was made, and Molly felt better for it. *But when?* Dare she wait until she was stronger and perhaps got together a few shillings? Or was time running out too fast now? Was the law closing in on her at this very minute? The thought made her tremble. And what to do about the bairns? In her deepest heart, Molly knew that Tilly was right. If she were to head for London with three young 'uns on her skirt-tail, it would certainly make things that much more difficult. But then, Molly reminded herself, she had travelled many foot-weary miles, through town and countryside alike, every step of the way followed by three pairs of little feet, all as determined and brave as her very own.

All of these memories brought a gentle smile to Molly's face, and a grateful warmth to her heart. But she could not ignore Tilly Watson's warning. She would be all kinds of a fool not to realize that trudging the roads and finding the occasional stopping-off place was altogether different from searching for both a permanent home and a secure position which would provide for them all. What employer would take her on with three young children beside her? And one a cripple. It was hardly likely.

Try as she might, Molly could not resolve her dilemma. Her task might prove impossible with the children along, but, oh dear God above, how could she leave them behind? Even in the safe hands of the good woman who had taken them in.

Suddenly Molly's terrible anxiety was thrust away by the thought of Jack. Jack-the-Lad! *Jack the Waster!* The boy who had never become a man. Too much of a coward to face up to life. The dreamer who had cruelly deserted them.

Molly had no illusions left where that was concerned.

Jack would *never* be back. She knew that now, and all of her worries were swamped by the anger such realization brought. Molly had loved him so. *Idolized him!* And in her blind love she would never have dreamed of a day when her feelings could be any different.

That day had been in the making when Tom was born and her man had fled at the sight of his tiny, deformed son. It hurt Molly to remember. She wondered whether she might ever forgive Jack for that. One thing she *did* know: her love for Jack had begun to die on that night, until now there remained in her heart only a cold, empty place where that love had been. To set eyes on him now would never revive that love. Instead it would only bury it forever, along with any future they might have had.

Yet if the thought of Jack brought distress to her, the memory of someone else made her weary heart soar. To her mind now came the image of Mick, strong and virile, protective and caring.

In a moment, Molly recalled something that dear old Sal had told her: 'We're all of us entitled to one big mistake in us lives, Molly darlin'.' Only now did Molly realize the profound truth of those words. Because hadn't she already used up her entitlement to 'one big mistake' when she had sent Mick away? To Molly's mind, she could never make a greater mistake than that one.

Where was he now? Molly tortured herself. Was he in some other, wiser woman's arms? Had he forgotten her entirely? What a fool! What a blind, ignorant fool she had been! And now, it was all too late. Suddenly the tears were burning in Molly's eyes, spilling over and trailing down her face. 'Oh, Mick! Mick! If only you knew,' she murmured into the darkness, leaning her head into the palms of her hands and gently swaying in the manner a child might do when comforting itself. Her sobs were so soft that they fell away on the still night air, unheard – except by Molly herself, and by the other who, for these past few moments, had stood at the top of the steps, discreetly out of the candle-light, becoming angered by the name he had heard on Molly's lips.

Joe Watson knew more of Mick the bargee's where-abouts than did either Tilly Watson or Molly herself. He knew, for instance, that Mick seemed very well in with the Tanners these days, or so the ale-house gossip had it. And that Mick's barge had been laid up at Liverpool for some time, while the fellow himself was said to be 'tramping the country like a soul with a purpose'. There had been much speculation. But nobody appeared to be familiar with the true facts as to what ailed Mick Darcy. None dared ask, for Mick was a very private fellow, it was said.

Since the day when Molly had arrived on his mother's doorstep, Joe Watson could so easily have mentioned the gossip concerning Mick Darcy. But being the cun-ning fellow that he was, his instincts had warned him to stay quiet. After all, he knew how the bargee had a liking for Molly and he suspected Molly was not altogether unimpressed by Mick Darcy's attentions. And since he himself had growing designs on Molly, it wouldn't do to discuss possible rivals, now would it? And deep down, Joe Watson had wondered whether it wasn't Molly herself that Mick Darcy was searching for! With all this in mind, he had not even confided in his own mother. What! Old Tilly would turn stark grey in a minute if she believed her own provider was considering taking on another woman – a woman with three brats an' all. Imagining the ensuing confrontation between himself and Tilly, and still somewhat under the influence of the jugs of ale he had sunk that night, Joe Watson was made to quietly chuckle.

'*Who's there?*' Molly thought she heard something and would have clambered to her feet if Joe had not quickly stepped into the moonlight. 'Oh, it's you, Joe.' There was relief in her voice. As he came down the steps towards her, she discreetly dried her eyes on the corner of her shawl. For one awful minute, Molly had imagined it might be little Sal standing there. Her eldest daughter had an uncanny knack of knowing when her mammy was most in need of comfort. Molly had been careful of late not to lean too heavily on that darling girl. For she was only a bairn, however much she tried to be 'growed up'. To her shame, Molly had been in real danger of forgetting that. Then there was the matter of schooling. Tilly mentioned only the other day that the authorities were sending men round to check on the children. It was all becoming a real nightmare.

'You're a strange one, Molly darling.' Joe eased himself on to the same step as Molly, casually smiling into her dark eyes and thinking how beautifully they sparkled in the soft moonlight. The tears were still bright in the blackness of her gaze as she returned his smile. Encouraged, he gently insisted, 'You ain't fooled me . . . I heard you crying, gal.' He was careful not to reveal that he had also heard her call out Mick's name, and that he could easily have strangled her because of it.

'Oh, don't concern yourself,' Molly was quick to tell him. She was embarrassed that he had seen her crying. 'Women do get weepy sometimes.' Her smile deliberately brightened as he continued to gaze at her. She wanted no sympathy. Though she was grateful that Joe had not complained about her and the children being here, she was in no mood to discuss her personal problems.

'So, it's mind me own business, is it?' Joe teased, boldly taking Molly's hand in his, and being pleasantly surprised by the warmth in those long, fine fingers. 'You needn't worry,' he told her with a cheeky wink, 'Joe Watson knows when not to poke his nose where it don't belong.' His hand on hers remained steady, even though inside he was trembling with excitement. 'Y'know, Molly . . . I've never said this to any woman, but *I admire you*. The way you manage to cope without a fellow . . . and you being made responsible for three young 'uns. There's not many women as'd gladly shoulder such a burden. Mind you, them three bairns o' yourn . . . well, they're great little troopers. Just like their mammy,' he grinned, priding himself on knowing the surest way to Molly's heart was through the brats. 'They do you credit, gal. And don't think I ain't seen how you spend many an hour walking young Tom up and down the yard . . . encouraging him to make the best use of his bad leg, so's he might grow up without being altogether crooked.' Here, he shook his head and was obliged to be truthful. 'You mustn't fool yourself on that score though, Molly, because it's as plain as the lovely nose on your face that one o' Tom's legs is a terrible lot shorter than the other.' When he saw the light dim in Molly's eyes, he cursed himself, 'Aw, now . . . I ain't saying as all your efforts is in vain, or that you should give up. No indeed!' Seeing his slender chances slipping away, he tenderly squeezed her hand and filled his voice with compassion. 'Take no notice o' me, Molly. You just carry on doing what you think best. It's amazing what a body can do, if they put their mind to it. There ain't a single thing wrong with a body holding faith in miracles . . . an' who says they can't happen, eh? Who says that? Not *me*, an' that's a fact!'

Molly was made to laugh at his desperation to make amends; although she did think he had held her hand quite long enough. 'We all have to hope for miracles,' she told him, gently drawing her hand from his grasp. 'I won't ever stop believing that one day something *will* be done to help my Tom.'

'O' course, Molly!' He was downhearted that she had felt the need to tuck her two hands beneath her shawl. If he were not careful, Molly would be up and away to bed, taking a golden opportunity with her. Oh, but not if he were cunning. Tread gently, Joe old pal, he told himself, or your chances of bedding this tasty creature will come to a sorry end. He could just imagine it! Milk-white skin, smooth and warm against his nakedness, open, inviting thighs waiting to draw him in, and soft round teats hardening beneath the tip of his tongue. Oh! It was all too much. How could he stop himself trembling? Why didn't he take her here and now, *against* her will if needs be? No! No, he wouldn't dare. Not with his mother in hearing distance. Besides, if he were wily, he might get far enough into Molly's good favour that she'd want him to bed her on a *regular* basis. Now then, wouldn't that be a fine thing, eh?

'Joe . . . I haven't really thanked you for letting me and the young 'uns stay under this roof so long,' Molly said, shifting her position so that she was looking full into Joe's face.

'Aw, you're very welcome, Molly,' he replied, thinking

how she'd be like an innocent child in his hands. 'Besides, don't forget . . . it ain't really *my* roof. It's me mam's.' He sidled closer. Molly's eyes were so unusually lovely, so darkly entrancing.

'I know, but it's *you* who keeps the family and pays the rent. Tilly's told me that often enough.' Molly was well aware that one harsh word from Joe might have obliged Tilly to turn them out on the streets. Although, to be fair to Tilly, she did have a strong mind of her own, and could be infuriatingly stubborn when she wanted. Many was the time Molly had witnessed a real clash of wills between mother and son. But these two had a great deal of love and respect for each other. She had seen that also.

'I'm not denying that I'm a good provider and a hard-working man,' boasted Joe Watson, deciding to play along that particular line. He had an instinct that Molly would be most impressed by that, being as her husband was neither, and because of it, Molly and the young 'uns were the ones to suffer. 'Oh, yes. To my mind, it's a man's duty to take care of his family.' He kept his voice soft and his gaze gentle. 'I'm not a fellow to shirk his duty, I can assure you of that!' Oh, how he ached to grab her into his arms!

'You're a good man, Joe. There's no denying it.' Molly was faintly amused by his glowing self-opinion. All the same, it was nothing less than the truth. He was a hard-working man, and he certainly looked after Tilly and her brood. 'Any woman would be proud to have you as her man. When the right girl comes along, Joe, well . . . she'll be very fortunate, that's for certain.' Molly began gathering the tails of her shawl together. The night air had grown bitterly cold and she found herself shivering.

Greatly encouraged by Molly's words, Joe reached out both hands, placing one on Molly's slim shoulder and the other beneath her chin, cupping it gently so as to raise her face towards him. When Molly looked at him with big, surprised eyes, a thrill raced through him. Quickly he asked, 'Would *you*, Molly? Would *you* be proud to have me for your man?'

Molly had been astonished when he had put his hands on her. She was even more astonished by his question. 'I didn't mean you to take my words that way,' she told him. 'I'm sorry, Joe . . . you misunderstood me.' She wriggled uncomfortably, but he made no move to release her.

'But you do like me, don't you Molly?' he murmured, his face so close to her that Molly could feel his warm breath against her mouth. The taint of booze filled her nostrils. *So, that was it!* Tilly's eldest had been drinking and was full of false courage.

'Well, of course I do. You've been very kind to me and the children.'

'And, you think me a pleasant-looking fellow . . . handsome, wouldn't you say?' His voice was low and caressing.

In her own mind, Molly could not deny that Joe Watson had a certain charm, a special attractiveness that might appeal to women; with that thick, wavy hair, warm blue eyes and his lithe, muscular figure, there was no doubt he had swept many a girl off her feet. All of this raced through Molly's mind, but in this situation she was most reluctant to voice it aloud.

'You *do* think I'm handsome, don't you, Molly darling? . . . Happen you even *fancy* me a bit, eh?' As he leaned forward, and Molly sensed his intention, she

296

made a determined effort to break free. Even then, however, being conscious of the fact that he was under the influence, she must be careful not to make him lose his footing. A tumble down the stone steps and into the flagged yard could easily prove fatal.

As it was, Molly found herself struggling more to keep Joe Watson upright than to ensure her own escape. 'For God's sake, Joe . . . let me pass!' There was a moment when the pair of them nearly went headlong. But instead of giving Molly the leeway she needed, Joe Watson was determined not to let his moment go. With a laugh, he swooped her to him and before Molly could even object, he kissed her full on the mouth – a long, demanding kiss that filled her with alarm.

His need of Molly was most obvious by the manner in which he pressed himself against her, pushing her back against the wall, and beginning to fumble at his trousers with his one free hand. In his growing excitement, his teeth sank into Molly's lips, causing a slight trickle of blood to escape.

With a last, determined effort, Molly twisted herself away from him, gasping with horror when he made a frantic grab at her and lost his balance! She was helpless as he stumbled sideways and fell on to the steps, before sliding ever so slowly over each stone rising, until with a muffled thump, he came to rest at the bottom, his jacket tangled round his neck, and his trousers limp round his boots.

For one awful minute Molly was petrified, staring down at the misshapen lump and fearful that he'd drawn his last breath.

When she hurried down the steps to investigate, however, Molly's fears were stilled. Joe had come to no harm, 'Come the morning, every bone in your body'll ache,' Molly told his prostrate form, 'and it's no more than you deserve, Joe Watson!' She couldn't help but chuckle at the poor fellow. Yet, all in all, the experience had not been a pleasant one. Certainly not one which she would ever hope to be repeated.

As Molly returned to the parlour, where she collected Joe Watson's greatcoat from the nail on the door, she recalled the ardour of that young man. The more she thought about it, the more serious her mood became. There was no doubting that Tilly's eldest had a yearning for her. A yearning that she had not been aware of. Until tonight.

Oh, it was true that Joe Watson had been influenced by the jugs of ale he had downed at the ale house. But wasn't it also true that, while the ale might have plucked up the courage for him to make advances to her, the wanting itself was already in him? That particular thought disturbed Molly a great deal. Suddenly she was made to recall how, on occasions, she had caught Tilly's eldest staring at her in a strange manner which she took to be disapproval of her and the young 'uns being there. Well! It was plain to see that *that* was *not* the case at all. The simple truth was that Joe Watson had a hankering to bed her! There could be trouble in that, thought Molly. Real trouble. Of a kind she could well do without!

On swift, silent feet, Molly returned to the place where Joe Watson still lay, open-mouthed, loudly snoring and out to the world. Where she had been amused before, she was now troubled. 'You've made my mind up, Joe Watson,' she told him, while carefully draping the heavy greatcoat over his figure, and tucking in his limbs out of the cold. 'I can't stay here another day. It's London Town for me. And the sooner the better!'

For some reason she couldn't fathom, Tilly Watson suddenly woke up in the early hours. Climbing out of bed, she went on bare feet to the window, shivering and moaning when the cold floorboards struck chilly to her toes.

At the window she peered out into the sky, still quite dark, but beginning to shimmer at the edges where the sun was coming up. 'Bloody cats, I shouldn't wonder!' muttered Tilly, wondering what had disturbed her at such an unearthly hour. 'Climbing atop o' one another . . . mating and marauding! Waking decent folk from their beds.'

Opening the window she leaned out, ready to throw the first thing to hand at any moving shadow. 'Get away with you!' she said in a loud whisper, shaking her fist and almost toppling over the window-ledge when she saw a movement in the yard below. Curious, she peered harder. 'That ain't no bloody cat!' she muttered. 'I'm buggered if it ain't a *fella*!'

Quickly Tilly closed the window and rushed back to the bed where she wrapped herself in a shawl. Grabbing the oil-lamp, which she had lit on waking, Tilly went from the room, satisfied herself that all the children were fast asleep, and then began her way downstairs. '*And where's that Molly?*' she muttered. 'What the devil's going on?'

On reaching the parlour, Tilly's temper was not improved by the discovery that her eldest son was not yet tucked up asleep on the couch. 'There'd best be some good reason for such goings-on,' she told the empty couch, 'or my name's not Tilly Watson!'

Passing through the back parlour to the scullery, Tilly was shocked: as she swung her lamp by the big table in the centre of the parlour, she caught sight of a folded note with the name 'TILLI' written on it in big, bold letters.

Setting down the lamp on the table, Tilly carefully unfolded the note, screwing up her eyes in typical fashion as she read, with great difficulty, the following large scrawl:

Tilli,
I've gon to London.
Pleez mind my babis til I can fetch them. Tell them
  I luv them.
I've put my trust in you and God.
Luv, Molly.

'Well, I'm buggered!' Tilly was so overcome that she felt the need to fall into a nearby standchair. 'Well . . . I'm buggered!' Suddenly it came to her that something untoward must have happened for Molly to have made such a swift and fearful decision to leave her precious young 'uns behind. Oh Molly knew right enough that they'd be well looked after and kept safe by Tilly – there was no question. 'But she were so *agin* it!' Tilly said aloud in a shocked voice. 'I thought she'd *never* agree to leave them young 'uns . . . though o' course *I* knew that it would be for the best. Oh aye! They'd be much better off with me . . . tucked up in bed of a night, with a proper roof over their heads and some'at substantial in their bellies. *And* they'll be waiting here when their mammy comes to fetch them.' Tilly had no qualms that

Molly had done the right thing. What she could not understand was what in heaven's name had driven Molly to run off in the middle of a cold, dark night? It weren't like the lass. Not at all. Molly were the sort who would have waited till morning, when she could have talked her plans over proper, and explained to the bairns why it were best to leave them with Tilly. 'And has she even a shilling to her name?' Tilly wondered out loud, 'Or a bite to eat with her?' A quick rummage in the pantry revealed that Molly had taken nothing from there. 'Though the Lord only knows, there ain't much in there to *begin* with!' tutted Tilly. Then Tilly received a second shock.

'Molly, you bugger . . . what did you push me away for, eh? I'm the best fellow *you're* likely to get in a hurry! . . . The *only* one, I shouldn't wonder. Come here, you flighty bitch!' Joe Watson stumbled up the steps and into the half-light of the scullery, one hand struggling with his falling trousers, and the other making a clumsy grab for the shawled figure which turned, startled, from the pantry door.

When Joe Watson's bloodshot eyes caught sight of the woman's disbelieving face, he almost fell back out of the door with astonishment. '*Mam!*' His voice was incredulous.

In a second, he was frantically drawing up his trousers, apologizing profusely and entreating Tilly, 'I didn't know what I were saying, Mam, honest! I've sunk too many jars at the ale house . . . went into the yard for a pee and . . . I must'a fell over or some'at.'

Tilly was having none of it! So! *Here* was the reason for Molly fleeing into the night. This bugger had tried it on. Frightened her. Made her feel it wouldn't be safe to stay where she was easy game. '*Why! You filthy swine, our Joe!*' Tilly was incensed that a lad of hers could take advantage of somebody who'd come to this door for shelter. '*Bloody men!* You're all the same . . . look at a woman and all you see is a bare arse!'

Time and again Tilly lashed out at the hapless fellow, who was losing the battle to hold up his trousers with one hand and fend her fierce blows off with the other. 'Well, she's run off to London Town! . . . You've frightened the poor little sod away. So, now you can work a bloody sight harder and feed the three extra mouths she's left behind in my care. And you'd better hope she comes back for them sooner rather than later.' With each word she landed a resounding clap round his ears. ''Cause they're not going short of *nowt*, d'you hear? Molly's three are to be treated the very same as my own, for as long as they're under this roof. *D'you hear? You fornicating bugger!*' She pushed him aside and angrily slammed and bolted the back door. 'Get out of my sight. You're not only drunk . . . You're shameful. *Shameful!* That's what you are!' She grabbed up the oil-lamp and swept past him, pushing him away with a look of disgust when it seemed he might fall against her. 'You want to thank your lucky stars that your dad ain't here to see this day, Joe Watson,' she called on her way through the parlour, 'because the thrashing *I* just gave you wouldn't be nothing to what you'd have had from him! *He* were a good man. Not the sort to take advantage of an unfortunate young woman deserted by her old man and left with three bairns to worry about. Well, now *you* can worry about them, can't you, eh? . . . Till their mammy's able to fetch them away!'

Alone in the darkness of the scullery, Joe Watson

leaned unsteadily against the wall, cold and aching in every inch of his body, both from the time he had spent crumpled at the foot of the steps, and from the angry attack made on him by Tilly.

But now Joe Watson was angry too. And smarting. And deeply humiliated. There was something painfully belittling in being thrashed by a woman, even if it were his own mother and he couldn't hit back, and even if he *had* deserved it! On top of all that he couldn't forget how Molly herself had also belittled him. Joe Watson never dreamed the day would come when he was turned down by *any* woman, let alone one who must be starving for want of a fellow. '*You bitch!*' he hissed into the darkness. A well of fury rose in him. 'You bloody trash, Molly! I'll not forgive you . . . and I'll not forget how you've turned my own mother on me!'

Long after Tilly Watson's gentle snoring sounded through the house, her eldest son lay on his couch downstairs, his anger and humiliation a burning pain inside him. His greatest fear was that the blokes at work or in the ale house might find out what had taken place here this night, and how he'd been so badly used by two women. If it was ever made public knowledge, his life would be made hell. The thought of all that had happened was like a sore inside him, a terrible hatred that simmered and spread until he could think of nothing but revenge.

Suddenly it came to him! And with such clarity that he was forced to sit upright in his bed, a smile of delight on his face, and a feeling of satisfaction in his wounded heart.

'The brats!' he cried in a whisper. '*Molly's three brats*.

So *I'll* be the one to provide for them, will I?' He chuckled. 'Like bloody hell I will!' He had no intention of doing any such thing. But how to rid himself of them, now that was another matter entirely.

Like a bolt from the blue it came to him. While mulling over the conversation he had overheard between his mother and Molly, Joe Watson was made to recall a name. A certain name that made even him shiver in spite of himself. Justice Crowther. Molly's self-confessed sworn enemy. 'Oho, Molly my darling . . . you'll rue the day you ever stirred up trouble in this house!' His laugh was awful to hear, but not so awful as his cruel intent.

'But when's me mammy coming back? . . . I want her to come back!' Little Sal's vivid blue eyes swam with tears as she looked up at Tilly beseechingly.

'Aw look, sweetheart. If I've told you once this morning, I've told you a hundred times . . . your mammy won't leave you here a minute longer than she has to.' Tilly had been under siege from the girl's questions ever since she'd got from her bed. She'd felt bad enough about leathering poor Joe the way she had; got up special early an' all, to make friends with him, she had. Although her intention was to make it plain that she thoroughly disapproved of the way he'd behaved! All the same, she hadn't behaved very well herself either going at him like that. After all, he was a grown man now. No, she'd done wrong, and meant to tell him so. But when she came down, all ready to mend the rift between them, he weren't there. The bugger had gone, and not even his snap-can with him. It worried Tilly, because Joe did a long, hard day at work. And if he had no snap-can with him, what would he have to eat, eh? After a while of fretting, Tilly decided that he must mean to come home at midday for some'at to eat. She'd talk to him then. Everything would be all right between them; she was sure of it. But then, she was *not* sure of it. 'Oh, Sal . . . I'm telling you, your mammy's only gone to get herself some work . . . and a place where you can all live.' She was wearied by little Sal's insistent questions, although she felt a deal of sympathy for the lass.

'Will she be back tomorrow?'

'Not tomorrow, no,' Tilly told her firmly. 'That don't give her much time to get it all sorted out, does it, eh?' She took her hands from the sink, where she was up to her elbows in dirty breakfast crockery, and with a gentle sigh she wiped them on her pinnie before resting them on the girl's small shoulders. 'Has your mammy ever left you before?' she asked.

'No.'

'Would she leave you at all, if she didn't have to?'

'I don't think so . . . *no*.'

'Your mammy loves you bairns more than anything in the world. You know that, don't you?'

For a long, painful moment there came no reply, and it was obvious to the onlooking woman that the child was fighting inside herself. When suddenly little Sal burst into tears and flung herself forward into the woman's arms, Tilly crushed her tight in a loving embrace. 'Go on, young 'un,' she said softly, 'you bawl your little heart out if you want.' Which the child did. After a while she stepped back from the haven of Tilly's arms. Wiping her eyes on the back of her hands, she looked up at Tilly, and the woman was astonished at the resolve in Sal's face. 'All right now, are you?' she asked.

Instead of an answer, she got yet more questions.

'Me mammy's not been *taken* away, has she? She's not in trouble, is she? That awful man from Miss Nelly's hasn't got her, has he?'

'Why! . . . I ain't got the slightest idea what you're talking about, sweetheart.' Tilly thought Sal's 'Miss Nelly' and 'that awful man' must belong to some misadventure or other that Molly and her young 'uns had experienced during the time when they were trudging the streets. She might have gone deeper into the matter but she was presently more preoccupied with her son, Joe. Something was troubling her. Something that wouldn't let her be. 'Your mammy *ain't* in no trouble . . . you've got my word on it.' Quickly, she fished Molly's note out of her pinnie pocket. 'Look here. Your mammy wrote this . . . she left it on the table for me to find. It were there when I got up this morning.' She handed it to the girl, who flattened it out on the slopstone, trying desperately to make head or tail of it. Thanks to Nelly, Sal could read a few words. Molly's spelling, however, posed a difficulty for the child.

'Well?' Tilly was amused to see how Sal turned the note every which way in order to decipher it. 'Can you tell what it says?' She assumed that Mollly must have taught the girl about words.

'I know my mammy's name,' Sal said proudly, pointing to the word 'Molly' at the bottom of the note, 'and I think that's your name there?' She showed Tilly her own misspelt name.

'That's a clever lass,' encouraged Tilly, pointing to the main body of the note. 'Can you tell what all *that* says?'

'Not properly,' Sal admitted.

'Right then!' Tilly ran her finger along each word,

carefully reading it for Sal's benefit. When she had finished, there was a brief silence, during which Sal was thinking hard on what her mammy had said. When at last she returned her attention to Tilly, her eyes were much brighter, and there was a little smile on her face.

'Are we going to live in London then?'

'It would seem so . . . *if* your mammy finds work and a place for you all.'

'She does love us! . . . And she *will* come for us soon, won't she?'

'She said so, didn't she?' Tilly asked kindly. When Sal eagerly nodded, she told her, 'There you are then. Now! . . . Can a poor woman get a bit o' peace round here? You go off and play in the cellar with the others. Keep them all outta sight mind . . . because that schooling fellow might come a-searching these 'ere parts!'

With serious face – that told Tilly how the girl would not be altogether happy until Molly was back – Sal went down the scullery steps towards the cellar, from where there came enough noise to satisfy her that Molly's two younger bairns were not fully aware that their mammy had gone so far away.

Tilly knew that Sal would not stay long in the cellar. After a short while, she was proved right when Sal emerged to seat herself on the front doorstep, where she gazed wistfully up the cobbled street, watching for the familiar and much-loved figure of her mammy to come round the corner at any minute.

If it weren't for her brother and sister depending on her, and the fact that she didn't know the way to London, Sal might have been tempted to follow her mammy there and then.

Though little Sal stayed on the doorstep for the best

part of the day, she was not rewarded for her vigilance. At suppertime she was told by Tilly, 'Come in off that cold step, my girl . . . you've been out there quite long enough!' Feeling both cramped and hungry, little Sal made small protest.

No sooner had little Sal sat herself round the big table in the centre of the parlour than Joe Watson let himself in the front door. On hearing his familiar footsteps, Tilly rushed into the passage. 'Don't you lot touch none of them muffins!' she warned the little hungry souls assembled round the table. 'Joe's here now. We shall *all* enjoy us supper . . . when grace is said.'

There was such a forbidding, sullen look on her son's face that Tilly's joy at having him home was cruelly quashed. 'Are you all right, Joe?' she asked, watching him take off his flat cap, which he flung over the nail in the door. She was concerned to see what a strange, brooding mood he was in. 'What's kept you so late? . . . I've been worried. D'you know what the time is, eh? It's gone eight o'clock.' Still he made no response. Instead, he pushed past her and made straight for the front parlour. His foot was already over the threshold when Tilly urged, 'Don't be surly, Joe. Supper's already laid out in the back parlour. We've none of us started, because I insisted that we wait for you.' Coming closer to him now, she was deeply disappointed to realize that he had been drinking again. 'Aw, Joe, you've never been drowning your sorrows in that ale house, have you?'

'What if I have?' His manner was strange to her, and most disturbing.

'Look . . . I'm sorry we had a fight, Joe. I was wrong to tackle you the way I did. And *you* was wrong to try and take advantage of Molly. You must have really

308

worried her . . . else she wouldn't have gone off like that in the middle of the night. Oh, she *had* to make a move, I know that . . . and I'd already asked her to leave the bairns with me till she were settled. But I don't like the idea that you forced her hand, Joe. I don't like it at all!' All this time, Tilly had deliberately kept her voice low, because of small, curious ears not too far away. 'She's a good sort is Molly. And she's had a bloody hard time of it.'

'Leave me be!'

'Aw, lad . . . don't keep bad blood between us,' pleaded Tilly. His answer was to close the door in her face. 'Have it your way,' she called out, 'but you did wrong, Joe Watson. You think on it, and you'll see your old ma's right. *You did wrong!*'

When there came no reply from the other side of the door, Tilly tutted loudly and, shaking her head angrily, she returned to the back parlour, where numerous little eyes turned to look at her, anxious and hungry.

Sensing that the children were made nervous by the raised voices between her and Joe, she promptly set about putting them at their ease. 'Oh, take no notice of grown-ups,' she declared, putting on a smile to cover her anxieties. 'They shout at nothing sometimes . . . just like you little tinkers.' Sitting herself on the standchair at the head of the table, she clapped her hands to draw their attention. When all eyes were looking at her, she bent her head, peering over her brows to ensure the children followed suit. Then, being satisfied, she quickly gave up a prayer of gratitude for the 'adequate spread of food on our table'. After which, the muffins and preserve were duly shared out, and everyone appeared to forget about the angry young man in the next room.

That is, all but little Sal and Tilly; the one hoping desperately that her mammy would soon be back to take them to their 'own place', and the other sad at heart that such a rift should ever come between her and her eldest. At the same time though, Tilly stood by her accusation that Joe had done wrong. She was made also to think on Molly – finding her way to London Town along dark and unfamiliar streets. What would she face once she got there, eh? Strangers? Hostility? Happen some'at far worse. Who knows, thought Tilly. Who knows.

Some time past midnight, Joe woke up in the throes of a terrible nightmare. Sweat was trickling down his back and the sound of a fist thumping against wood resounded in his head long after his eyes were open and his senses returned. Bang! Bang! The whole house seemed to tremble around him. Rising above the din came Tilly's voice, terrified and shocked. 'Joe! . . . What in God's name is happening? *Joe! Joe!*' Her cries became a scream.

Scrambling into his trousers, Joe raced to the bottom of the stairs. 'Quick, Mam . . . I'll fend the buggers off. *You get Molly's young 'uns away as fast as you can!*' He stared up at her with pleading eyes. 'Do as I say, Mam . . . for pity's sake, DO AS I SAY!' He knew now. It was no nightmare! Dear God above, what devil had possessed him to go to the Justice Crowther?

As she stared at her son's stricken eyes, Tilly was gripped with an awful realization. When she spoke, it was with a sinking sense of horror. 'Aw, no! Dear Lord, our Joe . . . you've never brought the authorities to the door?' The guilt on his face was her answer. 'Jesus, Mary and Joseph! *You have.* You've betrayed Molly's trust in old Tilly.' She threw her hands to her head and shook her whole body from side to side, as though fending off an attacker. 'What'll we do now? Dear God, what'll we do now?' All sense of reason fled her thoughts, as the noise outside grew more insistent. Now there were voices – angry, threatening voices, promising all kinds of terrible retribution 'if this door isn't opened straight away'!

By now the children too were out on the landing, some loudly crying, some softly whimpering. Only little Sal remained deathly silent.

On swift and silent steps, Joe bounded up the stairs. '*Please, mam!* Get the bairns out afore they break down the door!' he urged, taking Tilly by the shoulders and gently shaking her. 'I'll hold 'em off while you make your getaway. Head for the Navigation . . . tell them Joe's asking a favour. They'll give you shelter till it's safe.' At that minute, the thumping and shouting stopped and there followed a chilling silence. Tilly put her fingers to her lips, urging the children to be quiet. When gradually they did so, she murmured to Joe, 'They've gone, son. The buggers have gone after all, eh?'

'No. They haven't gone,' he told her in the softest of whispers, beginning to gather the children towards him while keeping an eye on the front door. He was mortally afraid that it might fly open at any minute. 'They'll not leave this house till they get what they've come for.' He looked at Tilly, and the warning in his eyes was like a knife through her heart.

'And what is it they've come for, our Joe?' she demanded, her condemning eyes drilling through him. 'What have you done, you bad 'un? *What is it they want?*'

Joe gave no reply, other than to shift his fearful gaze to

where Molly's three were huddled together. *It was enough!*

'Oh, you bad 'un, Joe. God forgive you,' Tilly muttered, making the sign of the cross on herself, and rushing back in the bedroom, from where she collected a shawl to cover her long nightshift. The children were not afforded such 'luxury', but nevertheless were warm and decent enough in their thick ankle-length garments. Quickly she ushered them down the stairs. 'Softly now, young 'uns. Stay close to Tilly.' Joe led the way, praying with every step that they might get away with it. In a long, silent line, they tiptoed through the back parlour. Joe had a mind to send them along the narrow ginnel that led to the brook. From there they could climb the bank and find their way along the alleys to the Navigation ale house. It would have been easier for them to go by way of the cellar but since the steps from these cellars led directly to the front of the house, he was left with no choice.

'Hurry up! For God's sake . . . get a move on.' He fed the small, trembling bodies through the back parlour door and into the scullery. Here Tilly was desperately fumbling with the bolt on the back door. 'I can't budge it,' she told him, 'it's stuck fast and my hands are that sweaty.' It was dark, too. Almost pitch black. Yet it was more than they dared do to light a candle. The only glimmer of light was the moon's soft glow as it played in through the small window panes.

Without a word Joe came forward, gently pushing Tilly to one side. When the bolt shot back, a sigh of relief filled the air. *But then came the worst*: it all happened so quickly that no one in that scullery could have prevented it. As the door swung open, they were pounced on!

Dark, fleeting figures in the moonlight, surging forward, intent on creating mayhem. In the furore that followed, both Tilly and her son fought to protect the children, who cowered together in a corner of the scullery, their sobbing pitiful to hear. Only Sal came forward, throwing herself again and again into the uproar, to be sent reeling backwards by flaying fists.

In a matter of minutes, Tilly and her son were overpowered. '*Bastards!*' Tilly spat the word out, employing the last dregs of her strength when, in one last determined effort she rammed her two fists into the chest of her attacker. His answer was to strike out a vicious hammer blow to her head. As she fell sideways, Tilly's temple cracked against the corner of the slopstone. With a strange, muffled cry, Tilly slumped to the ground. The brave fight was over, and Joe feared that, because of him, his own mother had paid with her life. Openly sobbing, he fell to his knees, collecting Tilly into his arms and begging her forgiveness.

'*Fools!*' The voice was cunning, dripping with satisfaction. 'Fools, the lot of you!' Justice Crowther stepped into the scullery where, with a quick, sure movement, he lit the candle which stood on the window ledge. In the flickering light his face became an eerie sight, the eyes narrowed to thin dark slits, his lower features embedded in a mass of thick, greying hair. As his gaze fell on them, the children clung to each other more fearfully, each struck dumb by the grotesqueness of those smiling, cruel eyes.

From the alcove in the far corner where she had been flung, Sal watched with wary eyes, afraid to move a muscle. *She had seen this man once before.* On a particular day outside Nelly's house, when she and her mammy had run away. Sal remembered how terrified her mammy had been on seeing this man. Now *she* felt that same terror. But mingled with the fear was a spiralling disbelief. Also shock and fury *Joe* had brought these men here! At first Sal couldn't bring herself to believe that he had done such a terrible thing, not even when Tilly had said so.

But if the child had any doubts before, they were dispelled in the moment when Justice Crowther laughed in Joe's face, telling him, 'I hope for your sake, Watson, that you haven't brought us here on a wild-goose chase.'

'You *lied* to me,' Joe accused, cradling Tilly's blood-soaked body, and the tears raining down his face as he glared up at the formidable, smiling features. 'You promised there'd be no violence.'

'So I did. And, if you hadn't had a change of heart like the coward you are, there would have been no need of any violence.' The smile slithered from his face. In its place came a look of malevolence. 'On your feet, man,' he instructed, glancing towards the children. 'Three of these are the urchins belonging to the woman called Molly, you say? Point them out! *Which are the three I've come for?*' He raised his cane and made a sweeping gesture over the children's heads.

'I'll tell you nothing more!' shouted Joe. 'You lying bastard . . . you've done for my mam . . . when you promised there'd be no harm come to us!' Suddenly he was on his feet and launching himself into that mountainous figure. 'I'll kill you!' he yelled, clutching his fingers round the thick, ageing neck with a cry that was terrible to hear.

In the chaos that followed, two of the men leapt

forward, and Joe was quickly prised away, eventually silenced by a heavy blow to the head. He slithered to the floor, unconscious, beside the crumpled figure of his mother. 'Damned fool! ' Caleb Crowther was seething. 'His sort never learn.' He might have had Joe run through there and then. But there were *more* important issues at stake here. What could be more important than Emma Grady's grandchildren?

The Justice glared at the children and chuckled aloud. When that fool Watson brought him news that a certain person had left her offspring in his mother's care – a certain person by the name of Molly, and whom he understood the Justice might have a warrant out for – he could not have known what a precious package he was bringing. A package so important that it could even be the means by which Emma Grady herself might be brought to heel!

Advancing on the small, trembling figures, he put on his most pleasant and cajoling voice. 'Which of you belong to the woman called *Molly*?' he asked, bending his face to them. 'There are *three* of you, I understand.' When he was greeted with big, frightened eyes and a stony silence, his manner became harsher. '*Those three will step forward!*' He waited a moment, enraged when his demands only made them huddle together all the more. Every child was in deep shock at what had taken place. Nothing he could do or say could persuade them to talk, or offer themselves up. Instead their eyes were drawn to the two lifeless figures on the floor, and they visibly trembled.

'I'm surrounded by dolts!' he declared, furiously thwacking his cane into the air. '*Take them all!*' he told the nearest man. 'If they think to get the better of me

. . . they would do well to remember how others were treated when they thought to do the very same!' He kept his steely glare on the small, terrified faces, while pointing with his stick to the pitiful figures of Tilly and her eldest. 'Get to it!' he snapped at the men, who appeared somewhat reluctant to carry out his orders. 'Damn and bugger it . . . you're being paid well enough, aren't you? *Do as I tell you!* Children such as these are no more than thieves and vagabonds in the making! *Scum! Ruffians!*'

In the face of such fury, it was only a matter of minutes before the children were bundled from the house and into the waiting carriage. By this time, their silence was broken. Cries of 'Mammy' and 'Sal . . . Sal' trailed behind the carriage as it fled away.

One by one the few neighbours who resided in Dock Street came hesitantly to their doors. Curious and afraid, they made their way to Tilly's door, now swinging back and forth in the gentle breeze. They couldn't begin to guess what had taken place there; they were afraid of what they might find. All they did know was that the children had been taken. *All of them!* Every last one, judging by the cries they'd heard. There were people in authority who could do that. People who had the right by law to commit such a crime against ordinary folk. You didn't go out of your way to pit yourself against such wicked creatures. Not unless you wanted them to turn on *you*, you didn't!

As the neighbours came in through the front door, nervous and afraid, a smaller, even more terrified creature sped through the dark, rat-ridden cellars below, then up the flight of steps on to the front pavement.

From there, her heart still beating furiously, Sal ran

along the cobbled streets, tears flowing down her face and occasionally crying out for her mammy.

After Justice Crowther and the men had taken away the others, Sal had remained pressed tight in the dark corner, desperately fighting the impulse to show herself in an effort to save her brother and sister, together with Tilly's brood. She knew instictively though that to betray her presence there would be a foolish thing to do. It had been hard, so very hard, to see the young 'uns all taken away and to be unable to do a single thing to stop it.

As she sped along the streets, Sal dared not think of Tilly, and the 'bad 'un'. In her mind's eye she could still see them lying there, and she was mortally afraid. What if her mammy had been there tonight? Oh, it didn't bear thinking about!

As she ran and ran, losing her way, then finding it again, Sal had one thought in mind. One person to whom she could turn. Even then, she was afraid. Because hadn't her own mammy told her that this one was *not* to be trusted! *Not* the friend they thought she was.

In her headlong flight Sal reminded herself of this. But she *had* to trust someone, didn't she? *She would trust Nelly!* Because, deep down, she had come to love that lady. *Nelly would help*. Nelly *must* help. There was no one else in all the world to whom Sal could turn. Tilly and Joe were badly beaten. The young 'uns had been taken. And her mammy was away to London Town, trying to find them a place to live.

Upstairs in the big house, Emma could not rest. She felt old and weary, afraid to hope in the wake of recent developments. Thoughts of the young woman called

Molly would not let her be. There were too many things still left unanswered, too much that played on her mind. The watch chain found by Nelly in this very house . . . the same piece that Emma's father had given to her shortly before he departed this world. The same piece that had been lost on a twilight morning so many years ago, when she had given birth to a girl-child, before being unjustly transported from these shores.

Something else even more disturbing had come to light since Marlow had taken Mick Darcy into his confidence. Only yesterday the young man who adored Molly had returned to Eanam Wharf, dejected and weary after scouring the country far and wide in search of her. The closest he had come to finding Molly was when he paid a seaman for 'certain information' which had taken Mick to a café beside the Liverpool docks. The proprietor – a surly creature by the name of Bill Craig – had spoken badly of Molly, calling her 'the worst kind o' trouble . . . a bad mistake that he had been glad to see the back of'. Apart from that, he would say little else, except to warn Mick 'if you've any sense at all, you'll steer clear o' that one . . . a wicked little baggage if yer ask me!' Mick's response was a sombre word of advice that left the disgruntled fellow in no doubt at all that if he should continue besmirching Molly's good character, he would find himself answering to Mick Darcy!

Since that particular encounter, there had been no word of Molly or the children. To the disheartened Mick, it was almost as though she had disappeared from the face of the earth. Disillusioned and hoping against hope that Marlow and Emma might have news of her, he had come home to Blackburn after many weeks away.

But there was no news. Even the private detective hired by Marlow Tanner had uncovered nothing of Molly's whereabouts.

Restless and afraid that she might disturb the sleeping Marlow, Emma draped a shawl about herself and went from the bedroom on soft footsteps. She still could not come to terms with it all; especially in the face of Mick Darcy's astonishing revelation that 'Molly was brought up by an old tramp . . . an eccentric old dear known as old Sal'. When Mick was questioned further by Marlow, it was discovered that the old tramp's full name was Sal Tanner – Marlow's very own *sister*.

Realizing that Molly was one and the same girl who had gone out of her way to ensure that old Sal did not suffer a pauper's grave, Marlow immediately set about moving heaven and earth to track her down. There was so much that he owed her, so much that he wanted to ask her with regards to the sister he had loved and lost. On top of which, Emma herself had a great need to speak to Molly, the question of her watch chain being paramount.

But to Emma's mind, there was something else. Something both unnerving and exciting. Some deeper instinct that would not easily be denied. A strange, insistent feeling in her bones that maybe . . . just maybe, this young woman called Molly might be *her own daughter*. The seed of her forbidden love with Marlow. The same girl-child she had given birth to, and who was pronounced stillborn, and left in the gutter as the prison-wagon drew away. Knowing how there was nothing to substantiate such a phenomenon, and in the wake of her own illness these past weeks, Emma had been careful not to voice her deep feelings to anyone. Not to Marlow, who had been deeply concerned for Emma's health of late. And not even to Nelly, who over so many long years in exile had been Emma's loyal friend and confidante. Nor could Emma bring herself to speak to the priest about her troubled soul, for she had turned her back on the Church when her only son had been so cruelly taken from her.

There was no one in whom Emma dare confide. So she tortured herself, recalling certain instances that were all pieces of a jigsaw split asunder by cruel circumstances so very long ago. The time between had been like a fast-running brook spilling into a vast ocean. Gone forever. And yet, and yet! Was it all to do with Emma's long and desperate wish that the girl-child might have survived? How could she tell whether it was all just wishful thinking born of a terrible loss which, even now, caused her great pain. How could she tell? Dear God, what was she to think?

For weeks now, Emma had been haunted by all those little encounters which only seemed to add to her confusion – the fact that old Sal never had any children of her own, and on a day not too long after Emma was transported, Sal was suddenly in possession of an infant . . . *a girl-child with the same black eyes and dark hair as Marlow himself!*

Oh if only it had been possible to discover *where* old Sal had got the infant! But until now, no one seemed to know; Sal claimed that 'the little people sent her to me'. Then there was the watch chain. Emma could not satisfy herself as to how it came to be in this house; not belonging to either staff or household, yet discovered soon after Molly's departure. And, if it *had* been in Molly's possession, then how did she acquire it? Had she stolen it? Certainly, as Nelly pointed out, Molly had stolen to survive. Had she been given it, perhaps by an admirer who was himself a thief? Or – and it was this possibility that tormented Emma – *had the piece been found by old Sal in the same spot as she had found the girl-child herself?*

If that 'spot' were none other than the cobbled street behind the prison where she and Nelly were held, Emma would be convinced that the dark-eyed Molly was her long-lost daughter. Hers *and* Marlow's!

So deep in thought was Emma that when Nelly came into the drawing-room carrying a lamp before her, Emma did not detect her presence. Instead, she remained by the casement windows, gazing out to a star-studded sky and wondering whether the heavens held the secret of all that went on below.

Placing the lamp on the mantelpiece beside the smaller lamp which Emma had brought down, Nelly took stock of her old friend. It hurt her to see how the slim shoulders were drooped, as though carrying an unbearable weight. Emma's whole countenance seemed greatly saddened. If only the boy had been spared, Nelly thought now; if only that particular source of joy had not been so heartlessly torn from her. It was true that Marlow was Emma's strength in these troubled times, and she adored him as always. But the love between a mother and her child was special, a unique and wonderful thing that could never be replaced.

Now, as she went forward, deliberately making a noise in order not to startle Emma unnecessarily, Nelly did so with a purpose. Unable to sleep herself, she had heard Emma leave her room. For a long time now Nelly had fought with her conscience. There were certain

321

things she should confess to Emma. Things of the past that had somehow found their way into the present, and possibly had the power to affect the future.

Nelly was afraid, convinced that her long-overdue 'confession' would signal the end of Emma's affection for her. All the same, and because she loved Emma above all else, Nelly had decided that on this night she would open her heart and afterwards beg Emma's forgiveness.

'Oh, Nelly!' Emma swung round on hearing her dear friend's noisy procession across the floor. 'Couldn't you sleep either?' She came forward. When Nelly seated herself in one leather chair beside the empty fire-grate, Emma seated herself in the other. In the lamp's soft glow, Nelly was pained to see how Emma's hitherto rich, chestnut-coloured hair was now heavily streaked with grey. The bloom of youth had long left her face, but now a terrible weariness seemed to draw the lines of age so much deeper. But for all that, Emma retained a certain grace and beauty that was timeless.

'I've a good mind ter wake Marlow and tell him how yer haunting the house in the middle o' the night!' Nelly chastized, her face a picture of annoyance. 'Yer knows very well what the doctor told yer. "Stay in yer bed," he said, "get yer strength back after being laid so low with the illness." And what d'yer do, eh?' she demand-ded, shaking her tousled head. 'Well . . . yer wanders about in the cold night air, that's what!'

Emma smiled at her old friend's sharp tongue. She knew that Nelly meant well. 'I couldn't sleep,' she said, 'and I was afraid I might wake Marlow. He's so ex-hausted . . . these past weeks haven't been easy for him.' She laughed, a gentle unhappy sound. 'We're none of us getting any younger, Nelly,' she said.

'Huh! . . The past few weeks ain't been easy fer none of us, my gal,' replied Nelly, 'what with this business o' Molly, an' you being took so poorly.' Suddenly her voice softened as she asked, 'Are yer feeling better, gal? . . . Feel stronger in yersel', d'yer, eh?' The doctor said that Emma had been struck down by 'a particularly nasty fever'. But Nelly knew better; t'weren't no matter o' the fever that had laid Emma low. It were *other* matters, much more powerful to a woman. Matters of the heart, that's what had struck Emma down: grief, and longing, and the loss of two children. Yes! *Two* children, because to Nelly's mind, Emma had *never* got over the loss of that new-born girl-child. Nelly could not ease that loss for Emma. Nothing she could say would ever ease it. Indeed, what she had to say could even make that loss *more* unendurable. Or, in the light of recent events, it might prove to be a godsend. Nelly didn't know. All she *did* know was that only days before, she had confided all to Marlow. Now, and on Marlow's insistence, she had to tell the truth of what happened on that terrible night so long ago. 'What yer been thinkin' about, Emma . . . down here on yer own, gazin' outside the window like a lost soul?'

'Life, Nelly . . . I've been thinking about life. How good it's been to me, and how bad.'

Nelly was compelled to broach the subject of Molly, because unbeknown to either of them, the very same suspicions that had been plaguing Emma had also been tormenting *her*. 'I've been doing that an' all, gal . . . y'know, thinkin' about how good life's been to me. In particular, how fortunate I was to have come across such a friend as you.' She saw that Emma was about to intervene. 'No. Let me finish, Emma darlin'. Y'see, I ain't never been entirely honest with you all these years. There's some'at I want to get off me chest, like. Some'at that yer 'ave ter know . . . an' I'm not altogether certain, mind . . . but well . . . I've a feelin' it all might 'ave some bearing on Molly.'

Emma's attention had been wandering, but now at the mention of Molly's name, she grew excited, leaning forward in her seat. 'What is it, Nelly? . . . What have you to tell me that might relate to Molly?' she urged.

Swallowing hard, Nelly prepared to launch into an account of how she suspected that Emma's new-born was still alive when the prison-wagon carried them away. But at that moment the room was filled with the sound of bedlam. '*Nelly! Help me, Nelly! . . . Let me in, please!*' The desperate cries were accompanied by a series of other, more violent noises like the kicking of a boot against the front door, together with the familiar, if more desperate sound of the heavy iron knocker being crashed again and again into its metal base.

'Good Lord above!' exclaimed Emma, her face ashen as she scrambled out of the chair. 'Who on earth is that?' Even before the last word was uttered, she was collecting the lamp from the mantelpiece and hurrying from the room.

'Sounds like bleedin' old Nick himself,' declared Nelly, staying close behind Emma, 'though I don't know why the bugger might be callin' my name!' In a moment of panic, it had crossed her mind that the sins of the past had caught up with her.

It was no time at all before Emma and the doubting Nelly were in the vestibule and struggling to reach the upper bolt of the front door when Marlow – awoken by

the uproar   rushed to Emma's aid. The parlour maid
and the cook stood someway behind, both unkempt and
wide-eyed, with the maid squashed close to the other
woman, fearful that upon the door opening some un-
speakable creature might clap its eyes on her and
devour her instantly. Even so, when Nelly insisted that
these two return at once to their beds, they went away
most reluctantly, their curiosity threatening to get the
better of them. They had no sooner gone a few paces
than the door was opened, and a sobbing mite fell
forward into Nelly's arms. 'Gawd almighty! . . . It's little
Sal . . . Molly's bairn!' Nelly clung to the small, trembling figure. 'What is it, child? Where's yer mammy?
What yer doing here?'

'*Don't* badger her, Nelly.' Realizing that the child was
in a state of shock and in danger of being overawed by
the presence of herself and Marlow, Emma thought the
best thing was to let the child recover enough to explain
lucidly exactly what had brought her to this door at such
a deadly hour, and in such terror.

'*No! No!*' When Nelly made an effort to help Sal into
the house, she was astonished at the vehemence with
which the girl fought her off. 'STOP HIM, Nelly . . .
we've got to stop him! *He's killed Tilly, and he's taken the
young 'uns.*' The memory of the awful scenes she had
witnessed that night was too much. Sobbing loudly, the
child fell to the floor, her arms doubled beneath her head
and her whole body helpless in the grip of convulsive
sobs.

As Nelly made to stoop and raise the child, Emma
came forward, gentle in her manner and soothing little
Sal with her low, soft voice. A terrible suspicion had
crept into Emma's heart. A suspicion which only this

small girl, *Molly's girl*, could answer. 'We will stop him, Sal,' she told her, 'but we need to know his name. *Who* killed Tilly? *Who* took the young 'uns?'

'*The man!* The man who wants to kill my mammy too!' Sal could hardly speak for the choking sobs, her vivid blue eyes raised to Emma's tender, loving face – the face of her own grandmother, although she was not yet aware of that. 'I want my mammy back,' she cried now, 'please, missus . . . I want my mammy back!'

'We'll get your mammy back, sweetheart,' Emma promised, 'but first . . . we need to know who the man is. Can you tell me his name?'

For one agonizing moment, when little Sal raised her head in response to Emma's question, it was thought that all would be revealed. She opened her mouth to speak. But the name they all waited to hear was lost in a whisper as the exhausted child sank away in a dead faint.

Tenderly Marlow carried the small, limp figure up the stairs, where it was put carefully to bed, and the doctor urgently summoned. 'Later, when she's rested,' he told the anxious Emma, 'we will know who "the man" is.' The intimate smile he gave her was a curious yet reassuring one. It came to Emma in that moment how Marlow also might have been secretly mulling over all the events that had taken place regarding Molly. Events that were deeply woven into his own life, and into the life and death of old Sal, the beloved tramp.

One thing Emma believed was that Marlow could not be agonizing over whether Molly was his own daughter. Because Emma had never confided the truth in him, and so he knew nothing of her either conceiving or giving birth to his girl-child. That was the way that Emma had wanted it, for it would have served no real purpose for

Marlow to know, except to cause him heartache.

Unbeknown to Emma, however, Marlow *did* know of the girl-child born to Emma all those years ago! And because of it, he also wondered just how deeply Molly's life was linked with his and Emma's. Since Nelly had recently confided in him, he had been driven that much harder to find Molly, because in his heart he wanted to believe that she was his daughter. *He prayed that it was so*.

Because Nelly had begged to be the one who would tell Emma of the possibility that her girl-child might have survived that night, Marlow had kept his own counsel. Now though, in the light of Molly's own child being here, under this very roof and in need of help from them, he felt that Emma should be told all there was to know. Not even one moment should be lost.

Marlow ushered both Nelly and Emma downstairs to the drawing-room. 'There is much for you to know, Emma,' he told her, the light of love as strong in his dark eyes as it was when they had first met: he just a boy, she a young and gently blossoming girl. The feelings that had stirred between them then were still as young, still as wonderful in both their hearts.

What he had to tell Emma now seemed to Marlow like a blessing from the Good Lord, in compensation for having taken their son. Nothing was certain, though. When all was revealed, it might be that Molly was *not* their own flesh and blood after all. But even before Nelly had unburdened her heart to him, Marlow had been deeply disturbed by something he could not understand – a certain feeling about the infant that his dear sister had found and raised as her own. No, nothing was certain. But there was always hope. And that hope would bind him and Emma closer still.

With lighter heart, Marlow followed Nelly and his beloved wife into the drawing-room. Between the three of them, they would find whatever truths there were. In all of his distress following Emma's illness and during the search for Molly, Marlow, like Nelly, had derived much comfort from their faith. It would have given Marlow so much joy to know that Emma's own faith had returned. Perhaps one day soon, he thought, when the pain of losing their son was not so unbearable.

How much sooner that would be if, by the grace of God, their first-born was returned to them. Was it too much to hope for, Marlow asked himself now as he closed the drawing-room door.

It was some time later when the messenger came: an ill-mannered lout of dubious character bearing news that struck both fear and joy into the hearts of all present. There was nothing delivered in writing, but the fellow was obviously well rehearsed. 'I've been sent by a certain gent,' he addressed Emma, 'a certain gent whose name I'm not at liberty to disclose, yer understand, but what I've to tell yer is this . . . the gent is in possession of a number o' brats. I'm to tell yer that *three* of 'em are yer own grandchildren.' When the colour drained from Emma's face, he seemed momentarily surprised. 'That's right, lady . . . *yer own grandchildren* . . . an' I was to make quite certain that yer understood that. The brats belong to a young woman by the name o' Molly . . . your daughter.'

'What proof d'you have of all this, you disgusting ruffian?' demanded Nelly. Emma seemed lost for words.

'Aha! . . . the gent said yer might ask such a thing. In the event I was to disclose certain information.'

'Out with it then!' Emma had recovered, and her tongue lashed him sharply.

The fellow went on in hurried voice, not caring much for the turn of atmosphere. He remembered all the Justice had told him concerning the origins of the one called Molly. 'Old Sal Tanner found the infant near the jail where Emma Grady was kept afore being despatched on the ocean voyage,' he revealed, adding that the information 'came straight from the mouth of the old salt who wet-nursed the abandoned girl-child'.

All the while he was speaking, Emma had her hand clutched to her heart, for his every word only served to confirm what she suspected – that she and Marlow were indeed Molly's parents. If there had been any vestige of doubt remaining, it vanished when the fellow stretched out his arm and opened his fist. There, nestling amongst the callouses of his thick, grubby fingers was a tiny, delicate timepiece. 'I'm to deliver this,' said the fellow, 'with the information that the young woman in question wore it round her neck even as a child. *T'weren't stolen!* It belonged to the child . . . right from the start.' Here he deliberately paused before going on in a cunning voice, 'Afore that, it belonged to your good self . . . this 'ere timepiece . . . an' the girl-child with it.'

Nelly had seen how his words were affecting Emma, Emma who had been so poorly, and she was incensed by it all. 'You blaggart!' she snapped, pushing at the fellow and threatening to tumble him out of the front door.

'No . . . leave him, Nelly.' The tears were flowing down Emma's face as she stepped up to look more closely at the piece of gold. It should have been twenty pieces of silver, she thought. Even without the fellow mentioning the name of the one who had sent him,

Emma knew it by heart. It could be none other than Caleb Crowther. *He* was the one who had betrayed her all those years ago. He was betraying her now. *He was an evil man!*

With tender reverence, Emma collected the tiny piece into her hand. 'Where are the children?' she asked, and in such a chilling manner that the fellow stepped back a pace. 'What does he want? . . . *Justice Crowther!*'

''*Ere!*' He was suddenly trembling, his eyes protruding with fear. 'I ain't said no name! Yer didn't get no name from me!' He was gabbling now, the words careering one over the other. 'Yer to cancel a certain court case that comes up shortly! . . . Drop all charges an' put an end to it once an' fer all. That's what the gent said . . . *If yer wants ter clap eyes on them brats while they're still alive, that is.*' He backed away, his message delivered and his every nerve-ending urging him to make a hasty retreat. 'That's it! That's it . . . I ain't saying another word,' he yelled, turning about and ready to run. Suddenly he was kicking and struggling. Pinned fast by two sturdy arms – *Mick Darcy's* arms. 'So, you're not saying another word, eh?' Mick asked with a half-smile. 'Then we shall have to change your mind!'

'At least the authorities will.' The rejoining voice was Marlow's. Grim-faced and struck to the heart by what he and Mick had overheard, he gestured to the bargee to get the fellow inside. 'You'll talk all right,' he promised the shivering fellow. 'When the authorities arrive, you'll have *plenty* to talk about.'

As Mick manhandled the unfortunate messenger into the library, Emma voiced her fears to the outraged Marlow. 'The children, Marlow . . . if we don't send this man back to my uncle, I'm desperately afraid that he will harm the children.'

Reaching down to kiss her greying head, Marlow gently assured her, 'He won't do that, sweetheart. He's a bad sort, a coward of the worst order. But he won't murder children . . . he thinks too much of his own precious neck to risk it on the gallows.'

Nelly felt the need to intervene. 'That's as maybe!' she declared angrily. 'But that's where the bugger will end up! *Stretched on the gallows* like any common criminal!' Loudly tutting, she went in a great fury towards the library. She had a thing or two to say to that grubby fellow, and it wouldn't wait.

Marlow explained how he had gone to Eanam Wharf where he had alerted Mick Darcy of the developments. From there, Mick had taken him to Dock Street where Tilly Watson lived. And no, it wasn't true that the Justice had killed Tilly, although she had been brutally knocked about.

'It's a bad business, Emma,' Marlow said, 'but our priority is to get Molly and the children back safe. The rest is a matter for the authorities.' He clung to her, saying softly, 'God willing, we'll have our daughter and grandchildren safe soon. Very soon.'

Chapter Twelve

Agnes Crowther stood with one hand on the ornate mantelpiece: a tall, regal figure in a blue taffeta gown, her aged features as chalk-white as the pearls about her wrinkled neck, a look of horror on her face. 'What is it you want with my husband?' she demanded curtly. Though thinly disguised, there was undeniably a trace of nervousness in her voice. Her manner, however, remained haughty.

The officer felt the need to be cautious. 'As my colleague explained, ma'am . . . we have reason to suspect that Justice Crowther might be able to assist with our inquiries.' The stocky officer with the drooping moustache and heavy eyelids made no secret of his delight at the reason for being at Breckleton House. His smile was infuriating to Agnes Crowther.

'Then you are fools!' she retorted now. 'How dare you suggest that a respected and eminent figure such as the Justice could possibly know *anything* with regard to a woman being "viciously attacked"? And it is absurd to think he could ever be involved in the "abduction of children".' Her indignation was amazing to behold, especially since she had already suspected that her 'respected and eminent' husband was up to no good. 'My advice to you both is to go away and find the real culprit. I don't mind telling you that, on his return, Justice

Crowther will have a great deal to say concerning your visit here.'

'I can assure you, ma'am . . . we're only doing our job,' explained the thinner of the two. 'Of course we're sorry if our visit has caused you distress. But we really do need to talk with the Justice.' He put on his trilby and seemed to make a little bow. 'And you have no idea of his whereabouts at present?'

'None whatsoever.'

'But should he return, you will inform us?'

'I will inform *my husband* of your visit. Oh, you may depend on it!' Agnes Crowther swept angrily across the library. Swinging open the door, she assured them in a cutting voice, 'And when he discovers *the reason* for your desire to talk with him . . . the "distress" will *not* be mine. It will be yours! Good day to you.'

On the two men leaving the house, Agnes Crowther hurried to the window in the great hall. From a discreet distance she watched them walk from the front door to the waiting carriage. She stepped back a pace when they half-turned towards the house, seemingly immersed in deep discussion. Then, when eventually they climbed into the carriage and were taken at some speed towards the road, she continued to stare after them, her face a study in confusion. Her fears were heightened when she realized that an officer was being left behind to stand guard outside the gates.

'Father will have their heads for this!' Martha Crowther had been sitting in the library throughout, stunned into silence by the conversation between the two officers and her mother. Now, as she led the way back to the library, her eyes were narrowed with anger, and her uneven nostrils grew to twice their size as she sucked in great helpings of air. '*How dare they?*' she said in an explosive voice. When her tantrum drew no response from the woman behind, Martha Crowther deliberately slowed her footsteps and turned her ungainly brown head to ask, 'What will you do, mother . . . ? Will you tell him?' Of late, her father's temper had been unbearably short. The thought of his reaction to this tiresome episode made her visibly tremble.

'Of course he must be told,' Agnes informed her. Martha's state of anxiety had not gone unnoticed, though; to Agnes Crowther's mind her foolish daughter had created her own deplorable situation, by constantly refusing to be a 'proper' wife to Silas Trent. Time and again he had begged her to join him in Australia, where he had taken on Emma Grady's already prosperous trading company, and expanded it even more. The man had worked hard and, as far as Agnes Crowther was concerned, he deserved the same support and loyalty from his wife as he got from his son, Edward. Martha, however, gave him neither support *nor* loyalty. And for too long now she had withheld all form of affection from him. Was it surprising, therefore, that her unfortunate husband had sought solace in the arms of the woman who worked alongside him? In Rita Hughes he had found a loyal colleague and, according to Martha's peevish innuendoes, a generous lover. There was no doubt that the marriage was over. Agnes Crowther, for one, was not surprised.

The conversation of mother and daughter was interrupted by a soft tap on the door. '*Come!*' Agnes Crowther called with some irritation. She was at once on her guard when she saw that it was the maid. Amy had been with them a long time, but she was far too curious about matters that did not concern her. 'Yes, what is it?' There were other, more pressing matters on her mind than domestic trivialities.

'It's Cook, m'lady.' Amy made an odd little curtsy, inclining her head to one side in the way she did when nervous. At this moment in time she did look exceedingly nervous and – because of the fact that she had come to the library earlier and overheard the riveting conversation that had taken place there – Amy was also acutely embarrassed. At the same time, she bubbled inwardly with excitement. Amy was very partial to a snippet of gossip, and here was a deal *more* than a snippet. What she had learned through a chink in the door was the most astonishing, the most awful and the most delicious revelations it had ever been her unpleasant lot to bear. She hadn't told Cook yet, because the last time she imparted a bit of juicy gossip to Cook all she got for her trouble was a belt round the ear. But she *would* tell her soon, because if she didn't, she would just burst.

'Yes, yes . . . what about Cook?'

'I'm to inquire, m'lady . . . whether dinner is to be served now. Or should we wait the master's return?'

Agnes Crowther appeared to give the matter small thought, but then she instructed, 'Tell Cook we will *not* be waiting the master's return. She may serve dinner as usual.'

'Very well, ma'am.' With another curious little curtsy, Amy left the room.

The lamps were burning long into the evening at Breckleton House.

Upstairs in the drawing-room, Agnes Crowther sat in

the deep comfortable armchair by the window, a look of disbelief and shock in her eyes as she gazed out to the two figures bathed in moonlight and discreetly positioned by the big gates. Earlier there had been only one man on duty, but a second officer had remained behind after yet another visit by the authorities. During this particular visit it had been revealed to Agnes Crowther that 'a certain man who had delivered a blackmail threat to the Tanner home' had been taken into custody. After lengthy interrogation he had reluctantly put forward a statement that incriminated Justice Crowther, and which also appeared to substantiate certain earlier allegations made by a Mrs Tilly Watson and her son, Joe. The charges were serious: the Justice was urgently wanted for questioning.

Cook sat in the upright, uncomfortable standchair, her chubby arms stretched out across the table, and a letter clutched tightly in her fist; a very old and condemning letter, written by a woman hanged many years before.

Cook had been stunned by the news regarding her employer, most of which had reached her ears via the parlour maid. Although it was all a most unexpected and shocking revelation, Cook was not altogether surprised by it. There was no doubt whatsoever in her mind that Justice Crowther was a bad, bad man; a tyrant of the worst order, if this letter were anything to go by. A heartless fiend who did not stop even at *murder!*

Cook shuddered. In her hand she held a statement that was far more damaging to Justice Crowther than any statement the authorities had in their possession. It was not to do with the abduction of children or the battering of a woman – though they were obscene enough crimes. No! This letter accused him of other things. Things beyond the imagination of normal, civilized beings. Things that made a body's blood run cold.

The letter pointed this 'respectable eminent man' out as the same creature who possibly *murdered both of Emma Grady's parents!* Her mother, following a secret affair with Caleb Crowther, and her father, when it seemed he might change his will to remove power over Emma from that evil man.

'What to do . . . ? Burn the blessed thing, or show it to the world?' Cook murmured, her breath fanning the candle-light and sending the shadows scurrying about; the ensuing gyrating shapes on the wall held her mesmerized for a moment. They look like him, she thought – dark and furtive, shifting this way and that.

Only a few months before, Cook would have suffered no dilemma where the letter was concerned. It had always been her 'insurance' against poverty and home-lessness in her old age. She had kept the letter hidden away, and would not have hesitated to use it for black-mail against the Justice if he had ever carried out his threat to put her 'on the streets'. Fortunately she had not been made to resort to such shameful means, mainly because of kindly intervention by Agnes Crowther herself. Only recently that same lady had confided to Cook, 'I may shortly be leaving this house and taking up residence in a smaller property of my own. I would very much like to retain you, in my new home'. Of course, Cook had been both eager and delighted at the sugges-tion, especially as there was a 'possibility' that Amy also might be 'taken care of'.

Her thoughts driven to the past, Cook was made to

think on the young, innocent girl that was Miss Emma. How unspeakably cruel Justice Crowther had been in deliberately keeping father and daughter apart and how devastated she had been at the death of her father. Soon after, he had married Miss Emma off to an unsuitable man. Then, when she was accused of murder, he had turned his back on her, afterwards ransacking her inheritance and building his own prosperity on it.

'But your sins have come home to roost, ain't they, m'lud,' Cook said now, looking accusingly towards the stairs that led from the kitchen to the upper hall. On her homecoming from Australia, Emma had put into motion a series of events to right the injustice towards her. These events were now set to culminate in a trial that would have the whole of Lancashire agog. There was no doubt in everyone's mind that the outcome of that trial would serve as the Justice Crowther's downfall. And there wasn't a single person – with perhaps the exception of his daughter Martha and his grandson Edward – who would wish it to be otherwise.

'Yet you're a crafty fox, Justice,' Cook said softly, 'and though the cards is set against you, it wouldn't surprise me at all if, somehow, you was to wiggle out of it.' The possibility was appalling to her. 'We *all* have to pay for our sins . . . and the likes of you should be made to pay twice over, because you've been blessed with the best that life can offer. *And you're still hungry for more!*' The one thing that turned Cook's stomach was the thought of Justice Crowther outwitting Miss Emma yet again. Oh, it was true that Miss Emma was now a rich and powerful lady when at the time she was ill-used by her uncle she had been little more than a child, but the man had some powerful and influential allies. He was a Justice, after all.

Suddenly Cook's mind was made up! She *would* make the letter known! Her first instinct was to show it immediately to Miss Emma, but then she recalled that Miss Emma was reputed to be not fully recovered from her illness. Mr Tanner than? No! There was no doubt in Cook's mind that he would likely strangle the Justice, and be hanged for it. The authorities? Well, yes . . . but they had an uncanny way of dragging an innocent body into the proceedings in a way that terrified a simple soul such as Cook.

At the point when the agitated woman was in her deepest thoughts, the bell on the wall behind her loudly jangled. 'Mercy above!' she gasped, clutching her two chubby hands to her breast and rising from the chair. 'It's a wonder I ain't struck dead!' With a bright red face and pounding heart she looked up to see who on earth could be summoning her at this late hour. 'It's the drawing-room,' she observed with interest, 'it can't be the master, because he's not back yet, I think. And it can't be his spoilt daughter Martha . . . because Amy took a glass of hot milk to her room some two hours ago, together with a headache powder to "soothe my aching head". No! That one would be out to the world and snoring like a good 'un,' Cook decided with a measure of indignation. That left only one other person to be ringing the bell. *Agnes Crowther*. 'What in heaven's name could she be wanting at this time of night?' Cook wondered, at the same time ramming the letter into her pocket, then straightening her pinnie and patting her grey curls into place. 'There's no peace for the wicked,' she told herself, mounting the steps as fast as her thick old legs would allow.

In the drawing-room, Cook found the mistress in a strange mood. 'I wasn't certain whether you had all gone to bed,' Agnes Crowther explained, being mindful of the fact that she had already informed Amy there would be no further need of her that evening.

'That's all right, ma'am,' Cook said, waiting her instructions, 'I wasn't ready for bed . . . had too many things on my mind, d'you see?'

'All the same, I would not have disturbed you at this late hour if it were not absolutely necessary,' Agnes Crowther said, thinking how Cook was not the only one to have 'too many things on my mind'. Looking away from Cook, she raised the long, slender fingers of her left hand to her temple, gently massaging the area with a look of discomfort on her face. 'I have the *most dreadful* headache.'

'I'll fetch you a powder at once, ma'am.' Cook put her hand on the door knob. 'Will there be anything else, ma'am?' She suddenly thought of the letter. Her heart beat furiously at the idea of revealing it to the mistress. She wanted to, oh so much, but she was half-afraid of what Agnes Crowther's reaction would be.

But then the anxious woman was afforded a golden opportunity when, in answer to her question, the lady of the house peered at her most intently, as though secretly debating some inner thought. Presently she said, 'You have been with us a very long time . . . you must know us all so well.' She smiled, but it was a sad, lonely smile. 'Of course, you recall the day when my brother Thadius Grady came to live at Breckleton House.' She appeared not to be directly talking to Cook now. Instead she seemed to be rambling, lost in thought. 'My brother . . . so trusting . . . so desperate that his adored daughter should be well taken care of.' Here she gave a small, cynical laugh. 'Like Breckleton House itself, Thadius was in a state of decline when he came here to live. Yet, because of his kindness and generosity, the house was restored to its former glory. And how did we manage to repay him?' Her head was lowered as though in shame as, with broken voice, she went on, 'By denying him the comfort of Emma by his side when he needed her most . . . cried out for her! And after his death, by betraying his most heartfelt wish . . . that Emma should be well taken care of.'

There followed a long, painfully drawn-out silence during which Cook remained silent and motionless. She was deeply shocked at the manner in which Agnes Crowther had uttered such shameful and private thoughts in her presence. Such a thing had never occurred in this household all the years Cook had been retained there. Yet, in some strange, instinctive way, in that moment it seemed so very natural. With tingling astonishment, Cook suddenly realized that the mistress had been drinking. There, on the table beside her, was a half-empty sherry decanter and a partly filled glass. So that was it! They did say that the drink loosened a body's tongue.

'I was not altogether innocent in the proceedings regarding Emma. I am not proud of that fact . . . and I have since lived to regret it.'

'I'll go and fetch the powder, ma'am.' Cook was suddenly afraid of hearing things she had no right to know – or perhaps of having the contents of that letter confirmed. She would have made a discreet exit there and then. But suddenly she was confronted by Agnes Crowther's direct question and it frustrated her intention.

'Have you seen the two officers guarding this house?'

'Yes, ma'am.'

'Do you know *why* they're watching the house?' She did not wait for Cook's answer. 'I'll tell you why . . . ! They're waiting for your master . . . *the Justice.*'

'I'll fetch the powder, ma'am.' It was all too much for Cook. She felt totally out of place, and convinced that, on the morrow, when the mistress realized the extent of what she had confided to *a servant*, no less, Cook would be sent packing forthwith.

'No . . . ! I want you to stay. You've seen it all, I know. You've seen everything over the years. You're no fool, I'm well aware of that. What do you *really* know, I wonder . . . ? Do you know that your master is accused of attacking a woman? Do you know that they say he is wanted in connection with abducting children?' She swayed on her feet.

'*What* do you know? All these years . . . what do you really know?'

At this point Cook remembered the letter in her pocket. She remembered also the awful possibility that Justice Crowther might yet outsmart Emma in this forthcoming court case. *That must not happen!* Without a word, she took the letter from her pinnie pocket and held it out to Agnes Crowther, who, being cautioned by the serious look in the other woman's eyes, took it hesitantly and went across to the lamp where she might read it more easily. Cook chose that moment to leave quietly, hoping that her departure would not be a permanent one, once the contents of that terrible letter were made known to Agnes Crowther.

* * *

Cook had waited in the kitchen for over an hour, bone-tired and preparing herself for the moment when Agnes Crowther would come bursting through the door. *But it never happened*. Eventually, unable to stay awake any longer, she laid her head back into the curve of the easy chair by the empty fire-grate, and dozed off into a troubled sleep.

She was not aware that, incensed and deeply shocked by what she had read, Agnes Crowther took it upon herself to rouse the groom and instruct him to quickly make the carriage ready. From the gate – where they were briefly questioned by the two men on duty – the flustered driver was told by Agnes Crowther to 'make haste to Park Street. *To the Tanner residence.*'

It was some two hours after Agnes Crowther's speedy departure that all hell was let loose. 'WAKE UP . . . ! *For Gawd's sake, Cook, wake up!*' Amy's cry was desperate as she shook the older woman back and forth in the chair, the tears running down her face, the look of a wild thing about her.

'Lord love and save us!' shouted Cook on being so rudely awakened, convinced that Agnes Crowther had ordered her execution. 'Whatever's the matter . . . ? Are we all to be murdered in our beds or what?' She scrambled frantically to get from the chair.

'Happen we will . . . if we don't get to a safe place smartish!' Amy told her. ''Cause there's a madman loose upstairs. *A bloody madman!*' Her two eyes stuck out like hat pins as she clutched the long shawl over her nightshift and made ready to escape.

Normally Amy would have received a severe scolding from Cook for using 'untoward language', but the moment was interrupted by an officer of the law, who repeated Amy's instruction that they should leave the house as quickly as possible.

As Cook was unceremoniously propelled from the house by a trembling, terrified Amy, she asked, 'What in God's name is going on?'

Amy replied in a fearful voice, '*It's the Justice*. He's locked himself in his room upstairs, and he's daring the officers to come and get him.'

'Good Lord!' exclaimed Cook, adding, 'Where's the mistress . . . and her daughter?'

'It seems the mistress went out on an urgent errand some time ago.' Amy hesitated to say more.

'Well? Are you deaf, girl?' Cook demanded, having recovered enough of her authority to put the parlour maid in her place. '*What about Mrs Trent?* I asked.'

Amy made a faint-hearted gesture with her tousled head, to indicate the upper reaches of the house. 'Martha Trent's in there . . . with her mad father,' she said in a low, irreverent voice. 'But I don't expect she'll ever again see the light o'day.'

'What are you talking about, you foolish creature?' Cook felt an awful panic rising in her.

'The Justice has threatened to kill her an' all, if the authorities move in. He will too! *He's got a shotgun!*'

Dawn was already lighting the sky when Agnes Crowther returned home, her conscience easier than it had been for many a long year. The information which she had carried in that letter had been badly received by Emma, outlining as it did certain suspicions that Caleb Crowther was directly responsible for the death of her father, Thadius, and that of her mother also. However, in view of the fact that Agnes Crowther had delivered the letter herself, condemning though it was, and because Emma's aunt held nothing back of her shame in the part she had played when Emma was imprisoned and desperate for help, there was a deal of forgiveness in Emma's heart for her father's sister. The letter itself was handed to the officer on duty at the Tanner residence.

Now, as the brougham travelled along the lane which led to Breckleton House, the driver was alerted by another carriage, manned and guarded by officers of the law, and stationed in the drive leading up to the big house. This observation was quickly reported to Agnes Crowther, who on leaning from her window as the carriage drew nearer was astonished to see how the house itself appeared to be under siege.

'Sorry, m'lady . . . you can't go no further, I'm afraid,' the officer at the gate told her. Being one of the men who had questioned her on leaving the house earlier, he recognized her at once and explained the situation, adding with genuine sympathy, 'I'm very sorry, ma'am.'

At that point, a loud shot rang out and the officer sped away to investigate. Defiant and afraid for Martha's life, Agnes Crowther clambered from the carriage and hurried after him. 'My daughter's in there!' she called. 'You must let me go to her.'

'*Stay back!*' The officer grabbed her by the arm and thrust her behind the shelter of an old oak tree. 'There's no question of *anyone* going in there just yet. The fellow's beyond all reason . . . firing at random. Every effort will be made to get your daughter out,' he promised, 'but we have to choose the right moment to move in.'

346

Before he could go on, there came another volley of shots. 'Stay where you are, ma'am. I'll send someone to escort you back to your carriage. It's too dangerous for you to remain here.' He went cautiously forward, staying low and occasionally slipping out of sight. Agnes Crowther followed at a discreet distance.

As she came closer to the big house, all manner of things careered through Agnes Crowther's mind. Suddenly she felt the years lying heavy on her shoulders. She felt old. She *was* old, and now it didn't seem to matter any more. Nothing did, *except Martha*. Martha, peevish, spoilt and with no thought for anyone but herself. That was not entirely true, because she adored her son, Edward, and she had always loved her father to the point of obsession, the same father who had callously rejected her from the day she was born. Agnes's heart went out to her now.

As she moved forward on slow, secret footsteps, nearer and nearer to the rear of the house, Agnes Crowther was made to reflect on other things of the past. That letter had planted so many distasteful seeds in her mind. It had opened up so many questions that had lain dormant all these years: questions regarding her husband's faithfulness during the early period of their marriage. She was under no illusion with regard to his infidelities these past years, but now that was not the issue any more.

Casting her mind back, Agnes Crowther remembered her brother's wife, Mary . . . unusually lovely, vibrant and captivating. She recalled how enchanted Caleb was in that young woman's presence, and how she herself had suffered agonies of suspicion and jealousy when the two of them were together. How she loved Caleb in

347

those days; he was so tall and handsome, so virile and overpowering. Strange, she thought now, how a love so deep and trusting could turn to cold indifference – even hatred – over the passage of time.

The letter had intimated that Caleb had murdered Mary following an affair, when Emma was but an infant. A terrible thought had entered Agnes Crowther's mind. Was *Caleb* Emma's real father? Could it also be true that he had suffocated the life out of Thadius, before that poor suffering man could change his will? *She had to know!*

'Jesus Christ! . . . There's a woman in there!' Agnes Crowther could be seen through the open doorway. With determination she mounted the stairs and pressed on, beyond restraining hands, beyond help.

Unafraid, she pushed open the bedroom door, her heart soaring when she saw that Martha was safe – the unfortunate creature was trussed into a chair, her unattractive face contorted with pain, and a faint cowardly whimpering emanating from her lips. When she heard her mother's voice, thick with emotion and authority, issuing the instruction, '*Let her go!*' Martha was at once silent. And more fearful than before. She knew at last how much her father loathed her – had *always* loathed her. She knew much more than that. Here in this room she had been her father's confessor. She knew his deepest secrets – and his madness.

Caleb Crowther swung round, his eyes wild and excited, the barrel of the gun aimed at his wife's throat. The chuckle started as a rattling sound deep in his chest. In a moment he was roaring with laughter – frightening, insane laughter that sent a chill down the spines of all who heard it. Outside, huddled together in a carriage and waiting to be transported to an even safer distance, Cook and Amy heard it also. 'God love and save us,' whispered Cook, hurriedly making the sign of the cross, 'it's the devil himself!'

As soon as the laughter had started, so it ended. The ensuing silence was more than the officer in charge could bear. '*I'm going in!*' he said in sombre voice. 'The rest of you stay here . . . there's no point in risking *all* our necks. Keep alert, mind!' he warned. 'He's a devious devil.'

No sooner had the officer gone a dozen steps than a shot rang out, causing everyone to dive for cover. The echo had barely died down when there followed a short burst of laughter, then a second shot.

For what seemed an endless moment, the startled birds overhead ceased their dawn chorus. A deathly hush prevailed.

On cautious footsteps the men inched their way forward, dreading what might await them. At any minute each one feared the shot that would mow him down. However, they had no choice. Two shots had been fired in that room, yet there were three people there. If the third was alive, it was their duty to get her – or him – out alive.

As they silently entered the house, there wasn't a man there who did not offer up a prayer for his own safety.

Chapter Thirteen

'Well now, sure *there's* a song to light up some lucky fella's life, eh?' The good-humoured Irishman came into the hotel bedroom, jauntily flinging his carpet bag on to the bed and appreciatively eyeing the slim, uniformed figure that emerged from the bathroom.

'Oh, I'm sorry, sir,' Molly said, obviously embarrassed at being overheard humming a merry tune as she went about her duties. 'I was just changing the towels . . . I've finished now.' She crushed the soiled towels to her breast and would have hurried by him if he hadn't called out, 'Won't you tell me what wonderful thing has happened to put such a jolly melody in your heart, eh?' There was a twinkle in his eye and a certain unsteadiness about him that told Molly he also had been doing some celebrating.

Molly warmed to his friendly manner. 'Nothing more "wonderful" than landing a proper job,' she said, smiling at him, 'and soon . . . I hope to bring my children to live with me.' Molly's smile was radiant, bathing her whole face with loveliness. Her dark eyes sparkled like black gems.

'Kids, eh . . . ? And where's your ol' fella?' His gaze was suddenly intense.

Molly was on her guard now. She thought the man was too interested. 'Excuse me, sir,' she apologized, 'but I've a deal of work that won't wait.'

'Aw, go on with you . . . there's never been work that won't wait.' He sauntered towards her.

It was when Molly put her hand to the door knob with the intention of making a hurried exit that there came a slight tap on the door, after which it was swung open to reveal a matronly figure with stiff, disapproving features, and a deep scowl on her face as she glowered at Molly. 'Go to my office,' she said, before instantly addressing the man. 'I do apologize. Staff have strict instructions *never* to intrude on a guest's privacy.'

'No, you've got it all wrong, darling. The little girlie was only doing her job.'

'That's perfectly all right, sir.'

'Hey, I hope she's not in any trouble on account of me?'

'Please don't concern yourself.' The proprietor's wife feared that a distasteful scene might be brewing. Checking first to see that Molly had reluctantly started her way down to the office, she leaned into the room, saying in a lowered voice, 'You should consider yourself very fortunate, sir. Lately there has been a spate of stealing.' She deliberately glanced after Molly's retreating figure. 'I'm thankful to say that we have tracked the culprit down.' Her intimation left the fellow in no doubt as to who 'the culprit' was.

'You don't say?' He was momentarily shocked, but mindful of the fact that only last night an innocent-looking whore had stripped his pockets bare. 'It just goes to show, eh?' he chuckled. 'My old ma was right when she warned me never to trust a pretty face.' Molly's dark, smiling eyes came into his mind. 'There's no need for the police, surely?'

'Don't worry, sir. It's our policy not to involve the police if it's at all avoidable,' she assured him, before closing the door.

Even before the proprietor's wife came into sight of the office, she could hear Molly vehemently protesting her innocence. She quickened her step, fearful that the fracas might be overheard. As it was, the entire episode had cast a shameful slur on their 'respectable' hotel. Thieving from the guests' bedrooms! Such a thing would damage trade badly if it were to get out. Thank goodness they had managed to nip it in the bud. It *was* that wretched young woman, however much she might deny it. There had been no such incidents prior to her arrival. What a fool her husband was to take the creature on without previous experience or references of any kind.

Storming into the office where her husband showed signs of believing Molly's protests, the woman slammed shut the door. 'I'll thank you to keep your voice down!' she warned Molly.

'But I'm innocent, I tell you!'

'*You're a thief . . . that's what you are.*'

'Now, now, let's keep calm,' the flustered proprietor intervened. 'This needs to be discussed quietly and sensibly.'

'Don't you give me that,' his wife rounded on him viciously. 'It was *you* who took her on. It speaks for itself . . . the thieving only started when she was put to work as a chambermaid.'

'It weren't only me who started then,' Molly reminded her. 'What about *Vera*?' Normally Molly would never point the finger at anyone, but she was desperate. She needed this job, and the big cellar room that went with

it. The proprietor had already promised that, if she
worked well, the children could live down there with her
'so long as they keep quiet and don't become a nuisance'. She knew it was an arrangement that his wife
had never agreed to. But the promise was made and
Molly had skivvied her fingers to the bone to keep him to
it. Besides which, she was innocent of the thieving. It
hadn't escaped her notice that the other new chambermaid – who also happened to be a relative of this surly
woman – had a full purse lately, and money to spare.
'Have you questioned *her*?' Molly wanted to know.

'How dare you suggest that my sister's daughter is a
thief!'

'Well, *I'm* no thief neither. I won't be sacked for
something I didn't do.'

The woman laughed at Molly's defiance. 'Oh, you
won't, won't you?' A particularly nasty smile came over
her face. 'In that case, we should send for the authorities
. . . don't you agree?'

Her words were met by a thick silence. Molly knew
she was bluffing, but she dared not take the chance.
What if they did come? What if they found out who she
was, and where she'd come from? What about the
children? She might be delivered into the hands of
Justice Crowther! Dear God! *The very thought filled her
with terror*. She'd be hanged for the murder of that café
owner, Bill Craig. Hanged, as sure as day follows night.
No, she couldn't risk it. *Daren't* risk it.

'Well?' The woman's voice was a sneer.

'I'll not leave without my dues though.' Molly braz-
ened it out, knowing that she had lost the argument.

'Your "dues", eh?' snorted the woman. 'You won't
get a brass farthing!'

'The lass is entitled to her dues.' The proprietor surprised them both by stepping forward and taking a sum of money from his pocket. This he handed to Molly saying, 'We'll not keep back what you've sweated for.' He cast a cursory glance at his wife, 'Because then *we'd* be the "thieves", wouldn't we, eh?' He pressed the money into Molly's hand. 'Best go quietly, eh, gal?' he suggested kindly. And that was just what Molly did.

As she pounded the streets of London, desperately searching for a new place of work and a home where she could bring the children, how different it might have been if only Molly had known that the best thing that could have happened was for the hotel proprietor's wife to call the authorities as she had threatened.

Molly's belief that the authorities were searching for her was very true, because even at that moment there were a number of people scouring the streets of London for Emma Tanner's daughter, including the frustrated private detective hired by Marlow. There was another also. The man who was never far from Molly's mind; the man she loved but, for so many reasons, had sent away. Mick Darcy was her strength and her comfort during the dark, lonely hours. He was also a great source of pain and unhappiness, for she was convinced that he was lost to her for ever. How it would have gladdened her heart to know that, even now, he was not far away, searching for her, determined that he would not go home without the woman he adored.

Chapter Fourteen

It was early in the month of June, in the year of our Lord 1887. The evening was hot and uncomfortably humid. During the day, the streets had been alive with people strolling about in their summer outfits; the women bedecked in pretty bright colours with the hems of their skirts swirling about the tops of their buttoned shoes, and looking very summery in their frilly hats and fancy waistcoats. The men too looked dapper and handsome in their stiff white collars with neat little dickie-bows, and bright, becoming boaters.

From early light there could be heard the cries of the many vendors who sold their wares in the streets: the muffin-man, the flower-seller, the costermonger, and even a man with a small cage alive with birds, strapped to his middle. But now it was evening, and the night creatures were stirring.

'Lonely are yer, darlin'? D'yer fancy a bit o' company, eh? I'm a fair enough fella . . . willing to pay, o' course.' The fat man doffed his hat and leered at Molly through cunning eyes. 'What d'yer say?'

Weary and disheartened by the many refusals of work and lodgings, Molly turned away from Piccadilly Circus, quickening her footsteps towards Hyde Park. The night was coming in fast, and she had a mind to find a quiet corner where she could hide herself away from prying eyes. Last night she had huddled in some dark alley. It had been a fearsome place, haunted by scavenging vermin and frequented by lovers who giggled and coupled, blissfully unaware of her presence. One poor fellow had been brought there for a beating, and a particularly nasty vagabond had warned Molly to 'stay off my patch'! Fearful that she might be robbed of the wages given to her the day before by the hotel proprietor, Molly had barely slept a wink.

All day Molly had trudged the streets, knocking on any door where she thought she might find work. But so far she had not been successful. Tomorrow, she thought, tomorrow I'll find work. Suddenly her courage threatened to desert her, and she felt close to tears. Every minute of every day, she kept certain memories warm in her heart: memories of happier days, of the children, and of Mick. Engulfed by these wonderful memories, she was tempted to make her way home. Home to Blackburn, to Tilly and the children. But then she was cruelly reminded that she *had* no home.

A well of gratitude for Tilly rose in Molly's tired heart. The children would be well looked after; she knew that. All the same, she wanted them with her. There had not been a single minute when she hadn't missed them, every one. She thought of little Sal, and her heart ached. Two other faces filled her mind, those of Peggy and of Tom. It was almost more than she could bear. She had been away for a fortnight now and, after believing that it was only a matter of days before she could collect the children and bring them to London where they could begin a new life, all her hopes were cruelly shattered yet again.

'Tea, is it?' The grinning woman wiped the table and

stared at Molly as she settled herself in an upright chair by the door. It occurred to her that here was a streetwalker, looking to pick up a client. But then she saw how proud were Molly's lovely features, even in spite of her poor, unkempt appearance.

'Yes please . . . and a muffin.' Molly had suddenly felt hungry, which wasn't surprising considering that in order to preserve her meagre savings, she had denied herself food all day. Besides which, she was loath to leave the busy, lamplit streets. A terrible feeling of loneliness had settled on her. For some strange reason, she felt restless and deeply disturbed, filled with a terrible sense of impending doom. The night was sultry, but Molly was cold.

'All right, are you dearie?' asked the woman, setting a mug of steaming tea before her. When Molly nodded and smiled back, she went on, 'We ain't got no muffins left. But if you look along the counter there, you'll see there's all manner o' pies . . . apple tarts and barm-cakes. Now then, you just tell me what takes your fancy, dearie.'

Inching forward in her chair, Molly let her dark eyes rove over the mouth-watering delicacies, her hunger like a sharp pain inside her. Her glance went from the barm-cakes to the apple pie. Then to the newspaper pages that lined the shelf beneath. The headline of a particular report blazed from the page.

CHILDREN ABDUCTED
JUSTICE OF THE PEACE
WANTED FOR QUESTIONING

Ashen-faced, Molly came closer. Her sense of horror was realized when she read:

> The distinguished Justice of the Peace, Caleb
> Crowther, now retired, is wanted for questioning
> by the authorities.
>   In the early hours of yesterday morning there
> was a break-in at the home of Mrs Tilly Watson of
> Dock Street, Blackburn, Lancs . . .

At that point the words disappeared beneath the folded
paper. Half-crazed with fear, Molly tore at the shelf,
spilling plates and pastries as she frantically tugged to
loosen the paper. Oblivious to the loud protests and
screams from the woman behind, Molly read on:

> Mrs Watson herself was brutally attacked, and a
> number of children were forcibly removed from
> the premises. No charges have yet been made.

The newspaper was dated some two weeks previous.
    'Hey! What the bloody hell d'yer think yer playing
at . . . ! POLICE! HELP! POLICE!' The woman had
been both astonished and terrified at Molly's puzzling
behaviour. When, wide-eyed with shock, Molly pushed
past her to run on to the streets, she yelled and shouted,
threatening to heap all manner of punishment on Molly's
head. But Molly couldn't hear her. All she could think of
was that he had got her children. THE JUSTICE HAD
GOT HER CHILDREN! Dazed and shocked to the
very core, she was aware of only one thing: she had to get
home. She must get home . . . *must* get home!

Having carefully avoided the many horse-drawn carriages that thundered along the busy roads to converge
on Piccadilly Circus, Mick Darcy leaned against a lamp

post, where he drew out his pipe and proceeded to light it. He was foot-sore and exhausted by the many miles he had covered these past weeks.

Mick had searched high and low, delving into every nook and cranny, questioning more people than he could ever hope to remember. But Molly was nowhere to be found. Dear God in Heaven, he thought now, where else am I to look? Even the detective hired by the Tanners had fared no better than himself. But then London was a big place, bustling with people and covering many square miles. All the same, he felt as though he had covered every available inch. Certainly he had followed up on what Tilly had told him, inquiring at all the big hotels. Molly had been to none of them, 'as far as we can recall'.

On the far side of the busy road, the uproar was so loud that it drew Mick's attention. For a moment, he took little notice – there were always people shouting and yelling, competing with the costermongers and fighting amongst themselves. He began to turn away, to bring his mind back to his Molly. But then, as though the image in his mind had suddenly materialized, *there she was*! Her black hair more unkempt than the last time he had seen her, and her figure painfully thin, but it was Molly right enough! His heart leapt inside him. There was something wrong. She was being chased. Molly was in trouble. '*MOLLY!*' His desperate cry cut above the noise. For a split second she half-turned. 'Molly . . . Stay where you are!' he yelled, running forward along the pavement and frantically seeking an opening where he might dash across the road to her.

Afraid that she had not seen him, Mick yelled again and again, 'Molly! Stay there!' Several times he made to run across the road, but was driven back by the many rushing carriages. Suddenly Molly was running in his direction, two men and a woman in pursuit. Mick could not be sure whether or not she had heard him. '*Molly! Molly!*'

When the horse and carriage careered alongside the kerb, the spin of a wheel catching Molly and flinging her across the pavement, Mick was momentarily paralysed. Then he surged forward, her name on his lips and a fervent prayer in his heart. 'Dear God . . . don't let her be dead. *Don't* let her be dead.'

Molly was not dead, although when Mick gathered her into his arms she at first appeared lifeless. After a moment, when he sobbed her name over and over, his warm tears spilling on to her still, white face, she opened her eyes to murmur his name. 'Mick . . . oh, Mick.' Then a look of terror darkened her face as she struggled in his tight embrace. 'My babies! He's *got* my babies!' The tears rolled down her face and her voice broke into sobs.

'No, sweetheart. Your "babies" are safe.' He would have added, 'with Emma . . . their grandmother, your *mother*', but Molly knew nothing of that. Not yet. He gently assured her that they were out of harm's way, and so, thank God, was she. When Molly tearfully confessed how the authorities would hang her and make her children orphans because she had murdered a café owner by the name of Bill Craig, Mick softly laughed. The relief flooded her lovely face when he explained how the man was not 'murdered' because he himself had lately spoken to Bill Craig in the flesh.

'Take me home, please, Mick,' Molly begged, her features contorted with pain and her arms clinging to this man whom she loved so much.

'Oh, Molly . . . my sweet darling,' he murmured, his heart heavy with love. He wanted nothing more in this world than to take his Molly 'home'. To take her and keep her, and love her forever.

Seeing that the young woman would live – and some feeling cheated because of it – the crowd began melting away. Only one man lingered a while longer: a man attired in evening suit and with an air of prosperity about him, a man with brown eyes and a serious look on his attractive face. In the dark, in the background, he remained unobserved, although he was in a position to see both Molly and Mick clearly. For one uncertain moment it seemed that he might make himself known. But then he abruptly turned away and climbed into the waiting carriage.

Now, as he smiled at the redhead waiting there, her slim shoulders wrapped in fur and her long fingers bright with diamonds, the seriousness of the previous moment swiftly left him. 'Drive on!' he urged the man up front.

'*Was* it an accident?' his companion asked, her pink-painted nails stroking the vivid scar down her cheek as was her habit.

Taking hold of her fingers, he put them to his mouth and began playfully biting them. 'Don't worry your pretty head about such things,' he told her with a twinkling grin. 'Just concentrate on me, darling. Because, now that the Justice has gone to his maker, *I* intend to be the only man in your life. And I won't complain if you should blackmail me to your heart's desire!' He laughed aloud. 'So long as it's me *body* you're after . . . and not my money!'

'*That'll* be the day, when you've got money of your own,' she chuckled. 'No wonder they call you Jack-the-Lad.'

The sound of their raucous laughter echoed behind them. There was a moment when his face peered from the back window to see Mick gently raise Molly from the pavement. His arms about her were strong and sure. She clung to him, and they looked so right together.

Turning to his vulgar, teasing companion, Jack kissed her full on her scarlet mouth, his fingers reaching inside her silken blouse. They laughed and drew closer. Suddenly he felt as though a mountain of responsibility had fallen from his shoulders.

Lapsing into a short, troubled silence, he realized that Molly would never willingly give herself up to any man while she believed herself to be wed to another. Suddenly he was filled with guilt. He should have told Molly long ago how their 'marriage' had been a carefully arranged sham. He was not one to be shackled by any woman, even one as captivating as Molly, and he knew she would not sleep with him unless it was with a ring on her finger. He had cheated her. Now, he must right that wrong. Somehow he must get word to her that she was a free woman. No doubt she would curse him for the rogue he was, but he hoped she would forgive him. He believed she would, for Molly was never vindictive. He chuckled aloud.

'What's taken your fancy then?' inquired his companion with a giggle.

'Nothing for you to worry about,' he replied, hugging her tighter. Nothing for either of them to worry about, he mused, wiping his mouth along her neck. He had his woman. Molly had her man. All was right with the world.

Chapter Fifteen

'How can I ever thank you, Miss Nelly?' Cook's round face was squeezed into a most uncomfortable expression as she tried to suppress her tears of joy. 'If you hadn't come forward with such a generous offer . . . well, I daren't think what might have happened to me and Amy.' She glanced at her smaller companion, who was seated demurely beside her on the couch, seemingly overawed by all that had happened. '*Amy!*' Even in her delight, Cook had not lost that air of authority with which she had kept the hapless little maid in check all these years. 'What have you got to say to this kind and benevolent lady who's saved us from the workhouse?' Her frown deepened when she saw Amy look gormlessly about. 'Amy! I asked . . . what have you to *say?*'

'I don't know what to say . . . I really and truly don't.' She raised her eyes and Nelly saw that they were swimming with tears. 'I was so afraid, you understand . . . I never wanted to go in no workhouse!'

Deeply moved, Nelly leaned forward in her chair and patted Amy's trembling hand. 'Don't you worry yourself, my gal!' she declared firmly. 'There ain't nobody gonna put you in no workhouse . . . nor Cook neither. You've got Nelly's word on that.' She pursed her lips into a circle of perfect wrinkles, waiting until Amy had finished loudly blowing her nose in a linen square. 'Right then, you two,' she said smartly, rising from the chair, 'take yersel's off ter Blackpool an' get that there tea-rooms open, while the summer's on us. There'll be many a thirsty tripper just waiting fer such a dandy little place, I'll be bound. What's more . . . you'll happen get a visit from the Tanner family afore long.' A beam of delight spread across her homely face as she went on, '*All* on us! Mr and Mrs Tanner with their daughter Molly and her fella, Mick Darcy. And the chillder o' course. Oh, without a doubt, the darlin' chillder.' She stared at the two women with a look of incredulity. 'Did yer know that them poor chillder ain't never paddled in the sea?' she demanded. 'Oho! We shall soon mend *that*. What! Me an' Emma's looking forward to it like no-body's business.' She clutched her chubby belly and chuckled aloud. 'So, get yersel's off like I said . . . 'cause ye'd best have that there tea-rooms open afore we get there!'

'We'll do our best . . . seeing as it's thanks to you that we've got the opportunity of our own little business.' Cook positively beamed as she, too, got to her feet, indicating for Amy to do the same.

'Well, it ain't no gift, is it, eh?' Nelly reminded her. 'I'll be looking for the monthly payments on the loan, soon as ever yer get the first customer through the door. *And* I'll be expecting a handsome bonus on my share of the takings.' Nelly prided herself on the fact that she had actually put some of her savings into a business venture. Huh! T'weren't only *Emma* as had a good business head, she told herself. She had told Emma the very same, and what more could that darling woman do than agree with her!

'Oh, you won't be sorry, I promise you,' Cook assured

her. 'Me and Amy . . . we'll have the busiest tea-rooms in the whole of Blackpool.'

'I should think so, too!' Nelly was eager to see the women gone now. She had other, more important matters on her mind. 'Go on then. Off yer go.' She stepped towards the door, leaving Cook and Amy with no choice but to follow her.

In the outer vestibule, Cook hesitated, before venturing seriously, 'I hope you don't mind me saying, but I'm so glad that things turned out right for Mrs Tanner, what with finding her daughter and her grandchildren. It fair broke my old heart to see the way she was betrayed.' Her eyes misted over, and she made a strange, coughing sound. 'Emma . . . I mean Mrs Tanner . . . well, she were always a very lovely, amiable girl.'

Suddenly Nelly felt ashamed. 'O' course! *You* knew Emma long afore I did.'

Cook nodded. 'Her father was a good man.' Her voice cracked with anger. 'And to think how he met such a terrible end.'

'There are some things best not talked about,' warned Nelly in a sombre voice.

Cook was at once repentant. 'No, no, of course not. All the same . . .'

'Good day to you.' Nelly began closing the door.

'Good day. And thank you again.'

Long after the two women had disappeared down the lane, Nelly gently propelled herself back and forth in the rocking-chair. Cook's departing words echoed in her troubled mind. What a wicked, wicked fellow the Justice had been. Not content with shooting himself and his unfortunate wife, he had put his hapless daughter Martha through such a devastating experience that she might never recover from it; not even with her son's tender care, nor with her husband on his way from Australia at this very minute. Although to Nelly's mind – and from what Cook herself had been given to understand by hearsay – that particular marriage was long dead and gone. It would be to her son Edward that Martha would turn for strength and comfort. No doubt Silas would return to the arms of his Australian comforter.

What the Justice had confessed to his own daughter were crimes of the most evil and sadistic nature. Into her unwilling ears he had poured out the most vile and corrupt secrets, which he had carried in his black heart these many long years – the illicit love affair with Mary Grady, even while his *own wife* was heavy with child. The fact that he had pressed a pillow into Thadius's face and suffocated the life out of him while the wretched man lay weak and helpless. How he had later abused that same man's trust, and prematurely married Emma off. Then when she was unjustly accused of murder, he had shamelessly blackmailed a fellow Justice in order to engineer Emma's transportation from these shores, so that he could take over her inheritance. An inheritance which had provided him with the means to gamble and keep the company of whores.

From his own lips, Caleb Crowther had proudly related all this to his daughter, actually *boasting* of adultery against her mother, Agnes; treachery, fraud and, most damning of all, the heinous deed of *murder*. Word by word, he had shattered every illusion that his daughter held of him. He also admitted with great relish how he had set Martha against her own husband, Silas. 'You're a dim-witted fool!' he had laughed. There had bccn so much more that he had told the gullible creature. Things that had cut her to the heart. Awful, soul-destroying things that she would not forget in the whole of her lifetime. Things that she could never bring herself to reveal, not to any living person. And certainly not to Emma. *Especially* not to Emma.

Rocking thoughtfully in her chair, Nelly reflected on Martha's state of mind when she had related the things her father had confessed to her. The ordeal was written in every line of that woman's face, thought Nelly now, as she realized how the dreadful experience appeared to have changed Martha somehow; made her softer and more understanding of others. Oh, but wouldn't it change anybody? First, to be taken hostage by your own father, and trussed up at gunpoint. Then, to be an unwilling and horrified confessor to his many sins. And finally, to witness the murder of her own mother before her disbelieving eyes, before her father turned the gun on his own miserable person.

Nelly visibly shivered. What a monster was Caleb Crowther. *Why*, in the name of all that was decent, could he not have spared his daughter such punishment? Dear God. It didn't bear thinking about. Suddenly Nelly brought the rocking-chair to a halt. *There was something not quite right.* Something with regard to Martha, and the telling of what had taken place in that room. Some furtive and secret look in Martha's brown speckly eyes. Something that had suggested to Nelly at the time that Martha was not revealing the full truth of what had been done, or said, in the final, desperate moments of her parents' lives.

Nelly began her rocking again; slow, methodical movements that seemed to suit her deep, thoughtful mood. 'You were keeping some'at back, Martha, my gal!' she muttered. 'What were it, eh? What could be so fearful that yer chose ter keep it in yer own broken heart? Surely to God . . . it couldn't be more terrible than the things yer disclosed to us all, could it? COULD IT?'

Distressed by her own imaginings, Nelly thrust the puzzling matter of Martha from her mind. Her thoughts flew to other, happier events. Like Marlow's pride and Emma's great joy at having found Molly and her brood. Now they not only had the daughter lost to them many years ago, but they had also been blessed with two adorable granddaughters, and a lovable, rascally grandson, whose crippled leg would receive the very best medical attention that money could buy.

Closing her eyes, Nelly cast her mind back over the long, eventful years, to when she and Emma had first come across each other in that rat-infested prison cell. So many years. So much had happened since that fateful day, when the two of them were little more than children; afraid and friendless, not knowing what the future held, or whether they might never see another day. 'Oh, but we did, didn't we, Emma, gal?' Nelly chuckled. 'We ain't so easy put down, are we, eh?' She blessed the day when she and Emma were flung together, because it had brought her the very best friend any woman could have. Suddenly Nelly's heart was filled with love for that darling woman who had suffered so much in her life, and yet had emerged all the stronger for it. 'Bless yer, Emma,' she said softly, the tears rolling down her lined face, 'bless yer yeart, Emma darling.' She clambered from the chair and went to the sideboard. From here she took out a bottle of gin which she quickly opencd and, with her feet doing a little jig, she tipped it to her mouth and gulped down a sizeable measure. Afterwards, returning to the rocking-chair with the bottle clutched to her lap, she closed her eyes and fell into a delightful slumber.

The last impression on Nelly's mind was that of Marlow and the children, who had all been ecstatic when Mick Darcy had returned with Molly that very morning. All six of them had gone to the church to reunite Molly with her mother. Too emotional to be patient, Emma had made her way there as soon as the news had come through that Molly had been found and would shortly be brought home.

The priest gazed on Emma from a discreet place at the back of the church, his face wreathed in smiles as she knelt at the altar, her eyes raised to the crucifix, and her lips murmuring a prayer of heartfelt thanks for her new-found grandchildren, and for Molly's safe return.

Silently the priest moved away, having already given his own prayer of gratitude and being overjoyed at the news that Molly was being returned from London this very morning. It was a miracle that Emma's grand-children were also safely recovered from a derelict warehouse along Bank Top. These were wondrous tidings. As was Emma's return to the Church – which she had so bitterly denounced on the tragic death of her son.

Seeing a group of people approaching, and at once recognizing Marlow, he hurried forward, eager to make the acquaintance of the new additions to the Tanner family.

* * *

Emma sensed that there was someone behind her. Suddenly, even in the heat of a blazing June morning, her every limb was trembling. When at last she was compelled to turn round, her heart almost stopped. '*Molly*,' she whispered, the name warm and loving on her lips. As she gazed at her daughter, the slim figure wrapped in a tattered shawl, her hair so rich and black, and those dark, beseeching eyes intent on her, Emma could not stem her tears. Through a bitter-sweet mist she continued to gaze on this girl, *this young woman*, who was her own flesh and blood – hers and Marlow's. Dear God above!

So many images rampaged through Emma's mind, the strongest and most painful being that of a cobbled street outside a prison. And of a girl-child, newborn and abandoned to the gutter. 'Oh, Molly! Can I really believe you're home with me now?' she cried brokenly. Through her tears, Emma saw that Molly also was crying. Taking a hesitant step forward, she stretched out her arms, unable to speak for the strength of emotion that overwhelmed her. Without a word, Molly fell into her mother's loving embrace. Together, in a silence that bound them like no words could, the two of them went at a gentle pace to where Marlow, Mick and the children had waited, and had witnessed the tender scene with full hearts. There was so much to talk about. So many memories to relive, and so many more to make.

Now, as the children surged forward to take their place with their mammy and their grandmother, Marlow took out his handkerchief and surreptitiously dabbed at his eyes. His voice was shaking as he told Mick, 'I'm a fortunate man, Mick Darcy . . . a very fortunate man.'

'No more than meself,' Mick replied, 'for I have the love of my Molly at long last.'

Emma stole a moment to go to her father's resting-place. Here, she whispered of her love for him, telling him with glad heart, 'It's all over, Papa. We must forget the heartaches now, and learn to live again with hope for the future.' She paused for a moment, remembering the man her father was. He had always been her strength. Her example. 'I love you,' she murmured, momentarily closing her eyes and bathing her mind with fond memories of him. How he would have loved Molly and the children, she thought. And now he could rest in peace because at long last, her life was fulfilled. Over the coming years she would tell his granddaughter and great-grandchildren all about him. Thadius Grady was a special man, a man they could be proud of.

The horse-drawn ensemble travelled slowly down the winding lane that passed the churchyard. From the carriage, Martha saw how proudly Marlow stood beside his grandchildren, and how occasionally he glanced lovingly towards Molly, who was safely enfolded in Mick's strong embrace.

In the foreground was Emma, bent over her father's tombstone, her handsome face so peaceful, so very proud. Fleetingly Emma saw Martha, and her smile was warm and genuine. Emma bore no grudges. She believed that Martha had suffered enough. They had *all* suffered enough.

Martha, too, was of the same mind. She returned Emma's smile, and settled back in the seat beside her son Edward, the awful truth kept hidden in her heart.

What her father had told her must remain her secret forever.

Martha realized with shame how, many years ago, she would have enjoyed inflicting a degree of pain on Emma. But not now. Not after all that had happened. The resentment was all a long time ago – to do with hate and love and passion.

Emma must never be told that Thadius Grady was not her real father. Nor that she was begot from an illicit affair between her mother and Caleb Crowther. Most damning of all, that it was Thadius himself who had murdered Emma's mother in a fit of insane jealousy, when she took a bargee for a lover. The bargee was Bill Royston. This unfortunate fellow had met his sorry end at the hands of Caleb Crowther. Later, both Caleb and Thadius had remained silent when that man's own wife, Eve Royston, was hanged for the murder in which she had played no part.

Thadius Grady and Caleb Crowther were cowards of the worst kind: each bound to protect the other. Emma, Molly and her children, were innocent pawns. Vagabonds on the road of life. Now though, because of hope and love, and the kinder hand of fate, they were vagabonds no more!

The very next evening the house on Park Street rang with laughter. Passers-by smiled knowingly. The story of Emma and Marlow's reunion with their daughter and grandchildren had been told far and wide. It was good that all had come right for Emma Grady. She was a fine woman who had known great heartache. Now it was only right that she should also know great joy.

'I do love you so, Emma.' Marlow had gently drawn

her from the table, where she had been helping Tilly Watson, Nelly and Molly to supervise the children's party. It was a noisy, happy affair. With Molly's three youngsters and Tilly's brood, the exasperated Nelly had earlier been heard to remark loudly, 'By! The whole bleedin' house is shakin' on its foundations!'

'Oh, Marlow, I'm so happy . . . so very happy.' Emma's grey eyes were awash with tears as she lifted her gaze to his.

Taking Emma's hand in his own, Marlow raised it to his lips, brushing it with a kiss and telling her, 'We have our family now, Emma, and so very much to look forward to.'

'Our family,' Emma repeated thoughtfully. She found untold comfort in those words. She pressed into the arm that lovingly encircled her. 'And oh, Marlow . . . aren't they all wonderful?' Emma was smiling now, softly laughing as she looked across to where Sal was causing mayhem by indignantly insisting that the other children should 'take proper turns at the jelly dish.' Nelly was red-faced from trying to keep 'order', and Tilly's brood were all complaining to their mam that 'Sal's being bossy again'.

Laughing aloud, Marlow told Emma, 'Our eldest granddaughter is going to be as cantankerous as her namesake. With my sister Sal . . . *nobody* could ever get a word in edgeways.'

At the far side of the room, Molly was helpless with laughter. In that moment, her dark eyes glanced towards Emma. A well of love rose between them, subduing them for an instant. The two of them had talked deep into the night and on into the dawn. There had been many tears, of both joy and regrets, yet through it all had emerged a bond so strong that nothing would ever weaken it.

'It's a glorious evening, me beauty,' Mick Darcy murmured in Molly's ear.

'That it is, Mick Darcy,' she replied in a teasing manner, her black eyes dancing mischievously. She thought of Jack-the-Lad, and of the hastily scribbled note telling her the two of them were never wed. But it was in the past now. 'I wonder if a certain fella would take a lass for a stroll in the garden?' she asked. She slipped her small hand into his and smiled up at him.

'If you mean *this* certain fella . . . he would follow the lass concerned to the far corners of the earth.' He bent his head to kiss the top of her unruly hair. 'I'd be a proud man to stroll with you in the gardens, sweetheart,' he said softly, 'on this night . . . and on every night for the rest of our lives.'

A moment later, Emma watched Molly and her man go quietly from the room. Her heart was full. The good Lord had answered her prayers.

Now, as Marlow's arm slid round her shoulders, Emma glanced up at him, at those familiar dark eyes that held a lifetime of love. For the rest of her days she would remember this day above all others.

BORN TO SERVE

Josephine Cox

'*I can take him away from you any time I want.*'

Her mistress's cruel taunt is deeply disturbing to Jenny. But why should Claudia be interested in a servant's sweetheart? All the same, Jenny reckons without Claudia's vicious nature; using a wily trick, she eventually seduces Frank, who, overcome with shame, leaves the household for a new life in Blackburn.

Losing her sweetheart is just the first of many disasters that leave Jenny struggling to cope alone. When Claudia gives birth to a baby girl – Frank's child – she cruelly disowns the helpless infant and relies on Jenny to care for little Katie and love her as her own.

Despite luring a kindly man into a marriage that offers comfort and security to them all, Claudia secretly indulges her corrupt desires.

Always afraid for the beloved child who has come to depend on her, Jenny is constantly called upon to show courage and fortitude to fight for all she holds dear. In her heart she yearns for Frank, believing that one day they must be reunited. When Fate takes a hand, it seems as though Jenny may see her dreams come true.

'Driven and passionate, she stirs a pot spiced with incest, wife beating . . . and murder' *The Sunday Times*

'Pulls at the heartstrings' *Today*

'Not to be missed' *Bolton Evening News*

FICTION / SAGA 0 7472 4415 4

MORE THAN RICHES

Josephine Cox

'*You'll never let it go, will you?*'

Taken aback by the hatred in her eyes, he wanted to tear out her heart. 'I'll let it go when you stop wanting him!' he hissed. Then he covered his head with his hands and cried like a child.

When Rosie's parents were involved in a train accident, her mother was killed and her father was left crippled, unable to earn a living and relying on Rosie to keep the wolf from the door.

With her mother gone and her sweetheart Adam away in the army, Rosie is lonely. She eagerly awaits the letters from him, but they never come. As she grows more disillusioned, Adam's best friend Doug goes out of his way to be charming and attentive. Alone and confused, Rosie blossoms under his evil influence. Soon she is carrying Doug's baby and her father has thrown her out of the house. Realising she has no choice, she agrees to marry Doug.

As if she isn't in enough trouble, Rosie's whole world falls apart when a warm and wonderful letter arrives from Adam . . . telling her he's on his way home.

'Driven and passionate, she stirs a pot spiced with incest, wife-beating . . . and murder'
The Sunday Times

FICTION / SAGA 0 7472 4657 2